T
Convenient Wife

These tall, dark and passionate Italian men
are about to marry

Three passionate novels!

In June 2008 Mills & Boon bring back
two of their classic collections, each
featuring three favourite romances
by our bestselling authors…

THE ITALIAN'S
CONVENIENT WIFE

The Italian's Suitable Wife
by Lucy Monroe
The Italian's Love-Child Bride
by Sharon Kendrick
The Italian's Token Wife by Julia James

MARRIED TO A MISTRESS

The Forbidden Mistress
by Anne Mather
Mistress to Her Husband
by Penny Jordan
The Mistress Wife by Lynne Graham

The Italian's Convenient Wife

THE ITALIAN'S SUITABLE WIFE
by
Lucy Monroe

THE ITALIAN'S LOVE-CHILD BRIDE
by
Sharon Kendrick

THE ITALIAN'S TOKEN WIFE
by
Julia James

⊙™ MILLS & BOON®
Pure reading pleasure

*Harlequin Mills & Boon Limited,
Eton House, 18-24 Paradise Road, Richmond, Surrey TW9 1SR*

THE ITALIAN'S CONVENIENT WIFE
© by Harlequin Enterprises II B.V./S.à.r.l 2008

The Italian's Suitable Wife, The Italian's Love-Child Bride and
The Italian's Token Wife were first published in Great Britain by
Harlequin Mills & Boon Limited in separate, single volumes.

The Italian's Suitable Wife © Lucy Monroe 2004
The Italian's Love-Child © Sharon Kendrick 2003
The Italian's Token Wife © Julia James 2003

ISBN: 978 0 263 86126 6

05-0608

*Printed and bound in Spain
by Litografia Rosés S.A., Barcelona*

THE ITALIAN'S SUITABLE WIFE

by

Lucy Monroe

100 Reasons to Celebrate

We invite you to join us in celebrating
Mills & Boon's centenary. Gerald Mills and
Charles Boon founded Mills & Boon Limited
in 1908 and opened offices in London's Covent
Garden. Since then, Mills & Boon has become
a hallmark for romantic fiction, recognised
around the world.

We're proud of our 100 years of publishing
excellence, which wouldn't have been achieved
without the loyalty and enthusiasm of our
authors and readers.

Thank you!

Each month throughout the year there will
be something new and exciting to mark the
centenary, so watch for your favourite authors,
captivating new stories, special limited
edition collections…and more!

Lucy Monroe started reading at age four. After she'd gone through the children's books at home, her mother caught her reading adult novels pilfered from the higher shelves on the book case…alas, it was nine years before she got her hands on a Mills & Boon® romance her older sister had brought home. She loves to create the strong alpha males and independent women that populate Mills & Boon books. When she's not immersed in a romance novel (whether reading or writing it) she enjoys travel with her family, having tea with the neighbours, gardening and visits from her numerous nieces and nephews. Lucy loves to hear from readers: e-mail Lucymonroe@Lucymonroe.com or visit www.LucyMonroe.com

Don't miss Lucy Monroe's exciting new novel
Forbidden: The Billionaire's Virgin Princess
out in July from Mills & Boon® Modern™.

To my critique partners, Erin and Kati.
Your friendship is something I will always
treasure. Thank you for being in my life and
being the special women that you are.

CHAPTER ONE

HIS lips hovered above hers.

Would they make contact? They never had before, no matter how much she ached for it. He started to lower his head and her heart kicked up its pace. *Yes. Oh, yes.* This would be the time. But even as she strained toward him, he began to back away. His image dissolved completely as the discordant note of a ringing telephone tugged her toward consciousness.

Gianna Lakewood picked up the cordless handset still half immersed in dreamland, a land where Enrico DiRinaldo was not engaged to supermodel, Chiara Fabrizio.

Her voice still husky from sleep and the emotions elicited by her dream, she said, "Hello?"

"Gianna, there's been an accident." The sound of Andre DiRinaldo's voice brought her eyes wide-open as tension immediately tightened her grip on the phone.

"An accident?" she asked, sitting bolt upright and flipping on the bedside light almost in the same motion.

"*Porco miseria.* How do I say this?" He hesitated while she waited with a premonition of dread for what was to come. "It is Enrico. He is in a coma."

"Where is he?" she demanded, jumping out of bed and clutching the phone to her ear, her green eyes wild with the fear coursing through her. She didn't ask what happened. She could find that out

5

later. She needed to know where Rico was and how soon she could get there. She started shucking out of her pajamas.

"He is in a hospital in New York."

New York? She hadn't even known Rico was in the States, but then she'd avoided news of him since his engagement to Chiara had been announced two months ago.

She hopped over to the nightstand, one leg still encased in cotton pajama bottoms, and grabbed a notepad and pen from the drawer. "Which one?" She wrote it down. "I'll be there as soon as I can!"

She hung up before Andre could say another word. He would understand. He had thought to call her even though it was the middle of the night whereas Rico's parents would have waited until morning in misguided courtesy. Because Rico's brother knew that Gianna had loved Enrico DiRinaldo since she was fifteen years old.

Eight years of unnoticed and unrequited love, even his recent engagement to another woman had not been able to dampen those feelings.

She rushed around her tiny apartment, throwing together the necessary items for her trip to New York. She considered checking into flights, but discarded the idea. It was a two-and-a-half-hour drive, but it would take longer to get to the airport, book a flight and make the plane trip to New York. She wasn't like the DiRinaldos. She couldn't command first class attention, or even hope to get on the next available flight unless an economy seat was vacant.

She didn't bother to take a brush to her chestnut-brown, waist-length hair, leaving it in the braid she slept in. Nor did she take time to throw on makeup.

She barely dressed, leaving off her bra and slipping into a worn pair of jeans, lightweight sweater and tennis shoes, no socks.

A scant two hours later she walked into the hospital and asked to see Rico.

The woman behind the information desk looked up and asked, "Are you family?"

"Yes." She lied without compunction. The DiRinaldos had always said she was family. The only family she had left. The fact she could claim no blood relation was irrelevant at the moment.

The woman nodded. "I'll call an orderly to take you up."

Five minutes that felt like five hours later, a young man dressed in green scrubs came to lead her to ICU. "I'm glad you're here. We called his family in Italy three hours ago," so just before Andre had called her, "and they won't be here for another five to six hours. In cases like this having loved ones around in the first hours can make all the difference."

Well she wasn't a *loved* one, but she loved and she supposed that had to count for something. "What do you mean, cases like this?"

"You know Mr. DiRinaldo is in a coma?"

"Yes."

"Comas are very mysterious things, even with all the medical knowledge we have today. There's a case to be made for the presence of important people in the patient's life bringing him out of the coma." The orderly said this with a certain acidic bite she didn't understand.

They stopped at the nurse's station and she was given instructions for her visit with Rico. She also

learned why the *orderly* had seemed so knowledgeable about Rico's condition. He was actually the intern working with the ICU doctor on call.

She walked into the ICU unit, her eyes not taking
in the medical paraphernalia surrounding Rico. All
she could see was the man in the bed. Six feet four
inches of vitality as lifeless as a waxwork doll.
Eyelids covered the compelling silver eyes she loved
so much. His face was badly bruised and one shoulder was splotched with purple as well.

He didn't appear to be wearing anything but the
sheet and blanket, which covered most of his torso.
His breathing was so shallow, her heart literally
stopped in her chest at first because she thought he
wasn't breathing at all.

She moved forward until she stood beside the bed,
her lower body pressed against the metal bedrail. Her
hand reached out of its own volition to touch him.
She desperately needed to feel the life force beating
beneath his skin. Seeing no bandages, she laid her
hand very lightly over the left side of his chest. Her
knees almost buckled with emotion.

The steady beat of his heart under her barely
touching fingers was proof that as still as he was, as
pale as he looked, Rico was still alive. "I love you,
Rico. You can't die. Please. Don't stop fighting."

She didn't realize she was crying until the intern
handed her a tissue to wipe at the tears sliding silently down her cheeks. She took it and mopped up
without once taking her focus off the man in the bed.

"What happened?" she asked.

"They didn't tell you?"

"I hung up before his brother had the chance.

Getting here seemed more important than getting details," she admitted.

"He was shot saving a woman from a mugging."

"He was shot?" The only bandages she saw were on his head.

"It was just a crease—" the orderly pointed at the white gauze strips "—along his cranium, but he fell into oncoming traffic and was hit by a car."

"The bruises?"

"Were from the car."

"Is there any lasting damage?"

"The doctors don't think so, but we won't know until he wakes up."

There was something in his voice and her head snapped around. "Tell me."

"The nature of some of his injuries could result in temporary or permanent paralysis, but there's no way of knowing for sure until he comes out of the coma."

"Where is the doctor?" She wanted more information, more than the opinion of an intern, no matter how knowledgeable he might be.

"He's making rounds. He'll be in to see Mr. DiRinaldo in a little while. You can talk to him then."

She nodded and turned her eyes back on Rico, immediately forgetting the intern was in the small cubicle. There was only Rico. He'd filled her world for so long, the prospect of a life without him in it made the pain she'd felt upon his engagement pale into insignificance.

"You have to wake up, Rico. You have to live. I can't live without you. None of us can. Your mother, your father, your brother…we all need you. Please don't leave us. Don't leave me.'' She even forced herself to mention Chiara and his upcoming wedding. ''You'll be married and on your way to being a papa soon, Rico. I know that is what you want. You always said you were going to have a houseful of children.''

She'd hoped with the naïve dreams of a girl that those babies would be hers, but she didn't care if Chiara was the mother, Gianna just wanted Rico to live. She kept talking, pleading with him to wake up, not to give up and she told him over and over again how much she loved him.

She was holding Rico's hand and willing him to come out of the coma when the doctor came by later.

He examined Rico's chart and checked the electronic monitors by the bed. ''All his vital signs look good.''

''Isn't there anything you can do to wake him up?'' she asked, her throat raw from swallowing tears.

The doctor shook his head. ''I'm sorry. We've already tried stimulants to no effect.''

Her hand tightened on Rico's unmoving one. ''I guess he'll just have to wake up on his own then. He will, you know. Rico's got more stubborn genes than a Missouri mule.''

The doctor smiled, his tired blue eyes warming a little. ''I'm sure you're right. It's my opinion, having family around does its part, too.'' His tone was censorious, but she didn't feel it was directed at her.

''His parents and brother will be here as soon as humanly possible. It's a long flight from Milan, even on the fastest private jet in the world.''

"I'm sure you are right. It's too bad his fiancée couldn't see her way to staying."

"Chiara is here, in New York?"

"Miss Fabrizio was contacted at her hotel. She came in and became hysterical at the sight of him, furious he'd risked his life for *a woman too stupid to know not to walk alone at night.*" This time the censure was blatant.

"But why isn't she here?" Perhaps Chiara had stepped out to use the facilities or something.

"She stayed for about an hour, but when we informed her he was in a coma and we didn't know how soon he'd come out of it, she decided to leave. She left a number to call when he *wakes up.*" There was a wealth of disgust in his words.

"She must be really upset." Gianna looked again at Rico's motionless countenance and had no trouble understanding his fiancée going to pieces over it. She couldn't imagine leaving his side, but then everyone dealt with fear in their own way.

"She'll sleep fine tonight. She insisted we prescribe her an oral sedative," the doctor added.

Gianna nodded absently, once again focused almost entirely on Rico. She rubbed the skin of his hand with her thumb. "He's so warm. It's hard to believe he isn't sleeping normally."

The doctor made some comments about physiological differences between coma and normal sleep that she only half listened to.

"Is it all right if I stay?" she asked, knowing it would take an orderly for each arm and one for her legs to get her to move from Rico's bedside.

Laughter rumbled in the doctor's throat. "If I said no?"

"I'd sneak back in wearing scrubs and a mask and hide under the bed," she admitted, amazed she could find any humor in a hospital room with Rico lying broken in the bed.

"As I thought. Are you his sister?" the doctor asked.

She felt the blood rush into her cheeks. Should she lie again? Looking at the understanding light in the doctor's eyes, she didn't think she would have to. "No, I'm a family friend."

Speculation flickered briefly in his expression before he nodded. "I won't tell if you won't. It's obvious you care. Your presence can't hurt and may very well help enormously."

Relief swirled through her bloodstream. "Thank you."

"It's all about what's best for the patient." The doctor exited the cubicle thinking it was a pity his patient wasn't engaged to the tiny woman who obviously cared so much instead of the gorgeous Amazon with a heart like a rock.

Gianna was only vaguely aware of the doctor's departure as memories of Rico assailed her. She picked up his hand. It was heavy and she kissed his palm before laying it back on the bed, her own covering it.

"Do you remember the year Mama died? I was five and you were thirteen. You should have hated having me tag after you. Andre called me a pest often enough, but you didn't. You held my hand and talked to me about Mama. You took me to Duomo Cathedral, such a beautiful place, and told me I could be close to Mama there. It hurt so much and I was scared, but you comforted me."

She suppressed the memory of how different it had been a year ago when her dad died. Rico had been dating Chiara then and the other woman had no time for Gianna and had made sure Rico didn't, either.

"Rico, I don't want comforting now. Do you hear me? I want you to get better. I thought nothing could hurt more than when you announced your engagement...but I was wrong. If you die, I don't want to go on living. Do you hear me, Rico?" She leaned forward, her head resting against the strong muscles of his forearm. "Please, don't die," she pleaded as tears once again bathed her skin and his.

She was dozing when a familiar voice repeating her name woke her up.

"Gianna? Wake up, *piccola mia*."

She lifted her head from its resting place by Rico's thigh. Sometime in the last five hours, she had lowered the bedrail and settled her head beside him. She needed the physical contact as a reminder that Rico was still alive.

Her eyes slowly focused as she blinked in the subdued lighting of the ICU cubicle. "Andre, where are your parents?"

He grimaced. "They left only two days ago on a cruise aboard a friend's yacht to celebrate their anniversary. Papa insisted on complete privacy and secrecy. They won't be back for another month and I know of no way to contact them. Rico was the only one with that information."

He left unsaid the obvious. Rico was in no condition to share his knowledge with them. Her insides twisted when she thought of the reaction Rico's parents would have to the news of their son's accident and Andre's inability to reach them.

"If he dies…" Andre's emotion-filled voice trailed off.

She glared at the younger version of Rico. "He won't die. I won't let him," she said fiercely.

Andre reached out and squeezed her shoulder, but said nothing. He didn't need to. They both knew she could not will Rico to live, but that wouldn't stop her from trying.

"The doctor said there has been no change in his condition since it stabilized after he was brought in."

"Yes." She'd been there for every blood pressure check, every time a nurse came in and read his monitors, marking the stats down on his chart.

"When did you arrive?" he asked.

She shrugged. "A couple of hours after you called."

"The drive is longer than that."

She just looked at him and he sighed. "It's a good thing you didn't get a ticket. Rico would have blasted you for it."

"When he comes out of his coma he can lecture me all he likes about my driving."

Andre nodded. "I know." Then his gaze skirted the room as if looking for something. "Where's Chiara? I thought she was supposed to be with him on this trip. She's modeling in some show while Rico attends the banking conference."

She told him what the doctor had said and Andre cursed eloquently in Italian, then switched to Arabic when he saw the way her face turned red. "I'm sorry. She's just such a bitch and my brother's too smitten to see it."

The image of a love-struck Rico was both painful and funny. "I can't quite imagine Rico's judgment completely obliterated by a pretty face, Andre. I'm sure there are things about Chiara that he genuinely admires. He's marrying her after all. He must love her." Even saying the words hurt, but she gritted her teeth against the pain of acknowledging Rico's desire for another woman.

Andre snorted. "More likely he's sexually obsessed with her. She knows how to use her body to its best advantage."

If her face had been red before, now it was flaming. "I..."

Andre sighed. "You are so innocent, *piccola*."

She didn't want to dwell on her twenty-three-year-old virginal status. She'd never wanted any man but Rico and he'd never seen her as anything other than a younger sister.

"How was your flight?"

Andre shook his head. "I don't know. I spent the entire time praying and worrying."

She reached out and gripped his hand, never letting go of her connection with the man in the bed. "He'll be all right, Andre. He has to."

"Have you eaten since you got here?"

"I haven't been hungry."

"It's hours past breakfast," he admonished her.

And that was how the next four days went. Rico was moved to a private room, per Andre's instructions. Gianna took the opportunity to shower. Other than that, she refused to leave Rico's room. She spent every moment, waking and dozing, by Rico's bedside. Andre bullied her into eating and drinking only by bringing the food and beverages into Rico's room.

Chiara came to see Rico once a day and stayed for five minutes each time. She looked at Gianna with a mixture of scorn and pity. "Do you really think this incessant vigil will make the least difference? He'll wake up when he wakes up and then he will want me by his side."

Gianna didn't bother to argue. No doubt Chiara was right, but it didn't matter.

It was three in the morning on the fifth day. The hospital halls were quiet, the nurse had taken Rico's vitals at midnight and no staff had come to disturb the silence of his room since. Andre was asleep on a reclining chair in the corner. Gianna couldn't doze, so she was talking again and touching Rico.

She brushed his arm and looked lovingly into his still face. "I love you, Rico. More than my own life. Please wake up. I don't care if it's to marry Chiara and give her all the babies I want to have. I don't care if you kick me out of your life after hearing what a besotted fool I've been the last five days. Just wake up."

She said the last on a note of desperation and was hoping so fiercely for him to make some sign he'd heard that when he moved, she thought she'd imagined it. The muscles of his arms spasmed and his head jerked from side to side.

She pressed the call button while shouting to Andre. "He's coming out of it! Andre, wake up!"

Andre came out of the chair fully alert. After that, everything was a blur. The nurse came running in. Soon she was followed by a doctor and then another nurse. Andre and Gianna were shooed out of the room. Then came the waiting. Gianna paced while Andre first sat and then stood, then paced, then sat again. Finally, the doctor came into the waiting room.

It was the same one who'd been on call the night Rico had been brought in. He smiled at Andre and Gianna. "He's awake, but he's a little disoriented. You can see him for five minutes one at a time."

Andre went first. He came back to the waiting room, his expression troubled.

She was desperate to see Rico and would have brushed by Andre without a word, but his hand snaked out and grabbed her. "Wait, *cara*. There is something I must tell you."

"What is it?"

Andre swallowed convulsively and then met her gaze head-on. The look of anguish in his eyes terrified her.

"What's wrong? He hasn't gone back into a coma, has he?"

"No. He…" Andre took a deep breath and let it out. "He can't move his legs."

CHAPTER TWO

Rico's eyes were fixed on the doorway when Gianna walked in. She couldn't miss the expression of disappointment that clouded his expression briefly before he masked it.

"Hello, *piccola mia.* Did Andre ask you to come and keep him company waiting for me to wake up?"

The endearment did things to her heart when Rico said it that didn't happen when Andre called her his little one. She smiled, her relief that he was talking so acute, she couldn't get a word past the blockage in her throat for several seconds. She stopped beside the bed, noticing someone had raised the guardrail.

"I couldn't have been kept away," she said with more honesty than was probably wise.

One corner of his mouth tipped up. "Always the nurturer. I still remember the cat..."

His words trailed off. He looked tired. Exhausted, really. "He turned out to be a lovely pet."

"So Mama thought. She gave him the run of the place until he died," he replied, speaking of a tabby cat she had rescued from the road after it had been injured when she was ten.

"Pamela was furious with me and wanted to call the animal people to come take it away," she said, speaking of her stepmother. Gianna smiled. "You wouldn't let her."

"What kind of cat do you have now?"

She'd always had pets, usually strays picked up

from somewhere, but once there had been a puppy her parents had given her when she was four. He'd been a wonderful friend and she'd cried buckets when he died. "I don't have any animals."

His face registered surprise. "That's not like you."

It wasn't by choice. She lived in campus housing and pets weren't allowed. She had no intention of burdening Rico with her problems, however. So she just smiled again and shrugged.

"You haven't asked how I'm feeling."

She gripped the bedrail to stop herself from touching him. She'd gotten so used to the freedom over the past five days. "You look like you've been pummeled on the playground by the school bully. I don't imagine you feel much better."

That made him chuckle and she rejoiced in the sound. Then he sobered. "My legs don't move." His expression and voice had gone blank.

She couldn't resist the urge to take his hand. "They will. You've got to be patient. You've had a terrible experience. Your body is still in shock."

His eyes remained unreadable, but his hand returned her grip with betraying fierceness. "Where is Chiara?"

Oh, Heavens. Gianna had forgotten to call the other woman. She felt guilty color stain her cheeks. "I was so excited you'd come out of coma, I forgot to call." She reluctantly pulled her hand from his. "I'll do it right away."

"Tell her to come round in the morning." His eyes closed. "I'll be more myself then."

"All right." She moved toward the door. "Sleep well, *caro*," she whispered. The endearment was so common it was like saying *hey you,* but she said it with a surfeit of emotion she prayed he could not hear.

He didn't reply.

Rico waited impatiently for Chiara to come. Andre and Gianna had both been in to see him again this morning and stayed until he had tired. Gianna looked exhausted and thinner than he remembered. He wondered if her job as an assistant professor was taking too much out of her. He'd have to talk to his mother about it.

But even exhausted, Gianna exuded an innocent sensuality that he'd never been completely able to ignore. At times it had made him feel guilty because his body reacted even though his mind saw her as more sister than woman. Regardless of his body's baffling response, he'd never once considered pursuing it. He didn't bed virgins and until recently, marriage had held no appeal.

His damn legs still wouldn't move and the doctors could not tell him if the paralysis was permanent or not. Gianna was convinced it was temporary and had said so again that morning. She was such a sweet little thing. He was surprised she wasn't married yet. She'd be twenty-four next year, but then American women married later, he thought. It was too bad Andre didn't see her as marriage material. Rico wouldn't mind having her in the family.

A surge of something dark and inexplicable stabbed him at the image of Andre walking down the aisle with Gianna. He tried to convince himself it was because Rico didn't know if he would be able to walk down the aisle with Chiara when the time came.

He could very well still be in a wheelchair. But something ugly had shifted in him at the thought of Gianna married.

Was he such an egoist he couldn't stand the thought of losing her innocent adoration? The thought did not sit well.

"*Caro!* You mustn't glare like that. You'll scare the nurses off and then who will bring you your lunch?" A trill of laughter accompanied Chiara into the room.

He watched his beautiful fiancée's entrance. Any man would be proud to claim Chiara for his own, but she belonged to Rico. "Give me a kiss and I won't feel like frowning any more."

She made a moue with her mouth. "Naughty man. You're sick."

"So kiss me and make it better," he taunted.

Something flickered in her eyes but she came forward and offered her lips for a brief salute. He wanted to demand more, but he allowed her to step back from the bed.

"You weren't here last night," he said.

Her eyes filled with tears and her expression was wounded. "That brother of yours and the *little paragon*," she must have meant Gianna, "they kept me out of it. They didn't call me for hours after you woke up."

Why hadn't his brother called Chiara right away? "They were here. You were not."

The tears spilled over. "That horrible girl! She's infatuated with you. She wouldn't leave your side. There wasn't even room for me next to the bed. Half the staff are convinced *she's* your fiancée."

He couldn't imagine Gianna doing something so cruel. "You're exaggerating."

Chiara spun away and her shoulders shook with misery. "I'm not."

"Come here, *bella*."

She turned around and returned to stand by the bed, her face wet with tears. "She lied to get into your room the first night. She told them she was related to you. And she never left, just like some pathetic clinging vine."

"Everyone was upset."

"But I'm your fiancée. I want you to tell her to stop acting like she is and not to spend so much time here at the hospital. I don't want to be tripping over her."

"Are you jealous?" he asked, the thought not unpleasant considering the state of his body.

She pouted with expert effect. "Maybe, a little."

"I'll talk to her," he promised.

Gianna walked into Rico's room an hour after she'd woken from the first unbroken stretch of sleep she'd had in six nights. Andre had insisted she take the other bedroom in his suite, saying it was just going to waste until his parents could arrive. She'd been grateful as her budget did not stretch to Manhattan hotel prices or taxi fares from a less expensive part of the city. She hadn't relished the thought of sleeping in her car or depleting her small savings account to nothing.

Rico looked up, his smile of greeting conspicuous in its shortness.

She stopped a few feet from the bed. "You look

better.'' And he did. His skin wasn't so pale under the tan and his eyes were clearer.

''Gianna, we need to talk.''

He'd found out how she had refused to leave his side. He knew she loved him and he pitied her.

She swallowed the knot of pain her pride had lodged in her throat. ''Yes?''

''You are like a sister to me.''

She hid the pain those words caused, but remained silent.

''You care about my health and this is understandable, but *cara*, you must not push Chiara aside in your concern for me.''

He thought she'd pushed his fiancée to the side? Gianna wanted to defend herself, but to do so would require telling him Chiara hadn't wanted to be with Rico when he was so sick. She couldn't do it. It would hurt him too much when he was vulnerable from his injuries.

''I didn't mean to push her aside,'' she said instead.

''I did not think you did. You are too tenderhearted to deliberately hurt someone like that, but you must be more considerate in future, no?''

She nodded, choking on the words she wanted to say. ''I'll try,'' she promised.

''Chiara does not want you visiting so often,'' Rico went on.

''What do you want, Rico?'' she asked helplessly.

''I want my fiancée to be happy. This is a trying time for her. I do not want her upset further.''

It was a trying time for him too, but Rico never considered his own needs. He thought only of protecting those he loved. "Andre said you refuse to contact your parents."

"There is no need for them to cut short their holiday."

"Your mother would want to be here."

"I do not want to be fussed over." The impatience in his voice made her smile.

"I'm surprised you're not working."

"*San celio.* Andre refused to bring in the laptop and the doctor ordered the phone removed when he found me talking to our office in Milan last night."

"What time last night?" she asked, pretty sure she knew the answer.

"What time do you think? When the office opened."

Which would have been roughly 3:00 a.m. No wonder the doctor had the phone removed. She shook her head. "You are supposed to be resting. How can you get better if you won't let your body recuperate?"

"What choice have I?" he demanded, indicating his still legs below the blanket.

She took several involuntary steps forward until she was next to the bed. She laid her small hand across his large one. "You don't have any choice right now, but you will get better."

His silver gaze caught hers and his hand turned until their fingers were entwined. "*Cara*, you always believe the best, no?"

She nodded, unable to speak. The feel of his hand holding hers was such a sweet torment she didn't want words to intrude.

"I believe the best also. I will walk again." He

said it with such arrogance, how could she help believing him?

"When have you merely walked, Rico?" she asked with a husky voice she did not recognize.

His free hand came up and cupped her cheek and a look she did not understand passed across his face. She went completely still, allowing every fiber of her being to absorb the delicious feeling produced by his touch. It would be gone all too soon and she didn't want to waste a moment of it.

His eyes narrowed. "Chiara believes you are infatuated with me, *cara*."

"I…" She swallowed.

"I told her you are like my *sorello piccola*."

Like his little sister? Yes, she knew he saw her that way, but she did not look on him as a big brother and her senses were running riot with his hand on her cheek and his fingers entwined with hers. "Right."

He brushed his thumb across her lips and she shivered.

Silver eyes turned gunmetal gray. "You are cold?"

"No," she whispered. Why was he touching her like this?

"What is going on in here?" Chiara's voice raised in furious censure, broke the spell of Rico's touch and Gianna jumped back.

She forgot her hand linked with his and was pulled up like a dog at the end of its leash as his hold on her did not lessen.

She tugged against her hand, but Rico didn't let go. He was looking at Chiara, his expression unreadable. "I am visiting with Gianna. She is not too busy to spend more than five minutes in my company."

Two things became apparent to Gianna at once. Chiara was jealous and Rico knew it.

"I've spoken to Gianna about letting you take your rightful place at my side, but you must be here to do so, *bella*."

Chiara's beautiful face turned red with temper and she glared at their entwined hands. "I am on assignment. You know I cannot spend every waking moment at the hospital like your pet limpet."

"She has her own job. Yet she finds the time."

He hadn't even bothered to protest the *pet limpet* remark, so she did it. She yanked on her hand. Hard. He let go. "I'm no one's pet, Chiara. I'm a friend and I didn't realize my visiting Rico would upset you so much."

Chiara's glare did not lessen. "You expect me to believe that, the way you've carried on for the last week. Andre treats me with contempt and you, he insists on keeping in his own suite at the hotel."

"You are staying with Andre?" Rico demanded, a tone in his voice that sounded very much like disapproval.

"There are two bedrooms in the suite. I'm using one until your parents arrive."

"They aren't coming."

"Because you won't call them," she said with some exasperation.

He ignored that. "It is not seemly for you to stay with an unmarried man alone in his hotel suite."

"It would be even less seemly for me to sleep in my car."

"*Per favore*, spare us the dramatics," Chiara jeered.

Gianna wanted to smack the beautifully painted red lips, but she wasn't a violent person…at least she never had been. She supposed there was a first time for everything. "Where I stay is neither of your business," she said firmly.

Chiara's eyes shot disdain at Gianna. "It is when you take advantage of the generosity of my fiancé's family to keep yourself underfoot and in the way."

"Stop playing the shrew and come here. I want my kiss of greeting," Rico demanded of Chiara.

He hadn't bothered to deny she was in the way and for all Gianna knew, he felt the same as his fiancée. He'd told her not to visit him as much. But he had taken Chiara to task for being rude. That was something at least.

Still, perhaps it was time for Gianna to go back to Massachusetts. She hadn't had her position long enough to accrue significant vacation time and since she wasn't related to Rico by blood, the university administration did not see her absence as a family emergency. The department head had already made one not very veiled threat regarding her job if she wasn't in class teaching the following Monday.

Chiara was obeying Rico with an overkill of enthusiasm. Gianna turned to give the couple some privacy, but the kiss lasted minutes. Finally, the pain of being in the room with the man she loved while he kissed another woman got to her and she walked out, sure they wouldn't notice.

"I told you she had a crush on you." Chiara's voice floated out the open door and down the hallway to where Gianna waited for the elevator.

Gianna felt waves of mortified color sweep up her skin. She'd spent eight years nursing a secret love and to have it laid bare for that witch to mock was more than she could bear. She was furious with Rico too. He'd used her to make his barracuda of a fiancée jealous. All that touching that had meant so much to her had been nothing more than a ploy to keep Chiara in line.

Evidently Rico didn't approve of his fiancée's flying visits any more than Gianna and Andre did.

"Gianna's feelings for me are of no concern to you." Rico could hear the bite in his voice and did nothing to mitigate it.

Chiara's kiss had not blinded him to her vicious attitude toward Gianna, an attitude he would not tolerate. "And you will not speak to her again as you did when you arrived. Her genuine concern for me is not something to mock."

Chiara's eyes widened in shock. "How can you say these things? Another woman's feelings toward you are definitely my concern."

"Gianna is no threat to you." But even as he said the words, he wondered at their truth. Would he have kissed the younger woman if Chiara had not arrived when she did? He didn't like to believe he was capable of such a dishonorable act. His affections were committed to Chiara, but he hadn't wanted to let go of Gianna's hand and the feel of her soft lips under his fingertips had caught at his emotions in a way Chiara's extended kiss had not.

"She's a little schemer and it devastates me that you can't see that." The tears welling in his fiancée's eyes did not move him as they once would have done.

She'd spent too little time at his bedside and her complaints about Gianna simply did not ring true. He wondered just who the schemer in this situation really was.

Gianna waited until the following evening to visit Rico again.

He was talking on a hospital phone and typing on a laptop set up on a desk across his legs when she came in. She smiled wryly to herself. Nothing and no one could keep Rico out of business circulation for long. He looked up and spotted her. He motioned to a chair near the bed and she sat down, waiting patiently for him to finish his call.

Lines around his eyes made him look tired, but he had more color and his jet black hair had been washed and styled in its usual neat fashion. He wore a navy-blue silk pajama jacket that looked brand new. It probably was. She didn't imagine Rico was the type of man to wear pajamas to bed.

He rang off and moved the desk with the portable computer aside. "Been busy sightseeing?" he asked with an edge to his voice.

"Sightseeing?" she asked incredulously.

"You have not been in to see me since yesterday morning."

He needn't sound so accusing. "You said Chiara didn't like me visiting so much."

"I did not mean for you to stop coming all together." Silver eyes snapped their disapproval at her. "For all you knew I had slipped back into a coma."

He was being totally unreasonable and for some

reason she found that terribly endearing. It was almost as if he'd missed her. "I'm here now," she said soothingly, "and Andre would have told me if you'd taken a turn for the worse."

"*Si*. Andre, whom you share your hotel room with."

"We don't share a room." She examined his face for a clue to the source of his irritability. "Are you in pain?"

He glared at her. "I have been shot and hit by a car driven by a man who could not see his hand in front of his face in a brightly lit room. Of course I have some pain."

He sounded so outraged, she had to stifle a grin. "I don't think the driver was expecting a man to fall in the street in front of him."

Rico dismissed that with a flick of his hand. "Blind fool," he muttered.

"Andre said you saved the woman's life. They caught the mugger and he had a list of prior offenses as long as your arm, most of them were violent assault and he'd already killed two women." Andre had also told her that the woman had come by the hospital to thank Rico, but he had told his security to keep out all visitors except her, his brother and Chiara. "You wouldn't let her thank you."

"I do not need this thanks. I am a man. I could not drive by and do nothing."

"If you ask me, you're more than an average man." She smiled at him, letting him see her approval. "You're a hero."

His eyes warmed slightly. "Chiara believes all this," he indicated his unmoving legs, "is my fault."

Gianna jumped up and laid her hand protectively

on his arm. "No. You mustn't think that. You were being the best kind of man. You paid a price, but you wouldn't let that stop you from doing it again."

His hand came up to hold hers and she was reminded of the day before, both of the wonderful feelings his touch invoked and the way she'd felt used when she realized he'd touched her only to make Chiara jealous.

She pulled her hand away and stepped back. "I don't plan to stay long," she said quickly, lest he think she was clinging like the limpet Chiara had accused her of being.

"Why? Do you have a hot date with Andre?" he asked scathingly, his unreasonable anger back in full force.

"He's taking me to dinner, but I'd hardly call it a hot date."

"Do not pin your spinsterish hopes on my brother. He is not ready to settle down."

She clenched her teeth. "I'm not pinning anything on him, much less a desire to marry. We're going to dinner because *he* doesn't mind my company."

"I do not mind your company." He pointed at his chest with an arrogant finger. "You could have dinner here, with me."

"What's the matter, can't Chiara get away from her busy modeling schedule to share a meal with you?" Gianna asked with uncharacteristic bite, still stinging from the way he had used her to make the other woman jealous the day before.

His remark about spinsterish hopes had done nothing to make her feel more charitable toward him, either.

His look could have stripped paint. "My fiancée is none of your business."

Gianna's heart melted. It had been a rotten thing to say and she just knew all that anger was hiding pain. Chiara was a totally selfish person who wouldn't know how to put herself out for another human being if her life depended on it. Worse, here was Rico, tired, in pain, not sure if he'd walk again and Gianna doing her best to act like a witch as well.

"I could call Andre and ask him to pick up dinner and bring it here," she offered by way of a peace offering.

"I will call him." And he did just that. He made arrangements with Andre in a burst of staccato Italian before hanging up the phone.

"I told him to get you your own room."

"I heard you, but it won't be necessary. I'll only be staying one more night. Surely my reputation and his virtue will be able to survive such a short test."

Rico looked disgruntled. "I did not say you would attack him."

"How else would a spinster like me expect to get a macho Italian male like your brother to the altar?"

"Why do you say you will only be staying one more night?" he asked, sidestepping her taunting words.

"I'm going home tomorrow."

"Why would you do this? I am not well. Do you see me ready to leave this place?" He sounded like a man ready to explode.

She couldn't imagine why. "You don't need me to stay and hold your hand. You've got Andre and Chiara. And your fiancée doesn't like having me underfoot." The words still rankled.

"You did not remain by my bedside for five solid days for Chiara's sake."

So, he knew about her vigil. Probably realized how much she loved him, too, which was all the more reason for her to leave. Her pride had already been dented but good by Chiara's nasty comments.

"You're better now."

He reached out and grabbed her wrist, pulling her close to the bed. His expression was intense, the hold on her wrist almost bruising. "I am not well. I am not walking."

"But you will walk."

Frustration was apparent in the set of his firm lips. "Yes. You believe this. I believe this, but my brother, my fiancée, they have their doubts."

"You'll just have to prove them wrong."

He nodded, heartwarming in his arrogant confidence of his return to full health. "I do not wish to do this alone."

Such an admission from Rico was astonishing and she couldn't gather her wits enough to respond.

"I need you here, believing in me, *cara*."

She almost fainted, she was so shocked at his words. "You need me?" she asked in a choked whisper.

"Stay." It sounded more like an arrogant command than a plea for her support, but Gianna knew what it had cost him to say it and she could not refuse.

"Okay."

He smiled and pulled her close for a kiss of gratitude.

At least that's what she assumed it was supposed to be, but Rico kissed her lips, not her cheek and the moment their mouths connected, their surroundings ceased to exist for her.

CHAPTER THREE

COLORS in every hue swirled around her as Gianna's lips tasted Rico's for the first time. His mouth was firm, warm and tasted faintly spicy. She inhaled and was engulfed in his masculine scent. *Rico.* She ached to run her fingers through his hair, to explore the contours of his chest under the pajama jacket. She probably would have, if he didn't have such a firm hold on her wrist.

Her other hand was gripping the bedrail with white-knuckle intensity.

He broke the kiss and she hung there, suspended in a world of sensation she was not ready to leave. Her eyes opened slowly to see him smiling at her.

''Thank you.''

''Thank you?'' For what? For kissing him?

''For staying,'' he replied, not without some amusement.

And it hit her. It *had* been a kiss of gratitude. Here she was, poised to reconnect with his lips and he was smiling at her like an indulgent older brother, pleased he'd gotten his own way. She straightened and spun away so quickly the long braid down her back arced over her shoulder to land against her left breast. ''N-no problem. I'll call the college and let them know I won't be returning right away.''

She had a feeling that phone call wouldn't go over very well, but even if it meant losing her job, she wouldn't leave Rico. Not as long as he needed her.

Andre arrived with dinner and Rico ate the beautifully prepared pasta dishes and steamed vegetables with fervor. "This is a great improvement over the food served here."

"You could have your meals delivered," Andre replied.

Rico shrugged. "It has not been my main concern."

No, Gianna thought, that would be reserved for business and walking again. Maybe even in that order.

"Something that does concern me is Gianna staying in your hotel room. I do not like this."

Andre gave his brother an interested appraisal. "Why not?"

"It is not good for her reputation."

Gianna couldn't help laughing at this. "Rico, you're a total throwback. No one cares if I stay in Andre's suite."

"I care," Rico informed her with an attitude that said that was all that should matter.

"Well, *you* are not my keeper. I haven't got the money for a prolonged stay in a hotel room." Particularly if she lost her job.

"I will pay for it."

She glared at him. "No, you will not."

"Besides, there is no need," Andre inserted. "My suite has two bedrooms and since you won't call Papa and Mama back from their cruise, the second one will go empty if Gianna does not stay in it."

She thought Andre's argument had merit. From the angry tilt to Rico's chin, he did not agree.

He pinned her with a look that sent shivers to places she had yet to discover. "You will allow

Andre to care for your needs, but you refuse my help?''

She barely suppressed the urge to roll her eyes. ''It's not the same thing. It doesn't cost Andre anything more to give me the extra room in the suite.''

''You think I begrudge you this trifling amount?'' Rico demanded.

Why was he being so obtuse? ''No. Of course, not. It's simply that I'm already there.'' She laid aside her fork and allowed herself to make direct visual contact for the first time in an hour. She'd perfected the art of talking to his shoulder since almost making a complete fool of herself over that kiss.

''I don't know what you're so worried about, Rico. My name doesn't make it into the social columns on a regular basis. No one cares where I sleep or who I do it with for that matter.''

His expression turned feral and she found herself scooting to the back of her chair, her body posed stiffly away from him.

''You have shared your bed with a man?''

Heat scorched up her cheeks until they burned like the Chicago fire of 1908. ''That's none of your business.''

''I do not agree.'' He looked ready to get up out of the bed and shake an answer out of her.

Even knowing that was not possible did not suppress the shiver of apprehension that skittered down her spine. She swung her gaze to Andre, appealing to him for help with her eyes, but he was obviously enjoying the conversation too much to step in on her behalf. She looked back at Rico.

His expression had not softened at all.

''I really don't want to talk about this with you.''

''You will tell me the name of the man.''

Heavens. When had her silence become an affirmative answer? And what right did he have to grill her like this? If Chiara were still a virgin, Gianna would dance naked on the top floor of the Empire State Building. ''Are you saying you and Chiara don't sleep together?''

''This is not under discussion.''

''Nothing is under discussion,'' she came close to shrieking.

''You are very red. You are embarrassed, no?''

Why bother denying it? He'd know she was lying. Her blush had already given her away. ''Yes.''

''A woman of experience would not be so discomfited,'' he said with smug assurance.

That set her over the edge. ''Are you sure about that? Maybe I've slept with tons of men. Maybe I'm even sharing Andre's bed now and the two room suite is only a ruse.''

She realized she'd let her temper lead her into deep, dark waters a second before he exploded. Mr. Cool Italian business magnate sent the portable table with his dinner on it careening across the room and started shouting at Andre.

Gianna spoke fluent Italian, but she didn't recognize some of the words. From the ones she did, she guessed they were curses. Andre's usually smiling face was stiff with shock. He tried to tell Rico it was a joke, but Rico's fury did not abate. His hands pounded the air, punctuating his angry speech and if he had been mobile, his brother would have been flat on his back. She was sure of it.

''For Heaven's sake.'' She jumped out of her chair and crossed to the bed, standing between Rico and

Andre. "*Calm down.* I said what if, not that I had. Rico—"

His arms snapped around her waist and she found herself sitting next to him on the bed, her chin cradled in a surprisingly gentle but firm hold. "Do you sleep with my brother?"

"No. I've never been with any man," she admitted, thinking nothing but the truth could completely diffuse the situation.

Rico's glare was sulfuric. "Yet you taunted me with the idea you had."

She couldn't begin to understand why it mattered so much to him. Perhaps he felt responsible for her in some way since her father had died. She wouldn't have known it by the way he'd ignored her for the past year, but maybe the feeling was there all the same.

"I wasn't taunting you. You embarrassed me and made me angry. Most women are not…not…" She couldn't make herself say the word. "Well, by my age, most women have some experience."

"But you do not."

"I do not." She agreed and stifled a depressed sigh. With him marrying Chiara, that wasn't likely to change, either.

He brushed her cheek with his fingers before dropping his hand from her face. "You should not be embarrassed to speak of these things to me."

She didn't know where he'd got that from. How could she help but be embarrassed to talk about it? She'd never even admitted her lack of practical application when discussing the subject with her girlfriends in college. But she didn't want to spark another outburst so she remained silent.

She went to get up, but his arm around her waist prevented her. "Rico?"

"You are very innocent."

She grimaced. That had been well and truly established. "If you're finished dissecting my lack of a love life, could I get up please? I want to go back to the hotel."

His hand was warm against her waist and he was idly brushing his thumb back and forth in a manner guaranteed to drive her mad or into a lustful frenzy. She wasn't sure there was much difference between the two.

"You will move to another room."

"No." Andre's firm denial surprised her into looking at him, regardless of the fascination Rico's small caresses held for her.

Andre's face was set in hard lines. "This is New York, Enrico. It would be inadvisable to allow Gianna to stay in a room by herself, even in a hotel with security."

"Then I will assign one of my security people to watch her room."

This conversation was growing more bizarre by the minute.

Andre shook his head in a short, decisive negative. "How can it be better for her to stay in a hotel room with a stranger than with me?"

Her attention swiveled back to Rico. He was scowling thoughtfully. "Perhaps we should get Chiara to stay in the suite as well."

"No!" Andre and Gianna chorused at once.

Rico's brows rose. "What bothers you about this?"

How did you tell a man you could not stand his

fiancée for dirt? Gianna cleared her throat, trying to think of a tactful way of putting her absolute refusal to share living space with the selfish witch.

"Gianna told me what Chiara said about her," Andre said, disapproval clear in his voice. "Your fiancée's unfounded jealousy was the reason Gianna considered going back to Massachusetts in the first place."

"Now you seek to protect her from my fiancée?" Rico asked with silky vitriol. "Are you sure there is nothing you two wish to share with me?"

She'd had about enough of Rico's overdeveloped sense of responsibility toward her. She was not some helpless female in need of his protection. She'd been on her own, if not physically then emotionally since long before her father had died. Or maybe Rico really thought she'd set her sights on marriage to the younger DiRinaldo brother.

"This is ridiculous. I'm not about to trip Andre and try to beat him to the floor."

Andre smiled, all Italian male. "Which is not to say, *cara,* that I will not be so inclined."

The hand on her waist tightened and Rico glared retribution at his brother. "Your humor is misplaced."

"So is your hand, considering you are engaged to marry someone else," Andre taunted.

Rico's hold did not loosen one bit. "She is practically family."

"Is she?" Andre asked. "I wonder."

"*What I am* is tired of this conversation." She yanked on Rico's hand at her waist. He let go and she stood up.

Setting both fists on her hips, she directed her next

words to Rico. "If you want me to stay in New York, it will be in Andre's suite and Chiara's services as chaperone will not be required. Even virginal spinsters have their standards and mine don't run to primitive, arrogant males who talk about me as if I'm not even in the room."

Rico winced at the word spinster and Andre's expression turned calculating. "It is true, Enrico is almost medieval in his outlook, but I am a modern man. I do not see anything wrong with a twenty-three-year-old woman remaining unmarried."

"Fine, *modern man,* take me back to the hotel. I'm ready for some of my own company."

Rico grumbled some more about her staying in Andre's suite, but in the end he acquiesced. He didn't have any choice. Gianna loved him enough to risk her job, but that didn't make her a doormat.

Doormat was the last thing Rico would have called Gianna over the next two weeks. She harangued him about working too much and not participating in his physical therapy sessions enough. She argued when he had the fast modem line installed in his room at the private hospital he'd moved to. That same day he had caught her unplugging the phone beside his bed and giving it to an orderly to take away. She'd been unrepentant.

Whereas Chiara spent very little time at the hospital and refused to attend his sessions at all. She'd left for Paris two days before to model in a Fall fashion show. Which was fine by him. No man wanted his woman around to see him helpless and that's how he felt with his damned useless legs refusing to do what he wanted them to.

If a part of him was relieved to see the back of his fiancée and her nagging comments about Gianna, who could blame him. He'd made her angry more than once defending the younger woman and was sure to do so again. He would not allow anyone to denigrate the girl he'd spent a good portion of his life protecting...even from himself. Chiara's attitude regarding his health had also worn thin. She said she believed he would walk again, but her eyes said not.

Gianna was not so reticent. She continued in her unwavering belief that feeling would return to his lower body in due course. She reminded him repeatedly that spinal shock injuries often resulted in complete recovery given enough time, something one of the doctors had asserted the first week. She also not only attended the physical therapy sessions, she participated in them. Which he did not thank her for. He needed her belief in him, not her interference.

"Get me back my phone," he gritted at her.

She shook her head, her long chestnut braid swinging gently from side to side catching the light and his attention. What would the richly colored hair look like unbraided? It was easily long enough to fall past her waist. Did she ever let it down? It would be beautiful.

"That was the third call in fifteen minutes." Gianna frowned at him like a diminutive schoolteacher lecturing a student caught passing notes in class. "You aren't going to walk again talking on the phone."

The physical therapist had the gall to nod his agreement. "Gianna is right, Mr. DiRinaldo. You need to concentrate on your therapy."

The therapist smiled conspiratorially with Gianna

and Rico's blood pressure climbed several notches. The overmuscled, blond Adonis was supposed to be the best physical therapist in New York, but Rico would gladly have flattened him.

"You wouldn't take a phone call in the middle of negotiating an important deal, would you?" Gianna asked.

"I am not negotiating. I am sitting here bored out of my skull while he," Rico pointed to the therapist with one hand, "moves my legs as if that will magically make them start working on their own."

"It's not magic. It's work and I wouldn't have thought you were afraid of hard work," she jeered.

"*Porco miseria!* I, Rico DiRinaldo, afraid to work? You are out of your mind."

"Good. I'm glad you said so." Her pixie chin set at a stubborn angle. "Then you understand why the phone is not allowed for the rest of the session."

"At least let me forward it to my answering service." Once she got back the phone, he could finish his call and *then* he would unplug it if she was so insistent.

She crossed her arms, pressing surprisingly feminine curves for such a small woman into prominence. "I already did it. You're not getting the phone back, you might as well accept it."

He gave her the look that sent bank presidents running for cover, but she just stood there, arms crossed and did not budge.

He turned to the therapist. "Give me something to do."

The other man jumped at the tone of his voice and Rico felt a small measure of satisfaction that unlike Gianna, the therapist found him intimidating.

* * *

Gianna knocked lightly on Rico's door, but heard no answering voice within.

She'd made it her habit to arrive after breakfast and stay through the morning's physical therapy. Perhaps Rico had already been taken down to the treatment room. She was running a bit late. She had overslept. The day before had been exhausting and ended in a late night.

She'd driven to Massachusetts and back all in one day so she could retrieve her belongings from the furnished university apartment that was no longer hers. Her prediction the department head would not see her staying in New York in an understanding light had been right on. But she'd finally found something to be grateful for in the debacle following her father's death.

When her stepmother had sold the house, Pamela had tossed everything she did not want to keep personally. Which meant that Gianna's belongings fit in her car and she would not have to go to the expense of renting a storage facility.

When there was no answer to Gianna's second knock, she pushed the door open. She wouldn't mind missing his session. They were getting more and more difficult for her to handle. The therapist insisted on Rico dressing in sports shorts and a body hugging T-shirt for his physical therapy. Every ripple of Rico's muscles was visible to her obsessive scrutiny.

She felt like a voyeur watching him exercise his incredibly gorgeous body.

It would be fine if she could encourage him and be the unaffected "cheerleader" on the inside she portrayed on the outside, but she wasn't. She had loved Rico since she was fifteen years old and wanted him almost as long. Apparently temporary paralysis and a foul temper were no deterrent to those feelings. She felt like some kind of depraved sex fiend.

The sight that met her eyes when she came into the room stopped her like a clanging train crossing. Rico sat on the side of his bed, wearing nothing but the sexiest pair of briefs she'd ever seen. Not that her untried eyes had seen all that many, but it wouldn't have mattered if she'd seen a thousand men in their skivvies. This was Rico.

He was the only man that mattered.

She practically swallowed her tongue trying to speak. "I… You… The door…"

His head swiveled round and the look on his face was a revelation. He looked elated.

"Rico? What…"

"You are having a difficult time with your sentences, *cara*."

She nodded mutely.

His mouth curved in a wide grin and his eyes glittered silver triumph. "I can feel my toes."

It took a second for the words to register, but when they did she flew across the room to hug him. She landed against his chest with all the momentum of a dead-on run. Rico went backward and she went with him, her arms wrapped around his neck, her mouth babbling her excitement.

"I knew it! I knew you could do it!"

His hard male body shook with joyous laughter under her. "And is it I, *piccola mia,* that has done this or *il buon dio?*"

Laughter trilled out of her to mingle with his. "A

bit of both, I think.'' She grinned down at him. ''When did it happen?''

''I woke before dawn with a tingling in my feet. The tingle became feeling as the morning advanced.''

The satisfaction mingled with relief in his voice tugged at her emotions and her heart just melted. ''Oh, Rico…''

''Do not turn into a waterworks on me, woman.''

Her smile was misty, but she managed to blink back any real tears. ''I wouldn't dream of it. I'm just so happy,'' she said in her own defense. Then she did something she would never have done had she been thinking clearly. She kissed him.

It was just a small salute on his chin, but her lips didn't want to move once they landed against Rico's warm, stubble covered jaw. She wanted to go on kissing him, tasting his skin, nibbling at his neck. She knew she had to move away, but she couldn't do it. She told herself she would let it last just one more second and then she would get off him and let him get dressed.

Then it hit her. Where she was. What she was doing. Rico was barely dressed and she was plastered all over him like a sticky blanket. She reared up, which had the effect of pressing her legs in a V over his thigh and pushing her skirt up at an indecent angle. She tried to get her knees under her to crawl off of him, but only managed to put her body into intimate contact with male flesh for the first time in her life.

It paralyzed her.

The thin silk of her panties were no barrier to the heat of his flesh and the erotic stimulation of his hairy leg between hers. She should have worn tights today instead of her short boots and slouchy socks. At least then her thighs would not be bare against him. She felt a flush crawl up her body from her toes to her hairline. The heat was caused by both embarrassment and physical pleasure. "Rico... I..."

"You have lost your words again, *piccola mia.*" Lazy amusement laced his voice.

She felt like anything but a little girl at that moment. In fact, she'd never felt more like a woman. "I'm sorry," she muttered as she once again tried to move away from him, but two very strong hands at her waist held her still.

"You have nothing with which to reproach yourself. Your excitement equals my own."

She doubted it. Where his excitement was limited to a very natural joy at the prospect of walking again, hers had a large dose of sexual awareness mixed in. The hands at her waist moved and she found her face directly above Rico's.

"I am happy, *cara.*"

"Me, too." She tried to control her breathing, but pulling air into her lungs had become an Olympic event.

His mouth quirked. "I could tell."

"Could you?" she asked stupidly, her mind focused on the ten different ways she wanted to close the gap between his mouth and hers.

Silver eyes flared wide and primal man came to the surface as Rico became aware of her preoccupation.

"Have many men kissed that luscious bow of a mouth?"

"W-what?" Had he just asked her if she'd done

much kissing? She couldn't take it in. Rico had no reason to be interested in her kissing history.

Her thoughts cut off midstream as Rico went about discovering her level of experience for himself. Though she was on top, she felt as if his lips were drawing hers, holding her captive with masculine domination of the most basic kind.

She felt a hand at the back of her head, holding her in place. She could have told him it wasn't necessary...if she could stop kissing him long enough to speak.

His lips molded hers with expert precision and she found hers parted without having been aware of opening them. His tongue ran along her lips before dipping inside her mouth, sharing an intimate sort of kiss that had disgusted her in the past. With Rico, she found it exciting beyond belief and she squirmed against him like a wanton.

Her hands explored his naked chest with abandoned delight while her tongue dueled shyly with his male aggressiveness. Soon, the entire world was reduced to his body under hers, his mouth against her mouth and their mingled breath.

"Rico!" The feminine shriek from the doorway brought Gianna out of her sensual haze with shattering speed.

CHAPTER FOUR

GIANNA tore her mouth from Rico's and rolled aside as his hands fell away from her. She jumped off the bed and straightened her short plaid wool skirt while her skin crawled with embarrassment to match the cherry-red of her ribbed turtleneck sweater.

"You filthy little slut," Chiara raged at her while Rico pushed himself back into a sitting position.

Rico rapped out something in Italian, but Gianna's senses were still so fogged up she didn't catch anything but his comment that he hadn't expected Chiara back in New York so soon. Whatever else he said, it caused Chiara to reel back like a drunken sailor and then glare at Gianna with undisguised malice.

Chiara stormed over to the bed, her high heels clicking on the floor, her eyes promising murder and mayhem. "That is obvious. I won't tolerate this sort of thing, Rico! Do you hear me?"

Gianna thought the entire medical staff probably heard her, but forbore saying so.

Just before reaching the bed, Chiara swung to face Gianna. "Do you think I don't know what was happening? I am not so stupid I believe Rico made a play for a plain little thing like you. It is obvious you were throwing yourself at him in some desperate attempt to get him to notice you as a woman, but you will never be enough woman for a man like Rico...even paralyzed."

Each word found their target in Gianna's vulnerable heart. She knew she wasn't Rico's type. Never had been. And she felt guilty because she knew Chiara was right. Gianna had thrown herself at Rico, kissing him, going all gooey-eyed on him when all he'd been doing was sharing his good news.

Of course, none of that explained why he'd kissed her back. But then with a man of Rico's machismo, maybe the reaction was automatic.

She opened her mouth to apologize, when Chiara spun away and addressed Rico. "You either send that wretched girl away, or I'm leaving and I won't come back."

Everything inside Gianna froze. Given a choice like that she knew what decision Rico would make. Hadn't he made it time and again over the past year when Chiara had made sure he had nothing to do with Gianna, even to the point of dragging Rico from Gianna's father's funeral with indecent haste?

"Well, Rico?" Chiara demanded, her full, glossy lips set in a pout, her eyes filled with crocodile tears that made Gianna grind her teeth.

"I think you know my answer," Rico replied.

They were the last words to register as Gianna spun and walked as fast as her wobbly legs could carry her from the room, real tears burning a path down her cheeks.

She thought she heard Rico call her name, but she dismissed the idea as fancy.

He'd made his choice.

He would send her away, but as of yesterday, she officially had nowhere to go. Which did not lacerate her heart with near the effectiveness as the fact Chiara had successfully evicted Gianna from Rico's life.

*   *   *

Gianna plopped down onto her bed in the hotel suite, grateful Andre was at a banker's meeting in Rome on Rico's behalf. She could do her packing and grieving in private.

She felt like she had when her father died: alone, lost and in pain. And humiliated. Though, humiliation was something she hadn't felt at her dad's death. The memory of her shameful reaction to being on top of Rico mortified her. How could she have been so brazen? Rico probably thought she was some kind of nymphomaniac virgin.

She groaned and buried her face in the bedspread covered pillow. Hiding her face did not hide her tormenting thoughts. She'd made an absolute fool of herself and she felt sick to her soul acknowledging it. The phone rang, but she ignored it to wallow in her misery. It was probably just housekeeping or something.

Or maybe one of Rico's doctors. Darn it. She forced herself to sit up and reached for the phone just as it stopped ringing. She couldn't work up any real chagrin she'd missed the call. She didn't want to talk to anyone right now.

But thinking the caller might have been one of Rico's doctors introduced another line of thinking to add to her misery. With her gone, who was going to make sure Rico focused on his rehabilitation? The therapist, big blond giant that he was, was afraid of Rico. Even Andre hesitated to cross his brother in Rico's current mood. Andre had been the one to arrange for the high-speed phone line to be installed in Rico's room at the hospital.

No one would be around to make sure Rico didn't

channel too much of his energy into business instead of getting better.

Tears burned the back of her eyes. She'd been such a fool and because of it, Rico would suffer. She wasn't so arrogant she thought he really needed *her*...but he needed someone to help him stay on track and Chiara certainly wasn't going to do it. The beautiful model was too self-centered to care.

Gianna curled into a fetal position and concentrated on not letting the tears fall.

She didn't know how long she wallowed in her gloomy despair, but she eventually got up and started packing. The sound of the door opening in the outer room alerted her to Andre's return. She hadn't expected him back from the banking conference until tomorrow. She'd have to face him sometime and tell him about her stupidity and Chiara's ultimatum. It might as well be now.

She trudged into the living room of the suite only to stop and rub her eyes, sure they were playing tricks on her.

"Why did you not answer the phone?" Rico raked at her, his face set in furious lines.

"I didn't know it was you," she said rather stupidly.

He was here. In the suite. Other than the streamlined wheelchair, he looked every ounce the powerful Italian businessman. His dark hair gleamed smoothly against his head and his Armani suit was immaculate.

More intimidating than that was the incandescent fury gleaming in his silver eyes. "You ran away."

"I thought you wanted me to go." His fiancée certainly had. "Where's Chiara?"

His mouth set in a grim line. "Gone."

"Because of me?" she asked, stricken to the heart at the thought her shameless behavior was to blame for Rico losing the woman he loved.

"Because I do not allow others to dictate my friendships."

Gianna bit her lower lip until she tasted blood. "I'm sorry I jumped on you like that."

"You were excited about my news. So was I."

"But I…" She swallowed and screwed up her courage to say it. "I kissed you."

"That is not the way I remember it, *tesoro mio*."

"I acted like a…a hussy. I attacked you," she said miserably.

"You behaved like a warm and vibrant woman when confronted with the unexpected physical proximity of a man you are attracted to." He rolled the wheelchair forward. "You are attracted to me, no?"

Her hands curled into fists at her side in an effort not to reach out and touch him. "Yes."

She ducked her head, breaking eye contact with him. She did not want to see the disgust he was bound to be feeling at her admission to being attracted to a man engaged to marry another woman.

Warm, masculine fingers touched her chin, lifting her head. "This is nothing for you to be ashamed of, *cara*."

"But, Chiara…"

"Is gone." The words sounded very final.

"You mean she's not coming back? Didn't you tell her it meant nothing? She knew I was to blame already."

"She does not wish to tie herself to a cripple."

Gianna felt the words like a blow and she dropped to her knees by Rico's feet. She grabbed his hands and held them to her breast. "You are not a cripple. It's just temporary. Doesn't she realize that? Did you tell her you felt your toes this morning?"

Rico's expression blanked. "What I told her is of no concern to you. She is no longer in the picture. Accept it as I have."

"I…" She felt so guilty, but what could she say?

He turned his head and looked through the open door to her bedroom. The suitcase on the side of the bed told its own story. "You were going to leave, no?" Strangely enough, he sounded angrier by her supposed defection than Chiara's.

"I thought that was what you wanted," she repeated.

"It is not. Did I not say I wanted you to stay?"

"Yes, but—"

"There is no but. You stay with me." *Mother,* he sounded arrogant.

"I—"

"You will not return to the university to teach. You promised me this."

"I couldn't go back if I wanted to," she admitted wryly, "they fired me."

She suddenly realized where she had his hands. She might as well be mauling him again. Dropping them with the speed of a lightning bolt, she jumped to her feet. His fingers curled possessively around her wrist before she could move away. He tugged until she found herself on top of Rico for the second time that day, but this time in his lap. She ended up sitting sideways to him, her legs dangling over one hard muscled thigh.

"You were fired?" he asked, his silver gaze probing hers.

"Yes. So, I'm footloose and fancy-free." She tried to smile about her lack of a job or any prospects in that direction. Getting an assistant professorship right out of university had been a fluke she couldn't expect to repeat. "I can stay with you as long as you need."

"What of Pamela?"

The mention of her stepmother's name did nothing to soothe Gianna's agitated feelings. Pamela had made it very clear after the death of Gianna's father that she did not consider their tie familial or binding. "She sold the house and pretty much everything in it and moved away two months after Dad's death. She's cruising the French Riviera with one of my father's former students."

Rico's eyes darkened. "She sold your home? She disposed of your family possessions?" He sounded incensed. He would be, of course. An Italian as traditional as Rico would find it impossible to understand the willful dismantling of the family home and all it represented. The DiRinaldos had been living in the same villa in Milan for over a century.

"Where have you been living?"

She was finding it increasingly difficult to concentrate while sitting in such close proximity to him. "What? Oh, in a furnished flat provided by the university."

"A furnished flat." His mouth twisted with distaste. "How long have they given you to move?" He caught on quick.

She grimaced. "I went up yesterday and packed everything into my car."

"You are homeless?" He made it sound like she was living under a bridge.

"I'm not. I'm staying here for now, but I'll find a

place when you're back on your feet—'' she meant that literally ''—and no longer require my services as cheerleader.''

"This is not acceptable.''

She smiled. "Don't let it worry you. I'm a big girl. I can take care of myself. I've been doing it since I was eighteen and went away to college. Pamela never wanted me to move home, even for the summers.''

"No wonder you spent vacations with Papa and Mama.''

"Your parents are wonderful people, Rico.''

"*Sì.* Yes, but I think you are also very special.'' His praise warmed her heart and made her smile again.

"Thank you. I think you're pretty special yourself.''

"Special enough to marry?''

Her heart stopped beating and then resumed at supersonic speed. "M-married?'' she squeaked.

"Perhaps, like Chiara, you do not wish to link your life with that of a cripple.''

Sheer rage filled her at his repeated use of the ugly word and she slammed her fist against his chest. "Don't you dare use that word to describe yourself! Even if you remained paralyzed for the rest of your life and we both know you won't, you would never be a cripple!''

"If you believe this, then marry me.''

"But you don't want to marry me!''

"I want children. Mama is expecting a daughter-in-law. I think she will like you in that role, no?''

The thought of having Rico's children left her weak, but... "This is ridiculous. You're angry with

Chiara, but you don't want to spend the rest of your life with me as your wife and you know it.''

"I want to go back to Italy. I want you to come with me."

"Of course, I'll come. You don't have to marry me to convince me to return with you."

"And to have my children? Are you content to do that outside of wedlock?"

She could feel her cheeks literally drench with color. "I don't know what you are saying."

"I'm saying I want *bambini.* Is this so difficult to understand?"

No. It wasn't. Rico would be an incredible father and had never made any secret of his desire to become one. "But..."

"You will have to undergo an IVF procedure. I cannot perform..." It was his turn to let his voice trail off and she knew it shattered his pride to say the words.

"Of course not. That's only to be expected, but it won't last," she tried to reassure him.

His expression told her she had fallen short of the mark.

The forbidden flirted at the edges of her consciousness. It was irrational. It was insane, but for just a moment she let herself picture what it would be like to be Rico's wife. To belong to him and to bear his child. It was all too easy to imagine herself round with his baby...and very, very happy to be in that condition.

"Perhaps you are afraid of the procedure."

"No." She looked at him and sucked in air in response to the intense will beating at her. "Rico—"

He cut her off with a finger over her lips.

"Consider it."

She nodded her head, mute. Even if she hadn't wanted to marry Rico more than she wanted anything else out of life, she would not have refused him flat out. After Chiara's rejection, such an action would be cruel.

"And while you are considering, think of this."

His lips replaced his finger and her brain short-circuited. Zinging electric charges shot from one part of her body to another. Her nipples beaded almost painfully against the silk confines of her bra and an ache of emptiness pulsed between her thighs. This was no kiss of discovery. It was an all out assault on her senses and when Rico's tongue demanded entry into her mouth, she gave it without a murmur.

The pulse in the heart of her womanhood increased its beat, tapping out a message of need she had never before felt.

She moaned and pressed herself against him, her fingers curled tightly around the lapel of his jacket. His hand tunneled under her sweater and caressed the vulnerable skin between her shoulder blades, making her shudder. Then she felt the clasp of her bra give and a masculine hand cupping the fullness of her breast. Shocked delight froze her. She'd never allowed any of her dates to explore and had never had a hand on her bra-covered breast, not to mention her naked flesh.

But this was Rico and she craved his touch. She cried out, the sound lost in his mouth as his fingers gently pinched and pulled her nipple into even more aching rigidity. The throb between her legs increased until she felt like screaming. She squirmed in his lap, unable to control the impulse to move.

He pulled his mouth from hers and she chased it with her lips. *He couldn't stop kissing her. Not now.* He didn't. He simply moved from her mouth to the sensitive spot behind her left ear. She shivered. She quaked. She moaned.

All the while his hand kept tormenting her breast while his lips wreaked havoc with her nape.

"You taste so sweet, *tesoro mio.*" Then he proved his words by tasting every inch of skin his lips could reach. The neck-high collar on her turtleneck sweater seemed to get in his way and he tugged at the hem. "Take this off."

Her eyes opened and she stared at him, confused. "What?"

But he didn't answer. He was already sliding the soft red knit up her torso. Her skin tingled where he touched it and she was naked from the waist up before she came out of the passionate daze he'd sent her into enough to realize what he had done. She blinked down at the plush carpet and the small pile of red knit and silk thrown there by his insistent hands.

The silk thing was her bra. She was completely uncovered—open to Rico's hot stare. And it was hot. His silver eyes looked like molten metal as they centered on her now blushing breasts. Her hands flew to cover the vulnerable curves. "You shouldn't look at me like that."

He did not shift his gaze, but gently curled his fingers around each of her wrists, brushing the undersides of her breasts in the process. She nearly came out of her skin at the contact and choked out some kind of inarticulate plea.

"Let me look."

"But…"

His head tilted up and he pinned her in place with his look. "You want me to see."

That was just too arrogant for words. "I don't."

"You do, *cara mia*. It excites you to have my eyes on your flesh, to let me see what you hide from others."

She shook her head, denying it—but knowing he spoke the truth. He could have been touching her, she was so impacted by his stare. He tugged at her wrists and she allowed him to pull her hands away. Then sat there blushing hotly while he looked his fill.

She'd never sunbathed topless, so her skin was pale, contrasting starkly with the reddened, excited flesh peaking each breast.

One long masculine finger reached out and touched the end of a hardened peak. *"Bella…"* he said with a reverence that brought moisture to her eyes. *"Bella mia,"* he added, his tone possessive as both his hands cupped her, one reaching around her ribcage from behind so she felt completely surrounded by him.

She quivered.

He molded her with his hands, gently squeezing, caressing her with an expertise of which she refused to consider the source. She watched in fascination as his head lowered. He closed his lips around her nipple. The sight of his mouth against her untouched flesh sent shards of excitement slicing through her.

Then everything went out of focus.

The feeling was so electric, she could have powered a small town with her excitement. He nipped at her and then soothed the small stabs of pleasure filled pain with his tongue. Her eyes slid shut and her head fell back, her chest heaving with sobs of pleasure. She cried out, "Please, Rico, please!"

She didn't know what she was asking for. But she needed something. Her body felt on fire. She could not concentrate. She was going to fly apart, explode like a bomb on a very short fuse. And Rico's touch was that fuse—his mouth the match to light it. How could it be anything else? She had dreamed of this moment for almost a decade and her fantasies had never come close to the reality.

In all the world, she had only ever loved this man.

Husky male laughter greeted her desperate pleas while one hand trailed up the inside of her calf. He tickled the back of her knee, making her squirm and then brushed the inside of her thigh. Her legs parted of their own volition and his touch continued its upward journey until he brushed the apex of her womanhood. She jolted with sensation and cried out. He brushed her through the silk of her panties again and she moaned, shamelessly pressing herself into his exploring fingers.

His thumb slid past the elastic band at her leg and touched her intimately, making her whimper with both pleasure and feminine fear. She had never done this. Had never, ever even considered allowing another man to touch her like Rico was doing. In some ways she was more naïve than an adolescent. "What are you doing to me?" she whispered.

"Loving you…"

The words sounded so good. She could pretend for just this moment in time that he really did love her, that his touch was spurred by his need for her. The sweet thought increased her pleasure to the point of mindlessness. For right now…Rico loved her as she loved him. If only in her mind.

He pulled her to stand beside him. *Was he done?* The thought sent distressed need coursing through her.

He unzipped her skirt and let the red and black plaid wool drop to the carpet. Then he pushed her silk panties that matched her bra down her thighs. They dropped to pool at her feet. ''Step out of them,'' he commanded her.

She obeyed mindlessly, toeing off her short boots and socks at the same time, wanting nothing more than to return to the safe haven of his lap. She had her wish almost instantly as he pulled her back into his arms and began again with the ministrations to her oversensitized flesh. He probed her warm depths with one finger while his thumb played a gentle sonata on her most sensitive spot.

The sobs returned. The shaking increased. Her body caught fire of the volcanic kind. She felt on the verge of a precipice, desperately wanting to jump off but terrified of what would happen when she did.

''Let go, *cara mia.*'' He moved his mouth to her lips, kissing her with passion she had only ever dreamed of feeling. ''Give me the gift of your pleasure.''

She went over the edge into starbursts and earthquakes. The pleasure went on and on while she screamed and cried, begging him to stop, begging him to go on. He touched her until her body's convulsions almost tipped her off his lap. His hold on her torso was too tight. His touch was too much.

She tried to say it, but no coherent words would leave her mouth and she found herself shuddering in a series of climaxes that left her spent and barely conscious in his arms. He tucked her up against him and guided the wheelchair into her bedroom. He rolled up to her bed and pulled back the covers before lifting her gently onto the cool white sheets. He tucked the blankets around her.

"Sleep, *tesoro*. We will talk tomorrow."

Gianna woke sometime before dawn, the feel of the bedclothes against her naked flesh an unfamiliar one. It only took a few seconds for the events of the day before to come flooding back. Heat traveled up her body as she remembered what she had allowed Rico to do to her. He'd touched her every intimate place. He'd made her scream with pleasure and beg with abandon. And he hadn't even taken off his suit coat.

Why had he done it? Until yesterday, Rico had never so much as noticed she was a woman—except maybe of the sisterly variety. Now, all of the sudden, he'd made love to her with a passionate expertise that had left her nearly comatose. Okay, so they hadn't technically had intercourse, but she wasn't sure she could feel more intimately touched. He'd been inside of her, with his hand.

Just remembering the way he had dominated her body with pleasure had her breath sawing in and out and her heart beating an arrhythmic pattern. It had been a fantasy fulfillment so spectacular that she could live on the memories for the rest of her life.

But she didn't have to, an insidious voice reminded her. He'd said he wanted to marry her. If she agreed, he would not withdraw the offer, even if he wanted to. He had too much Old World honor to even consider it.

He couldn't really want to marry her though. Chiara had rejected him and he had responded with typical DiRinaldo action. He'd asked another woman to marry him and made love to her so incredibly well, her response had to have boosted his male ego. Rico was a macho man and being ditched by the beautiful but shallow Chiara would have left him feeling the need to prove that in some way.

Well, he'd done it.

He'd completely convinced Gianna that his machismo rating was off the Richter scale. Of course, she'd never been in any doubt. Just walking into a room with him in it bombarded her with enough testosterone to set her female hormones raging.

She hesitantly touched the places of her body that still felt achy from his attention. They felt no different than normal…no more or less feminine than they ever had washing those bits in the bath. And yet she felt different. Infinitely more womanly.

Rico had given her that gift—he had made her feel like a complete woman.

The least she could do would be to give him the gift of her understanding in return. She would not use his emotional reaction yesterday to trap him into a marriage he could not possibly want in the cold light of a new day.

She ruthlessly crushed the glowing dreams of being his wife and carrying his child. She would get up and shower and get to the hospital first thing so she could let Rico off the hook before he had too much time worrying about it.

CHAPTER FIVE

GIANNA dressed more carefully for her visit to Rico than usual. She dithered between wearing a doeskin skirt and short jacket set and a long denim skirt with black raw-silk long sleeve T-shirt. The doeskin skirt was short, hitting her right above the knees and even with tights—she felt exposed. She pulled it off and slid into the other outfit before brushing her hair into a large black oval clip at her nape.

She didn't know if her clothes would be sufficient armor against memories of Rico holding her naked body and making her sob with pleasure. She hated the idea of facing him at all, but she refused to be a coward. Yesterday would have to be dealt with and then they could move on. Of course, the less said about the embarrassing episode the better, in her opinion.

This time when she knocked on his door at the private hospital, she did it loudly and waited for him to call for her to enter. She pushed open the door to his room, which resembled Andre's suite at the hotel more than a hospital. Rico was sitting at his desk, wearing the skimpy shorts and form-fitting T-shirt that were de rigueur for his therapy sessions.

His concentration was on the computer, not her, so she took the time to compose herself in the face of his sexy attire. It didn't do much good. She wanted desperately to fall on him and beg for more of what he'd given her yesterday.

The urge left her feeling shaky and she moved to a chair to sit down. "Good morning, Rico. I see you're already at work."

He turned his chair to face her. "*Buona mattina, bella mia.* Did you sleep well?"

And that quickly she felt her composure slipping to the wayside. "Yes," she answered in a strangled tone.

"You were exhausted when I left you."

Her gaze flew to his and she read smug satisfaction in the silver depths.

"You made sure of it."

His smile was all conquering male. "There can be no doubt I will satisfy your needs in marriage, *tesoro.*"

Rico had needed to prove his manliness to himself and he'd done it. One part of her hurt that she'd been little more than another form of therapy for a man frustrated by his limitations. Another part of her— the part that loved him—rejoiced in the fact she could give him back a small part of his pride by admitting her reaction to his touch.

Still, she had never questioned her level of satisfaction married to him. "But you won't be happy, Rico. You don't want to marry me."

"You said this yesterday, but I proved differently, no?"

What did she say to this? She had no desire to tromp on his male ego by telling him she thought he had needed to prove something to himself. On the other hand, how could he seriously contemplate marrying her when only yesterday morning he had still been engaged to Chiara?

"Chiara will come back, Rico. She was angry, but

she'll realize her mistake and you don't want to be tied to another woman when she does.''

His expression hardened. "It is over with Chiara. I said this already."

And he didn't like repeating himself.

"But—"

"Do not argue. You want to marry me."

She gasped at his arrogant claim. "Says who?"

"I say."

"It wasn't so long ago you were using me to make your inattentive fiancée jealous." Or had he forgotten that bit?

His eyes registered genuine surprise. "This I did not do."

He'd never lied to her before and she couldn't tolerate him doing so now, even for the sake of his pride. "You did."

"When did I do this?"

"You touched me that day and you knew she would see. I'm not even sure yesterday morning's kiss wasn't for her benefit," she admitted, getting the worst of her fears out in the open.

"I have only ever touched you because it is what I wanted to do, *mi tesoro*. How can you believe otherwise? Am I a scoundrel that I would use you in such a way?"

Put like that, she had to pause. His expression said she'd really offended him.

His hand sliced through the air. "I do not deny her initial jealousy at your attentiveness did not please me, but I have never courted such a thing. I, Rico DiRinaldo, do not need to do such a thing."

Great. Now she'd offended not only his sense of integrity, but his pride as well.

It did not help her equilibrium that the gesture drew her attention to his sculpted muscles. Weren't only weight lifters supposed to have that kind of definition? "Do you lift weights?"

"What is this?"

Her face burned when she realized what she'd said and she dragged her attention back up his body to the amused expression on his face. "Never mind. It's not important."

"This is true. We have other things to discuss. Will you be disappointed not to have a big wedding?"

"It doesn't matter." She wouldn't care if they got married in the register's office if she believed Rico really wanted to marry her.

"Good. I want to marry before we return to Italy."

"I haven't said I'll marry you." She should not even be considering it. "Look, if this is about what you said yesterday. You don't need to worry. I knew you weren't serious at the time. You were distraught."

"I, Rico DiRinaldo, do not get distraught. This is an emotion for old women and young girls."

What about young women? She was fast approaching that state. "My point is, I'm not holding you to what you said yesterday."

"But I am holding you, *cara*."

The image of him doing so interrupted her normal thought pattern for several seconds.

He smiled at her as if he knew what she was thinking. He probably did, the fiend.

"What are you holding me to?" she asked, quite proud of herself for remembering the thread of conversation.

"You let me make love to you. That implies a certain commitment. I am holding you to that commitment."

He was devious and too smart for his own good.

She didn't even attempt to say they hadn't made love, because for all intents and purposes they had.

"Women make love with men all the time without marrying them," she said instead.

"Not you."

She glared at him, wanting to wipe that look of overconfidence right off his face. "Maybe I do."

He laughed and she wanted to scream. "You have already admitted your untouched state to me. You cannot prevaricate now."

"Just because I haven't had sex does not mean I've never let a man touch me," she pointed out.

How had she forgotten his unreasonable fury when she'd taunted him similarly before? One second, his chair was several feet across the room and the next he was in front of her, his hands clamped around her shoulders. The hold was not painful, but it was unyielding all the same. "Tell me the truth," he bit out, each word a sharp bullet.

"Why are you so angry?" she asked, feeling helpless in the face of such an irrational reaction.

"You ask this after yesterday?"

Funny, but somehow she had seen the day before as happening to her only. Sure Rico had made it happen, but she hadn't thought of it affecting him in any way. Apparently, giving a woman her first orgasm, or several of them, made a guy feel possessive.

"I've never let another man touch me like you did," she admitted grudgingly. She wasn't about to deal with another eruption like the other day when first she, then Andre had goaded Rico.

His hold changed to a caress on her upper arms. "I believed this. Do not tease me again."

"You're so bossy."

"It comes with being the oldest."

"You'd be that way if you were the youngest of six children," she postulated.

He shrugged, clearly dismissing the subject. "The doctors say there is no problem with returning home within the week."

"What about your therapy?"

"I have arranged for an eminent therapist to treat me in our home in Milan."

There he went, assuming her agreement again. "Rico, do you still love Chiara?" she asked baldly.

Everything else could be dealt with, but she wasn't about to marry a man in love with another woman.

His upper body tensed and he moved away from her. "My feelings for Chiara are of no concern to you."

"How can you say that?" She shook her head. "You want me to marry you thinking you love another woman. That's cruel, Rico."

"Because *you* love *me,* no?"

Love him? She wanted to brain him. "Don't put words in my mouth. We're talking about your feelings here."

"No. We are not. Anything I felt for Chiara is in the past, as she is."

That sounded somewhat reassuring. If it were the truth.

"Why do you want to marry me?" Perhaps if she

made him face his reasons, he would realize how unrealistic he was being.

"I told you yesterday. I am of an age to marry. Mama, she is expecting a daughter-in-law and I want *bambini*. You and I, we get along, *cara*. We always have. You will make an admirable wife and mother."

That was quite a speech for a man like Rico. "You want to marry me because you think I'll make a good mother?"

He shook his head. "I also believe you will be a good wife. You know my schedule. You know my limitations. You will not expect more than I can give."

Wouldn't she? Perhaps not, but that didn't mean she wouldn't want it. One phrase stuck in her mind though, *she knew his limitations.* He was still hung up on the temporary paralysis. She realized there never had been any real choice. He was vulnerable right now and for a man like Rico that was an anathema. She could not compound that vulnerability by rejecting him.

But she couldn't fool herself into believing her decision was entirely altruistic. If she married Rico, she would once again have a family. She'd been lonely since her mother's death, but never more so than after her father remarried and Pamela had efficiently cut Gianna out of the family circle in everything but name.

The DiRinaldos had been kind, but they had not belonged to her. She had not belonged to them, but if she married Rico that would change. She would once again have a real home, a place in the world she could call her own. And when the babies came, she would have so much more. She could once again share the type of bond she'd shared with her mother.

Only this time she would be the doting mamma.

"I'll marry you."

Andre came back to New York later that night. Gianna was curled up in an armchair watching television in the suite's living room when Andre came in. She knew he'd been to visit Rico and warily waited to see how he would respond to the news she was marrying his brother.

Andre peeled out of his trench coat and hung it over the back of the sofa before sitting down across from her. He measured her with a look. "So, you're going to marry my brother. That's pretty fast work considering he was engaged to Chiara not so long ago."

Gianna felt heat crawl up her neck. "I didn't set out to trap him."

Andre gave her a lazy smile and shrugged. "But you succeeded, *piccola mia*. This is a good thing."

Was it? She'd been plagued with doubts since leaving Rico's room shortly after dinner. She bit her lip, abusing the tender tissue until the pain made her realize what she was doing and she stopped. "He doesn't want to marry me."

"He assured me he did."

"He only thinks that. He's feeling down because he isn't walking yet and Chiara broke off their engagement. As soon as he calms down, he'll regret this craziness."

Andre's smile disappeared. "It is not crazy." He leaned forward, his brown gaze set intently on her. "Rico needs you right now and he recognizes that fact. Hell, I think he has always needed you. He just didn't realize it until he thought he'd lost you for good.'' So Rico had told Andre about the confrontation with Chiara. ''My brother's answer to his need is marriage. Considering how you feel about him, it's the ideal solution.''

Men could be so dense. ''He won't even tell me if he still loves Chiara.''

''He is not that stupid.''

''I thought I was pretty smart myself until I agreed to marry Rico.'' She'd been questioning her intelligence and sanity ever since. What sane woman agreed to marry a man who did not love her, who made no pretense of loving her? Even if that marriage fulfilled the deepest desires of her heart.

Andre shook his head. ''But this is a good decision. It is what he wants. It is what you want. What could be better?''

Rico wanting her for the right reasons. She didn't bother saying so. Andre wouldn't get it. In some ways, he and his arrogant brother were too much alike.

''Come. You will have Mama and Papa as your new parents. I as your brother.'' He pointed at himself with an expansive wave of his hand. ''This can only be good.''

She was too agitated to respond to his attempt at humor and all too true comment. ''You really think I'm doing the right thing?''

Andre reached out and took her hand, squeezing it with his own larger one. ''Yes, not only the right thing, but a good thing, *piccola mia*. I will be very pleased to welcome you into our family. And will it not please you to become my sister?''

She nodded, smiling slightly, her worries temporarily assuaged by Andre's wholesale support of her marriage to Rico. But what would his parents think? Would his mother believe Gianna had trapped Rico in a moment of weakness as Andre had jokingly suggested?

The worries kept her awake most of that night and the next two before the wedding.

"Mama will be furious about this register office business." Andre's comment came as he, Rico and Gianna were ushered into the judge's chamber for the short civil ceremony three days after Rico proposed.

Rico turned his head, "She will get over it."

"More likely she'll insist on a church blessing and all the expected conventions of a traditional wedding to accompany it," Andre replied with some humor.

Rico shrugged. "This is fine with me, but she will wait to arrange such a thing until I can walk to the altar."

Rico's insistence on a speedy civil ceremony began to make sense. Gianna had wondered if he had seen their marriage in such a clinical light that he did not want to be bothered by the traditional ceremony. Instead, Rico had not wanted to put himself on display for family and friends in his current condition. Which only drove home the knowledge that his decision to marry her had been made under duress. Andre had told her not to worry about it, but how could she help it?

Rico didn't love her.

As she repeated the short vows, she could not make herself meet Rico's gaze. She kept her eyes lowered, her focus on the small bouquet of white roses Rico had provided. However, when he spoke his vows, he tipped her chin up and said them to her, promising fidelity and honor in a voice that left no doubt to his sincerity. She couldn't help being moved.

The judge gave Rico permission to kiss her and he did, pulling her forward, their heads almost level because he was sitting in the streamlined wheelchair again. The kiss was soft and sweet, leaving her wanting more and yet comforted.

"Congratulazioni, fratello." Andre hugged his brother and kissed Rico's cheeks with typical Italian warmth. Then he turned to Gianna and lifted her off her feet in a bear hug. "Welcome to the family, little sister."

Gianna laughed, despite her misgivings and hugged him back exuberantly. *"Grazie!"*

Andre returned her to her feet and she turned to smile at Rico only to be hit with the unreadability of his expression.

They arrived in Milan in the wee hours of the morning and Gianna sleepily went through customs and then slid into the waiting limo with a tired feeling of relief. She'd slept so little over the past days, it was all she could do to keep her eyes open. Rico and Andre sat on the seat opposite and she knew there was something wrong with that picture.

She was married, but she didn't feel married. It was all so unreal. Rico had pretty much been treating her like a piece of furniture since the wedding. She hadn't expected his undivided attention on the DiRinaldo jet. There'd been several other people present after all. Andre was flying back with them along with the usual complement of security staff and Rico's personal assistant who had been in New York for the past week working with Rico.

Yet, even with the others on board, she hadn't expected him to forget she was even there. He'd spent almost the entire eight-hour flight working. The only time Rico had acknowledged her presence had been at dinner, when the flight attendant, a gorgeous, tall brunette had made a completely unnecessary fuss over Rico.

If Gianna had fussed like that, Rico would have torn strips off her, but he smiled indulgently at the flight attendant. Images of a dinner plate dumped in her new husband's lap had done little to assuage the feeling of jealousy that had plagued her. Which was why Rico was sitting across from her.

She'd waited to get into the limo until he had done so and then sat on the opposite seat. Andre had taken a place beside Rico after only the slightest hesitation.

Focusing her attention out the window, she ignored her new husband's watchful regard and tried to pretend she was alone. It hurt less.

"Papa and Mama will return from their holiday next week." Rico's voice broke the silence.

Gianna said nothing, assuming he'd been speaking to Andre. It wasn't like he'd bothered to speak to her for the last eight hours.

"Gianna."

She didn't turn her gaze from the dark window. "What?"

"You will be happy to see Mama, no?"

"Of course." But was that true? She was still afraid that Rico's parents were going to think she had somehow manipulated Rico while he was vulnerable and wrung a marriage proposal out of him.

"You do not sound enthusiastic."

"I'm tired."

"I do not like speaking to the side of your head, *cara*."

She shifted until their gazes met. It was difficult to read his expression in the limo's dim interior lights. "I got the impression you weren't particularly fond of speaking to me period."

"What is this? When have I ever said such a thing?"

"Actions speak louder than words." The trite saying tripped off her tongue with more venom than she'd meant it to.

He sucked in a breath. "What is your problem?"

Gianna slid her gaze from Rico to Andre to see what he was making of their exchange. The younger man had an inexplicable look of satisfaction on his face. He liked watching his brother argue with his new wife?

"I asked you a question, *cara*."

"And I chose not to answer it." With that, she dismissed him and the irritatingly amused Andre.

In an obvious bid to smooth troubled waters, Andre asked Rico a question and soon the men were making plans for their parents' return. Gianna tuned them out. She was struggling with a horrendous fear that she'd made the biggest mistake of her life. It was obvious Rico was regretting his decision to marry her, but why he couldn't have woken up to reality before the ceremony eluded her.

When they arrived at the DiRinaldo villa, Gianna waited outside the limo for Rico's wheelchair to be unloaded. Rico noticed her waiting and waved her off. "Go inside. There's no reason for you to hover."

Her eyes widened with hurt and she turned on her heel, doing just as he suggested. When she got inside the house, she went directly to the room she always used when she stayed at the villa. There was no way she was going to risk getting kicked out of the master bedroom.

She found a nightgown she'd left behind the summer before and took it into the bathroom. She wrapped her hair turban style in a towel and took a quick shower, washing the feel of extended travel from her skin. Later, she was sitting in front of the vanity mirror, brushing out her hair from the French roll she'd styled it into for her wedding when Rico came in.

"What the hell are you doing *here?*" he demanded.

"Brushing my hair." She flipped her hair over the opposite shoulder and started on the other side. There was absolute silence from where Rico remained near the door.

When she had removed every tangle from her hair, she parted it into three sections and started braiding it for sleep.

"Don't."

The harsh demand startled her and her fingers stilled in their task. She heard the wheelchair moving across the floor, but she couldn't make herself face him.

"*Per l'amore di cielo,* it is beautiful." His fingers threaded through the tresses, undoing the beginnings of the braid. "I have wanted to see it like this, but it is more than I could imagine."

She peeked a look at him through the curtain of her hair and her breath caught at the look of intense concentration on his face. "You like my hair?"

It seemed like such an inconsequential thing. She wore it long because her mother had liked it that way and letting it grow had been a way to feel close to her. It would never have occurred to her that Rico might find her very ordinary locks so fascinating, but he did.

His attention was riveted.

"Come here." He went to pull her into his lap, but self-preservation had her shooting to her feet and moving away.

"I'm tired. I want to go to bed."

Rico's eyes glittered silver messages at her she did not want to read. "I too wish to go to bed."

"Then you'd better get to it, hadn't you?"

He drew himself into a stiff and imposing stance. Even in the wheelchair, he was easily as tall as her and a hundred times more intimidating. "You plan that I should return to my bed, while you sleep here?"

She shrugged, trying for an insouciance she did not feel. "What difference does it make?" She'd meant that since he did not love her or particularly want her, he shouldn't care where she slept.

His head reared back as if she'd slapped him. "Indeed, what difference, *cara?* I cannot perform the usual wedding night ritual and undoubtedly the thought of sharing my bed is not a welcome one."

"That's not what I—"

"It does not matter," he said, cutting across her words. "It is just as well to me if you do not expect me to perform my husbandly duties. They hold little appeal when I cannot participate fully and are unnecessary to the conception of our child.''

The words were like icy rain stinging her with their frozen cruelty. She stood there in mute pain while he spun his chair and left her room.

She walked to the bed, feeling like an old woman, all the energy necessary to braid her hair drained by Rico's cold rejection. He saw the most beautiful experience of her life as a duty…an unnecessary one at that. And unappealing. How he must have despised her wanton eagerness to experience pleasure at his hands while incapable of giving any back.

Even if Rico had not been paralyzed, she would not have known how to return his caresses. Chiara had been right. Gianna was not enough woman for a man like Rico, regardless of his condition. Why had he wanted to marry her, then?

The answer came in another blinding wave of pain. Because he didn't love her or want her. She could give him babies, but she would not be a constant reminder of what he could not have. She didn't know what would happen when Rico regained feeling in the lower half of his body. Regret for their marriage would play a major role in his feelings, she was sure of it.

CHAPTER SIX

RICO sat on the balcony above the swimming pool and watched Andre and Gianna cavort in the water. It was a scene like so many he had witnessed in the past. Gianna and Andre had always played together, being of almost the same age. But now she was his wife and Rico was seeing his brother as a rival male rather than her childhood playmate.

The feelings of jealousy surging through him were unwelcome. He had not expected them to be part of marriage, but then he had not expected to sleep alone in the marital bed either. Even so, he didn't want to feel jealous of his own brother and the woman he had married. He simply had not anticipated experiencing such an emotion toward Gianna. He'd never been particularly jealous of Chiara. Possessive, yes, but jealous, no.

It made no sense. It was not as if he was in love with his wife. He cared for her. Of course he did. She had been a part of the fabric of his life since her birth.

Their mothers had been best friends as children and behaved as sisters as adults. Gianna's mother, Eliana, had married an American professor and returned to the States with him, while his mother had moved to Milan after marrying his father. But the two women's families had shared holidays and visits until Gianna's mother died. Gianna had continued to come to stay with his family, more frequently after her father remarried.

She did not play emotional games like Chiara. Chiara had used sex to manipulate and even before the accident, Rico had been growing increasingly intolerant of her tactics for getting what she wanted. He had believed marriage to Gianna would have all the benefits of the wedded state without making him vulnerable again to a woman. Gianna was too innocent and too good to manipulate him as his former fiancée had done.

Even so, he'd been wrong.

He'd felt damn vulnerable when she rejected him sexually the night before. He'd been sure that in this area he could at least give her the semblance of a normal marriage. She'd gone to pieces in his arms when he touched her in the hotel suite, letting him make love to her with a sweet trust he'd found addictive.

He'd suspected she had tender feelings for him before that. She had made it to his bedside after the accident before his brother. And according to a scornful Chiara and equally admiring Andre, Gianna had not left Rico's side until he came out of coma. Awareness of her devotion had buoyed him when so much had seemed hopeless.

After making love to her, he had been sure she had stronger feelings than friendship toward him. No woman responded with such speed and abandon without feeling something powerful for the man making love to her.

So, why the hell had she rejected him last night?

They hadn't spent much time together on the plane. He'd had to work. At least making money was something he could do unhindered without the use of his legs. At dinner, she hadn't seemed to care when the flight attendant flirted with him, and for some reason that had irritated him. So, even though he'd found the other woman's cloying attentions annoying, he had suffered them in some ridiculous attempt to get a rise out of Gianna.

It hadn't worked and he'd ended up feeling angry and stupid. Hadn't he told Gianna that he did not play those kind of games? He had enjoyed feeling like an idiot even less than his present jealousy. So, he'd been short with her in the limousine and felt guilty for being that way. But she'd got her own back. She had ignored him.

He still had not expected to find her occupying a guest room instead of his bedroom when he made it up the stairs. He'd gone to her room breathing fire to be poleaxed by the sight of that gorgeous hair streaming down her body. It had rippled like living silk and he had wanted to touch it with a hunger he had not been willing to analyze.

He'd done so. And it had only made him want more. More of her soft skin. More of her. But when he'd gone to pull her to him, she had backed away. She'd lost no time making it clear she had no interest in sharing his bed.

The rejection still stung and watching his brother play with her in a way he could not, was doing nothing to improve Rico's temper.

Gianna approached the room set aside for Rico's physical therapy with some trepidation. She'd avoided him the entire morning, shared stilted conversation with him and Andre over lunch and had only ventured down here in order to meet the new physical therapist. It was silly, but she needed to assure herself that Rico was truly in good hands. Besides, she'd been participating in Rico's therapy since the beginning.

She stepped into the room that looked so much like the one used for the same purpose at the hospital and stopped to marvel at how quickly the transformation had taken place. The warm wood décor had been replaced with exercise mats, a set of parallel bars, a treatment table and assorted weight lifting equipment. The big windows still allowed the sun to stream in through the clear glass, which was a great improvement over the hospital's fluorescent lighting.

Rico lay on the treatment table. A man with steel-gray hair and a very fit body encased in white cotton trousers and T-shirt put Rico's legs through the usual stretching exercises. Rico's own clothes resembled those he'd worn for sessions in New York and had the same destabilizing effect on her nervous system. She had to concentrate on getting her breath to come more naturally before she greeted the two men.

"Good afternoon."

Rico's head swiveled toward her, an expression she could not decipher in his eyes. *"Buon giorno."*

The therapist turned around. "Hello. You must be Mrs. DiRinaldo. I am Timothy Stephens. Rico tells me you are newlyweds. Congratulations."

"Thank you, Dr. Stephens. I didn't realize you would be English," she blurted out.

"Canadian, actually, and please call me Tim. A colleague of mine in New York recommended me to your husband."

She felt foolish for not distinguishing the accents.

Her only excuse was the shock she'd experienced that the therapist wasn't Italian. "I hope your temporary relocation wasn't a problem for you."

Tim laughed. It was a warm, rich sound, reminding her of her father's laughter when her mother had been alive. "My wife would have killed me if I had turned down an opportunity to work in Milan, all expenses paid. She's out shoe shopping as we speak."

Gianna felt her mouth crease upward in response to the man's friendly manner. "You'll have to bring her to the villa for dinner after Rico's parents return from their trip. I'm sure they'll want to meet her."

"Thank you. I will."

The whole time they'd been talking, Tim had not hesitated in his ministrations on Rico's legs. He now laid the one he had been exercising on the table and began an examination, testing for feeling. Not only did Rico confirm feeling in his toes and feet, but he actually moved his right foot in the beginnings of a rotating movement.

Gianna rushed to his side and grabbed his arm. "You didn't tell me you'd regained some movement."

"It is hardly more than a twitch, *cara*. Nothing to get so excited about."

She stared at him, unable to believe his cool demeanor. "You've got to be kidding! I was ecstatic when you felt your toes…that twitch you're so nonchalant about is cause for major celebration."

"Is it really, *tesoro?*"

And suddenly memories of what had happened when she had *celebrated* his first milestone filled her mind. She'd leapt on him and they'd kissed. Her gaze skittered to his lips. They were curled in a sardonic smile, but all she could think about was matching her mouth to his.

"I think all celebrations of the sort you are contemplating will have to wait, no?"

His mocking tone brought her back to the present with a bump. He didn't want her. He found kissing her a duty, a chore, not his preferred method of celebration.

She turned her heated face away from the men and pretended an interest in the parallel bars at the other end of the room. She was embarrassed by his comment as well as hurt remembering how little she fulfilled his needs as a woman.

"How soon do you think before Rico will be using these?" she asked Tim regarding the parallel bars.

"That's difficult to gauge. Every patient has their own timeline of healing, but your husband has a strong will and with a new wife, a pretty good incentive to recover as quickly as possible. We could see him using those in as little as seven days."

She spun around at such good news, only to be stopped short by Rico's cold voice. "I am a man, no? I do not need to be spoken of as a child who has no say in his future."

His masculine ego was definitely out of kilter.

Gianna wasn't sure how to assuage Rico's anger, but Tim just smiled.

"It's a bad habit family members and doctors can fall into. Talking about a patient as if he's not there. Thanks for calling us on it. How do you feel about targeting a goal of seven days for preliminary work on the bars?''

''It is doable,'' Rico replied with a confidence that pleased Gianna.

That confidence seemed well placed as he steadily regained feeling up his legs. Rico pushed himself mercilessly, doing more therapy sessions than he had in the hospital. Gianna still attended the sessions with him, but he seemed to need her encouragement less and less.

It was as if something inside him had clicked and even the DiRinaldo bank and Enterprises took backseat to his drive to walk again.

''Still, there is no feeling from the knees up,'' he said to Tim a few days later. ''How can I use the bars with only half my legs working?''

Tim smiled as he helped Rico move from the weight lifting machine back to his chair. ''You're doing great. You'll be on the bars in no time.''

''It has been six days. Tomorrow is seven.''

''You're almost there,'' Tim said with an insouciance Gianna envied as he packed up his supplies.

She wished she could respond in such a relaxed fashion to Rico, but she couldn't.

Tim promised to be in early the next morning for a session.

''It is easy for him to dismiss this. He does not sit useless in a wheelchair.'' Rico's frustration didn't surprise her, but his voicing it did. He'd been stoic about everything since returning to Italy. And very distant.

She handed him a small towel to wipe the sweat from his brow. He'd been working on his upper body tone and his muscles rippled with the effects of weight training.

''Only a fool would call you useless, Rico.''

''But what else can I be? My wife, she sleeps in a separate bed. My business, it must run itself while I retrain my body to function normally. Do not spout these happy platitudes at me.''

She felt herself blushing. They'd never discussed their wedding night. She assumed he was glad she stayed in the other room considering his attitude toward making love to her.

''If your business is running itself then why do you spend so much time on the computer and phone, not to mention attending board meetings at the bank?'' He'd gone to one yesterday, intent on proving to the other stockholders that all was well.

According to Andre, Rico had been very convincing.

She wasn't surprised.

''I notice you ignore the reality of separate beds.''

The blush intensified and she turned away, wanting to hide her vulnerability to him. ''We both know why I don't sleep with you, Rico. It's not as if our marriage is real.''

Strong fingers curled around her wrist and pulled until she faced him. ''And why is our marriage not real?'' The molten metal of his gaze burned into her. ''You agreed to have my baby, to be my wife. I made vows to you. What is not real about this?''

''Y-you weren't thinking straight. Now that you've had some time to think about it, I'm sure you've come to your senses.'' She tried to smile as if the words she was saying weren't tearing her into a million pieces. ''We can get an annulment. No one need ever know about our crazy wedding.''

He tugged her a step closer, his body exuding dangerous energy. "Andre knows. I know. You vowed to be my wife."

"But you didn't really want to marry me. You know you didn't. I knew you'd come to your senses and you have."

"On what do you draw this conclusion?"

What could she say? *You find kissing me a chore.* That would sound like she cared, which she did, but she didn't want him to know that. She had very little pride left where he was concerned, but she didn't want what remained lacerated.

When she didn't answer immediately, his eyes narrowed. "Perhaps it is not that you believe I have changed my mind, but that you have changed yours."

She shook her head. "No. I feel the same way I did when I agreed to marry you," she answered honestly.

He held her gaze captive with his own, his eyes drilling into her with ruthless determination. What was he looking for?

For her part, she was becoming increasingly aware of his physical person. His scent tantalized her, made her think of things she'd tried desperately to forget since leaving New York. He smelled earthy, his sweat-covered skin irresistibly drawing her gaze and to look was to want. To want was to remember and to remember was madness. Yet, she could not turn off the images in her mind.

"You pity me?" he asked, shocking her.

"What?"

"You pitied me. You did not wish to marry me, but you felt too sorry for me to reject me. You hoped I would let you go, but I have not done this."

She stared at him, completely aghast. "Pity?" she squeaked. Who could pity Rico? He was too vital, too much a man. "You've got the wrong end of the stick."

He glared at her and she felt guilty even though she knew she wasn't guilty of what he'd accused her of. "Is it also this wrong end of the stick for me to believe my parents will share in your pity when they realize my wife will not share my bed?"

"I didn't refuse to share your bed," she practically shouted.

"Then you will not be bothered to learn I have instructed the maid to move your things to my suite."

He'd done what? "But, Rico—"

"If you married me out of pity, I ask you allow that emotion to prompt you to sleeping in my bed. It is not as if I am a risk to your virtue."

"I don't pity you!"

"But you also do not wish to be married to me."

"I didn't say that."

"Then what is this talk of annulments?"

"I thought you wanted out."

"I did not say this. I do not want this," he said with emphasis. "Marriage is for a lifetime."

She groaned. "I knew you thought that."

"I do not think it; I know it."

"But, you don't *have* to stay married to me."

"Enough of this." He threw her hand from him in violent repudiation. "You want out of our marriage. You say so. Do not hide behind a false concern for *my* wants. You are my wife because I chose you for my wife. You cannot really believe I want to end our marriage before it has even begun."

The hot sulfur of his glare singed her tender emotions. "You do not want to be the mother of my *bambini*. Fine. *Non è un problema*. Go." He waved his hand toward the door. "But go before my parents come tomorrow. I will have enough sympathy to deal with without explaining a wife who is no wife."

Pain coursed through her so she could barely breathe. For the second time, she was being told to leave Rico's life. Only this time by him. If she went, would he ever let her back in?

Apparently, he truly did want to remain married. Knowing that, could she leave him? *Did she want to leave him?* The answer was simply no.

"I don't want out of our marriage." She whispered the words because she couldn't speak more loudly past the obstruction in her throat.

"Then you sleep in my bed."

She nodded and turned to go, her heart aching from a choice that had been no choice at all. Share a bed with a man who saw touching her as an unpleasant duty or be evicted forever from the life of the man she loved.

Crunch time came that night when she walked into Rico's suite to find him getting ready for bed.

The cool blue tones and Mediterranean-style wood furniture hardly registered on her consciousness.

He was sitting on the edge of the huge bed, half dressed. He'd taken off the immaculate suit he'd worn at dinner. His tie was gone and his shirt hung open on his torso. Short black hair curled across his chest and down to the navy-blue silk boxers that rode low on his hips.

He was just so gorgeous, it was criminal. No one man should be allowed to have so much sex appeal.

How was she going to sleep tonight with all that male perfection lying within inches of her body? Okay, on the oversize king bed, maybe it would be feet, but she didn't think the width of the room would be enough. What if he slept naked? She didn't think she could handle it. She was already on sensory overload and he still had his shirt and boxers on.

She gulped and met his eyes, her breathing already erratic.

He was looking at her with an arrested expression.

Maybe he'd never seen a woman do an imitation of a blushing, gasping fish before. Must be entertaining from his perspective.

"I... Where's my nightgown?" she asked, for lack of anything better to say.

"Do you need it?" he asked, with a positively wicked gleam in his eyes.

"Do I need it?" she repeated, her mind finding it impossible to wrap around the concept of going to bed naked.

"Many husbands and wives sleep together without wearing anything, no?"

Was that humor in his voice? She could hardly credit it, not after his mood earlier. "Are you going to sleep that way?"

"What way?"

He was tormenting her and loving it.

She took a deep breath and let it out. "Without your shorts." She was proud of the ability to get the words out when her mind had gone on an erotic vacation.

"I do not like confinement in my sleep."

"Oh... I think I prefer wearing a nightgown."

He shrugged as if it did not matter one way or the other to him. Which she was sure it didn't. He wasn't the one practically hyperventilating at the thought of sleeping together in the same bed.

"Uh—where is it?"

"In there." He indicated the walk-in closet on the other side of the room.

She almost tripped over her feet in her haste to get to the relative privacy of the closet. She found her nightgowns hanging at one end of the wardrobe. She chose a white one with an embroidered yoke and no sleeves. It was unseasonably warm for late September in Milan.

She took her time in the bathroom, hoping Rico would already be under the covers when she returned to the bedroom.

She got her wish, for all the good it did her. He sat, propped up against pillows, his upper body naked and the bedclothes hitting him low enough to be indecent. She stopped and stared at the sight he presented for several seconds.

"Are you coming to bed, *cara?*"

She swallowed and nodded, speech beyond her.

It took all her strength of will to cross that room and climb into the opposite side of the bed from him. What would she do if she snuggled up to him in the night? What if she had one of the sensual dreams that had plagued her since the night in New York? The dreams in which he played center stage. And what if her body acted out the fantasy with him so close? She'd woken up wrapped around a pillow on more than one occasion, her lower body throbbing.

She lay beneath the covers, stiff with nerves.

"You look like a thirteenth-century bride waiting to be ravished by her despot husband."

Her head whipped sideways to see gleaming silver eyes and a sardonically twisted mouth on his handsome face.

"I'm not used to sleeping with anyone."

"We established that in New York."

She nodded.

"I thought we also established you liked my touch, no?"

She thought about denying it. Her pride begged her to, but innate honesty wouldn't let her. "Yes."

"Yet you have refused to share my bed since our wedding night."

"You said it was a duty. You didn't like it." Tears pricked her eyes with pained remembrance.

His look sliced into her. "A man may say many things after his woman rejects him, no?"

"I didn't reject you." How could he believe that? She wanted him. Desperately. It had to be obvious.

"You did."

Remembering how she'd pulled away, she bit her lip. "Maybe a little, but I didn't mean it the way you took it."

"And how should I have taken it?"

"Not as a big rejection," she answered rather lamely and then added, "I was jealous and angry," with more honesty.

"Of what were you jealous?"

"You seemed to ignore me on the flight and then you let the flight attendant fawn over you, but when we got here, you took me to task for just waiting outside the limousine for you."

He sighed, his expression pained. "I thought you

did not notice. I thought you did not care. So, I tolerated her annoying behavior to try to make you care. I felt really stupid afterward and that made me lash out at you.''

Was he telling her the truth? He hadn't tried to make Chiara jealous, but he'd admitted to wanting to make Gianna jealous. That was a major admission for a man like Rico. ''It wasn't meant as a big rejection,'' she repeated, with more conviction this time.

''For a man, any sexual rejection is big, *cara mia*. Did you not know this?''

''No.'' She sighed. It was hard to believe he had not realized how very much she wanted him, but as impossible as it seemed to her, she had hurt him. ''I'm sorry.''

''Are you really, *tesoro?*''

Her heart just melted every time he called her that. It was so much more intimate than *cara*. An endearment reserved for her alone…or that is how she felt. She'd never heard him use it with Chiara, or anyone else.

''Yes,'' she replied, a little breathless. Who wouldn't be, two tiny feet from a man as sexy as Rico?

''Show me.''

CHAPTER SEVEN

GIANNA didn't move, unable to believe what Rico had just said. Show him? How?

He reached across the width dividing them and tugged on her wrist. *"Venuto a me."*

His huskily growled command to come to him sparked an instant ache deep in her core while his grip on her wrist kindled an uncontrollable desire for more of his touch. She stared at him, feeling like a small animal mesmerized by a predator ready to pounce.

Did he mean what she thought he meant?

"W-why?" she managed to stutter out in a whisper past a throat as dry as the sand in the Sahara.

The tug on her wrist increased. "Come here and you will find out."

How could seven little words short-circuit her brain and send her pulses rioting? She loved him. She wanted him. She'd been pining for his touch since New York. She felt more alive right now with just his fingers circling her wrist than she had any time in the week since their wedding.

That knowledge along with a trick of the light that made him look vulnerable undermined any resistance she might have considered putting up. At least that is what she told herself as she docilely allowed him to pull her to his side. Once there, she lay in total silence, wondering what came next.

"Sit up."

Captivated by the intense sensuality that seemed to come off him like an electric force field, she did as he said without a murmur. She knelt beside him, her knees centimeters from his powerful thigh. She could now see he'd left on the silk boxers. In deference to her feelings?

"Unbraid your hair, *tesoro*."

She didn't know why, but she felt compelled to obey the enthrallingly sexy voice of her husband. She carefully undid her braid, finger-combing the long chestnut strands into a curtain down her back and over one shoulder. He watched her with deep concentration that made her hands tremble.

When she was done, he reached out and ran his fingers through the hair covering her shoulder and breast. "So soft."

She shivered as the pads of his fingers brushed over her nipple in their path to the end of her hair. He smiled and repeated the entire process, beginning his long caress in the hair at her nape and following it down again, but this time when he reached her breast, he stopped. He cupped her and rubbed her nipple into more pronounced arousal. The sensation of hair brushing against the thin fabric of her nightgown over her very sensitive flesh sent her nerve endings into orbit.

"Take off your nightgown," he commanded gutturally.

Her breath caught somewhere between her breastbone and expelling. She didn't think she could do it. She wasn't one of his experienced lovers, used to undressing for a man. Gianna had never been nude with any man but Rico. She shook her head.

"Do you want me to stop touching you?"

How could he ask such a stupid question? He'd barely begun and she felt as if her entire body had gone on red alert. "No."

"Then take off your gown." The sensual threat in his voice enervated her, but he merely dropped his hand to his side and watched her. Waiting.

"You're being bossy again," she whispered.

He shrugged.

That's all. Just a shrug. No words. No other movement. He was leaving it completely up to her. She could either remove her gown or…or what? Turn over and go to sleep? She almost laughed at the ludicrousness of that thought. Her sane mind demanded she give it credence, but her body throbbed for what it knew Rico could give…pleasure beyond comprehension.

Did it really matter if he saw this as some kind of duty when he did it so well?

When he touched her, she felt loved. She knew she wasn't, but she would face that truth afterward— for now the heated potential of fulfilled passion lured her like a siren's song. If she ended up crashed and broken on the rocks of unrequited love, at least the journey there would have been more satisfying than the endless ocean of loneliness she'd known for so long.

Her decision made, she began pulling her gown up her body and over her head. Warm, sure hands cupped the undersides of her breasts when the fabric was still blocking her head. The sensation was so incredible, her entire body stopped movement in arrested delight. Which left her literally in the dark.

Rico abraded her nipples with his thumbs. Drawing concentric circles around them until she thought she would go mad with desire. She groaned and arched into his touch, her entire being focused on those two small peaks and the pleasure they were receiving.

He gave a growling laugh and one hand abandoned her breast. She made a sound of protest and then felt her nightgown being pulled the rest of the way off. Suddenly she could see him as well as feel him. And what a sight it was. His eyes were lambent with desire, his chest rippled as he moved to pull her into the circle of his arms. She landed against the short curling hair of his chest and shuddered in reaction to the feel of her body against his without the barrier of clothing, except those barely there silk boxers, for the first time.

"*Si*, yes, it feels right, no?"

She kissed the hollow between his neck and shoulder, lingering to taste the salty goodness of his skin and inhale the spicy scent that was distinctly Rico. "Yes."

The arm around her waist tightened and she squeaked, finding it difficult to breathe. He loosened his hold immediately, but she was so proud of the reaction she'd caused she repeated the kiss, this time licking his skin delicately along his collarbone. He molded her breast, pinching her nipple and sending arcs of sensation to her most feminine place.

Then his other hand moved until he was cupping her backside, his fingers flirting with the vulnerable softness at the apex of her thighs. She squirmed against his touch, seeking remembered pleasure with blind passion. He flipped her onto her back and loomed above her, his body angled and resting on one elbow. "I want to make love to you."

"Yes."

The word was barely out of her mouth when his lips were over hers. She gasped in a mixture of shock and bliss. He immediately deepened the kiss, taking command of her mouth in a way that left her breathless and aching for more. While he kissed her with a fervor she found completely overwhelming, his free hand brushed up and down her body in repeated erotic caresses that left her shivering and craving a more intimate touch.

He broke the kiss and her starving lungs sucked in air.

"You are so responsive, *piccola mia*."

She'd never felt less like a child, but she wasn't sure her all out abandoned response was a good thing. Maybe he liked a more composed partner. Judging by Chiara, Gianna knew he was used to a more sophisticated one. "I can't help it," she admitted, not without a little embarrassment.

His look was pure, primitive male. "I don't want you to."

"Oh."

She bit her lip, wondering why he'd stopped kissing her, why his hand was motionless against her waist.

Then he did something she found very odd. He carefully arranged her hair over the pillow, taking so much time she was throbbing for more of his touch when he was finished.

"Why did you do that?"

"I have dreamed of seeing you like this."

Could that be true? "You dreamed of me?" She couldn't accept that a man who saw touching her as some kind of chore would dream about it.

He didn't answer. Instead, he picked up a lock of her hair and using it like a paint brush, began to "paint" her body, paying particular attention to her breasts and nipples. He was so focused in his efforts, she felt unsettled by his attention. He didn't seem to notice that her body was a little too curvy by today's fashion standards. If the look on his face was any indication, it didn't bother him a bit that she was easily six inches shorter than Chiara and both a bra and dress size bigger.

The length of her hair allowed him to tease her bellybutton and he did so, in such an erotic way she was soon moving shamelessly in a mindless search for relief from the torment pulsing between her legs.

She wanted to touch him and reached out to do so, but he stopped her. "No."

"Why?"

"This is for you, *tesoro*."

"I want it to be for you too," she replied.

He ignored her words, kissing her into total submission. Speaking in Italian, he told her how sexy she was, how beautiful he found her body and its assorted bits. Some of his words were so frank, they embarrassed her, but she found them all arousing.

Why wouldn't he touch her where she needed to be touched?

She realized she'd made the demand out loud when he laughed. "In time, *tesoro*. Making love to a virgin should not be rushed, no?"

"This virgin wouldn't mind," she assured him.

But he just laughed again and continued with the maddening caresses. She cried out in relief when his mouth closed over one nipple. But her relief soon turned to wanton need that remained unfulfilled. He suckled her until she was crying with desire. She begged him to stop. He moved to the other breast. By the time he was done with that one, she was a shaking, gasping bundle of over sensitized flesh.

His hand moved to the soft curls between her legs and teased her with light touches. ''You belong to me.''

''Yes.'' How could he doubt it?

His finger dipped between her legs, finding the evidence of her excitement. She widened her legs, no longer caring if her actions betrayed her overpowering need for him. He caressed her like he had the last time, gently circling her bud of feminine pleasure and then rubbing it in alternative movements until she came with an ecstatic scream that reverberated in her eardrums long after it was over.

His hand stilled, but he did not take it away. She lay, inert, wondering if he would do as he had in New York and touch her into senselessness.

He kissed her. Softly. Possessively.

His hand moved and she felt flesh inside her body for the first time as he probed her opening with the tip of his finger. The sensation was incredible.

''That feels good,'' she blurted out.

He smiled, elemental male claiming his woman. ''It will feel better,'' he promised and his finger dipped in further.

Incredibly, her body responded with renewed ardor and she could feel the build of yet another explosion in her innermost places. He probed further and suddenly she felt pain. She tried to back away from it, but he wouldn't let her move.

''Trust me.''

She met his silver gaze and stopped trying to get

away. She nodded as tears stung her eyes from the discomfort.

His thumb teased her sweet spot while he pushed inexorably forward into her until the burning became almost unbearable. His mouth closed over her left nipple as he pushed through the barrier and pressed into her body in an intimate way she would not have believed possible in their current circumstance.

Then pain turned to unutterable pleasure as he made love to her with the moves of a man who knew exactly what he was doing.

Pleasure built and built and built until her entire body was shaking on the edge of going over. He gently bit her nipple and everything inside her convulsed in the most incredible wave of ecstasy she could ever have imagined.

Fireworks were too tame to describe it.

A supernova too distant to express the intimacy of it.

Love was the only word that could possibly describe her body's reaction to her husband's lovemaking.

She shuddered every time he moved his hand, experiencing aftershocks course through her time and again until she fell into a dozing stupor.

She felt him move beside her and then the depression of the bed as he lifted himself off and onto his chair. She couldn't get her glued eyelids open enough to see what he was doing.

Time went by. She didn't know how long, but at some point he returned to their bed. She felt a warm washcloth between her legs. She twitched, made self-conscious by his actions, but he gentled her with a caress. "Shh, *tesoro*. Let me do this. It is a husband's honorable right."

Still reeling from the other "honorable right" he had exercised, she relaxed and let him complete his ministrations, feeling cherished if a little embarrassed.

Afterward he pulled her to his side, his solid, muscular arm closing around her with the warmth of a security blanket. "This, what I do with you. It is not a duty."

Remembering his words of praise, his passion filled kisses, she believed him. They'd both lashed out and said things they hadn't meant, but he liked touching her. He'd made that very, very clear. She smiled, sleepily, content. She snuggled into him and mouthed words of love against his skin before settling against his body.

On the verge of unconsciousness she heard him say, "There can be no annulment now."

She wanted to ask him what he meant, but she was too tired.

Gianna swam to wakefulness with a sense of disorientation. Why was her bed so warm? She couldn't move her head. Panic at the thought lessened only fractionally as she registered the fact her hair was trapped under something preventing her movement. A heavy weight was settled across her ribs as well. An arm. An arm whose hand was positioned possessively over one of her breasts. *Rico.*

Oh, Mother. Her eyes flew open to warm Italian sunshine and the supine form of the man beside her. Neither of them was wearing a stitch of clothes. The sheet covered the lower half of his body, but both

their upper bodies were cast in stark relief by the
bright morning light. His dark hand over the pale
skin of her breast sent a shiver of alarm through her.

What had she done?

She'd let Rico make love to her. That's what. A
very personal ache between her legs attested to it.

She hadn't known a man could do what he had
done to her with his hand. Thinking of how intimately he had touched her brought a rush of embarrassed heat up her skin and her gaze was drawn irresistibly back to his sleeping form.

His face was relaxed in sleep, appearing younger,
not so intimidating; but not even unconsciousness
could dispel the arrogant set of his mouth. His dark
hair was mussed and stubble shadowed his jaw.
Seeing him like this felt infinitely special, as private
as what they had shared the night before.

But they hadn't shared it, her mind taunted her.
He'd refused to let her touch him. Why? Unable to
resist the urge, she reached up and very softly
brushed back a lock of black hair falling rakishly
over his forehead. After his insistence she keep her
hands to herself the night before, she felt like a cat
burglar, sneaking in to steal the family silver.

Emboldened when he did not wake up, she allowed her fingers to trail over his hair-roughened
chest as she had longed to do before. It felt strange.
The hair was both soft and springy, different from
her own body hair which was much finer and of
course nowhere near as prevalent. She tentatively
pressed her finger into his flesh and reveled in the
hard strength of his muscles. He was just so beautiful. A secret smile tipped the corner of her lips.

It would mortally offend Rico to be described as

beautiful, she knew. But to her, he was everything masculine beauty could be. Strong. Virile. Hard. And big. He was so much bigger than her. Lying beside him emphasized the difference in their sizes. It made her feel safe. He stirred and she snatched her hand back, her heart palpitating at a terrifying rate at the thought of getting caught both ogling and touching him like a small child with a new toy.

He didn't move again and she let out a rush of air from tight lungs. Would he be bothered to waken to her touch? She wished she knew more about men and what made them tick. Rico was the only man she'd ever been interested in and he was as incomprehensible to her as a Chinese word puzzle.

But he'd shared a little of himself last night. He'd admitted to wanting to make her jealous. He'd also told her that touching her was not a duty. It was a fair start.

And he had been emphatic that he wanted their marriage to continue. Comprehension of the meaning of his final words hit her with the force of a Tae Kwon Do ax kick. Rico had "consummated" their marriage last night. She was no longer a virgin and that ruled out an annulment. He'd done it on purpose. Of course he had, but she couldn't be angry about that. Not when his actions were further proof of just how permanently he wanted them to stay together.

She smiled at the thought even as Rico's arm shifted, telling her he was waking for real this time.

He opened his eyes and silver light caught her gaze as inexorably as a high-powered magnet trapping a paper clip.

"*Buona mattina.*" His voice was husky from sleep.

She was now very aware of his hand against her breast. "Good morning," she croaked with something less than sophisticated cool.

"Is it?" His eyes probed hers.

He needed her reassurance. She didn't mind giving it to him. "Yes." Feeling embarrassed by their new intimacy, she tried to move away, but his arms gave no quarter. "We need to get up. You have a session in less than an hour." Now that he was awake, she realized she wanted to avoid a postmortem on the night before.

He might want to stay married to her, but he didn't love her and that colored the night before gray around the edges.

"What is wrong, *cara?* Are you sore?" he asked, with what she considered an extreme lack of tact.

She averted her gaze. How did other women deal with this first morning after? "A little."

His hand tipped her chin until she was forced to look into his eyes. "I regret I had to hurt you."

She could read the sincerity in his expression. She didn't want him to feel guilty for something so natural. "No big deal." She tried to sound as sophisticated as she wished she felt. "It's usually at least a little painful the first time, I've always heard."

"Less painful maybe than if it had been a normal first time, no? You are very tight, little one."

This was going too far. "Rico! I don't think we need to discuss the particulars."

His smile sent her thoughts exploding in different directions, none of them rational. "It is nothing for which you should feel shy with me, *tesoro.* I am your husband."

Remembering a similar statement he had made after goading her into admitting her virginity, she said, "Rico, your idea of what should and should not embarrass me is nowhere near my own."

"You are very innocent."

"Not anymore," she was provoked into saying.

He looked so smug. "No, *tesoro*. Not any longer. Now, you belong to me."

"For better or worse." A tinge of unexpected bitterness laced her voice. What was wrong with her?

He frowned. "You are not happy to be married to me? I do not believe this after last night."

Could a guy get any more conceited?

"Face it, Rico. This marriage is not what either of us envisioned for our future." And it was only as she said the words, she realized how true they were. Rico had planned to marry supermodel beauty and she, well she had planned to marry for love.

He brushed her cheek in an oddly tender gesture. "This is true, but life is rarely what we expect, no?"

"I guess you're right." She let her hand rest against his chest, over his heart. The steady beat was reassuring. "I always expected to marry because of love."

His arm tightened around her and an expression she could not identify hardened his features. "You love me."

She opened her mouth, to say what she didn't know.

He forestalled her. "Do not deny the gift of your heart to me." He put his finger over her lips, sealing them shut. "I will treasure it always."

Rather than confirm or deny his words, she voiced her own worry. "You don't love me."

What had been a difficult expression to interpret

became no expression at all. "I care for you, *tesoro*. I will be faithful." Again that soft brush of fingers along her temple and cheek. "We will have a good life."

She didn't answer. She couldn't. Knowing something and hearing it were two very different animals she discovered at that moment. She'd known Rico didn't love her, but secretly she'd nursed a hope that his insistence on marriage and keeping their marriage had meant something more than it did. Hearing him say he only cared for her and they would have a good life was like taking a mortal blow and yet having her opponent expect her to remain standing.

Rico wasn't her enemy, but at that moment he hurt her more than all her stepmother's petty cruelties over the years had been capable of doing. Years of loneliness in her marriage, longing for a love he did not feel stretched out before Gianna. But, perhaps the most lowering thought of all was that those years looked infinitely more devastating without Rico in them.

She took a deep breath and let it out, concentrating on not allowing her devastated emotions to show in her voice. "We still need to get up."

He looked like he was going to pursue the discussion further. She could not stand it.

"Please," she begged, not caring if she sounded pathetic at that point. She could not bear one more minute of their current conversation.

He wasn't feeling merciful because he shook his head. "I cannot let you go looking as you do. You must trust me that our marriage will be all that a marriage should be."

"Did you love Chiara?" she asked with masochistic fervor.

"With Chiara, it was sex. I thought there was more at the time, but I find now my memories of our time together center on one activity."

She didn't like the thought of him remembering sex with Chiara. Complete sex. Something they could not yet experience. "And with me?" she asked.

"It is infinitely more."

"But not love," she said, wondering why she was putting herself through this.

His mouth hardened while his mind searched for words. When they came, they were not what she needed to hear. "We have a history."

"You and Chiara have a history, too."

"Chiara is the past. You are the present."

"The wife you don't love, but refuse to let go."

"And do you wish to go?"

She swallowed, incapable of uttering a face-saving lie.

He pulled her across his chest, exciting her flesh even as she tried to come to terms with her emotions. He stopped when her face was directly above his, her lips only centimeters from his own. "I know you do not."

"You're right." Leaving him would be like severing a limb from her body without anesthetic. But living without his love would be as painful as constantly chafing an open wound.

"I do not wish you to go either."

Looking into eyes that demanded she believe his words, she felt a small spark of hope ignite. He did not want to let her go. That had to mean something.

Maybe he did not love her, but they had a lifetime together. Surely he would eventually figure out she was the best woman in the world for him. After all, Rico was smart.

He gave up on words at that point and kissed her.

The kiss turned carnal in less than five seconds and soon his hands were roaming over the naked contours of her back and exposed bottom with possessive assurance.

She fell into the lovemaking without protest, needing the physical intimacy more than ever after the denial of emotional ties.

They were late for Rico's physical therapy, but Tim only laughed, ribbing them about being newlyweds. He said he could understand how a woman like her could make Rico run late in the mornings. She wondered if Tim would find it equally easy to understand the fact her husband still would not allow her to touch him? Or would he be as perplexed as she was?

Because Rico had done it again. He had seduced her into blind response and successfully deflected her every attempt to explore his body as he explored hers. She couldn't help wondering why and if she didn't believe Rico would see it as the grossest act of betrayal to their privacy, she would ask Tim if there were a physiological reason for Rico's reticence.

Rico slammed back against the rowing machine's resistance and then yanked himself forward with a jerk made powerful by his frustration. He wanted to walk, damn it. He wanted to make love to his wife. Completely. With his whole body.

He'd thought that might be a possibility the night before. His sex had become semierect when he started touching her, but it hadn't lasted and he hated the feeling of sexual helplessness that experience had left him with.

That morning, she'd wanted to discuss their emotions. He didn't know what he felt. He needed her in his life in a way he had not needed Chiara. His inability to experience sexual release underscored that truth. He wondered if his innocent wife realized that. She'd been upset when he hadn't said he loved her, but didn't she realize that what they had was more permanent and lasting than some kind of romantic ideal?

He was committed to her. He knew she was committed to him. In time there would be children. He had begun to hope he would be able to father them in the normal way, but this morning's repeat performance of only a semierection and a temporary one at that, put paid to those thoughts.

He wanted Gianna pregnant with his child. He'd thought consummating their marriage would help her to settle into her role as his wife, but he still sensed a restlessness in her. Once she was pregnant with his child, she would not consider leaving him again.

CHAPTER EIGHT

RICO'S parents arrived back from their anniversary trip late that afternoon to the news of both their son's accident and his first time standing with the parallel bars.

Renata hugged Rico, kissing his cheeks with typical Italian exuberance. "Oh, my son, you are ever the achiever, yes?"

"It was hardly the accomplishment of the century," he dismissed, glaring at Gianna for bringing it up.

She refused to let him make light of it. Besides which his mother's tearful sympathy would have worn thin with him very shortly. Both his parents had been gratifyingly admiring of Rico's choice to help the woman being mugged. Then, not unexpectedly, Renata had gotten emotional at the sight of her son in a wheelchair. Gianna had mentioned Rico's achievement in an effort to focus Renata's attention on the strides he was making, not the results of the accident.

Gianna shifted in the chair she had taken upon entering the drawing room twenty minutes earlier and met his look without flinching. "It is proof positive that you will be walking again soon."

Renata smiled mistily toward Gianna, "Of course Rico will walk again."

Understanding Rico's male pride, Tito said nothing about Gianna's revelation. "Look at how she

stands up to him,'' he commented instead. ''No simpering little miss, our Gianna.'' Rico's father's
brown eyes twinkled at her with approving humor.

''*Ay, ay, ay.* I still cannot believe my son had the
good sense to marry our girl,'' Renata responded,
going back to sit beside her husband on the sofa facing Rico.

Tito, a commanding man, only a couple of inches
shorter than Rico, hugged his wife of over thirty
years. ''He has good taste like his papa.''

Renata blushed, her still beautiful skin taking on
a rosy hue. ''Oh, you!'' She slapped Tito's arm play-
fully.

Andre's low masculine laugh brought Gianna's
gaze around to him. He grinned at his father. ''I'd
say Rico's taste has certainly improved over six
months ago.''

Tito nodded, his expressive face showing his
agreement. ''*Si.* That one. Her heart is as empty as
my bank account after your mama went shopping on
Corfu.''

The others laughed, but Rico scowled. ''You imply I showed no discernment in choosing my fiancée.''

Gianna stifled a groan. Rico's pride wouldn't allow him to take his family's ribbing in stride.

Andre shrugged. ''You showed better taste in selecting a wife, in my opinion.''

''We can thank the good God he came to his
senses in time,'' Tito said with tactlessness allowed
only in a parent.

''Or maybe the driver of the car?'' Renata asked,
her expression thoughtful.

Gianna gasped and Rico's scowl had grown worse,

but Renata shook her head, a look of gentle wisdom in her loving eyes. "Things happen for a reason. Rico will heal, but this accident…it has stopped him from making a bad mistake in his marriage." Her expression turned to one of distaste. "He could have been stuck with such a wife! *Ay, ay, ay.* A conceited little miss who took her clothes off for a living!"

Gianna winced and she shot a glance at Rico, her every concern justified by his cold expression.

"Chiara is a model, not a stripper, Mama." Rico's voice dripped icy censure.

Gianna bit her lip. For a man who didn't still love his ex-fiancée, Rico was reacting with singular offense to criticism of her. She tried to tell herself it was just his pride talking. Rico's standards for himself were very high, so high in fact, he found it almost impossible to admit when he was wrong. Even knowing this, his defense of the other woman hurt.

Renata pursed her lips. "In my day, decent Italian girls did not undress for strangers, or parade themselves on a stage in clothing that covered less than their underwear. Can you see Gianna doing such a thing?"

Rico looked at Gianna with enough consideration to imply he was trying to picture it.

She deliberately looked away from those musing silver eyes. She hated the thought he might be comparing her physical attributes with Chiara's. "I'm inches too short and a stone too heavy to even compete for a modeling contract," she said to Renata.

"I don't know. I think you would do things to lingerie Chiara and those other skinny models could never manage," Andre said with a truly wicked intonation. "I've already seen what you do for a bikini." He kissed his fingertips and opened his hand in a gesture of approval.

It was Renata's turn to gasp.

"Andre, it is not appropriate to make such a comment about your sister-in-law."

Andre moved shoulders encased in a well-cut gray Italian suit in a careless gesture. "If I have offended her, I am sorry." He turned devilishly laughing eyes on Gianna. "Have I offended you, *piccola mia?*"

She shook her head, unsure what to say. His comment had embarrassed her, but it hadn't made her angry. She could hardly mind when his expressed sentiments were so good for her feminine ego. Besides, she knew he saw her as more sister than woman and took his remarks in that light. They were the bland teasing of an older brother.

"You have offended me," Rico declared with freezing cool.

"You cannot be serious," Andre taunted. "Had you married Chiara, you would have had to accustom yourself to such comments being made in the newspapers, not just by your brother."

What was Andre trying to accomplish? She couldn't believe he really wanted to bait Rico into losing his temper and yet that event was fast approaching.

"But I did not marry Chiara, did I?" Rico asked, his voice dangerously soft.

"No, and we are grateful," Tito answered for his younger son, doing nothing to lessen Rico's smoldering anger.

Although the subject changed soon after that, the next hour spent bringing Rico's parents up to date about what had happened while they had been on vacation was a tense one for Gianna. She couldn't forget Rico's defense of Chiara, or his angry reaction to criticism of her.

When the conversation moved into business channels, the women excused themselves so Renata could show Gianna the things she'd bought on her trip with Tito.

Gianna ran loving fingers over a hand-embroidered duvet cover. "It's so beautiful. It must have taken a year to finish." The pale lavender silk was covered with purple irises, their dark green stems and leaves intertwined like ivy.

Renata smiled the smile of a woman who has made a killer purchase. "The woman who did it told me it took her several months to finish." She pulled out a white lace mantilla she'd bought off the coast of Spain. "Now this would have been beautiful as a wedding veil."

Gianna felt herself color under the heavy hint. "It's lovely."

"A register office. DiRinaldos do not marry in such cold surroundings. No friends. No priest to bless the union. No gifts." Renata stood up and laid the mantilla over Gianna's hair and settled it around her shoulders, then stood back to admire the effect. "*Si.* This is how you should have looked on your wedding day."

"Rico didn't want to expose himself to the curious stares of wedding guests while he was still forced to use the wheelchair to get around."

"Then he should have waited, that son of mine. To marry without even his parents present..." She shook her head, her disapproval obvious.

Gianna said nothing.

"We will have to plan a proper blessing on the marriage after Rico has regained his mobility."

Gianna made a sound that could be taken as acquiescence and soon Renata was deep in plans for a big Italian wedding which would include everything but the actual ceremony. A formal church blessing would replace it. She shooed Gianna out of the room, saying she had lists to make and thinking to do. Gianna did not point out that as the bride, she should have some say in the preparations. If her own mother were still living, she would be doing exactly as Renata was, only she would have called Renata for advice.

Gianna went to the library and tried to lose herself in a book, but thoughts of the afternoon kept intruding. Although she was horribly relieved that Rico's parents apparently approved of their marriage, she worried that their voiced dislike of Chiara would cause problems with Rico.

Her worry was justified later as she and Rico dressed for dinner. She had gone into the bathroom to change and came out wearing a demure sheath dress in chocolate-brown silk with a gold pendant formed in the shape of a rose and matching earrings she'd inherited from her mother. She'd left her hair down, pulling only some of it back into a gold clip she fastened on the back of her head.

Rico's eyes flared when he saw her and then grew cold.

"Attempting to live up to my parents' image of you as the Madonna bride, *cara?*" His voice was lethally sarcastic and the endearment sounded like an insult.

She looked down at her dress. It wasn't so different than the outfits she'd worn to dinner over the past week at the villa. "I don't know what you mean."

His dark brows rose in mocking disbelief. "Don't you?"

Her fingers curled into her palms until she felt her nails dig into the soft flesh. "No."

"Chiara complained about how you and Andre made her feel unwelcome at the hospital and I dismissed it at the time, but after the visit with my parents and Andre earlier I have to wonder if she saw things more truthfully than I did."

Gianna remembered the accusations. She'd been relieved at the time that Rico hadn't taken the blatant lies seriously. It irked her unbearably that they'd come back to haunt her now, when there were already enough issues in her marriage causing her pain. From the look on his face, Rico wasn't going to believe her version of events, but she had to try anyway.

"Your brother may not be fond of her, but that does not mean he treated her with anything other than courtesy while she was your fiancée. He respects you too much to do otherwise."

"You think so?" Rico had moved until they faced each other with less than a foot separating them.

She swallowed, made nervous by his proximity and the brooding anger emanating from him. "I know it. I was there, remember?"

"*Si.* You were there, but if you aided my brother in dispossessing my fiancée of her place by my side, you would hardly advertise the fact, no?"

Fury filled her. How dare he question her integrity? Chiara was a royal pain in the neck and Gianna refused to submit tamely to an indictment on her character based on the other woman's manipulative games.

"I didn't dispossess anyone because she wasn't there to begin with. When I arrived at the hospital, your fiancée," she said the word sneeringly, "was nowhere to be found. She'd taken a flit while you lay in that bed in a coma despite the fact the doctors had told her having a loved one by your side could make all the difference in your recovering consciousness."

She yanked her hair from his hand, bringing stinging tears to her eyes as the action caused a painful pull on her scalp. "If you don't believe me, ask Andre."

"My brother has made it clear where his affection lies."

"Are you saying you think he would lie to you?"

"For you? Maybe."

"That's ridiculous."

"Is it? My brother has made no secret of his admiration for you."

She looked into his eyes and read anger and something else. "You're jealous," she said on a gasp.

Making a sweeping arc with his hand to indicate the chair, he glared at her. "Is that such a surprise?"

Funnily enough, it was.

"I didn't marry Andre." She'd never wanted to marry Andre. Only Rico. Only ever Rico.

"And yet you found his compliments on your body in a swimsuit pleasing."

"Did you think I should have been offended?"

She didn't know why she bothered to ask. The answer was obvious.

"You should not desire the admiration of other men."

"I don't desire his admiration, but that doesn't mean that when he says something nice I'm going to tell him to stuff it, either. He's my brother now."

"And I am your husband."

How had this crazy conversation gotten started? Oh, right. "Do you really believe I kept Chiara away from you in order to keep you for myself?"

His sensual lips twisted in a grimace. "No. I spoke in anger."

Remembering another time he'd spoken in anger, she smiled. "You were jealous."

He sighed long and loudly, his expression of disgruntlement for once easy to read. *"Si."*

She grinned and did something she'd never done before. She plopped down on his lap and clasped her hands behind his neck, then kissed him on the chin before laying her head against his chest. "Don't be. You have no reason."

His arms came around her in a hug that was almost hurting. Eventually his hold loosened, but kept his arms around her and rubbed the top of her head with his cheek. *"Cara."*

They sat that way for several minutes in complete silence before going down to dinner.

Rico entered his bedroom after two late night international calls to find his wife sleeping, her hand curled under her cheek like a small child. He was still reeling from how much having her sit in his lap voluntarily had meant to him. He had felt like he had his entire world in his arms. The feeling had not been wholly pleasant. It implied a lack of emotional independence he'd never before experienced. Definitely not with Chiara.

He got himself into bed.

His mobility had increased greatly over the past week, but still he could not walk. And things he had always taken for granted were impossible tasks to perform. Like right now. He wanted to pull Gianna across the bed and into his arms. He finally managed it, but only after a lot of maneuvering.

It was worth it to feel her small body curled so trustingly against him. She automatically snuggled into his side, as if they had been sleeping together for years, not a single night. Perhaps in her dreams like his, they had.

Remembering his irrational accusations earlier, he grimaced. Jealousy, he was discovering, could be hell. He'd never been jealous of Chiara. No matter how skimpy the outfit she modeled in. Andre had gotten that right, but just the thought of Gianna in a bikini within fifty feet of another man made Rico see red. He'd ask his mother to find her a modest one piece.

Getting his independent wife to wear it would be something else entirely, he admitted to himself. While in some ways Gianna was traditional Italian to the core, in others she was very American in her thinking and actions.

Her small hand rested against his chest, while one leg insinuated itself over his thigh. He could feel the sensation of her weight, but had to touch her with his hand to experience the softness of her skin. It was maddening.

When would he be whole again?

He let one hand rest possessively over her bottom, keeping her pressed against him in a way that should have caused a certain reaction in his male anatomy, but did not. Would it return with the complete return of his mobility?

The metallic taste of fear accompanied the possibility that it would not. No man wanted to be half a man. He would not let Gianna touch him in case she discovered his lack of true virility. Yet, he ached to allow those small hands to roam over his body in a way he had never wanted Chiara, or any other woman's touch.

One thing was certain. Half a man or a whole one, he would never let her go.

Gianna woke in the morning curled around a pillow scented with Rico's masculine fragrance. She was warm and had the vague impression of being held through the night. Had she been, or was it just wishful thinking on her part?

Rico was the only person at the breakfast table when she went down less than an hour later. She slid into a chair across the table from him. "Where is everyone else?"

"Papa and Mama are still sleeping and Andre is at a breakfast meeting on behalf of the bank."

She smiled. "It's nice to have your parents home."

His expression of approval warmed her insides. "They are thrilled to have a new daughter."

"Renata wasn't happy about how our marriage took place." Gianna smiled ruefully. "Your mother wants to have our marriage blessed. I think Andre

was right about her using it as an excuse to have all
the trappings of a wedding.''

Rico's smile made her melt inside like milk chocolate on a hot sidewalk. ''She will enjoy it. Do you
mind, *cara?*''

''No. When she was making plans yesterday, it
made me think of what it would be like if my mother
was still alive. It felt nice.''

''Then we will let her have her way.''

She nodded and started eating the fruit she'd
served herself from the bowl on the table.

Rico checked his watch. ''Hurry with your breakfast. We have an appointment in an hour's time.''

''An appointment?''

''*Si.* With the fertility specialist,'' he elucidated.

''But why?'' He was weeks, if not days from
walking. Why go through IVF if they didn't have to?

''So we can begin the process of making you pregnant with my baby.'' He said it as if speaking to a
slow-witted child.

''But…''

''Were you hoping I would forget that side of our
bargain?''

Sometimes he could be very paranoid. ''No. I want
to have your baby.''

''Then, finish your breakfast so we can be on our
way.''

''But, you're almost walking,'' she blurted out.

Something flickered in his silver eyes, but then it
was gone. ''There is no guaranteed timeline for that
eventuality. I want to begin on a family right away.''

And a baby would be another bond between them,
something else to build emotional connections
around. ''All right.''

CHAPTER NINE

SHE was still trying to comprehend Rico's desire to try for conception with IVF when they were shown into the doctor's office. The only thing she could think was that he didn't believe he would be capable of fathering her child any other way. She hated the thought of him tormented by such fear, but she knew too little about such matters to assuage those fears.

Maybe she would talk to Tim.

"You realize the more invasive procedure, intravenous fertilization, will not be necessary," the doctor was saying, bringing Gianna's attention back firmly to the matter at hand. "We will be performing TESE on you, Mr. DiRinaldo," the doctor said, talking about the process by which they would collect Rico's sperm, "a fairly painless, outpatient procedure."

Rico nodded, his expression bland.

The doctor turned to her. "You will have to go through intra-uterine insemination, Mrs. DiRinaldo."

Gianna found the ensuing conversation with the doctor embarrassing to say the least. He discussed options and asked questions about her fertility cycle that left her stuttering for answers. She'd never been one of those women who marked things like that on a calendar.

After her third stammering answer, Rico sighed. "Would you prefer I left while you discuss such details with the doctor?"

She felt her face heat with an even stronger blush. "Yes." Her eyes pleaded with him to understand.

His half smile told her that he had. He turned and left the room, closing the door behind him.

The doctor laughed. "I'm surprised he offered to go. Mr. DiRinaldo strikes me as a man who likes to maintain control and his protectiveness toward you is apparent."

But his understanding for her feelings was greater than his need for control, she thought with a warm gratitude. In that, their relationship had grown, at least. He might believe she should not be embarrassed discussing anything with him, but he now apparently accepted that she was.

"What were you saying about the IUI?" She wanted the consultation over so she could get back to Rico.

"The procedure is one of the least complicated treatments for infertility and little cause for concern."

She nodded, encouraging him to continue. The doctor went on to explain what she needed to do to prepare for the procedure and how to keep track of her temperature and other physiological indicators in order to determine the optimum time for the procedure.

Finally, the doctor smiled benevolently. "Although it is a simple procedure, it can be a trifle painful. You understand this, *si?*"

She nodded her affirmative, though she wasn't quite sure why or how it would hurt. Discussing such private matters with two men, even her doctor and husband, held no appeal.

The doctor made a notation in the file open on the

desk in front of him. "You will experience anything from minor discomfort to lingering pain from the procedure. Though to be honest, less than three percent of women undergoing treatment complain of anything more than the most minor of discomfort."

That was comforting, but even with the low percentage...not something she was willing to share with Rico. He might not allow her to undergo the procedure and she wanted his baby. Very much.

"I'm not worried about it," Gianna asserted.

"It often takes as many as six attempts before conception happens," the doctor warned her.

She hoped Rico would have regained full functionality by then, but she nodded in understanding and acceptance.

Rico was called back in and the doctor loaded her down with a lot of paraphernalia that was supposed to let her know when the optimum time for the procedure would occur. She eyed it askance. "I'm supposed to take my temperature every day?"

"Yes. And—"

"Never mind. I'll read the instructions," she hastily inserted before he started explaining the other methods of measuring her productivity in front of Rico. It had been bad enough the first time around with only the doctor in the room.

They left the private clinic after making an appointment for Rico's TESE on the following Tuesday.

It was the day after his appointment when Gianna followed him into the room where he had his physical therapy sessions. Tim had not yet arrived, but Rico settled himself into the rowing machine and started exercising with the same intense concentration he gave everything in his life.

His thigh muscles corded as he forced the machine through its rotation with his arms.

Gianna filled a water bottle and placed it on the mat beside him. "Tim said you took several steps yesterday."

She had gone shopping with Renata and hadn't found out about Rico's progress until Tim and his wife came for dinner. Gianna had been seeing them out, the rest of the family still in the sala, when Tim had mentioned it. He'd tactfully ignored her shock at the news.

The knowledge Rico hadn't shared his progress with her hurt and confused her. She thought they had been growing closer.

"*Si*. Can I expect a big announcement at dinner tonight?"

She flinched at the sarcasm. "Your parents and brother are interested in your progress."

He grimaced. "You are right, *cara*. I should not snap at you. Tell them what you like."

She couldn't help wondering if he were in pain from the procedure the day before. She bit her lip as he continued pushing his body to the limits. "Are you sure you should be going at it quite so hard after yesterday?"

His jaw tensed and he pushed through three more rotations before answering. "I do not need a nursemaid, Gianna."

He hardly ever called her by her first name and she couldn't help feeling it wasn't an indication of intimacy at the moment. "I'm not trying to be one."

"Then why are you here?"

Good question. She'd attended his sessions at first to cajole him into working on his rehabilitation rather than his company. But since their arrival in Italy, he had given more than enough attention to walking again. She continued to come to his sessions to spend time with him because the rest of the day his business kept him occupied. She saw him at dinner, but rarely otherwise.

Half the time she was asleep before he came to bed. Even when she was not, he never wanted to talk. He made love to her, but steadfastly refused to allow her to touch him. She enjoyed sleeping in his arms, but an underlying sense of insecurity accompanied his rejection of her attempts to give back a small measure of the pleasure she enjoyed in his embrace.

She still hadn't worked up the courage to discuss their intimacy with Tim. She wondered if she ever would. Perhaps if she could convince herself it wouldn't be a betrayal of Rico's privacy.

"I thought you liked having me here," she replied quietly, realizing even as she spoke, she'd clearly become surplus to requirements. "I'll leave you to your exercise."

She turned to go.

"Gianna."

"Was there something you needed?" she asked without turning to face him.

Several seconds passed in silence.

"I enjoy your company." Spoken after an uncomfortable pause and in such a stilted voice, she wasn't buying it. Rico was too polite to tell her to get lost, but it was obvious he wanted to. Had probably been wanting to for several days now.

She squared her shoulders and forced a lightness

into her voice she did not feel. "I think I'll find Renata and see if there's anything she wants me to do." At least his mother made her feel welcome, pulling Gianna into her social life and charity work at every opportunity.

"*Cara.*"

"What?" Maybe she'd been wrong. Maybe he would ask her to stay.

"Did you take your temperature this morning?"

The question was like a douse of ice water. The only thing Rico apparently wanted from her was her womb. "No."

"Why?"

"I started." He could figure out for himself what that meant. "I'll be going in for the procedure in less than three weeks if my body follows the normal cycle."

She didn't wait around to hear his reaction. She knew what he wanted. A baby. She was the necessary appendage to the body of his dream. Nothing more. Sometimes, in the night, when he touched her with tenderness that brought tears to her eyes, she convinced herself *she* meant something to him. But she didn't and the sooner she accepted that, the faster she would stop butting her head against the wall of his indifference.

Rico watched Gianna leave and wanted to call her back again, but what could he say? He hated the fact he had to use a sterile medical procedure to impregnate his wife with his child. It made him feel like less of a man. Added to that, having her witness his struggles to return to mobility was becoming more and more difficult. She treated him like an invalid.

She'd gone from cajoling him to work harder to reproaching him for expending too much energy.

The only time he felt like her husband was when he made love to her at night. Then, it made no difference he had less control over his legs than a two-year-old. She responded to him with such passion, he soon became addicted to the sounds of pleasure she made and the feel of her body as she convulsed in release. He found it so gratifying, it was like finding his own satisfaction.

According to Tim, that could very well be the only gratification Rico would ever know again. Asking the therapist about his lack of recovery in that area had been lowering for Rico, but he did not shrink from doing so. He had to know. Tim's comments had been both encouraging and discouraging. In many cases, full capability was restored, but there were the small percentage of men that even after mobility was restored were unable to maintain an erection.

Fear he was one of those men made him short with Gianna. She was his wife, his woman. *He loved her.* He didn't know when the knowledge had seated itself in his brain, but he'd known since waking in his hospital room in New York that he needed her in a way he had never needed another person.

And he wanted nothing more than to be whole for her. Which meant giving his rehabilitation everything he had. Exercising his legs. Going with Tim through the muscular rotations. Trying to walk no matter how many times he fell in humiliating defeat to the exercise mat. It wasn't defeat, though. Not if he didn't give up and with the impetus of becoming whole for Gianna…he never would.

*   *   *

Gianna saw almost nothing of Rico for the following weeks. She didn't visit him during his therapy sessions and he did not seek her out. He had business meetings during dinner three nights out of seven. The nights he was home for dinner, she kept the conversation centered on his mother's plans to celebrate their wedding.

Gianna avoided any sort of intimate conversation, wanting to sidestep the possibility of rejection. Rico seemed just as intent on avoiding her, coming to bed long after she'd gone to sleep each night. Once, he woke her when he came to bed and she coldly told him she was too tired. She hadn't wanted to deal with the pain and pleasure mixture that accompanied his making love to her. He hadn't tried again.

But there were nights she could have sworn she slept in his arms. He was always gone before she woke and she had to wonder if she had dreamed the sense of warmth and security.

In the middle of the third week, she came out of the bathroom after her shower to find him in their bed. "What are you doing here?"

His brows rose. "I sleep in this bed, no?"

"I meant now. You don't usually come to bed so early."

"So, tonight it is different."

There was something different all right...something about him. Triumph glittered in his silver eyes. Triumph over what? And then it hit her. "Where is your wheelchair?"

"Gone."

"*You're walking?*" she practically shrieked. He'd said nothing.

"After a fashion. I must use a stick, but this is progress, no?"

"Yes!" she shouted and threw herself across the bed to hug him in exuberant joy.

His arms locked around her and she found herself sitting across his lap, her hands locked behind his neck. "You're walking," she whispered with awe. "I knew you could do it!"

"With the right incentive, a man can do anything."

She smiled, her eyes tearing up. "Oh, Rico…" She didn't know what had altered his focus so completely, but whatever it was had her eternal gratitude.

"I thought we could celebrate, no?"

His husky voice brought back memories of their first "celebration" of his progress. A kiss that had irrevocably changed their relationship. Was he thinking the same thing? The sexy gleam of a predator in his eyes said he was. "Yes," she said with a sigh against his lips.

He let her kiss him for several seconds, allowing her to explore his lips with her tongue. It was heavenly. Finally, he was going to let her be an active participant in their loving. She tunneled her fingers into the silky black strands of his hair and deepened the kiss.

He growled against her lips as his hand cupped possessively over her breast. She arched into the touch, joy coursing through her veins from his achievement and this new, more evenhanded lovemaking. She let her hand trail down his neck to his collarbone. She outlined it with one fingertip.

He shuddered under her and she felt feminine power surge through her for the first time. It gave her the confidence to be bolder than she had ever thought possible. She shifted until she was straddling his thighs and placed both hands on the hot skin of his chest. It was her turn to shudder. She had wanted this for so long. The freedom to touch him. She could feel his heart beating a rapid tattoo against one palm and the protrusion of his male nipple against the other.

She wanted to touch him everywhere.

Her hands slid lower and lower as she edged toward that mysterious part of his body, she found so fascinating. She'd never seen a completely naked male in the flesh and she desperately wanted to see Rico. Her husband.

Suddenly his hands gripped her wrists like manacles. "No."

Her eyes flew open and she stared into an immovable gaze of molten metal.

"I want to touch you," she practically begged.

"It is better that I should touch you, *tesoro.*"

No. No. No. She wanted this to be equal. "Please."

He ignored her, bending his head to capture her mouth in an incendiary kiss. Her body reacted with its usual mind-numbing pleasure, but a small part of her brain remained functioning. And that part protested this further rejection.

He didn't want her to touch him. He. Did. Not. Want. Her. To. Touch. Him.

The refrain went round and round in her head until it drowned out even the nerve centers clamoring for more pleasure from the hands now roaming over her body.

She tore her lips from his. *"No."*

His eyes opened, a dazed expression in them that almost gave her hope. "Why won't you let me touch you?"

"Is it not enough I give you pleasure, *tesoro?*" he asked in a thickened voice.

Something cracked inside her heart. "No."

"You can say that when your body is already throbbing for release, when you are aching for my touch?" He illustrated his point by gently pinching her nipple, causing her to groan and arch in involuntary desire.

His expression was no longer dazed, if it ever had been. It was calculating and she couldn't stand it. Reasons for their lovemaking when he so clearly did not want her presented themselves to her conscious. None of them were good.

It was all about control. His over her. It renewed his male ego to have a woman so blatantly under his sensual thrall. Then there was pity. He felt sorry for her. It had to be obvious to him that she was in love with him. He'd even said so once. So, he made love to her because he pitied her. Maybe there was even some element of payoff for her willingness to have his baby.

She didn't want to be paid off. She wanted to be loved. A sob welled up and she ripped herself out of his arms, landing on the floor beside the bed. "I want my own room."

He reeled back as if she'd hit him. "What?"

"I don't want to sleep with you anymore."

He threw back the bedcovers, revealing wine-red silk boxers and the hair roughened contours of his legs. "Like hell! You are my wife. You sleep in my bed."

She was so angry, she was shaking. "I'm your incubator," she screamed at him, "not your wife!"

His olive skin turned pale and silver eyes registered shock. "No!"

He reached for her, but she spun away and ran to the bathroom. She slammed and locked the door.

She heard a thump and voluble cursing in Italian. Seconds later, he was pounding on the door. "Come out of there, Gianna."

"No!" Tears streamed down her face. She couldn't stand one more bout of pity sex.

Silence met her defiance. Long moments of utter silence.

"Come out of there, *tesoro*. We need to talk." He spoke calmly, but she didn't feel calm.

"I don't want to."

"Please, Gianna."

She stared at the door as if it might suddenly dissolve and leave her with no defense. "I d-don't want you t-touching me anymore," she said between sobbing breaths.

"Okay. I will not touch you."

"Do you p-promise?" Part of her mind acknowledged she was overreacting, but her emotions were out of control.

"You have my word."

She unlocked the door. He opened it and then leaned against the frame. His expression was almost as tortured as she felt and a white line of stress outlined his firm lips. "I am not a rapist."

She stared at him, appalled chagrin adding to her pain. "I know that."

"Then come to bed, *moglie mia*."

His wife. Was she his wife? Or was she just his

baby maker? At that moment it really did not matter. Too drained to fight anymore, she silently climbed between the sheets.

He followed her at a slow pace, taking careful steps, his expression one of grim determination. She realized belatedly that the thump she had heard earlier had probably been him falling. Guilt washed over her even as a sense of unreality accompanied it while she watched as her husband walked under his own power for the first time since the accident. Happiness at his accomplishment mitigated some of the pain of his rejection.

He eventually made it to the bed and he slid into place next to her. She reached over and turned out the light.

"Tesoro—"

"I don't want to talk," she slotted in before he could say anything more.

"I need to tell you—"

"No! There's nothing to say. Please. Just let me go to sleep." She started crying again and he pulled her into his arms, cursing under his breath.

She struggled feebly against him, but he just tightened his hold. "Shh, *tesoro.*" He stroked her hair and whispered words of comfort in a mixture of Italian and English.

Her tears finally ceased and he tried to talk to her again, but she begged him to let her be. She would do anything to stave off his explanation of why she wasn't woman enough for a complete intimate relationship with him. Even if he was afraid of an inability to perform, if he wanted her, wouldn't he want to try? Wouldn't he want her help?

A heavy sigh was the only response to her pleas, but his arms remained warm and strong around her throughout the night.

The next morning, Gianna woke up before Rico. Her histrionics of the night before brought a wave of shame. He had wanted to talk to her and she had refused. Stupid, stupid, stupid. But even after her refusal, he had held her and comforted her throughout the night. She loved him so much, but she certainly hadn't let love guide her actions the night before. Well, today would be different.

She absorbed his warmth and allowed herself the luxury of feeling cherished for several minutes before slipping from the sanctuary of his arms and the bed.

Fifteen minutes later, she surveyed the results of her daily tests to measure her body's readiness for the intrauterine insemination. Well, that explained at least part of her irrationality, she thought wryly.

A sound from behind her alerted her to Rico's presence. She turned to face him, her hand gripping the lapels of her robe together at her neck.

He stood framed in the doorway, all six feet four inches of him exposed but for what his silk boxers covered. His hair stood endearingly on end and morning stubble shadowed his jaw, giving him a dangerous air.

Eyes the color of stainless steel surveyed her with intense concentration. "We need to talk, *cara.*"

She nodded and swallowed. Yes, they did, but right now they had things to do. "My body is at optimum temperature for the procedure."

His eyes flared. "What did you say?"

"I need to contact the clinic and make an appointment for today."

"Today?" He looked dazed.

"Yes."

He closed his eyes as if he was battling something mentally.

Had he decided he didn't want her to have his baby after all? "Have you changed your mind?"

His eyes flew open. "I do not know…"

She couldn't believe it. "Does what I want matter at all?"

He looked so grim. "It matters a great deal, *tesoro*."

"I want to try."

His jaw clenched, but his head went up and down in a short affirmative movement.

She called the doctor from the phone beside the bed. Turning to Rico after she hung up, she felt a faint tremor of nerves attack. "He wants me to come in right away. It's better if I don't eat anything first."

"I'll be ready to leave in fifteen minutes."

She stared at him. "You want to come with me?" She hadn't considered that. He'd gone to his procedure alone. She assumed she would be on her own for hers as well.

"*Si.*"

"But there's no need." Did he think she was a basket case after last night? She wouldn't blame him.

"There is every need." The words were implacable, his expression even more so.

She chewed on her bottom lip and nervously pleated the soft velour of her robe. "They're going to put something inside me," she said, her gaze firmly fixed on the plush pale blue carpet.

"And this embarrasses you?"

Give that man a cigar. "Yes."

"I will keep my eyes on your beautiful face, *cara mia.*"

That brought her gaze up from the carpet. "I'm not beautiful," she blurted.

"You are the most beautiful woman I have ever known."

"You don't mean that." He couldn't, not unless he loved her. Only love would put her physical attributes above the gorgeous women he had dated.

He grimaced, as if in pain. "I do, but I do not expect you to believe me."

But she wanted to. Oh, how she wanted to. "Rico…"

"Will you allow me to accompany you?"

"Can I stop you?"

Again, the grimace. "In honesty? It is not likely." He said it apologetically, like he was sorry he had his own ideas and intended to follow through on them.

The embarrassment aside, the thought of having him with her was comforting. "You can come. I want you to come."

CHAPTER TEN

SHE realized halfway to the clinic that she'd forgotten to take the prescription-strength pain reliever she'd been instructed to take an hour before the procedure. She quickly swallowed a couple of over the counter meds from the pillbox in her handbag. The dose only called for one, two should make up for the fact it wasn't prescription strength.

Rico was instructed to wait in the waiting room while she undressed and donned an ugly blue hospital gown. She looked down at it ruefully. Somehow it seemed incongruous with an event that was supposed to leave her pregnant with her husband's baby, but then she'd never considered getting pregnant in the sterile environment of an outpatient procedure room, either.

It did not matter, though. She wanted Rico's *bambini*, no matter what she had to do to get them.

Rico was ushered into the room after her vital signs were measured and the nurse confirmed Gianna's morning test results. He smiled as he came in, leaning only slightly on the walking stick.

She smiled back nervously. "Like my new togs?" she asked, indicating the utilitarian gown.

He leaned down and kissed her gently. "I like what is in them better."

His words rendered her speechless with pleasure.

"Did you remember to take your pain medication?" the nurse asked Gianna.

She flushed guiltily and shook her head. "But I took a double dose of the meds I take for period cramping on the way here."

The nurse, a middle aged brunette with a kind smile, patted Gianna reassuringly. "That should be fine."

Rico had tensed beside her at the first mention of pain. "What pain medication? I thought this procedure was pain free. What is going on?"

Gianna reached out and took hold of his arm. "It's just a precaution. Nothing to worry about. The doctor and I discussed this."

He looked unconvinced. "Are you sure? Perhaps we should consider waiting."

"No." She took a deep breath. "This is what I want."

His frown said he wasn't happy about it. He turned to the nurse. "Perhaps she should take some now. Surely you keep a supply for such an occurrence."

The nurse looked doubtful. "We do, but I don't think it would be wise to mix the two medications. Some pain relievers wouldn't be a problem, but…"

She didn't finish her statement, but Gianna got the message. She reached out and took Rico's free hand. "I'll be fine. Please, Rico, don't make such a big deal about it."

Twenty minutes later her grip on Rico's hand was like channel locks around a water pipe and she was bitterly regretting her blithe assurances. The discomfort of having the catheter inserted to her womb hadn't been unbearable, but now she was cramping painfully and the entire lower half of her body felt like it was sharing in the experience.

Tears filled her eyes and she clung more tightly to

Rico, whose eyes reflected the tortures of the rack. He had tried to get her to abandon the procedure at the first sign of her pain, but she had refused. He'd stood by her side willing his own strength onto her. It was a small glimmer of the support she could expect having the baby and even amidst the physical pain, it pleased her.

"Is it almost over?" Rico demanded of the doctor in a voice that implied a negative answer would have a very bad affect on Rico's temper.

"Yes, just another few seconds and we'll be finished."

The man was as good as his word and within minutes everything had been removed. Her hips were elevated with a wedge and the doctor informed her she would have to remain like that for an hour. It would have been fine, if the cramping had stopped, but it hadn't. She didn't say anything, however, already feeling like a wimp for making such a big deal about the procedure.

Rico seemed to know anyway. He didn't say anything, but held her hand and massaged her tummy with a light, gentle circular motion. After a few minutes of the lulling treatment, she slipped into a doze despite the painful cramping.

She was startled when the nurse returned to the room and told her she could change back into her street clothes. Rico had kept up the soothing touch for the entire hour. Normally shy, she made no demur when he showed every sign of staying in the room while she dressed. She found his presence comforting and wasn't about to give it up.

"Is it getting any better?" Rico asked as he helped her into her clothes like a parent with a small child.

She let him zip her dress and settle her braid down her back before she turned to face him. "Yes. Next time, I'll remember to take the prescribed pain relievers, I can tell you." She smiled at him, but he did not return the gesture.

He looked like she'd said something repugnant. "There will not be a next time, *piccola mia*."

His words left no doubt he meant what he said.

She wanted his baby and was preparing to argue with him, but everything went fuzzy and her head felt like she'd been on a spinning ride at the county fair. She reached out for Rico, her hand colliding with his torso as she felt her knees give way.

She woke on the bed to the sound of Rico shouting. He was chewing the doctor out for everything from her cramping to the state of the world economy. Or at least, that was how it sounded to her still fuzzy brain.

"Rico?" The word came out a whisper, but he spun around midshout, his attention focused in on her with instant probing intensity.

"How do you feel? The pain, is it still there?"

"Only a little bit. I feel kind of woozy."

"I told your husband it is probably the lack of food. We'll give you a glass of juice to bring your blood sugar level up before he takes you home." The doctor's normally calm demeanor appeared a bit frayed around the edges.

She nodded, but Rico scowled.

"If this is so, such a thing should have been attended to before she was instructed to dress. What if she had been alone? She could have hurt herself falling to the floor." His voice rose with every word until he was shouting again.

She winced and touched her hand to her temple.

His jaw tautened. "I am sorry, *tesoro*. You do not need your out-of-control husband shouting right now, no?"

"Did you catch me?" she asked rather than answer his rhetorical question.

"*Si*. It was doubtful for a moment if I could keep us both up, but you are such a tiny thing, *cara mia*. I was able to lift you onto the bed."

A nurse arrived with a glass of apple juice, which Rico took from her with a look that sent the other woman scurrying from the room. He put his arm around Gianna's shoulder, lifting her into a sitting position and placed the glass to her lips.

She drank the juice, cheered by Rico's coddling.

She looked into his metallic gaze as she finished the juice. "You're going to be a wonderful papa."

His features contracted in bleak lines. "Not if it requires a repeat of today."

And if she couldn't have his baby, would he want her still? His actions pointed to an answer she was terrified of believing.

Rico insisted on her going back to bed as soon as they reached the villa. She knew she was supposed to stay horizontal for the rest of the day, to increase chances of conception, but she'd planned on doing so on a couch in the sala. She had not intended being cooped up in the bedroom.

"But I don't want to stay in bed. I can lie down just as easily downstairs," she argued with Rico even as he undressed her and put a nightgown over her head.

"You are in pain. You must rest."

She ground her teeth. "I don't want to."

He smiled, the first lightening of his expression since that morning. "You sound like a recalcitrant child."

"Don't make the mistake of thinking you can treat me like one. I want to go downstairs."

"No, *tesoro*."

"How would you like being bored and cooped up in a bed all day?"

He raised his brows and she felt like shouting. Last night being a rare exception, she never shouted. She glowered at him. "I know you were in the hospital, but you worked. You had your personal assistant around. I visited you. Andre visited you. Even the wicked witch of the west visited you."

"Do you want me to call Chiara and see if she'll pay you a visit?" he asked, showing he knew just exactly who she'd been speaking about. "I hear she's in Milan."

Heard from whom? Had Rico asked? The thought he was still interested in the comings and goings of his ex-fiancée made her angrier. She flounced onto the bed and fluffed her pillows as a backrest with more energy than necessary. "The last person I want to spend the day with is your former fiancée."

"How about me?"

Was he saying he had planned to stick around and visit her?

"*You* kept *me* company in the hospital."

"But I thought you would be going back to work." He'd spent so much time lately at the bank and DiRinaldo industries office, she hardly ever saw him.

"No way am I leaving you alone after your ordeal this morning."

She smiled in receipt of that statement. "Thanks."

"Do not thank me." He picked up the phone, pressing the inside line button. "I'll ring for some food."

She nodded and he spoke into the mouthpiece, ordering a late breakfast for them both. When he hung up, he went to pull a chair over by the bed, but she scooted toward the center, making room for him to sit beside her. "You can sit here if you like."

"I'm not sure that is a good idea."

"Why?"

He made a face. "Having you next to me in bed sends my brain down a path you cannot take at the moment, *cara*."

She thought he was teasing, so she responded in kind. "I'm sure you can control yourself."

"You are only certain of this because you do not understand the workings of a man's mind, I assure you." He sounded so serious, but lowered himself onto the bed beside her, propping his walking stick against the small table with a lamp on it. "How are you feeling?"

"Hungry," she answered honestly.

He smiled. "I too am hungry."

"You could have eaten breakfast," she reminded him.

"Not when you did not."

"Is that some kind of macho guy thing?"

He reached out and brushed her lower lip, making all the air in her lungs freeze between exhaling and inhaling. "It is a Rico DiRinaldo thing."

"You're a pretty special man, aren't you?" Her

lip moved against his finger and it was all she could do not to suck the digit into her mouth. But she wasn't leaving herself open for another physical rejection. Even if maybe she was beginning to understand why he did so, it still hurt.

She pulled her head back and he dropped his hand, an emotion like pain flaring briefly in the silver depths of his eyes.

"I am so special I allowed my wife to undergo a painful procedure rather than face up to my own fears," he evinced in a driven undertone, his head bent the light glinting off the black smoothness of his hair.

She stared at him, flummoxed by what he had said. "I don't understand, *caro*. What fears?"

His head reared back and something powerful burned in his eyes. "You never call me that. You use endearments frequently with Andre, but with me, it is always my name."

She felt like she was walking through the woods early in the morning, when the fog had not yet lifted and she could barely see one step in front of her face. She didn't want to trip on a fallen log and yet felt compelled to take the next step. "Does that bother you?"

"Si." Painfully honest. Painfully vulnerable. Doubly hard for a man of Rico's temperament to admit.

"With Andre, it's natural because they don't mean anything." She wanted to repay Rico's honesty with her own, but it was hard. "With you, they mean too much."

His hand curled around her own. "So, you do not say them."

She swallowed and went for broke. "To me, your name is like an endearment."

He lifted her hand to his lips and kissed the center of her palm. A noise near the doorway heralded the arrival of their breakfast and the discussion was abandoned while they ate.

She yawned when she finished. "I can't think why I'm tired. I shouldn't be. It's not as if I've run a marathon today." He hadn't even let her walk to the car, insisting on pushing her in a wheelchair. She had the sense that if he were just a tad steadier on his feet, he would have carried her.

"It has been a difficult time for you."

"I feel a lot better," she tried to reassure him.

He looked at her for several seconds, as if trying to read her mind, then without a word, he stood up and took the tray to the door and left it in the hallway. He came back toward her, an expression so grave on his features, she felt a physical hurt seeing it.

He did not sit down again, but went to stand at the window, his hand gripping the cane with white-knuckle ferocity. "When I married you, I was not sure I would walk again."

She'd known that—deep in her heart, she had known. If he had believed absolutely in his own recovery, he would never have married someone as ordinary as herself.

"But you believed in me and I needed that." Each word sounded ripped from deep inside him. "I was not thinking about what was best for you and it shames me to admit it."

"You were frightened."

His shoulders stiffened, but he didn't deny it. *"Si."*

"I understand."

He spun around to face her and torment gave his face a haggard look. "Do you? How can you understand me when I do not? I was selfish, *tesoro.* I did not care for your happiness, only my own."

She shook her head, remembering his infinitely tender introduction to lovemaking. "I don't believe that."

"Perhaps you are right. I thought in my arrogance that being married to me, sharing my bed, it would be enough for you."

She had thought so too. It had certainly beaten the alternative…life without him. "I accepted, knowing that was all that was on offer."

"Because you love me and I shamelessly used that love to get what I wanted, what I needed."

"You can't use what is freely given." She didn't want him wallowing in guilt. They couldn't go forward if he was regretting the past.

"Was it freely given?"

She met his gaze, her own steady. The time for hiding behind face saving generalities was over. "Yes."

"You can say that when I seduced you into accepting my marriage proposal, when I took your virginity so you could no longer speak of annulments?"

He really was feeling guilty.

"But I wanted you. I love the way you make me feel when you touch me."

"If that is true, *tesoro,* then what happened last night?"

"You wouldn't let *me* touch *you.*" And it had hurt so much.

"I was afraid."

Okay, he'd owned up to being scared when she'd said it, but she never, ever, ever expected those three words to come out of Rico's mouth. "Why?" She thought she knew, but she had to be sure.

"I do not know if I can perform as a man."

"You're afraid I won't turn you on enough to make love to me?" she asked painfully.

"*Porco miseria!* Where did you get this idea?"

"You said…"

"I said I did not know if I could perform. I said nothing about the beauty and sexiness of your body."

"But if I were the type of woman you usually went for, wouldn't it be easier on you?"

In her mind, it made sense, but he stared at her as if she'd gone mad. "You are my type of woman."

She closed her eyes against the pity she was sure was in his. "You don't have to say things like that."

Weight settled next to her on the bed and a fingertip outlined the contours of her face. "Have you ever known me to lie, *piccola mia?*"

She shook her head, her eyes still tightly shut.

"Then if I say that you are the sexiest woman I have ever known, you will believe me, no?"

At that, her eyes could not remain closed and she opened them to his gently mocking smile. "You… I…"

"I have never made love to a woman who made me feel more like a man."

"But you said…"

"That I did not know if I could sustain an erection,

but when I love you, your response gives me joy without my own body's involvement.''

Part of her wished he'd stop tossing the l-word around so flippantly and another, much bigger part of her—her heart—wished he meant it the way she needed him to mean it.

''Have you... Did you... I mean, has there been...''

He laughed huskily. ''If you are asking if I have reacted physically to you, the answer is yes. It did not happen that first time I touched you and this worried me, but I thought when I regained feeling, I would regain this as well.''

She had assumed the same thing. ''Didn't you?''

''I do not know.''

His hands framed her face, his own expression tortured. ''I let you go through the pain today because I, Rico DiRinaldo, was afraid to find out.''

But he hadn't known it would be painful. She'd hidden the possibility from him because instinctively she'd known he wouldn't let her go through with it. ''It's not your fault.''

He shook his head.

''You said you'd had a response.'' She couldn't make herself say the word erection for all her love for him.

''Yes. Many times when I have touched you, I felt a stirring, never more so than last night.''

''But you stopped me.''

''*Sí.*''

''Why? I don't understand.''

''If it did not last. If I could not climax...'' His voice drifted into nothingness, but she knew what he meant. He would have been humiliated.

"I would do anything for you."

"*Si,* today you proved this." He dropped his hands from her face and turned away. "I will never forget the sight of you falling to the floor, or the tears in your eyes when they performed the procedure."

"It wasn't your fault," she repeated. "The doctor told me that first day that some women experience lingering pain, but I didn't tell you. Honestly, I thought I wouldn't be one of them and I wanted your baby so much."

"If I had faced my own cowardice, perhaps you would not have felt that sacrifice necessary."

She reached out and turned his face toward her. So typical of Rico to take responsibility for the whole world and its population on his shoulders. "You are not a coward, Rico. You faced your paralysis. You fought it."

"But I did not face my fear and for that you paid."

Incredibly, his eyes glistened. She couldn't stand it anymore. To heck with worrying about if she'd been horizontal long enough for conception to take place. She sat up and threw her arms around his neck. "No, Rico, *no.* I wanted to try for a baby with you. I didn't care how we had to do it. I want to have your *bambini* so much."

He kissed her, softly, sweetly, like a benediction. "How are you feeling?"

"Better."

"No more cramps?"

She shook her head.

"Then maybe we should see if I can give you my child with more pleasure than you felt this morning, no?"

She sucked in air, her heart pounding arythmically. "Are you sure you want to try?"

"Si, mi amore bella."

His beautiful love. If only he meant it. Then she smiled. The tender look in his eyes, his willingness to risk failure…all for her. It was enough.

CHAPTER ELEVEN

RICO'S head lowered. His lips brushed hers. Once. Twice. Three times before she whimpered in protest to his teasing.

She turned her head, trying to catch his lips for a more satisfying kiss, but he was busy nibbling his way down her neck.

"Rico, *please*." She didn't want the gentle touch. She needed more. All of him. All of his passion.

"Shh...*tesoro*." His tongue dipped into the shell of her ear. "This will be perfect." His voice and sensual touch sent shivers of anticipation and delight cascading along her nerve endings.

Her lips parted on a breathless sound and he finally let his lips settle over hers with firm possession and he took control of the warm recesses of her mouth. The evocative kiss had her moaning and tightening her arms around his neck.

Then she remembered. *She could touch him.* She broke her mouth from his, panting with excitement, but adamant that this time things would be different.

"Take off your clothes, Rico."

He went still. His eyes slid shut and she watched as an internal battle raged within him. Instantly, she doubted her actions. Maybe she should just touch him and worry about getting him naked later. The raw vulnerability on his face hurt her. She was about to tell him to kiss her again, to ignore her demand, when he gently, but firmly removed her hands from around his neck and stood.

''You don't have to—''

He shook his proud head. ''I want to. You deserve this. I deserve this. I want to make you mine in the most elemental way a man can possess his woman.''

She loved it when he referred to her as his woman. It implied a chosen intimacy, not a marriage of convenience he was stuck with because of his strong sense of integrity.

The removal of his suit jacket acted like a catalyst to her body's response centers and it felt like everything inside her went on hyperalert. The movement of the very air around her became a tantalizing precursor for what was to come.

She watched, enthralled, while long, dark, masculine fingers loosened his tie and pulled it off. He let the patterned silk fall to the carpet with a soft swish of sound. The jet black buttons came next. First those at his cuffs and then the ones down the front of his shirt. One by one, he undid them, revealing the well-muscled contours of his chest in tantalizing bits until the white silk hung open. Black, curling hair made a V pattern on his chest. It disappeared enticingly at the waist of charcoal gray pants that clung to a dauntingly large bulge and the hard, defined muscles of his thighs.

She waited with suspended breath as he shrugged the shirt from his broad shoulders before moving to undo his slacks. He toed his shoes off at the same time he let the pants fall in another crumpled pile of fabric on the floor beside his shirt. He stepped out of them without looking away from her rapt face.

His socks came next and then he stood before her.

Proudly male.

Nude but for the black silk boxers riding low on his hips. He hooked his thumbs in the waistband and she expelled her held breath as he pushed the shorts down his thighs. An unintelligible sound came from her throat as she watched the most intimate of his male flesh come into view.

She swallowed.

She opened her mouth. Nothing came out. She closed it.

She closed her eyes. She opened them again.

She shook her head.

None of it helped.

"Does it get bigger?" she asked in a truly mortifying squeak.

Rumbling laughter had her gaze flying from his incredibly impressive form to his face. He looked amused, darn him. It wasn't funny. How was she supposed to face *that* with any equanimity, she asked herself furiously.

Rico shook his head, unable to believe his wife's reaction. He'd expected concern, perhaps even a little pity. An attack of feminine nerves and genuine fear at the sight of his only semierect flesh had never even made it on the agenda.

She was scared to death of the prospect of his complete arousal and that boosted his morale in a way nothing else could have. She didn't see him as a eunuch. Far from it. By the look on her face, she thought he was too virile. He felt himself stir in reaction and watched in fascination as she blanched. She really was worried, the poor little thing.

And she was little. Over a foot shorter than him and built on delicate lines that made women like his ex-fiancée seem like Amazons. Yet, he had no doubt they would fit together as *il buon Dio* intended. "Your body was created to accommodate mine."

She licked her lower lip, igniting more flames of desire low in his belly. "Are you sure? Maybe, I'm not made right." She chewed that same sexy lip. "I feel full with your finger. I don't think we'll ever get that in."

If he laughed at her, he was dead. He knew it, but still it took all his self-control to bite back the amusement her words invoked in him and the relief.

"You'll stretch, *cara*. Trust me."

He watched as she visibly swallowed and then squared her shoulders as if preparing to face the firing squad. "All right."

He walked slowly to the bed, his bare feet whispering across the carpet. His balance was improving all the time, but he wasn't about to risk falling. She seemed to shrink back into the pillows as he approached, her beautiful emerald eyes wide with apprehension. He stopped when his legs were against the side of the bed.

"Do you want to touch me?"

It was a hard question to ask. He was reacting to her physically already, but still the fear that he would not enjoy the full sexual response he had once been capable of plagued him. If she caressed him and he remained only semi aroused, or worse, lost what hardness he did have, it would be an unspeakable blow to his pride.

But watching her endure pain for his cowardice that morning had made him see becoming whole for her meant taking this risk.

She hadn't answered his question. She simply

stared at him, her gaze seemingly permanently fixed on his manhood. Then her lashes lowered and she shuddered.

"Yes." It was such a quiet whisper, he almost hadn't heard her.

"Maybe it would help, *tesoro,* if you started somewhere else?"

Wide, glistening green eyes, pleaded with him silently.

He reached out and pulled her to her knees on the high, oversize bed. Then he guided her hands to his chest, placing her small palms over the already stimulated flesh of his male nipples. They both shuddered at the contact. She leaned forward and kissed him, flicking a sweet exploring tongue out to taste his skin.

He groaned. "Do it again," he demanded hoarsely.

She obeyed without pause, this time nipping at his flesh with her sharp little teeth. Then her hands began moving. Just as they had the night before, but this time he made no effort to stop them. Small circles over his hardened nipples, fingernails kneading him like a cat. He pulled at her nightgown until she allowed him to slip it off over her head.

Then he pulled her to him, pressing his hard flesh against her yielding softness and they both stilled, their breathing shallow as they absorbed the sensation of body against body. He felt his sex pressed up against the smooth skin of her stomach and it was all he could do not to toss her on her back and impale her. The knowledge he *could* do it flooded his senses as excitement surged through his hardened flesh.

Oh, Mother. He was getting bigger. She could feel

him swelling against her. Her forehead rested against his chest while her fingers dug into the hard wall of muscle in front of her. She'd wanted to touch him, but now that the moment had arrived, she was terrified. What if she did it wrong? What if she turned him off with her clumsy, inexperienced fondling?

Then he was taking the decision out of her hands and putting himself into them. Literally. He pressed his hand over the back of hers and meshing them together, slid them down his torso until they reached the mat of hair at the base of his shaft. It felt silky and springy at the same time. She pressed her fingers into it and his big body trembled, building her confidence. Gently, but with firm purpose, he guided her hand to the rocklike hardness protruding from his body.

"Touch me, *amore*. Touch me, here."

And she curled her fingers around him, awed by the feel of velvetlike skin stretched taut over steel rigidity. She tentatively caressed him from the tip to the base, rejoicing as he made guttural sounds of excitement low in his throat. She wasn't turning him off. His hand closed over hers, forming her fingers more closely to him and showing her a rhythm and a level of pressure that gave him obvious pleasure.

He dropped his hand and she continued to caress him, shocked by the swaying tenseness of his body. She raised her head, taking in the expression of ecstasy on his face, the flushed heat of his skin, the stiffness of his nipples, all bespeaking a level of excitement she had never dreamed she could generate in him.

"You want my touch," she whispered in wonder.

His eyes opened, liquid silver gleaming down at her. "*Si*. Very much."

Tears flooded her eyes. "I thought you didn't," she admitted on a ragged breath.

His body jerked and he pushed her back on the bed, dislodging her hold on him as he settled between her splayed thighs. "I ached for you."

"But—"

He placed his finger over her lips. "Do not talk, *amore*. Feel."

And what she felt. He caressed every inch of her body, first with his hands and then with his mouth. When he buried his lips in the center of her feminine desire, she screeched. "No! Rico... I... You..." Soon her incoherent words turned to moans of the most incandescent delight.

He made love to her with his mouth in a way that sent her orbiting into space almost immediately. She screamed his name as the cataclysm of pleasure burst in her. She writhed under him, the pleasure so great it was almost pain, but he didn't stop and soon his clever tongue was sending her into an oblivion of bliss again.

Pleasure built upon pleasure until it felt like one, prolonged wave. Her body bowed off the bed, every muscle taut with her reaction to his ministrations.

But this time she knew there was more and she wanted it. Needed it. Demanded it with hoarse shouts that would have mortified her if she wasn't so lost to the feelings he gave her. She was shaking with her need by the time he returned to his position above her.

"I want you," she cried.

"*Si*. This I can see." The smug satisfaction in his

voice should have irritated her, but she was beyond irritation at male posturing. He probed her entrance, pushing inside a little bit. "Now we make love."

She stared up at him, sure they could not possibly continue but equally positive she would not pull away. This was too important to him and therefore to her, for her pseudovirginal fears to hold sway.

He smiled down at her, but there was no amusement in his expression. It was the smile of a predator, of primordial man establishing his place in the hierarchy of priorities in his woman's life...at the top.

"You are mine, Gianna. *Always.*"

The mesmerizing intensity in his molten eyes rendered her mute, but she nodded her head. Incredibly she felt her body stretch to accommodate him and then swollen, tender flesh molded around his hardness to leave her feeling completely possessed, filled with him and surrounded by him.

It was more intimate than anything she could have imagined. More emotionally devastating than anything they had done before.

She didn't realize she was crying until he licked the trail of her tears from the corner of her eyes to her temples. "Am I hurting you?" he asked in a shaken voice.

"No." She shook her head frantically, unable to utter another coherent word, but he seemed to understand because he began moving his body.

He slid almost all the way out of her, making her catch at him with her hands, desperate for a return of the feeling of intimate connection. But he did not withdraw, he surged back into her and began a rhythm that quickly escalated to something poundingly hard and fast.

The ecstasy built inside her, making her shout his name and utter other less intelligible noises. How could it be more, better than what he'd already done? She didn't know, but it was. Infinitely more intense. Maybe because they were sharing it. She arched up to meet him, matching his beat, matching his fierceness with her own sensual aggression.

Then the world exploded around her, going black around the edges and she came close to losing consciousness for the second time that day. A scream echoed in her head and she realized vaguely that it had been her own. Then a shout reverberated in her ears as Rico joined her in this ultimate pleasure between a man and a woman, his body bowing, his manhood growing impossibly large inside her.

The tension drained from his body increment by increment until his torso met her own as he allowed his body to settle against her. She hugged him with both her arms and legs, wrapping herself around him in exuberant delight.

"You're a wonderful lover, *caro*."

His body jolted. With a growl, he started raining kisses all over her face. He interspersed them with words of gratitude and extravagant approval. It was all so unreal. Rico, thanking her for making love. Rico, telling her she was the most beautiful woman alive. Rico, kissing her with totally uncool enthusiasm.

He rolled onto his back, taking her with him. She landed astride him, his flesh still firmly embedded in her. She laid her head on his heart and listened to the rapid beat with a sense of the miraculous.

"*Grazie, mi amore bella.*"

She smiled against his chest. "Thank *you*, my love."

His arms tightened around her. "You have restored to me wholeness."

Was that anything like the gift he had just given her?

"I love you," she said, unable to keep the words inside.

"*Si*. With you. This was safe," he said with deep satisfaction. "A man can be vulnerable with a woman who loves him."

She pushed herself up on her arms, causing him to press more deeply into her, and looked into his content face. "I'm glad." Simple, but heartfelt.

"Not as glad as I am." And incredibly she felt a renewed expression of that gladness swell inside her.

She sucked in air on a shocked gasp. "Rico?"

"*Si?*"

"What…" But even as the question was forming, his body was giving her the answer as he arched under her, sending her quivering body on a new voyage of discovery.

He really was intent on letting her share more equally in the loving was her last coherent thought as he taught her to set a pace to bring them both sexual satisfaction.

Gianna woke to the soft caress of lips against her temple. She smiled, her eyes still closed and husky male laughter blanketed her in its warmth.

"*Buona mattina, tesoro*. Open your eyes."

She obeyed him and felt joy well up from the depths of her being. "Good morning." She reached up to wrap her arms around his neck and lifted her face for a kiss, secure in their physical intimacy after a night of making love.

He kissed her, his lips moving over hers with possessive pleasure and soon she was plastered against his shirtfront, her tongue dueling with his. Groaning, he pulled away.

She stared up at him, not comprehending why he had stopped.

"I must go, *tesoro*. I have a meeting this morning. I would cancel it if I could."

Then she noticed the immaculate suit, conservative tie, his perfectly groomed hair and the smooth skin on his jaw from a recent shave. His eyes devoured her with hungry force and she believed he was leaving under duress.

She shifted and winced as her body reminded her just how many times they had made love in the past twenty-four hours.

He brushed her cheek, letting his fingers twine into her hair, which he had unbraided in the most erotic way yesterday afternoon. "Perhaps it is best for you that I go, no?"

She grimaced, but could not deny the twinges of discomfort. "I don't want you to leave," she said regardless.

"I will return as quickly as possible."

She felt her lips curve into a pout and part of her mind was shocked. She'd never pouted in her life.

He gave a groan of male appreciation and nipped at her protruding lip. "I promise."

She caught his mouth for a lingering kiss and then pulled back. "All right. If you promise."

His gorgeous face creased in a smile of sexy approval. "On my life." He kissed her briefly again, as if he couldn't quite make himself leave. "I will cut the meeting short if I can. Take a long, hot bath, *mi moglie.*"

"Will it help?" she asked with projected innocence.

"Si." He stood up, a serious expression passing across his face. "We will talk when I return."

They hadn't done much talking last night. She nodded and smiled.

He moved toward her as if he would kiss her again, but then stopped, a look of grim determination crossing his sculpted features and left. She watched him walk from the room, a sense of foreboding that overshadowed her joy from their lovemaking coming out of nowhere. What did he want to talk about?

Despite the mysterious sense of apprehension, she refused to consider it might be something bad. Rico had spent almost twenty-four hours doing everything in his power to give her pleasure and impregnate her with his child. She should feel a deep sense of security in her marriage, she chided herself.

With that thought firmly in mind, she followed Rico's instruction and had a long spa bath, the water softened and scented with expensive oil that had been a gift from her mother-in-law on one of their many shopping expeditions. The hot, swirling water soaked away the unfamiliar aches in her muscles and feminine flesh.

Later that morning, after a solitary breakfast because the rest of the family was gone from the villa, she was told she had a visitor in the sala. She walked into the room and as it always did, her gaze first went to the rich murals on the ceilings and down one third of the wall. The villa had been in the DiRinaldo family for many generations and boasted artwork by some of Italy's greatest masters.

A sound near the window brought Gianna's gaze around to her visitor.

Chiara stood outlined in the autumn sunlight, her face cast in shadow so Gianna could not read her expression. "I suppose you think you've been very clever," was her opening gambit.

"I don't know what you mean."

Chiara stepped toward Gianna, revealing the look of condescending pity on the other woman's face. "You're a little fool. He won't stay with you now that he is a man again."

How could Chiara know what Rico had only discovered yesterday? He wouldn't have called her. He couldn't have. Gianna's stomach heaved at the thought and she had to breathe slowly and shallowly to stop herself being sick.

"What are you talking about?"

"Don't play the ignorant with me. I know Rico's walking again."

So she didn't know about the other. A shudder of relief shook Gianna. But how had Chiara learned about his walking? Gianna had only found out the day before yesterday. "We always knew Rico would walk again."

"If he'd believed that, he'd never have let me go," Chiara said scathingly.

After his revelation that he *had* had his doubts, Gianna could not bring herself to give Chiara the putdown she deserved. "I don't know what difference you think that makes," was the best she could do.

"You really are a stupid little cow, aren't you?"

Gianna stiffened at the insult. "You clearly have something to say. I suggest you say it and then leave my home."

"Your home? How long do you think that will last? Until you give Rico a baby. That's how long. He knew I wasn't keen on getting pregnant and spoiling my figure. Once you've done your broodmare bit, he'll come back to me, the woman he really loves."

"Rico's not like that." He had far too much integrity to abandon the mother of his child.

Chiara smiled viciously. "When a man wants something enough, he'll sacrifice anything to get it."

"What makes you think he wants you? He let you go."

"He thought he couldn't be the man I needed him to be. He let me go for my sake. Now, we both know differently."

Gianna's hands fisted at her sides and she felt tension filter into every muscle group in her body. Chiara was more right than she knew. Rico's biggest fear, that he would be incapable of making love, not that he would not walk again, had been laid to rest only the day before.

"You don't love him."

Chiara's laugh was ugly. "When you have sex as good as Rico and I had it, you don't need maudlin emotions like love."

Gianna could not bear the image of Rico touching Chiara the way he had touched Gianna, so she forced such imaginings from her mind. "You're very crude and I think it's time you left."

"Not so fast. There are still things I want to say

to you and then I think I'll wait around for Rico to show up. I need to congratulate him on his walking.''

Gianna could not believe the audacity of the other woman. ''If you want to see my husband, you'll have to make an appointment with his secretary. You aren't welcome in *my home*.'' She emphasized the words, reminding both herself and Chiara that it was she Rico had married.

Chiara's catlike eyes narrowed. ''I'm not going anywhere.''

''Rico's security staff will say differently, I think.''

''You wouldn't kick me out. You haven't got the guts.'' Chiara sounded shocked and just the tiniest bit unsure of herself as if Gianna's threat had been completely unexpected.

Gianna opened her mouth to answer when she was interrupted by the sound of Rico's voice.

''I didn't realize you planned on company, *cara*.''

Gianna spun to face him, finding his expression maddeningly unreadable. ''I didn't. She came uninvited.''

''And your wife threatened to have me thrown out.'' Chiara's voice had gone husky with hurt and much to Gianna's disgust, tears now sparkled in the other woman's feline eyes.

Rico's black brows rose in sardonic question. ''Did she really?''

Chiara rushed across the room. Clutching at Rico's jacket with red lacquered nails, she said, ''Yes. It isn't enough she's married to you. She wants me out of your life completely.''

Rico carefully removed Chiara's clinging hands and turned his silver gaze to Gianna. ''Is this true?''

Did he expect her to deny it? "Yes. I told her if she wanted to see you to make an appointment with your secretary. I don't want her in my home."

Gianna wasn't going to put a polite façade on for appearance's sake. Chiara had lied about her in New York, had threatened her marriage just now and Gianna was certain would do anything in her power to seduce Rico back into her bed. She was not a person Gianna was willing to embrace in her circle of friends.

Rico nodded, as if taking in her words. "I don't think an appointment will be necessary, however." He looked down at Chiara, so he missed the spasm of pain that tightened her features that Gianna could not repress. "We can talk now, no?"

Chiara practically purred. "Yes, Rico. Please. I just wanted to see you and tell you how happy I am that you are walking again."

Rico stepped away from her, moving to the drinks cabinet. He poured himself a Scotch. "How did you find out?"

"I met your therapist's wife quite by accident while shopping one day. We struck up a friendship. You couldn't blame me for wanting to keep track of your progress, not after all we were to each other."

The words, the nauseatingly sugar sweet voice and Chiara's obvious duplicity were enough to make Gianna sick. Rico might not have supported her throwing his ex-fiancée from the house, but that didn't mean Gianna had to stand around and watch the other woman work her wiles on her husband.

She spun on her heel and walked out of the room.

Rico called her name, but she ignored him, just as she tried to ignore Chiara's voice telling him to let Gianna go.

CHAPTER TWELVE

GIANNA walked upstairs in a fog of pain. Why had Rico allowed Chiara to stay?

She stopped outside the bedroom door and realized she could not go in. She couldn't face the bed, couldn't face the memories in light of that poisonous woman's threats. She spun around and headed back down the stairs.

She went to the garage and climbed behind the wheel of the first car she found with a key in the ignition. It was a Mercedes sedan. It was bigger than she was used to, but she didn't care. She just had to get away.

The security guard was waving wildly at her to stop when she pulled out of the driveway after pushing the automatic gate opener. Rico and his father had been adamant she and Renata only leave the villa with a security escort, but Gianna wasn't in the mood for company. Any company.

She drove around the city mindlessly until she found herself in the vicinity of the *Duomo*. Memories of Rico bringing her here after her mother's death guided her in bringing the car to a halt. She found parking, which in itself was a shock, and left the car to venture inside the huge cathedral.

She was no longer a child, but she hurt and the vast open space inside the church was just as awe-inspiring to her now as it had been when she was a little girl. She needed the peace she'd found then inside the cavernous structure. Her feet took her of their own volition to the rose windows. Rico had brought her here, to this exact spot. He had told her she could talk to her mother, that even though Mamma was in Heaven, she would hear.

Had she started loving Rico that day?

She hadn't identified it as sexual love until she was fifteen, but Rico had always been the cornerstone to her heart. The only man she could give herself to. The only man she had ever wanted to marry, but he hadn't seen her for dirt. Not until the accident and his beautiful, but excruciatingly selfish fiancée had ditched him.

Gianna leaned against a column, letting her body soak in the sense of peace hundreds of years of pilgrims had felt before her. Rico was hers, but for how long?

After almost twenty-four hours in his bed, she refused to believe he still did not see her for dirt. He'd proven to her over and over again that she was a desirable woman in his eyes.

That didn't mean he loved her, but then again, it certainly did not indicate a lack of feeling, either.

He'd let Chiara stay.

The memory of something he had said the day before intruded with ominous significance. He had said he felt *safe* assessing the level of his virility with her—because she loved him. Did that mean he had only been using her as a testing ground to determine if he could go back to Chiara whole? The very prospect was enough to make her knees buckle and she sagged against the pillar.

But Rico wasn't like that. She knew he wasn't. So, why was she imagining all sorts of ugly scenarios?

"I thought I would find you here, *tesoro*."

Her head snapped up. "What are you doing here?"

His expression was somber. "Looking for my runaway wife."

"I didn't run away." She straightened against the pillar.

"You did not take a bodyguard. You drove yourself off the property, though my security men tried to wave you to a stop."

He made it sound like she'd committed cardinal sin number nineteen. "I wanted to be alone, all right?"

He shook his head, his hair looking black in the muted light of the *Duomo*, his expression bleak. "No, it is not okay."

She glared at him. "You can't dictate my every movement."

"I do not desire this."

Right. "Then why are you here?"

"Because you are here."

"You let Chiara stay in my house," she accused him.

"I had things to say to her."

She angled her head away from him and said nothing.

"Do you not want to know what those things were?"

"No." She didn't want to hear if he still had feelings for his ex-fiancée.

"How can you doubt me after what we shared yesterday and last night?" he asked in a driven tone.

Her head snapped back and she met his glittering,

accusing gaze. "We shared our bodies. According to Chiara, that's nothing new to you."

"We shared our souls and that, *mi moglie*, is something I have never done with another woman."

She wanted to believe him so much. Tears burned her eyes and ached in her throat. She shook her head.

"Si."

"You married me for all the wrong reasons," she said, fighting to talk around the crying.

His jaw clenched. *"Si."*

The tears fell faster and she turned from him, but she found no peace in her surroundings. There was too much pain slicing through her. A sob welled up and broke past her tightly clenched teeth.

His hands gripped her shoulders. "Do not do this to yourself. The past cannot be changed."

She twisted from him, knocking his hands away. She felt like a wounded animal, wanting to lash out. "Don't touch me."

He spun her back to face him. Pain easily equal to the hurt she was experiencing glittered in his eyes. "Does not forgiveness come with love?"

Forgiveness for what? Did he expect her to forgive him for not loving her? It wasn't that easy, nor was it a matter of forgiveness but learning to accept. "I don't know if I can," she said, speaking to herself rather than him.

She knew she had to learn to live without his love, but she did not know how to do that.

Rico's features set in chilling resolve that even amidst her emotional turmoil made her feel apprehensive. "I will not let you go, *mi moglie*. You are mine."

"I never wanted to be anyone else's." The words came of their own volition, in a pain-filled whisper.

"Then what is this *do not touch me?*"

"I hurt," she admitted.

"Turning from me will not make it better."

Her lower lip trembled and she felt another sob well up.

He cursed and stepped forward. "Come, *cara.* Let me take you home where we can talk in privacy."

She found herself swung high against his chest, his arms unbreakable bonds around her.

"Where is my home?" she asked, thinking of Chiara's smirking face when Gianna had left the sala.

"Where I am." His voice vibrated with purpose and his mouth came down over hers in a bruising kiss.

She responded with a passion released by her anguish. She didn't know how long they stood there, his lips staking claim on her, but eventually the sound of a child asking his mum what the man and his girlfriend were doing penetrated her conscious mind. She pulled her mouth away and it was at that moment, the significance of her position hit her.

"Rico, put me down." The thought of the English tourists watching while she and Rico kissed made her cheeks burn with embarrassment.

Inimical rage burned into her from eyes the color of molten metal. "No."

Why was he so angry? "Think of your legs. It's too much, too soon." What if he fell and hurt himself?

"You are worried about my well-being?" he asked, his ire fading slightly.

"Yes."

"You are not trying to push me away again?"

She sighed, linking her arms around his neck and letting her head fall onto his shoulder. "I can't."

He nodded, the anger completely gone now. She could feel it drain out of him as surely as if it had been herself.

He turned and with amusement and what she could have sworn was masculine pride in his voice, said to the little boy, "She's not my girlfriend. She's my wife."

The child said, "Okay," with the ageless wisdom reserved for the very young while his mother blushed scarlet.

Rico winked and then turned to leave the *Duomo*. He still hadn't put her down.

"Rico—"

"I told you, I will not let you go."

"I didn't realize you meant it so literally."

"If holding you in my arms is how I keep you with me, then you will spend the next fifty or so years in my constant company." The words should have sounded amusing, but they didn't. They sounded more like a threat from a man perfectly capable and willing to carry it through.

She said nothing else as he carried her out to the limousine waiting in a no-parking zone. The chauffeur opened the door and Rico let her down to get inside. Once they were seated, he pulled her back into his arms and onto his lap.

"What about the car?" They couldn't just leave it.

"Tell Pietro where it is and he will collect it."

So, she told the young security man where she'd parked and handed him the keys, all the while aware of Rico's hard body surrounding her and his hand laying possessively across her thighs.

She looked into his eyes and emotion she was terrified of naming burned in the silver depths.

"Why didn't you kick Chiara out?"

The hand on her thigh moved in a provoking caress. "I did."

"But…"

"She came to our home and dared to upset you, *cara.* I could see it in your beautiful green eyes and the tense way you held your delectable body so erect."

"But…" She didn't understand. "Then why the heck did you let her stay?"

"I needed her to know that I would tolerate no more interference in my life or that of my family, that if she attempted to hurt you again, she would answer to me. I do not play nice, she knows this. She will leave us alone."

"You were warning her off?"

"*Si.* I had barely enough time to make my position clear and have her escorted to the door when Security came with the news my wife had run away."

A twinge of guilt niggled at her. "I didn't."

"You did."

She didn't bother reminding him she had wanted to be alone, to have time to think. The excuse had carried no weight with him at all. "Where do we go from here?"

"Home, *mi moglie.* Back to bed maybe…"

She was tempted to give into the promise in his voice, but she wanted more than a physical satiation of their bodies' desires. "That's not what I meant."

He sighed. "It is up to you."

"What do you mean?"

"I cannot force you to stay if you want to go."

The tight band of his arms around her said otherwise. "And if I don't want to go?"

"I will be the happiest of men."

"You did not love me when we got married."

"You were with me when I came out of coma," he said, she thought apropos to nothing.

"Yes."

"It was your voice, your words that brought me out of it."

She bit her bottom lip. Had it been her voice, her words? "I don't know. Maybe it was just the right time."

"No, *tesoro*. It was not. Do you know how I know this?"

She shook her head, incapable of speech in the face of the warmth emanating from him.

"I remember the words. You told me you loved me."

He could be guessing.

He smiled. "You do not believe me, but it is true. I heard and I woke."

"I could not stand the prospect of a world without you in it." She laid her hand over his heart, even now needing affirmation of the life pulsing in him.

"*Si*. There has been no doubt in my mind of your love for me from the moment I woke. It sustained me, gave me strength when I had little of my own."

"But you don't love me." Even saying the words hurt.

"Do I not?"

"You said you only cared for me."

"And caring, it is not part of love?"

"What are you saying?" Hope was starting to unfurl in her heart like the petals of a rose exposed to the sun.

"How could your love bring me back from a living death if there was no corresponding love in my heart to meet it?"

She shook her head, terrified of believing.

"I did not realize it at first. I tried to stick with the familiar...the safe."

"Chiara."

"*Si*. She wanted nothing from me but my money."

"And your body," she slotted in.

"Without love, it is only that. A body. Any man would do, but for you it is only me, no?"

"Yes."

"Did it never make you wonder when I demanded we marry before leaving New York?"

Of course it had. Nothing about their marriage had made any sense to her. "I didn't understand your wanting to marry me at all, much less so quickly."

"I did not want to risk losing you and I knew you would take your wedding vows seriously, but my reasoning was selfish, *amore*. I wanted you, but was unwilling to admit I loved you. I would have deserved it if you had decided you preferred Andre as I feared."

"You thought I wanted your brother?" Was he blind? She thought Rico's anger toward her time spent with his brother had been possessive pride, not the result of any real fear.

"*Si*."

"But I never even flirted with him."

"He flirted with you." And from the remembered

anger in her husband's eyes, he had liked it even less than she'd thought at the time.

"But you said you didn't love me," she reminded him, hurting a little less, but still not sure what to believe.

"I broke it off with Chiara in New York."

"What?"

"I told her I no longer wanted to marry her. I told her this because my dreams were filled with a tiny green-eyed sprite who nagged me and stood up to me in a way no other woman would dare to do."

"You broke it off with her over me?" She thought it had been his inability to walk. "She said—"

"She convinced herself I had done it for her and that when I started walking again, I would want her back. I didn't. I don't. I only want you, Gianna."

She stared at him, her chest tight with emotion.

His expression was more serious than she'd ever seen it. "I love you."

"You can't," she said, crying again.

"*Mi amore bella,* I can and I do. You are my heart. My life. Without you, nothing matters. I did not tell you of my love because I was afraid. Afraid I would not walk again. Afraid if I did, I would not be able to perform as man—"

"Even if you were paralyzed from the neck down for the rest of your life, you would still be everything a man should be to me," she said stopping his flow of words.

His eyes closed and he shuddered. Then they opened and he kissed her gently. "A man would give his very life for that kind of love, *amore.* It is so beautiful, so real, I thought I could not match it."

''But now you can?'' she asked, desperately hoping the answer would be *yes.*

''I realized I could yesterday morning during the IUI. You were hurting and I knew that no matter the sacrifice, I would never allow you to hurt like that again.''

She didn't think it was the time to remind him that childbirth wasn't exactly painless. She had the feeling he'd decide to adopt and she wanted to have his *bambini.*

His hands cupped her face and his eyes grew suspiciously bright. ''I love you, *tesoro,* with all that I am and ever will be. You are the other half of my soul and I thank *il buon Dio* for that mugger and the driver of the car that hit me because if it had not happened, I would have lost you, the only treasure worth having in my life.''

Her heart almost stopped beating. ''You can't mean that.''

''*Si.* I now understand my mother's views. She knew I would be miserable with Chiara, that my life with you would be superior in every way. What is a little pain, a little work in the face of such a gift as your love?''

She would not have used little to describe the work or pain he'd gone through. ''You could have had my love without it.''

He wiped at the wetness below her eyes with gentle fingers. ''You would have given it yes, but I was not ready to receive it. I was blinded to your beauty and how important you have always been in my life.''

She would never agree with him or his mother that the accident was a good thing. It had hurt him too much, but she would not deny the joy his words placed in her heart.

"I love you."

"*Si.* You can never say this too often, *mi amore.*"

So she said it again, and again, and again, interspersed with kisses until they reached their home and continued saying it far into the night as he gave the words back to her in both action and voice.

The blessing of their marriage was everything an Italian mother could want it to be. Renata spared no effort in making sure every wedding tradition was observed. This included her daughter-in-law wearing a traditional white gown for the blessing ceremony and the lace mantilla Gianna had tried on the day Rico stood for the first time since the accident.

Doing his part to provide as much authenticity to the occasion as possible, Rico insisted on taking Gianna away for a honeymoon. When they reached the luxury hotel in Switzerland and were once again behind the closed door of their room, she expressed her love for him in the most intimate way she could.

Remembering his fascination with her hair, she unbound it and used it like he had taught her, painting his body with erotic strokes, eventually driving him to a passionate, almost bruising possession. Afterward, they lay entwined whispering words of love in Italian and English.

"My baby, it is here. I feel it." Rico laid his big hand over her stomach.

She smiled mistily. "I do, too."

"I love you, *tesoro.*"

"No more than I love you, *caro.*"

*   *   *

Eight months later, they were proved right when she gave birth to paternal twins. Rico was convinced he was so potent for her that both the IUI procedure *and* their making love had borne fruit. Who was she to doubt him?

Her love had brought him back from a living death, why couldn't his love conceive life not once, but twice in her womb?

THE ITALIAN'S
LOVE-CHILD

by

Sharon Kendrick

Sharon Kendrick started story-telling at the age of eleven and has never really stopped. She likes to write fast-paced, feel-good romances with heroes who are so sexy they'll make your toes curl!

Born in west London, she now lives in the beautiful city of Winchester – where she can see the cathedral from her window (but only if she stands on tip-toe). She has two children, Celia and Patrick and her passions include music, books, cooking and eating – and drifting off into wonderful daydreams while she works out new plots!

Don't miss Sharon Kendrick's exciting new story, *The Greek Tycoon's Convenient Wife*, out in July 2008 from Mills & Boon® Modern™.

For the *charmant* Laurent Droguet,
Who not only has the most dazzling smile,
But also the most wonderful friends

CHAPTER ONE

EVE saw him across the other side of the room and her world stood still. It was like watching a film, where fantasy took over and made real life fade away and it had never happened to her before.

That click. That buzz. That glance across the room which held and hung on in glorious disbelief as you met the eyes of a man and somehow knew that he was 'the one'. But of course it was fantasy, it must be—for how on earth could you see someone for a minute or a second and know that this total stranger was the person you wanted to spend the rest of your life with?

Except that this man was not a total stranger, though maybe that was fantasy, too. After all, it had been a long time.

She quickly glanced down at her drink and pretended to examine it, before risking another look, only this time he had turned away, and although her heart lurched with disappointment that he obviously didn't share her fascination, at least it gave her the chance to study him without embarrassment.

She was almost certain he was Luca, but he was certainly Italian; he couldn't have been anything else. Jet-dark hair framed the head he held so proudly and she drank in his perfect features as if trying to memorise them. Or remember them. The hard, intelligent black eyes, the Roman nose and an autocratic mouth which was both luscious and cruel.

He was striking and innately sexy, with a careless confidence which drew the eye and made it stay. In a room full of rich, successful men he stood out like some beautiful, exotic creature—his golden-olive skin gleaming like softly oiled silk, his body all packed, tight muscle. He looked like the kind of man who would command without even trying—an arrogant aristocrat from another age, yet a man who was essentially modern.

Eve was used to assessing people quickly, but her eyes could have lingered on him all evening. He wore his clothes with elegant assurance—a creamy shirt which hinted at a sinewed body beneath and dark, tapered trousers emphasising legs which were long and hard and muscular. He was very still, but that did not mask some indefinable quality he had, some shimmering vibrancy, which made every other man in the room fade into dull insignificance.

He had slanted his head to one side, listening to a tiny blonde creature in a sparkling dress who was chatting to him with the kind of enthusiasm which suggested that Eve wasn't alone in feeling a gut-wrenching awareness that she was in the presence of someone out of the ordinary. But why should that surprise her? A woman would have to be made out of stone not to have reacted to that package of un-mistakable, simmering sensuality.

'Eve?'

Her reverie punctured, Eve turned her head to see her host standing beside her, holding a bottle of champagne towards her almost-empty glass. 'Can I tempt you with another drink?'

She hadn't been planning to stay long and she had intended her first drink to be her last, but she nodded gratefully, welcoming the diversion. 'Thanks, Michael.'

The drink fizzed into the flute and she glanced around the room. The blinds had been left open, but with a view like that you would never want to draw them. Moonlight and starlight dipped and dazzled off the lapping water outside and the excited chatter, which had reached fever-pitch, gave all the indications of this being a very successful evening indeed.

She raised her glass. 'Here's to birthday parties— your wife is a very lucky woman!'

'Ah, but not everyone likes surprises,' he said.

Eve's eyes strayed once more to Luca. 'Oh, I don't know,' she said slowly as her heart began to bang against her ribcage. 'Great party, anyway.'

Michael smiled. 'Yeah. And great you could make it. Not everyone can boast that they have a television personality at their party!'

Eve laughed. 'Michael Gore! You've known me since I was knee-high to a grasshopper! You've seen me with grazed knees in my school uniform.' She gave him a wry smile. 'And I hardly think that presenting the breakfast show on provincial television classifies me as anything as grand-sounding as "television personality".'

Michael smiled back. 'Ah, but the girl's done good,' he said.

Maybe the girl *had*, but right then she felt as vulnerable as that schoolgirl with grazed knees. And, to her horror, she realised that she had gulped most of the drink down and that Luca—if indeed it *was* Luca—was still listening to the animated blonde. And that the last thing she needed in her life was the complication of a charismatic, complicated kind of man who was every woman's dream. Eve had learnt early in life that it was important to have goals, just so long as you kept them realistic.

'And the girl needs her sleep,' she sighed. 'Getting up at three-thirty every morning tends to have a negative effect on your long-term energy reserves. You won't mind if I slip away in a while, Michael?'

'I will mind very much,' he teased. 'But not if your legion of fans are going to blame us for deep, dark shadows under your eyes! Go when you like—but why not come back for lunch again tomorrow, when the show's over? There will be stacks of stuff left and Lizzy and I have hardly had a chance to talk to you all evening.'

Eve smiled. It would give her the opportunity to play with her god-daughter who had been tucked up in the Land of Nod all evening. 'Love to,' she murmured. 'About twelve?'

'See you at twelve.' He nodded.

She was tempted to ask him what Luca was doing there, but she was not a guileless teenager now—and what could she say, even if she was being her most casual and sophisticated? Who's the man talking to the blonde? Or, Who's the tall, dark, handsome hunk? Or even if she plucked up courage to say, Is that Luca Cardelli, by any chance?—all those would make her sound like a simpering wannabe!

But maybe Michael had seen her eyes straying over to the dark, still figure.

'You know Luca Cardelli, don't you?' he asked.

'Vaguely.' She gave it just the right amount of consideration and kept her voice casual. 'He was here one summer, about ten years ago, right?'

'Right. He sailed on a big white boat,' said

Michael, and sighed. 'Absolutely beautiful. Wonderful sailor—he put the rest of us to shame.'

Eve nodded. 'I didn't know he was a friend of yours?'

Michael shrugged. 'We were mates that summer and we've kept in touch, though I haven't seen him for years. But he emailed to tell me he was in London on business, and so I invited him down.'

She wondered how long he was staying, but she didn't ask. It was none of her business and it might send out the wrong message. There would be enough women here tonight fighting to get to know him, if the body language of the blonde was anything to go by.

'Oh, look—someone's setting off fireworks!' she murmured instead as in the distance the sky exploded into fountains of scarlet and blue and golden rain, and luckily Michael went to refuel someone else's glass, giving her the opportunity to go and stand by the window and watch the display, alone with her thoughts and her memories.

Luca watched her, at the way her bottom swayed against the silky green material of her dress as she walked towards the window. People were covertly watching her and he wondered why. But he had noticed her before that, even before she had started staring at him, and then pretending not to, but then, that was nothing new.

He had grown up used to the lavish attention of women right across the age spectrum ever since he could remember. He didn't even have to try and sometimes he wondered what it would be like if he did. The most rewarding business deals he had pulled

off had been the ones he had really had to fight for—
but women weren't like business deals.

He had been born with something which attracted
the opposite sex like bees to honey and, when he had
reached the age of noticing women, had quickly discovered that he could have whoever he wanted,
whenever he wanted and on whatever terms he
wanted. Very early on, he had learned the meaning
of the expression, 'spoiled for choice'.

'Luca!'

He narrowed his eyes. The tiny blonde was pouting. He raised a dark eyebrow. 'Mmm?'

'You haven't been listening to a word I've been
saying!'

She was right. 'Sorry.' He smiled, gave an expansive shrug of his broad shoulders. 'I feel guilty. I
have been monopolising you, when there are so
many men here who would wish to speak to you.'

'You're the only man I want to talk to!' she declared shamelessly.

'But that is unfair,' he responded softly. *'Sì?'*

The blonde wriggled her shoulders. 'Oh, I just love
it when you speak Italian,' she confided.

He stared down into the widened blue eyes—deep
and blue like a swimming pool and just begging him
to dive in. Unconsciously, she snaked the tip of her
tongue around her parted lips, so that they gleamed
in invitation. It was almost too easy. She could be in
his bed within the hour. At twenty-two, he would
have been tempted. A decade later and he was simply
jaded.

'Will you excuse me?' he murmured. 'I must make
a quick telephone call.'

'To Italy?'

'No, to New York.'

'Gosh!' she exclaimed, as if he had proposed communication with Mars itself.

He smiled again, his mouth quirking a touch wearily at the corners. 'It was delightful to meet you.'

He made his escape before she asked the inevitable. How long was he staying? Would he like her to show him around? Unless she was bold enough to replicate the incredible time he had met a woman and within two minutes she had asked him to take her to bed!

The woman in green was still gazing out of the window and there was something intriguing about her stillness, the way she stood alone, part of the party and yet apart from it. Like a woman secure in her own skin. He made his way across the room and stood beside her, his eyes taking in the last rainbow spangles of the fireworks, set against the incomparable beauty of the sea.

'Spectacular, isn't it?' he murmured, after a moment.

She didn't answer straight away. Her heart was beating hard. Very hard. Funny how you could react to someone, even if you told yourself you didn't want to. 'Utterly,' she agreed, but she didn't move, didn't turn her head to look at him.

Now he was a little intrigued. 'You aren't enjoying the party?'

She did turn then, for it would have been sheer rudeness to have done otherwise, mentally preparing herself for the impact up close of the dark, glittering eyes and the sensual lips and it was as devastating as she remembered, maybe even more so. At seventeen you knew nothing of the world, nor of men—

you thought that men like Luca Cardelli might exist in droves. It took a long time to realise that they didn't, and that maybe that was a blessing in disguise. 'Why on earth should you think that?'

'You're here all on your own,' he murmured.

'Not any more,' she responded drily.

His dark eyes glittered at the unspoken challenge. 'You want me to go away?'

'Of course not,' she said lightly. 'The view is for free, for everyone to enjoy—I shouldn't dream of claiming a monopoly on it!'

Now he was very intrigued. 'You were staring at me, *cara*,' he observed softly.

So he had noticed! But of course he had noticed—it was probably as much a part of his life as breathing itself to have women staring at him.

'Guilty as charged! Why, has that never happened to you before?' she challenged mockingly.

'I don't remember,' he mocked back.

She opened her mouth to say something spiky in response, and then pulled herself together. He had been sweet and kind to her once, and just because a girl on the brink of womanhood hadn't found that particularly flattering, you certainly couldn't blame *him*. It wasn't *his* fault that he was so blindingly gorgeous and that she had cherished a schoolgirl crush on him which hadn't been reciprocated. And neither was it his fault that he was still so gorgeous that a normally calm and sensible woman had started behaving like a spitting kitten. She smiled. 'So what do you think of the Hamble?'

'It isn't my first visit,' he mused.

'I know.'

'You *know*?'

'You don't remember me, do you?'

He studied her. She was not his type. Tall and narrow-hipped where he liked his women curvy, and soft and small. Her face was not beautiful either, but it was interesting. A strong face—with its intelligent grey-green eyes and a determined mouth and soft shadows cast by her high cheekbones.

It was difficult to tell what colour her hair was, and whether its colour was natural, since she had caught it back severely from her face, and tied it so that it fell into a soft, silken coil on the base of her long neck. Her dress was almost severe too, a simple sheath of green silk which fell to her knees, showing something of the brown toned legs beneath. The only truly decorous thing about her was a pair of sparkly, sequinned sandals which showed toenails painted a surprisingly flirtatious pink, which matched her perfect fingernails.

He shook his head. 'No,' he said. 'I don't remember you. Should I?'

Of course he shouldn't. 'Not really.'

She gave a little shrug and turned her head to the view once more, but he put his hand on her bare arm and sensation shivered over her.

'Tell me,' he murmured.

She laughed. 'But there's nothing to tell!'

'Tell me anyway.'

Eve sighed. Why the hell had she even brought it up? Because she liked things straightforward? Because the probing nature of her job made her explore people's feelings and reactions?

'You came here one summer, a long time ago. We met then. We hardly knew each other, really.'

Luca frowned for a moment, and then his face

cleared. So it had not been a woman he had bedded and forgotten. There had been only one woman during that long, hot summer and she had been the very antithesis of this keen-eyed woman with her scraped-back hair. 'Unfortunately, *cara*, I am still none the wiser. Remind me.'

It had been a summer of making money, which had never really been in abundance in Eve's life. Ever since her father had died, her mother had gone out to work to make sure that Eve never went without, but there had never been any surplus to buy the things that seventeen-year-old girls valued so much in life. Dresses and shoes and music and make-up. Silly, frivolous things.

Eve had been overjoyed to get the summer job as waitress at the prestigious yacht club. She had never been part of the boating set—with their sleek boats and their quietly expensive clothes and all-year tans and glamorous parties. She'd had precisely no experience of waitressing, either, but she'd been known and liked in the village for being a hard-working and studious girl. And she'd suspected that they'd known she'd actually *needed* the money, as opposed to wanting the job in order to pick up a rich boyfriend.

And then Luca Cardelli had anchored his yacht one day, and set every female pulse in the vicinity racing with disbelieving pleasure.

The men who had sailed had been generally fit and muscular and bronzed and strong, but Luca had been all these things and Italian, too. As a combination, it had been irresistible.

She had been breathlessly starstruck around him, all fingers and thumbs, her normal waitressing skills deserting her, completely dazzled by his careless

Italian charm. On one embarrassing occasion, the plate of prawns she had been carrying had slipped so that half a dozen plump shellfish had slithered onto the floor in a pink heap.

Biting back a smile, he had handed her a large, linen napkin.

'Be quick,' he murmured. 'And no one will notice.'

No one except him, of course. Eve wished that the floor could have opened up and swallowed her. But she told herself it was just a phase in her life, of being utterly besotted by a man who saw her as part of the background.

Their conversation was limited to pleasantries about wind conditions and her uttering unmemorable lines such as, 'Would you like some mayonnaise with your salmon?' which made his act of generosity so surprising that she read all the wrong things into it.

The end-of-season yacht club ball was the event of the year, with the ticket prices prohibitedly high, unless you got someone to take you, and Eve had no one to take her.

'You are going dancing on Saturday?' Luca questioned idly as he sipped a drink at sundown on the terrace one evening.

Eve shook her head as she scooped up the discarded shells from his pistachio nuts. 'No. No, I'm not.'

He lifted a dark, quizzical eyebrow. 'Why not? Don't all young women want to dance?'

She ran her fingers awkwardly down over her apron. 'Of course they do. It's just...'

The brilliant black eyes pierced through her. 'Just what?'

Humiliating to say that she had no one to take her, surely? And not very liberated either. And the tickets cost more than she earned in a month. She wished he wouldn't look at her that way—though what way could he look for her not to feel so melting inside? Maybe if he put a paper bag over his head she might manage not to turn to jelly every time he was in the vicinity. 'Oh, the tickets cost far too much for a waitress to be able to afford,' she said truthfully.

'Oh.' And his eyes narrowed.

Nothing more was said, but when Eve went to fetch her coat that evening there was an envelope waiting for her and inside it was a stiff, gold-edged ticket to the dance. And a note from Luca. 'I want to see you dance,' it said.

Eve went into a frenzy. She was Cinderella and Rockerfella combined; it was every fairy tale come true. She borrowed a dress from her friend Sally, only Sally was a size bigger and they had to pin it into shape, but even after they had done it still looked like what it was. A borrowed dress.

Eve surveyed herself doubtfully in the mirror. 'I don't know.'

'Nonsense! You look gorgeous,' said Sally firmly. 'You definitely need some make-up, though.'

'Not too much.'

'Eve,' sighed Sally. 'Did or did not Luca Cardelli give you a ticket? Yes? Well, believe me—no man splashes out that much if he isn't interested. You want to look sophisticated. Mature. You want him to whisk you into his arms and dance the night away, don't you? Well, don't you?'

Of course she did.

But Eve felt like a fish out of water when she walked into the glittering room, feeling an outsider and knowing that she *was* an outsider. Everyone else seemed to be *with* someone, except for her.

And then Luca arrived, with a woman clinging to his arm like a limpet, a stunning vision in a scarlet dress that was backless and very nearly frontless.

She remembered almost everyone's eyes being fixed with envious fascination on them as they danced in a way which left absolutely no doubt about how they intended to end the evening and Eve felt sick and watched until she could watch no more. He said hello to her and told her that she looked 'charming'. It was a curiously unflattering word and she wondered how she could have been so stupid.

She crept home and scrubbed her face bare and carefully took off Sally's dress and hung it in the wardrobe. Luca left for Italy soon after and she didn't even see him to say goodbye. She didn't even get the chance to thank him.

But that experience defined her.

That night she vowed never to make her ambition overreach itself. To capitalise on what she was and not what she would like to have been. And she was no looker—certainly not the kind of woman who would ever attract a man like Luca Cardelli. She had brains and she had determination and she would rely on those instead.

Time shifted and readjusted itself, and it was an altogether different Eve who looked into the dark eyes with their hard, luminous brilliance.

Well, here it came, in a fanfare, with a drum roll!

'I was a waitress,' she said baldly, but smiled. 'At the yacht club.'

He shook his head. 'Forgive me, but—'

'You bought me a ticket for a dance.'

Something stirred on the outskirts of his mind. A hazy recollection of a sweet, clumsy girl who was trying to look too old for her age. His eyes widened ever so slightly. How little girls grew up! He nodded slowly. 'Yes. I remember now.'

'And I never got the chance to thank you. So thank you.' She smiled, the brisk, charming smile she used to such great effect in her professional life.

'You're welcome,' he murmured, thinking how time could transform. Was this sleek, confident woman really one and the same person?

His dark eyes gleamed and suddenly Eve felt vulnerable. And tired. She didn't want to flirt or make small talk with him—for there was still something about him which spelt danger and unobtainability. A gorgeous man who was passing through, that was all, same as last time. Stifling a yawn, she glanced at her watch. 'Time I was going.'

Luca's eyes narrowed in surprise. This was usually *his* line and never, *ever* had a woman yawned when he had been talking to her—not unless he had spent the previous night making love to her. 'But it's only nine o'clock.' He frowned. 'Why so early?'

'Because I have to work in the morning.'

'I am not sure that I believe you.'

'That, of course, is your prerogative, Mr Cardelli,' she returned sweetly

He stilled. 'So you remember my surname, too?'

'I have a good memory for names.'

'Unlike me.' He glittered her a smile. 'So you had better remind me of yours.'

'It's Eve. Eve Peters.'

Eve. It conjured up a vision of the first woman; the only woman. It was a small, simple and yet powerful name. It spoke of things lush and coiling. Of a fallen woman, driven by lust and the forbidden. He wanted to make a mocking joke about serpents, but something in those intelligent eyes stopped him. 'So what kind of job gets you up so early, Miss Peters? You're a nurse?' he guessed. 'Either that, or you milk cows?'

Eve laughed in spite of herself. 'Wrong!' She didn't want to be charmed by him, or made to laugh by him. She wanted to get away and she wanted it now. He unsettled her, made her feel like the woman she wasn't. She liked to be in control. She was calm, and considered and logical, and yet right now she was having the kind of fantasy which was more suited to the naïve adolescent she had abandoned that night along with the borrowed dress. Wondering what it would be like to be in Luca Cardelli's arms and to be made love to by him.

The filmy cream shirt meant that she could faintly see the whorls of hair which darkened the tight, hard chest and for one wild and crazy moment she imagined herself pressed against him, the strong arms enfolding her in a magic circle from which no woman would ever want to escape.

Luca saw her green-grey eyes momentarily darken and he felt an unexpected answering ache. 'Don't go,' he urged softly. 'Stay a little while and talk to me.'

His body had tensed and a drift of raw, feral male

scent began to intoxicate her. 'I can't,' she said, with a smile she hoped wasn't weak or uncertain. She put her glass down on the window-ledge. 'I really must go.'

'That, of course, is *your* prerogative,' he said mockingly.

Her resolve was beginning to fail her. 'Goodbye,' she said. 'It was nice to see you again.'

'*Arrivederci, cara.*' He stood and watched her weave her way through the room, his face giving nothing away. And maybe the blonde had been watching, for she reappeared by his side, looking like a tiny, overstuffed cushion in comparison to Eve's slender height and suddenly her simpering presence was cloying and not to be endured.

'I thought you were going to make a phone call, Luca,' she pouted.

Did she spend her whole life pouting? he wondered with a faint air of irritation.

'I was distracted,' he drawled. 'But thank you for reminding me.'

It hadn't been what she had meant to happen at all, and the blonde's mouth fell open in protest, but Luca had gone, pulling his mobile phone out of his pocket, and he went to stand outside, for privacy and for a better signal.

And better to watch the shadowy figure of Eve Peters as she walked down the path with the moonlit water dappling in the soft night air behind her.

CHAPTER TWO

EVE knew that people thought that working in television was glamorous, but people were wrong.
Waking up at three-thirty had never been easy and
the following morning was no exception, made worse
by a foul, chill wind blowing in, which had the kind
of drizzle which could turn the straightest hair into
a frizzy cloud.

On automatic pilot, she showered and drank strong
black coffee, and when the car arrived to collect her
to take her to the studio she sat in the back with the
newspapers as usual, only for once it was hard to
concentrate on the day's news.

The truth was that she had had a disturbed night
and that it had been disturbed by Luca Cardelli. He
had burst into her dreams like a bright, dazzling me-
teorite, his brilliant black eyes mocking her and tantalising her and making her feel that she had missed
an opportunity by leaving the party early.

But dreams were curious and capricious things,
and unlike life you had no control over them. All he
had done was to awake something in her subcon-
scious, some forgotten teenage longing which had
never quite gone away.

And dreams were soon forgotten. They weren't
real. Neither was the ridiculous fluttery feeling she
felt at the base of her stomach when she thought of
him and there was a simple solution to *that*. She tried

her best not to think of him but he stubbornly stayed on her mind.

She wished now that she had asked Michael how long he was here for—but surely it would be a flying visit? His life wasn't here, was it? His life was in Italy—a different, unknown life in a country as foreign to her as he was.

That morning's show contained the usual mix of items, including a dog which was supposedly able to howl in time to the national anthem. Unfortunately, the animal refused to perform to order—the poor thing cowered and was terrified and then was sick in a corner of the studio. Johnny, her co-host, threw a complete wobbly afterwards, and Eve was relieved to get away after the post-show breakdown.

The car dropped her off just after eleven and she closed the door of her tiny cottage with a sigh of relief. She went upstairs, wiped off all her heavy studio make-up, stripped off her clothes and took a long, hot shower, blasted her hair dry and knotted it into one thick plait.

Feeling something close to human again, she put on a pair of black jeans and a charcoal-grey sweater, aware that she would have grubby little fingers crawling all over her, then set off for Michael and Lizzy's, stopping off on the way to buy a colouring book and some crayons for Kesi.

She rang the bell and Lizzy answered it, a look of repressed excitement on her face, as though the party were just about to happen, rather than having taken place the night before.

'Eve! You look gorgeous!'

'No, I don't. No make-up and slouchy old jeans.'

'Well, you looked pretty amazing on the box this morning!'

'Ah, but that's the magic of the make-up artist. Did you see the sick dog?'

'*Did* I? Michael recorded it for me. Poor thing! Come on up. He's taken Kesi out, but he shouldn't be too long.'

'And how *is* my gorgeous little god-daughter?' asked Eve as they walked into the bright, first-floor sitting room. 'I thought—' But what she had been thinking flew completely out of her mind, for sprawled on one of the long sofas, reading a news-paper, was Luca Cardelli.

He glanced up as they entered and his dark eyes glittered with what looked like mischief, but under-pinned with something else, something which Eve couldn't quite work out. Something which made her wary and excited all at the same time. She found herself wondering whether he looked at every woman that way, and whether it had the same dis-concerting effect on them. Probably.

But even so, tiny goose-bumps still prickled at the back of her neck.

'We thought we'd invite Luca, too,' smiled Lizzy.

Luca rose to his feet, observing the startled look on Eve's face change into one of suspicion. Was she so prickly with all men, he wondered, or just him? He smiled, her frozen face presenting him with a challenge which stimulated him. He threw her a lazy look. 'You didn't mind me gatecrashing your lunch?'

What could she say? That she did? And that wouldn't be entirely truthful, would it? Because her heart was racing with something which felt very close to elation. For here he was, only this time without the hoardes of people there had been last night.

'Of course not,' she said calmly.

Lizzy frowned, as if sensing that something was up and not quite able to work out what it was. 'Um, can I get you both a drink? There's loads of champagne left.'

Eve opened her mouth to ask for something soft and then shut it again. She felt wired up. At a loss. And curiously incomplete. She, who felt at ease in almost any social gathering, suddenly felt an urgent need for something to help her loosen up. 'That would be lovely.'

'Luca?'

'Please.' But he barely heard his hostess speak. He wanted to be alone with Eve, to break down the armoury he had seen her begin to construct from the moment she had walked into the room.

He rose to his feet, with all the grace of some lithe, dark panther and as he moved towards her Eve thought that there was something of the predator in him today. And how did vulnerable animals cope with predators in the wild? They didn't run away, that was for sure. They stood their ground and faced them.

But, dear Lord in heaven—they surely didn't share *her* feelings that this predator—if indeed predator he was—looked good enough to eat.

Like her, he was wearing jeans—faded and washed out and clinging to the hard shaft of his thighs—the pale sweater emphasising the glowing olive skin and the jet-dark eyes. His black hair was ruffled and he was smiling and Eve was aware that, while she had been fiercely attracted to him a decade ago—then she had been teetering on the brink of womanhood with precisely no knowledge of men and their power over women. But now she was experienced enough to know that there were few men of Luca's calibre around.

Achievable goals, she reminded herself and flashed him a bland, pleasant smile.

'So, Eve,' he began. 'Did you make work on time?'

'I did.'

'But you didn't sleep.'

Her eyes widened, for one crazy moment imagining that he had witnessed her fretful night. 'Yes, yes, I did,' she denied automatically.

'Liar,' he murmured as without warning he lifted his hand to lightly touch the delicate skin beneath her eyes. 'This gives you away. Dark shadows, like the blue of an iris, so dark against your pale skin.'

The invasion of her personal space was both unexpected and inappropriate and yet his touch made her tremble, the innocent contact feeling as highly charged as any intimate caress. She wanted to tell him to stop it, to ask him what the hell he thought he was playing at, but she was mesmerised by him, lulled by the deep, honeyed Italian accent. She felt like a weak, tiny kitten, confronted by the blazing strength of a lion. And Italians were tactile, she told herself—that was all.

'I'm not wearing any make-up,' she said, as if that explained everything, bizarrely missing the contact as he moved his hand away.

'I know you're not.' And her scrubbed, pure face intrigued him, too. She must be very assured not to wear any cosmetics, and self-assurance was a potent sexual weapon in itself. 'I didn't sleep myself, if it makes any difference.'

'Should I be interested?'

'Maybe you should, since it was for exactly the same reason as you.'

She pulled herself together. Pretend he's one of those men who plague you, she thought. One of those boring, vacuous men who are attracted to you simply because you're beamed into their homes every morning.

'Lumpy mattress?' she guessed. 'Or simply indigestion after a late night and too much party food?'

He laughed. 'No.'

And then she found herself saying, 'Perhaps there were rather more enjoyable reasons for your lack of sleep.'

'Such as?'

'Oh, I don't know. The blonde woman you were talking to seemed very attentive. Maybe she kept you awake.'

'And does that make you jealous, *tesora*?'

Eve stared at him. Her heart was thumping in her chest. Yes. Yes, it did. 'Don't be so ridiculous.'

He smiled. 'I slept alone.'

'You have my commiserations.'

'Did you?' he drawled.

'Are you in the habit of asking people you don't know their most intimate secrets?'

'I asked you a straight question.' He paused. 'Unlike you, who merely hinted at it.'

'Who you sleep with doesn't interest me in the slightest and I'm certainly not going to tell you *my* bedtime secrets!' she bit back angrily, and wished that she could have disappeared in a puff of smoke as Lizzy chose just that moment to walk back into the room, carrying a bottle of champagne and four glasses.

'Wow!' she exclaimed, her eyes widening like saucers. 'Shall I walk right out and then walk back in again?'

Luca took the bottle from her and began to remove the foil. 'Eve and I were just discovering that we like to get straight to the heart of the matter, weren't we, Eve?'

Eve glared at him, feeling the heat in her cheeks. What could she say? What possible explanation could she give to her friend for the conversation they had been having? None. She couldn't even work it out for herself.

'Well, that's what she does for a living, of course,' giggled Lizzy.

He poured the champagne and handed both women a glass, his eyes lingering with amusement on the furious look Eve was directing at him. 'And what exactly is that?' he questioned idly.

'Go on, guess!' put in Lizzy mischievously.

It gave him the opportunity to imprison her in a mocking look of question. 'Barrister?'

In spite of herself, Eve was flattered. Barrister implied intelligence and eloquence, didn't it? But she hated talking about her job. People were far too interested in it and sometimes she felt that they didn't see her as a person, but what she represented. And television was sexy. Disproportionately prized in a society where the media ruled. Inevitably, it had made her distrust men and their motives, wondering whether their attentions were due to what she did, rather than who she was.

But she wasn't going to play coy, or coquettish, or let Luca Cardelli run through a whole range of options.

'No,' she said bluntly. 'I work in television.'

'Eve's a presenter on *Wake Up!*, every weekday morning from six until nine!' confided Lizzy proudly. 'I've got her on video—would you like to see?'

'Oh, Lizzy, *please*,' begged Eve. 'Don't.'

Luca heard the genuine appeal in her voice and his eyes narrowed. So that would explain why people were watching her at the party last night. Would that explain some of her defences, too? The guarded way she looked at him and the prickly attitude? He shook his head. 'It will be boring for Eve. I'll pass.'

Eve should have been relieved. She hated watching herself, and especially when there was an audience of friends; it made her feel somehow different, when she wanted to be just like everyone else. But, perversely, the fact that Luca *wasn't* interested in watching her niggled her. How contrary was that?

'Well, thank heavens for small mercies.' She sighed, and the sound of the front door slamming and the bouncing footsteps of Kesi were like a blessed reprieve. She put her glass down and turned as a small bundle of energy and a mop of blonde curls shot into the room, straight for Eve, and she scooped the little girl up in her arms and hugged her.

'Arnie Eve!' squealed the little girl.

'Hello, darling. How's my best girl?'

'I hurted my knee.'

'*Did* you?' Eve sat down on the sofa with Kesi on her lap. 'Show me where.'

'Here.' Kesi pointed at a microscopic spot on her

leg as Michael walked into the room, beaming widely.

'Champagne?' he murmured. 'Jolly good. You must come more often, Luca—if Lizzy has taken to opening bubbly at lunch-time!'

'It was only because it was left over from last night!' protested his wife.

'How very flattering,' murmured Luca, and they all laughed.

'I'm *starving*,' said Michael. 'Some of us have been chasing after toddlers in the sea air and working up an appetite!'

'Well, Eve's been up since half-past three,' commented Lizzy.

Luca raised his eyes. 'When you said early, I didn't realise you meant *that* early. Still night-time, in fact.' He looked at her, where only her grey-green eyes were visible over the platinum mop-top of the child. 'Must be restricting, working those kind of hours,' he observed. 'Socially, I mean.'

'Oh, Eve's a career woman,' said Michael. 'She wouldn't worry about a little thing like that!'

Eve twisted one of Kesi's curls around her finger. 'Am I allowed to speak for myself? I hate the term "career woman"—it implies ambition to the exclusion of everything else. As far as I'm concerned—I just do a job which means I have to work antisocial hours.'

'Like a nurse?' interjected Luca, his dark eyes sparking mischief.

'Mmm.' She sparked the mischief right back. 'Or a dairy farmer.'

Their gazes locked and held in what was essentially a private joke, and Eve felt suddenly unsafe.

Shared jokes felt close, too close, but that was just another illusion—and a dangerously seductive one, too.

Lizzy blinked. 'Come and wash your hands before lunch, poppet,' she said to Kesi.

Kesi immediately snuggled closer to Eve.

'Want to stay with Arnie Eve!'

It gave Eve the out she both wanted and needed—anything to give her a momentary reprieve from the effect that Luca was managing to have on her, simply by being in the same room.

'Shall I come, too?' she suggested. 'And we can wash your hurt knee and put a plaster on it—how does that sound?'

Kesi nodded and wound her chubby little arms around Eve's neck and Eve carried her from the room, aware of Luca's eyes watching her and the effect of that making her feel self-conscious in a way she thought she had grown out of long ago.

But when she returned, lunch was set out on the table by one of the windows which overlooked the water, and Luca was chatting to Michael and barely gave her a glance as she carried the child back into the room and, of course, that made her even *more* interested in him!

She settled Kesi into her seat and frowned at Lizzy, who was raising her eyebrows at her in silent question. Just let me get through this lunch and I need never see him again, she thought. And the way to get through it was to treat him just as she would anyone else she was having a one-off lunch with. Chat normally.

But she spent most of the meal talking to Kesi, whom she loved fiercely, almost possessively. Being asked to stand as her godmother had been like a gift, and it was a responsibility which Eve had taken on with great joy.

Lots of women in her field didn't get around to having children and Eve was achingly aware that this might be the case for her. She told herself that with her god-daughter she had all the best bits of a child, without all the ties.

She had just fed Kesi an olive when she reluctantly raised her head to find Luca watching her, and knew that she couldn't use her as an escape route for the entire meal.

'So whereabouts are you living now, Luca?'

He regarded her, a touch of amusement playing around the corners of his mouth. She had barely eaten a thing. And neither had he. And she had been playing with the child in a sweet and enchanting way, almost completely ignoring him, in a way he was not used to.

He wondered if she knew just how attractive it was to see a woman who genuinely liked children. But perhaps he had been guilty of stereotyping—by being surprised at seeing this cool, sophisticated Englishwoman being so openly demonstrative and affectionate. He pushed his plate away. 'I live in Rome—though I also have a little place on the coast.'

'For sailing?'

'When I can. Not too much these days, I'm afraid.'

'Why not? Michael said you were a brilliant sailor.'

He didn't deny it; false modesty was in its way a kind of dishonesty, wasn't it? Sailing had been a passion and an all-consuming one for a while, but passions tended to dominate your life, and inevitably their appeal faded. 'Oh, pressure of work. An inability to commit to it properly. The usual story.'

The words *inability to commit* hovered in the air like a warning. 'What kind of work do you do?'

'Guess,' he murmured.

He had the looks which could have made him a sure-fire hit on celluloid, but he didn't have the self-conscious vanity which usually accompanied an actor. Though he certainly had the ego. And the indefinable air that said he was definitely a leader. 'I'd say you're a successful businessman.'

'Nearly.' He let his eyes rove over her parted lips, wishing he could push the tip of his tongue inside them. 'I'm a banker.'

'Oh.'

'Boring, huh?' he mocked.

She met the piercing black stare with a cool look. 'Not for you, I presume—otherwise you wouldn't do it.'

'Luca!' protested Lizzy. 'Stop selling yourself short!' She leaned across the table towards Eve and gave the champagne-softened, slightly delighted smile of someone who had landed a lunch guest of some consequence. 'Luca isn't your usual kind of banker. He owns the bank!'

Eve felt faint. He *owned a bank*? Which didn't just put him into the league of the rich—it put him spinning way off in the orbit of the super-rich and all the exclusivity which went with that. And there she had been thinking that he might have been impressed with her small-town media status!

She knew he was watching her, wanting to see what her reaction would be. That type of position would be isolating, she realised. People would react differently to him because of it, just as they did with her—only on a much larger scale, of course. On camera she had learned *not* to react, a skill which came in very useful now.

'I didn't realise that individuals *could* own banks,' she said interestedly. 'Isn't that rare?'

He felt as if she was interviewing him! 'It's unusual,' he corrected. 'Not exactly rare.'

'It must be heady stuff—having that amount of power?'

He met her eyes. 'It turns women on, yes.'

She didn't react. 'That wasn't what I meant.'

He ran a finger idly around the rim of his glass. 'It is like everything else—there are good bits and bad bits, exciting bits and boring bits. Life is the same for everyone, essentially—whether you clean the bank or own the bank.'

'Hardly!'

The black eyes gleamed. 'But yes,' he corrected softly. 'We all eat and sleep and play and make love, do we not?'

She willed herself not to blush. Only an Italian could come out and talk about making love at a respectable family lunch! 'That's certainly something to consider,' she mused. 'How long are you staying?'

This was interesting. So what had made her soften? The mention of sex or the fact that he was in a position of power? 'I haven't decided.' His eyes sparked out pure provocation. 'Why? Are you going to offer to show me round?'

'Of course I'm not! You already know the Hamble, don't you?' she reminded him sweetly. 'No, I just thought that maybe you might like to come into the studio one morning—I'm sure our viewers would be interested to hear what life as a bank-owner is like!'

The jet eyes iced over. So she was inviting him onto her show, was she? As if he were some second-rate soap star! 'I don't think so,' he said coldly.

She had offended him when she had only meant to distance herself, and suddenly Eve knew that she had to get out of there. He didn't live here. He owned a bank, for heaven's sake—and he had the irresistibly attractive air of the seasoned seducer about him. Achievable goal, he most definitely was not!

'Pity,' she murmured. 'Well, any time you change your mind, be sure and let me know.' She pushed her chair back. 'Lizzy, Michael—thank you for a delicious lunch. Kesi,—do I get a hug and a kiss?' She enveloped her god-daughter, then took a deep breath. 'I'll say goodbye then, Luca.'

He rose to his feet and caught her hand, raising it slowly to his lips, his eyes capturing hers as he brushed his lips against her fingertips in a very continental kiss.

Eve's heart leapt. It felt like the most romantic gesture she had ever experienced and she wondered if he was mocking her again, with this courtly, almost old-fashioned farewell. But that didn't stop her reacting to it, wishing that she hadn't said she would leave, wishing that she could stay, and…then what?

He's passing through, she reminded herself and took her hand away, hoping that the smile on her face didn't look too regretful.

'Goodbye, everyone,' she said, slightly unsteadily.

CHAPTER THREE

ONCE outside, Eve felt a sense of relief as the cool air hit her heated cheeks. Her pulse was racing and her stomach felt as churned as if she had been riding a roller coaster at the fairground. Though maybe that was because she had only picked at the delicious lunch at Lizzy and Michael's.

But deep down she knew that wasn't true. It was simply a physical reaction to Luca, and in a way it was a great leveller. She wasn't any different from any other woman and she defied any other woman not to react in that way, especially if he had been flirting with you. And he had, she was acutely aware of that. She might not be the most experienced cookie in the tin, but she wasn't completely stupid.

She walked over the rain-slicked cobblestones towards her cottage, listening to the sound of the masts creaking in the wind and thinking how naked they looked without their sails. It wasn't that she didn't meet men—she did—she just rarely, no, *never* met men like that. Which wasn't altogether surprising. Outrageously rich, sexy Italians weren't exactly turning up in the quiet streets of Hamble in their hundreds—or even in the TV studio.

She would go home and do something hard and physical—something to bring her back down to earth and take her mind off him. What did her mother always used to say? That hard work left little room for neurotic thoughts!

She changed into her oldest clothes—paint-spattered old khaki trousers and an ancient, washed-out T-shirt with 'Hello, Sailor!' splashed across the front. Then she put on a pair of pink rubber gloves, filled up a bucket with hot, soapy water and got down on her hands and knees to wash the quarry tiles in the kitchen.

She had just wrung out the cloth for the last time when the doorbell rang, and she frowned.

Unexpected callers weren't her favourite thing. She liked her own space, and her privacy she guarded jealously, but that came with the job. One of the reasons she had never moved away from the tiny village she had grown up in was because here everyone knew her as Eve. True, local television wasn't on the same scale as national—she had never been pestered by the stalkers who sometimes threatened young female presenters—but she was still aware that if your face was on television then people felt a strange sense of ownership. As if they actually *knew* you, when of course they didn't.

She opened the door and her breath dried her mouth to sawdust. For Luca was standing there, sea breeze ruffling the dark hair, his hands dug deep into the pockets of his jeans, stretching the faded fabric over the hard, muscular thighs.

'Luca,' she said. 'This is a surprise.'

'Is it?'

The question threw her. Helplessly she gestured to her paint-spattered clothes, the garish pink gloves, which she hastily peeled from her hands. 'Well, as you can see—obviously I wouldn't have dressed like this if I was expecting someone.'

The black eyes strayed and lingered on the message on her T-shirt and he expelled an instinctive little rush of breath. 'And there was me, thinking that you had worn that especially for me,' he murmured.

'But you don't sail much, any more, do you?' she fired back, even though her breasts were tingling and tightening in response to his leisurely appraisal. 'And strangely enough—the shop was right out of T-shirts bearing the legend: "Hello, Banker!"' She wanted to tell him to stop staring at her like that and she wanted him to carry on doing it for ever.

He laughed, even though he had not been expecting to, but it was only a momentary relief. His body felt taut with tension and he ached in a way which was as surprising as it was unwelcome. He did not want to feel like some inexperienced youth, so aroused by a woman that he could barely walk. And yet, when she had left the lunch party, she had left a great, gaping hole behind.

'Are you going to invite me inside?' he asked softly.

She kept her face composed, only through a sheer effort of will. 'For?'

There was a pause. 'For coffee.'

It was another one of those defining moments in her life. She knew and he knew that coffee was not on top of his agenda, which made her wonder what was. No. That wasn't true. She knew exactly what was on his mind; the flare of heat which darkened his high, aristocratic cheekbones gave it away, just as did the tell-tale glitter of his eyes.

She could say that she was busy. Which was true. That she needed a bath. Which was also true. And then what would he do?

'I need a bath.'

'Right now?' he drawled. 'This very second?'

'Well, obviously not *right* now.'

He looked at her curiously. 'What have you been doing?'

'Scrubbing the kitchen floor,' she answered and felt a sudden flare of triumph to see curiosity change to astonishment.

'Scrubbing the kitchen *floor*?' he echoed incredulously.

'Of course. People do, you know.'

'You don't have a cleaner?'

'A cleaner, yes—but not a full-time servant. And I've always liked hard, physical work—it concentrates the mind beautifully.'

The hard, physical work bit renewed the ache and Luca realised that Eve Peters would be no walkover. He decided to revise his strategy. 'Well, then—will you have dinner with me tonight?'

She opened her mouth to say, Only if I'm in bed by nine, but, in light of the tension which seemed to be shimmering between them, she thought better of it. And why the hell was she automatically going to refuse? Had she let her career become so dominating that it threatened to kill off pleasure completely?

'Dinner is tricky because of the hours I work, I'm afraid, unless it's a very early dinner and, as we've only just finished lunch, I don't imagine we'd be hungry enough for dinner.' She opened the door wider. She was only doing this because he had once been kind to her, she told herself. And then smiled to herself as she thought what an utter waste of time self-delusion was. Why not just admit it? She didn't want him to go.

'So you'd better come in and I'll make you some coffee instead.'

The innocent invitation caught him unawares and something erratic began to happen to his heart-rate even though he was registering—rather incredulously—that she had actually turned down his invitation to dinner.

Her eyes glittered him a warning. 'But I don't have long.'

'Just throw me out when you want to,' he drawled, in the arrogant manner of someone who had never been thrown out of anywhere in their lives.

He closed the door behind him with a certain sense of triumph, though he could never remember having to fight so hard to get a simple cup of coffee. 'These houses were not built for tall men,' he commented wryly as he followed her along a low, dark corridor through into the kitchen.

'That's why a woman of average height lives in it! And people were shorter in those days.'

The kitchen was clean and the room smelt fresh. An old-fashioned dresser was crammed with quirky pieces of coloured china and a jug of copper-coloured chrysanthemums glowed on the scrubbed table. From the French doors he could see the sea—grey and angry today and topped with white foam. 'I love the Hamble,' he said softly.

'Yes, it's gorgeous, isn't it? The view is never the same twice, but then the sea is never constant.' She studied him. 'What's it like, coming back here?'

He stared out at the water, remembering what it had been like when he had first sailed into this sleepy English harbour, young and free, unencumbered by responsibility. It had been a heady feeling.

'It makes you realise how precious time is,' he said slowly. 'How quickly it passes.' And then he shook himself, unwilling to reflect, to let her close to his innermost thoughts. 'This house is...' he searched for just the right description '...sweet.'

Eve smiled. 'Thank you. It's the old coastguard's cottage. I've lived here all my life.'

'It isn't what I was expecting.'

She filled the kettle up. 'And what was that?'

'Something modern. Sleek. Not this.' And today *she* was not what he expected, either. His pulse should not be pounding in this overpowering way. He tried telling himself that he liked his women to be smart and chic, not wearing baggy clothes with spots of paint all over them, and yet all he could think about was her slender body beneath the unflattering trousers, and his crazy fascination for the flirty pink varnish on the toes of her bare feet.

Eve made the coffee in silence, thinking that he seemed to fill the room with his presence and that never, in all her life, had she been so uncomfortably aware of a man. Maybe, subconsciously, she was unable to make the transition from starstruck adolescent to mature and independent woman. Maybe, as far as Luca was concerned, she was stuck in a timewarp, for ever doomed to be the inept waitress with a serious crush. Her heart was thundering so loudly in her ears that she wondered if he could hear it. 'How do you like your coffee?' she asked steadily.

'As it comes.'

But the kettle boiling sounded deafeningly loud, almost as loud as her heart. She turned and looked at him. He was leaning against the counter, perfectly still, just watching her. And something in his eyes made her feel quite dizzy. 'So?' she questioned, in a voice which sounded a million miles away from the usual way she asked questions.

He smiled. 'So why am I here?'

'Well, yes.'

He let his gaze drift over her. 'I couldn't help myself,' he said, with a shrug, as if admitting to a weakness that was alien to him.

Eve stared back at him. She tried telling herself that she wasn't like this with men. She worked with men. Lots of them—some of them gorgeous, too. Yet there was something different about Luca—something powerful and impenetrable which didn't stop him seeming gloriously accessible. Sensuality shimmered off him in almost tangible waves. He was making her feel vulnerable, and she didn't want to be.

She could feel the slow burn of a flirtation which felt too intense, and yet not intense enough. Part of her was regretting ever having asked him into her house, where the walls seemed to be closing in on her, and yet there was some other, wild, unrecognisable part of her that wished that they could dispense with all the social niceties and she could just act completely out of character. Take him upstairs and have him make love to her, just once. That was what he wanted; she knew that.

But life wasn't like that, and neither was she.

'Explain yourself, Luca,' she commanded softly.

There was only one possible way to do that and it wasn't with words. He moved towards her and noticed that she mutely allowed him to, her eyes wide with a mixture of incredulity and excitement. As if she couldn't quite believe what he was about to do.

But she made no move to stop him, and he could not stop himself. He brushed his fingertips over the strong outline of her jaw with the intent preoccupation of someone who was learning by touch.

He felt her shudder, even as he shuddered, and then he caught her in his arms, his breath warming her face, his lips tantalisingly close to hers.

'What do you think you're *doing*?' she gasped.

'I am about to kiss you,' he said silkily. 'Surely you can recognise that, *cara*?'

'You mustn't.'

'Why not?'

'Because…because it's *inappropriate*!' she fielded desperately. 'We hardly know each other!'

'Have you never kissed a man who is nearly a stranger?' he murmured. 'Isn't there something crazy and wonderful about doing that?'

Nearly a stranger. There was something so forbidding about that comment, and she tried to focus her mind on it, but all she could feel was the fierce heat of his body and it was remorselessly driving all rational thought from her head. She pushed her hand ineffectually at his chest. 'That's beside the point, and besides—how do you know I don't have a boyfriend?'

He gave a low laugh. 'You should not have boys in your life, Eve—there should be only men. And there is no one.' He drifted a careless fingertip to trace the outline of her lips. 'Even if there is, he is nothing to you. For you do not want him, *cara*. You want me.'

It was ruthless, almost cruel, but it was true. She did.

He read the invitation in her widened, darkened

eyes and brought his mouth crushing down on hers, and as her own opened in sweet response he felt desire jackknife through him with its piercing, flooding weight.

'Oh,' she sighed helplessly. *'Oh!'*

He smiled against her lips, sensing capitulation, and Eve dissolved, her fingers flying up to his shoulders, her nails biting into his flesh as she felt her knees begin to buckle and threaten to give way. She could taste her breath mingling with his and her body melting against his as he pulled her hard against him.

Vainly, she fought for control, for some kind of sanity. 'Luca, for God's sake—'

He lifted his head and looked down at her, his dark eyes almost black as they burned into her. 'What?' he whispered.

'This is crazy. Mad. I just don't *do* this kind of thing!'

'You just did,' he pointed out arrogantly. 'And you want to do it again.'

Yes, she did. She had given him the bait to play masterful and he had taken it and she liked it. Maybe too much. She wondered if he was masterful in bed and the hard, luminous brilliance in his dark eyes told her that, yes, he probably was. But would he give as well as take?

'You do.' He laughed as he felt her move restlessly against him. 'Oh, yes, you do.'

It was a statement, not a question and she didn't answer, just pressed her hips against his and she felt him jerk into hard life against her, heard the almost tortured little moan he made.

'Signore doce in nel cielo!' he groaned. He couldn't remember the last time it had felt like this.

And although he couldn't work out why it should feel that way—and why with this woman—at that moment he didn't care. Deliberately he circled his hips against her, so that she could feel the rock-hard cradle of him.

The tight band of wanting inside her snapped, exploded into a need so fervent that Eve was swept away by it. She ran her fingers through his hair while he kissed her, his lips moving from mouth to cheek, to neck and back to her mouth again, and she was transported into a whole new land. A place where nothing mattered other than the moment, and the moment was now.

'Luca!'

It was a strangled little cry. A pleading. A prayer. A need which matched his. He had thought that she might try to resist him and he was taken aback by her eagerness. With an effort he dragged his lips from the pure temptation of hers, his breathing ragged, his normal sang-froid briefly deserting him. For this was wild and sweet and instant and unexpected. Like being driven by a terrible aching hunger and stumbling upon a feast.

He captured her face between his hands, his eyes burning into her. 'Your bed?' he demanded. 'Take me there—now.'

Dear Lord! Her blood was on fire—any minute now and she would go up in flames. She felt strength and weakness in equal measures, overwhelmed by a desire which banished everything other than the need to have him close to her, as close as it was possible for a man and woman to be.

But it was not right. It could not possibly be. How did he see her—as one of those women driven only by some kind of carnal hunger? And, more importantly, how would this make her feel about herself?

With an effort she tore herself away from the temptation of his arms. 'No. Stop it. I mean it. I can't.'

He stilled, his eyes narrowing in question, feeling the deep, dark throb of frustration. He steadied his breathing. 'What?' The word came out as hard and clipped as gunfire.

'I shouldn't have done that. I'm sorry, Luca. I got carried away.' His face was like stone, but she guessed she couldn't blame him. She had behaved like the worst kind of woman—she had led him on and left him wanting, and left herself aching into the bargain.

'You certainly did.'

'It's just…hopeless, isn't it?'

He arched her a look of imperious query. 'Hopeless?'

She shrugged her shoulders as if in a silent request that the sudden icy set of his features might melt, but she met no answering response. 'Of course it's hopeless—you live in Rome, I live in England.'

His laugh was sardonic. 'I thought we were going to spend the afternoon in bed,' he drawled. 'I wasn't planning to link up our diaries for all eternity!'

She stared at him. 'How very opportunistic of you!'

'Only a fool doesn't seize opportunity when he is presented with it.'

And only a fool would give him house-room after a statement like that.

'I think you'd better leave, don't you?' she said, in a low voice.

'I think perhaps I had.' The black eyes were lit now, sparking with angry fire. 'But perhaps I could give you a word of advice for the future, *cara*.' He drew a deep, unsteady breath. 'Don't you think it unwise to lead a man on to such a point if you then change your mind so abruptly? Not every man would be as accepting of it as I am.'

She stared at him incredulously. 'What are you saying?' she demanded. 'That I have no right to change my mind? That "no" sometimes means "yes"?'

'That is not what I am saying at all,' he ground out heatedly. 'I mean that a lot of men might have attempted to *persuade* you to change your mind.'

'Well, they wouldn't have succeeded!'

'Oh, really?' The black eyes mocked her, challenged her. 'I think you delude yourself, Eve. I think we both know that if I had continued to kiss you, then your submission would have been inevitable.'

'Submission?' she demanded incredulously. '*Submission?* Tell me, just which century do you think you're living in?' She stared at him furiously. 'Words like that imply some kind of gross inequality. When I make love with a man, I don't *submit*, and neither does he! It's equal. It's soft. It's gentle—'

He gave a short laugh. 'You make it sound like knitting a sweater!'

Her cheeks flamed as she instantly understood the implication behind his words. That it would *not* be soft and gentle with *him*, and her pulses leapt even as she steeled her heart against him. 'Just go. Go. Please.'

'I am going,' he said, in a voice which was coiled like a snake with tension, though not nearly as tense as his aching body. 'But something like this cannot be left unfinished.'

Oh, but it could!

His eyes glittered. 'Goodbye, *cara*,' he said softly.

She watched him go with a terrible yearning regret, standing as motionless as a statue as she heard his footsteps echoing over the flagstones in the hall, her body stiff and tense like a statue's—and when she heard the front door slam behind him she should have felt an overwhelming sense of relief.

So why the hell did she feel like kicking her foot very hard against the wall?

CHAPTER FOUR

ALTHOUGH he wasn't due to fly back until the following morning, Luca changed his ticket and returned to Rome early that evening and remonstrated with himself for the whole two-hour journey. What in the name of God had come over him? What had he been playing at? Coming onto her with all the finesse of some boy just out of high school, acting like some hormonally crazed adolescent.

He stared out of the window, the dull ache in his groin still nagging at him, perplexed by the intensity of need she had aroused in him.

He could have clicked his fingers and had any number of beautiful women and—far more importantly—she was most definitely *not* his type. So why her?

Because she had at first been chilly and offhand with him—studying him calmly with those intelligent grey-green eyes? Because she had answered him back? And then resisted him? Had all these combined to make Eve Peters into a woman he had never before encountered?

Unobtainable.

He was home in time to shower and change, and on impulse he took Chiara out. He hadn't seen her in a long while and she was eager to tell him about her new film. It was late, but she agreed instantly to have dinner with him, and yet her suppressed excitement acted like a cold shower to his senses and he began to regret the invitation the moment he had made it.

Her black hair fell like a sultry night to a waist encased in silver sequins and he thought of Eve in her paint-spattered T-shirt, and glowered at his menu. She flirted outrageously with him all night and laughed at all his jokes and gazed at him as if he were the reason that man had been invented.

The paparazzi were waiting when they left the restaurant and in the darkened light of the taxi Luca narrowed his eyes at her suspiciously.

'Did you tell them where we were eating?' he demanded.

She shook her head. 'No, *caro*—I promise you!'

He didn't believe her. Women said one thing and meant another. They plotted and they schemed to get what they wanted. She tried to drape her arms around his neck. He could smell expensive scent and he found it cloying.

Gently, he pushed her away.

'I will drop you off at your apartment,' he said tersely.

'Oh, *Luca*!' Her voice was sulky. '*Must* you?'

He thought of Eve. Of the melting taste of her lips and the way she had exploded into life in his arms. The cool, composed exterior masking the surprisingly hot and sensual nature which lay beneath, of which he had seen only a tantalising glimpse. He sighed as he stared out at the bright lights of night-time Rome and realised that he must have her.

Should he send flowers? Few women could resist flowers. But then her job probably provided her with plenty of bouquets, so that they would be nothing out of the ordinary.

No, definitely not flowers.

'Goodnight, Chiara,' he said gently.

The car drew to a halt, and the actress flounced out.

'Take me home—and quickly!' he shot out, and the car pulled away again.

Eve tried not to think about Luca at all, though it took a bit of effort.

She never underestimated the cruelly dissecting power of the camera for it picked up on just about everything and then magnified it tenfold. A kilo gained made you look like a candidate for the fat camp and a spot seemed to dominate your face like a planet. And not just the external stuff, either. Doubt and insecurities became glaringly obvious under the lens. If you lost your nerve and your confidence, the audience stopped believing in you and started switching off, and once that happened, you didn't have a job for long.

So she tried to put Luca Cardelli out of her mind by analysing it and putting it into context. It wasn't as if it was anything major, after all. She had simply met a man she had once been mad about, and she was mad about him still. It just happened that he was living in another country, was the wrong kind of man to fall for, and had made a pass at her, clearly expecting her to fall into bed with him at the drop of a hat.

Thank heavens she hadn't.

She decided that she needed to get out more. Meet more people. Spread her wings a little.

She signed up for an afternoon course in French and decided that the next time the crew went out for lunch on Friday, she would join them. And she would take Kesi out for the day on Sunday.

But when she arrived home from work a few days later there was a postcard sitting on the mat, its glossy colour photo providing welcome relief in between all the boring bills and circulars. She liked postcards, though people never seemed to send them much any more—she guessed that was the legacy of travel becoming so much more accessible and unremarkable, and the advent of the email, of course. But there was a magic about postcards which electronic stuff somehow lacked.

She sucked in a sharp, instinctive breath of excitement when she saw where the postcard was from.

Roma.

The photo was unusual and bizarre—it showed a sculpture of two boys and a rather threatening and grotesque animal.

She didn't need to turn it over to know who it was from; she knew only one person who was there. And she didn't need to see his name signed at the bottom to recognise the writing, because somehow she had guessed that he would write like that.

Like a schoolgirl with a crush, she let her gaze drift longingly over his handwriting, like someone discovering a lover's body for the first time. In black ink, it curved sensuously across the card, like a snake.

It said: 'I expect you know the cherished legend that Rome was founded by Romulus—here is a photo of him with his twin brother Remus, suckling on a she-wolf! Any time you're in Rome, then please look me up. It was good to see you. Luca.'

And his phone number.

Eve read it and re-read it, her heart beating fast, feeling ridiculously and excessively pleased while trying to tell herself she shouldn't. It was only a post-card, for heaven's sake! And there was no way she would ever ring him.

But she propped the card against the kitchen window, with the backdrop of the sea behind it, and she looked at it, and smiled, because that simple and civilised communication made her able to put that whole passionate yet unsatisfactory scene out of her mind.

But Luca couldn't get her out of his mind, though he did his level best to—that was when he wasn't incredulously checking his phone messages.

She hadn't rung him!

He shook his head in slight disbelief. Did she not realise the intense honour...? He frowned. No. Honour would be too strong a word, and so would privilege—but he wondered just what Miss Eve Peters would say if she realised that he *never* gave his phone number out to a woman he had only just met!

He stripped off his clothes and stepped into the shower, standing beneath the punishing jets of water with a grim kind of anticipation. Maybe she was playing hard to get. He smiled as he reached for the shampoo. Give her until the end of the week, and she would be bound to ring.

Eve was just setting off for her car when one of the production assistants stopped her. 'Eve—a man rang for you.'

'Did he say who he was?'

The production assistant assumed the expression of someone who had been dieting successfully all week, only to be offered a large cream cake minutes before she was due to be weighed. She was getting married in a month, Eve remembered.

'No.'

'Oh, well—thanks, anyway. If it was important, I expect he'll ring again.'

'He was…' the assistant gulped '…*foreign*.'

Annoyingly, Eve's heart went pat-a-pat, then missed a beat completely. 'Oh?' she said, with just the right amount of studied casualness.

'Italian, I think,' the assistant continued. 'He sounded absolutely *gorgeous*! All deep and accented and sexy. You know what they say about a come-to-bed voice? Well, he must have been the man who invented it! Who *is* he?'

'I have absolutely no idea,' replied Eve airily, feeling a brief pang of sympathy for the girl's fiancé. 'And it irritates the hell out of me, when someone doesn't bother to leave their name!'

Which wasn't quite true. What was irritating the hell out of her was her irrational response to the fact that it had undoubtedly been Luca. What was he doing, ringing her? Ringing her at work, too!

And would he ring again? At home? Until she reminded herself that he didn't have her number. But she was in no doubt that someone like Luca could always get hold of a woman's number…

It had been many years since Eve had made excuses to hang around the house, hoping that someone might call her, and she hated it almost as much as she couldn't seem to stop herself from doing it. Every time the phone rang she jumped like a startled rabbit, but it was never him.

Finally, frustrated with herself—and with *him*, though she wasn't quite sure why—she went round to see Kesi and ended up staying for afternoon tea. And it was predictably typical that when she arrived home the red light on her answering machine was winking at her provocatively.

With trembling fingers, she clicked the button and his deep, dark, rich Italian voice began to speak. Just like him, she thought as she listened. Deep and dark and rich.

'Eve? I find that business brings me to London next week. How would you like to meet for dinner?' A tinge of amusement entered the voice. 'An early dinner, of course—leaving you plenty of time to get home for your allotted hours of sleep. Ring me.'

She was appalled to find herself replaying it four times, while silently wondering whether or not to return his call, even while, deep down, she knew with unerring certainty that she would be unable to resist.

But she left it for three days, even though the self-restraint it took nearly killed her. And when she finally got round to it, she had to field her way past a very aloof-sounding secretary who, once she had switched from Italian to perfect, seamless English, sounded very doubtful as to whether Signor Cardelli would wish to be disturbed.

Clearly Signor Cardelli would.

'Luca?' said Eve tentatively, wishing that she could rewind the time clock and never have dialled the wretched number.

Luca felt his body instinctively tense. So the *strega* had made him wait, had she? He couldn't remember ever having had to wait for anything in his life.

'Eve?'

'Yes, it's me! I got your message.'

'Good.' He waited. Now let her see how it felt.

Eve clutched the telephone tightly. Damn him! 'About dinner.'

'Mmm.'

She felt like slamming the phone down, and realised that might be overacting by just a tad. Did she want to have dinner with him, or not? Well, yes and no.

Luca's eyes narrowed. Did she always make it this difficult for men? And then he remembered the way she had been in his arms. They had been so close to going up to her bedroom, and… The tension increased. 'Would you like to have dinner with me, Eve?' he questioned silkily.

Yet another defining moment. Her life seemed to be full of them, and Luca Cardelli always seemed to have something to do with them. Eve swallowed. Pretend you're live on camera. Give him a briskly pleasant, take-it-or-leave-it attitude. It would be so much easier if she *could* just leave it, if the thought of not seeing him again didn't seem as if her world would then take on a rather dull and monochrome appearance.

'That would be lovely. When?'

She was making it sound as though she had been invited to tea with a maiden aunt!

'I arrive on Friday evening,' he said coolly. 'So how about Saturday?'

She supposed that she could pretend to be busy— but what would be the point in playing games if the outcome would only make her miserable?

'Saturday sounds good,' she said evenly, but her heart had started racing.

'Excellent. I'll ring you when I'm in England. *Ciao, bella.*'

Eve found herself staring at the handset, to realise that he had hung up. Her mouth had dried with pure excitement, which quickly changed into another emotion she didn't quite recognise and wasn't up to analysing because there was only one thought dominating her mind right then.

Dinner on Saturday. An early dinner so that she could get back in plenty of time for the early night necessary for her early start.

But she didn't work on Sundays. She knew that and he knew that.

Sunday was her lie-in day.

CHAPTER FIVE

THE hotel was one of those modern, quietly expensive places which often seemed to be featured in glossy magazines and were a million miles away from the featureless anonymity of the large chains.

Eve walked into a foyer painted a deep, dark navy with shiny wood floors and expensive-looking rugs. She had to look hard for the reception desk, which was clearly designed not to *look* like a reception desk. It was half hidden by vases of clashing scarlet and violet flowers and the sleek blonde who eventually gave her a smile looked as if she should be modelling in a glossy magazine herself.

She guessed that this was one of those exclusive places, so hip and cool that it was almost icy, and she shivered at the thought of what she was about to do. Although, as she reminded herself fiercely—she didn't have to do anything. Not if she didn't want to.

'Can I help you?' said the blonde.

'Um…' Oh, for heaven's *sake*—when did she last preface a question with the word, 'um'? 'I'm meeting Mr Luca Cardelli here at six.'

The blonde's cool face didn't flicker. '*Signor* Cardelli,' she corrected, 'should be here—'

'Any minute now,' came the honeyed tumble of his words and Eve's mouth dried as she turned round to see him emerging from the lift. 'Hello, Eve.'

He looked, she thought rather desperately, utterly

ravishing—in a dark linen suit, and a blue silk shirt which was unbuttoned at the neck, showing a tantalising glimpse of olive skin and the arrowing of dark hair.

'Luca,' she said, her voice very low. She forced a smile. 'Hello.'

He narrowed his eyes. This was not the behaviour of a woman who wanted him to make love to her. In fact, she looked as though she were dancing on pieces of broken glass. Did that mean she was nervous, and if so—wasn't that rather endearing? At least it showed him a chink in her sophisticated armour.

He smiled and moved forward, kissing her on each cheek, his hands on her shoulders, continental style, and Eve felt herself relax slightly. Anyone would think she was a timid little mouse of a thing, with no experience of men whatsoever!

But as she breathed in some subtle, heavenly aftershave he was wearing, and felt the faint rasp of his chin against her cheek, it struck her that she felt completely naïve and inexperienced. Why, give her a plate of prawns and she would probably drop them all over him!

'You look wonderful,' he murmured. More than wonderful—though distinctly understated. Some floaty little silk skirt and a soft, pink sweater, which moulded itself to her perfect breasts. A pair of high suede boots and her hair caught in a plait and tied at the end with a pink ribbon. It was both sexy and yet wholesome and it had the effect of making him want her even more.

'Thank you.'

'Shall we go and eat?' He glanced briefly at his watch. 'What time do you have to leave?'

'Oh, well, I can decide later,' she prevaricated. She met the look of curiosity in his eyes. 'That is—um, there's a train at nine-thirty.' Which wasn't answering his question at all, and she had said 'um' *again*!

'We could eat here, if you like. Or find somewhere local?'

Oh, heavens. Normally sure and decisive, she suddenly felt a quivering mass of uncertainty, until something happened which made her get real. Maybe it was the fleeting side-glance which the sleek blonde at Reception sent her, as if she would give anything to be in Eve's shoes.

Enjoy this, she told herself. Just enjoy it. 'What's the food like here?'

'I have no idea.' He glanced around. 'My secretary booked it for me—it's a little—antiseptic for my taste. But there's a sushi bar around the corner—do you like sushi?'

'I love it.'

'Come on, then.'

Outside, the whirr of traffic and the people walking made Eve feel more relaxed, and the sushi bar was gorgeous.

'I think this restaurant might have been designed by a feng shui expert,' she commented as they were shown to a low table, next to a blurred and restful painting.

'Because you have to be a contortionist to sit down?'

She smiled. 'Don't you think it has a rather restful air about it?'

Restful?

He thought that he could have been given some long sleeping draught and he still would have felt the constant heat of desire, but maybe that was because he had been on a knife-edge of delightful anticipation and uncertainty all week. And uncertainty could be a heady emotion—as if you had discovered some new and delicious food you had not realised existed.

Like a natural predator finding itself in undiscovered terrain, he narrowed his eyes and handed her the menu as the waitress hovered.

'Shall we order?'

They discussed the menu together, but Eve might as well have been selecting sawdust and treacle for all the notice she took of the food which began to arrive, on stark, square plates, pretty as individual pictures. She did her level best to eat it, determined to act as normally as if she were out with any attractive man, and not one who seemed to have the power to reduce her to a kind of melting jelly with just one hard, brief smile and one glitter of those brilliant, yet unfathomable dark eyes.

She sipped her wine and felt about seventeen, and just hoped to goodness that the face she presented was calm and serene.

Luca leaned back in his seat. 'So tell me how you came to be a television star.'

'*Presenter,*' she corrected immediately and caught his look of mocking question and smiled. 'I know I'm a bit defensive, but the job comes with so much baggage that it's almost instinctive.'

'People wanting to know you for the wrong reasons?' he guessed.

'Something like that.' She sipped at her wine. 'I expect you've been a victim of it yourself.'

'Never a victim, *cara*,' he murmured. 'And it is not a word I would have associated with you. So tell me about it.'

She loved the way he curled his tongue around the word *'cara'* and found herself, bizarrely, wishing that he would speak to her in Italian, even though she barely knew more than a few words of the language. 'I did a degree in meteorology at university. The weather had always fascinated me, but when you grow up in a place where so much is determined by it, it seemed kind of natural. Then the local station was looking for a weathergirl, and I applied for the job, without really thinking I'd get it.'

'Because?'

'Oh, because I wasn't blonde and busty—and most of the other candidates were!'

'Yet they chose you,' he observed softly.

'Yes, they did—it seemed that they weren't looking for a pneumatic blonde, but someone who actually knew what they were talking about, and the viewers seemed to like me. Then the regular presenter left to have a baby, and the next thing I knew they were asking me to fill in for her—temporarily, at first. But they asked me to stay on, and I did, and that was nearly three years ago, which is actually quite a long time in television.'

'And you like it?'

She hesitated. 'Yes, I do—though sometimes it doesn't really seem a serious job, something that matters, like being a brain surgeon. But I'm aware that I'm lucky to have it—and realistic to know that it won't last for ever. Television jobs rarely do.'

'And when it ends?'

She met his eyes, and shrugged. 'Who knows?'

'So you have no other ambitions, other than what you do now?'

Eve twisted the stem of her glass between her fingers, wary of how much to tell him. But why be a closed book? What would be the point? 'Oh, well, one day I hope to have children, of course.'

He nodded, noting the 'of course', but also her omission of the normal progression of falling in love with a man and marrying him first, but he knew that women were shy of talking of such things, for fear that men would think them needy.

Eve felt exposed. She had done all the talking, and he very little. 'What about you? Did you set out to become the owner of a bank?'

'I don't think anyone does that.' He shrugged. 'I set out to become successful, and somehow it never seemed successful enough. There was always a new challenge, a new obstacle to be overcome and, once I had overcome it, something else to move on to.'

'So now you own a bank, does that mean you've stopped moving on?'

'Oh, no. There's always something else to achieve.'

He stopped speaking abruptly and something about the suddenly wary look in his eyes told her that he had already said more than he was comfortable with.

'I see,' she said slowly, but she thought how restless and nomadic it made him sound. It should have had the effect of distancing her but she found that she wanted to reach her fingertips out and play them along the silken surface of his skin.

He could feel the tension surrounding them as palpably as if it had been a third person sitting with them at the table. Would she play games with him tonight? he wondered.

'Shall I get the bill?'

Something about the way he was looking at her was making her heart pound so loudly that it was as if an entire percussion section had taken up residence in her head. Mutely, she nodded, excusing herself to make her way to the bathroom where she splashed cold water on her wrists, as if hoping that the icy temperature might dull the fevered glitter of her eyes, but to no avail.

They walked out into the darkened street and he turned to her as her hair gleamed like liquid gold beneath the street-lamp. 'Do you want to catch that train?'

She heard a taxi pass them, and she thought of this passing her by. She looked up at him, aware of what hinged on her answer. She looked up into his face and in that moment her heart turned over. 'No.'

He smiled as he bent his head and kissed her in the street. He told himself that he would not have done the same in Rome, where curious eyes would have registered that Luca Cardelli was behaving in a way which would have distorted the image of his cool persona for ever. But that here in London, it was anonymous. And yet it was more than that. She had captivated him, with her cool, intelligent eyes, the way she had made him wait. For a man used to having whatever he wanted whenever he wanted it, it had proved a powerful aphrodisiac. And he could not wait any longer to kiss her again.

'Eve,' he groaned against her moist, sweet lips.

She threaded her fingers into his thick, dark hair as his lips worked a kind of magic, allowing him to pull her closer into his body until she began to tremble uncontrollably, almost relieved when he pulled away, his eyes as black as the night.

'Come,' he said shortly.

He took her hand and they walked in expectant silence back to the hotel, where she saw the receptionist staring at them, and as the lift doors closed on them it occurred to her that it must have been pretty obvious where they were going and what they were doing.

But who cared?

She was a free agent, and so was he. And she wanted him so much that she could barely think, let alone speak, but words were unnecessary because as soon as the lift doors had closed he took her in his arms again, kissing her with an unrestrained passion which took her breath away.

She barely registered the room, except to note that it was heady with the fragrance of flowers and softly lit for seduction. She felt a momentary qualm, half wanting to tell him that this felt slightly out of her league, but wouldn't that just sound like a woman wanting to safeguard her reputation?

But then he began to stroke her, murmuring softly in Italian, threatening to send her already heightened senses spinning out of control, and all her doubts and fears dissolved. Pulling away from him, she met the distracted question in his eyes, and she stroked the hard jaw, as if to silently reassure him. Did he think she was going to change her mind?

'What is it?' he demanded.

'Luca, I don't…I don't have anything.'

He frowned. 'What are you talking about? What don't you have?'

This was worse than one of those sex education books they forced you to read at school, graphic and matter-of-fact, but it was precisely because she *had* read them that she found herself blushing, which seemed slightly ridiculous in the circumstances.

'Contraception. I'm not on the pill. I'm not prepared.'

He gave a slow, sensual smile, her statement appealing to his undeniable machismo. So she was not on the pill—which meant that she did not do this freely with others, and that pleased him more than it had any right to please him.

'Aren't you?' he murmured silkily and moved his hand beneath her skirt, roving it up between her stockinged thighs. He slipped the panel of her panties aside and heard her gasp of pleasure as he pushed a finger into her moist, warm heat. He smiled when she moaned out a protest as he took the finger away and, slowly and deliberately, sucked on it, his eyes capturing hers in a look of erotic promise.

'On the contrary, *cara*,' he whispered, 'it occurs to me that you are very well prepared indeed. And you taste absolutely delicious.'

'Luca!' Her voice trembled briefly and she closed her eyes, feeling strangely shy at his blatant and unashamed enjoyment.

'And fortunately, I am, as you say—prepared.'

Her eyes flew open again to see that he had produced a pack of condoms from his pocket and, while the logical side of her was glad that he had thought of protection, some unrealistic, romantic side of her wished that he hadn't. For didn't that make it somehow *clinical*? Or did he always have them with him, just in case? And even if he did, would that be so bad? Wasn't it better to be careful, and didn't some of her more liberated girlfriends actually carry them around in their handbags?

He saw the brief, vulnerable look which crumpled her mouth and bent his lips to it, teasing it with tiny kisses until it had softened again.

'Stop frowning,' he whispered.

'Make me.'

'With pleasure. But first I want to see your body.'

He pulled the pink sweater over her head and sucked in a raw breath of pleasure as he saw what lay beneath. A sheer bra, sprigged with roses, and the pink-dark tips of her nipples looked as though they were a continuation of the flowers themselves.

'Beautiful,' he murmured. 'Beautiful. Do you always wear such exquisite lingerie? Did you wear it for me, Eve?'

She felt a feline glow of pleasure. 'But of course.' She tiptoed her fingers beneath his shirt and luxuriously began to trickle her fingers over the silken flesh, to alight on one small, hard nipple and to circle it.

He closed his eyes. 'That's good.'

His appreciation gave her the encouragement to begin to unbutton his shirt. She might not have done this for a long time, but she wasn't a complete novice and she sighed with pleasure as, bit by bit, she bared his chest, then peeled his shirt off and dropped it on the floor. Then she dipped her head and gently bit on his nipple, and he groaned before shaking his head. He wanted her naked, and quickly.

Yet he had never felt quite so preoccupied while

undressing a woman, revelling in the sensation of laying her bare. He skimmed off the skirt, the stockings and the panties and then, finally, untied the pink ribbon which bound her hair in the plait.

'Like unwrapping a birthday present,' he said as the hair spilled down over her shoulders, all over her tiny breasts.

She kissed a nipple and felt him shudder. 'When's your birthday?'

'August,' he said distractedly as he kicked off his shoes and swiftly divested himself of the rest of his clothes.

August was months away, and fleetingly she found herself wondering whether they would still be lovers then, but at that moment he lay down on the bed and pulled her on top of him and their warm flesh mingled as he began to kiss her and Eve stopped thinking completely.

He touched her and kissed her with expert lips and fingers, which soon had her making tiny little yelps of disbelief that something could feel so good. But he did it with a certain sense of wonder, too, as if she were the first woman he had ever made love to, and fleetingly she found herself thinking that he had seduction honed to a fine and flattering art.

His eyes were glittering with hot, black fire as he moved above her and she felt strangely and inexplicably shy when at last he entered her with one long, silken thrust.

He wrapped a strand of her hair possessively around his finger as he felt her tighten around him. 'Is that good?'

'It's…' But then he moved and the words were forgotten, her nails digging into his shoulders and her legs wrapping themselves sinuously around his back, pleased when he gave a low moan of pleasure.

'And that?'

'Yes!'

He moved inside her until she felt that she would die with the sheer pleasure of it, and when finally the slow stealth of pleasure exploded into unstoppable fulfillment she was taken aback by the sheer, devastating power of it. Her body continued to tremble as she felt him shudder helplessly in her arms.

They lay there for a while, sweat-sheened bodies locked in the trembling aftermath, until eventually he raised his dark head, kissed the tip of her nose and looked down at her, a rueful smile touching his mouth.

'Well?' he sighed.

She met his eyes. 'Well?'

He laughed, and while the rich, warm sound made her feel safe, it also made her aware of her own insecurities. But that was what happened, wasn't it? She didn't know his sense of humour, or his favourite colour or even where he lived. You met a man and you began an affair with him, and there was always uncertainty about what the future would bring.

He kissed her, his body beginning to ache again and, instinctively, he moved once more, but Eve stilled him with a cautious finger to his lips. 'Be careful.'

He understood immediately and slowly withdrew from her, and the regretful little sigh he made at leaving her made Eve lie back against the pillows, a contented smile of satisfaction on her face. She pillowed her head on her hands and her hair spilled over her like syrup.

'Let me use the bathroom,' he groaned as his eyes lingered on her rose and white nakedness. 'Stay right there.'

Wild horses couldn't have dragged her away. She wasn't going anywhere, she could never imagine wanting to leave until she had to and she wasn't even going to think about it. Dreamily, she gazed up at the high ceiling until Luca came back into the room and joined her on the bed.

'You,' he murmured, kissing her shoulder, 'are amazing. Beautiful.'

She pulled him fiercely against her, and he entered her quickly, but the love he made to her was long and slow and indescribably sweet, and when it was over she snuggled against him, fighting sleep.

He shook her gently. 'Don't you have to catch a train?'

'No.'

'Oh, I see,' he murmured. 'So the train was your escape route, was it, Eve?'

'Mmm.' But now she had no desire to break free. She rested her head against his chest, but he reached over to lift his watch from the locker and gave her a brief smile.

'Forgive me, *cara*.' He yawned. 'I must make one very, very quick phone call. Don't go away.'

But the phone call brought her crashing back down to earth as she lay there and listened while he spoke in rapid Italian. God knew what he was saying or whom he was speaking to. It was only a little thing, but maybe it helped her not to start dreaming impossible dreams.

Luca had another life in another country and she was only a tiny part of it, and who knew for how long?

Maybe for no longer than the morning.

CHAPTER SIX

EVE opened her eyes and in the split-second moment between waking and sleeping she found herself wondering where she was. She saw the rooftops of a London skyline through the uncurtained window, and a man asleep on the bed beside her, and felt the warm laziness which bore testimony to a night of rapturous love-making.

Quietly, she turned her head to look at him. He was truly beautiful in sleep, the deep, regular breaths making his hair-roughened chest rise and fall. He was lying on his side, one hand cupping his face, the long lashes making two ebony arcs which contrasted against the olive-gold of his skin. He looked innocent and indolent.

Turning back to study the ceiling again, she let out a tiny sigh, satisfaction mingling with regret that the night was over.

She hadn't been in this situation for a long, long time, and in fact she had never been in this particular situation, having shed all inhibitions and taken as a lover a man who was, to quote Luca's own words, 'nearly a stranger'.

In fact, she hadn't been in a relationship for almost... She frowned, shocked to realise that it was almost two years. And that had been so different. A slow build-up to a romance that she had known from the beginning would end yet with this one she had absolutely no idea what her feelings were.

71

It was out of character for her—the cool, calm and considered Eve Peters—to have fallen into bed simply because she found him irresistible. But it must happen to him all the time, she thought.

'So why the frown, *cara*? I thought I had kissed that goodbye, last night.'

She started. She had been so deep in thought that she hadn't realised he was awake. The dark eyes were watchful and shuttered by the lashes, his long-limbed body as still as a tiger lying in the full heat of the sun. Outwardly, so relaxed, but with all that pent-up strength and power lurking just beneath the surface.

She affected a careless smile. 'Was I?'

'Mmm.' Idly, he reached out and began to run his fingers through the rich satin of her hair. It had been an incredible night, but he had known it would be. He had been so hungry for her that it couldn't have been anything else, but now with morning came a desire that was transmuted into a different feeling altogether, as inevitably as night followed day. Then it had been the excitement of the unknown and the undiscovered, the delicious anticipation of waiting to see if she would be his.

And now?

Now he was left with the familiar, and, no matter how wonderful it had been, there was a certain protocol to be followed. There were unspoken rules and he wondered if she understood them as well as he did. Rules about boundaries and expectations. He would not be owned. He had never been owned.

'Come over here and kiss me,' he murmured.

But Eve had seen something in his eyes which had made the tiny hairs on the back of her neck prickle in apprehension. There was something very controlled about him this morning, no matter that she could see for herself the evidence that he wanted her very badly. Physically, in any case. But emotionally? Wasn't there a cool kind of distance in the black eyes which were studying her as one would a horse that had not yet been broken? Waiting to see what she would do next, how she would react.

Was he frightened that she was going to come on all heavy? Afraid that she would become clingy or needy or demanding or any of the other things which women sometimes instinctively did when a man had possessed and pleasured them? Well, he need not worry!

She curved her mouth into a smile, so grateful then to the job which had allowed her to make a living out of hiding what was going on inside. Why, even after the death of her mother, she had been back in the studio within the month, her heart breaking inside and yet able to keep a calm and controlled exterior.

True, a couple of the regular and more perceptive viewers had written in to ask if she was okay, and on the editor's advice she had mentioned the death. Which had led to a whole programme on bereavement, after she'd been flooded with letters from people who had gone through exactly the same thing and were anxious to share their experience and the strength which had grown from it. Television taught you lots about controlling your emotions; very early on she had discovered that the camera *could* lie.

'Why don't you come here and kiss me instead?' she suggested.

He rolled towards her, a lazy smile on his lips. So she was not one who would festoon him with kisses and tell him that he was the most marvelous lover she had ever had?

He lowered his mouth onto hers. 'Like that?'

The sweet, aching beauty of that kiss threatened to take her breath away. Eve closed her eyes.

'Exactly like that,' she whispered huskily.

He made love to her for a long time, seeming to go out of his way to demonstrate his finesse as a lover, and twice she sobbed his name out loud. It had never been like this with a man. Never. But that was the kind of thing you should never admit to—especially to a man with an ego the size of Luca's.

He relaxed as he noted her smile of dreamy contentment, smoothing a few stray strands of hair away from her damp forehead. 'How long can you stay?'

'I'll go after lunch. When's your flight back?'

'At five.' He very nearly offered to change it, but he smiled as he touched his lips to hers. It was a very clever woman who made no demands on a man—someone ought to tell them that that was what kept interest alive!

She didn't leave until three and for the whole train journey home Eve was on a high. Her cheeks were rosy and flushed, her eyes bright and her hair very slightly mussed and she bore all the signs of a woman who had been very thoroughly made love to.

He was gorgeous. Utterly, utterly gorgeous, but she hadn't been stupid enough to go all gooey-eyed on him. She recognised that he was that hard, rare breed of man who was essentially a loner, living life on his terms and his terms alone—and why shouldn't he? Wasn't that exactly how she lived her own life?

And as long as she remembered that, there was no

reason why they couldn't have a wonderful and mutually fulfilling love affair.

The green fields rumbled by and she closed her eyes, recalling the lazy morning they had had, not getting out of bed until just after noon, and then strolling to a nearby pub for lunch, where Luca had been engaging and amusing company.

It would be all too easy to fall for him, hook, line and sinker, and she knew instinctively that she must be on her guard against losing her heart to him. She would play it slow and careful. He had told her that he would ring, and she would be very patient and wait.

Well, no—that wasn't *quite* true. She wasn't going to *wait*—for what use was a life spent waiting as if that were the only thing which mattered? She would live her normal life, she reasoned. She would be happy and fulfilled, and look forward to his phone call when it came.

Her state of euphoria lasted for precisely three days, by which time he hadn't rung and Eve fell into the age-old trap of feeling insecure and stupid.

Why had she launched straight into a love affair with him, when she had known nothing of his expectations of it, nor been given a chance to express her own? Though, how could she have done? Wouldn't it have been the kiss of death to have quizzed him about what he wanted, or tell him what she wanted—especially when she didn't know?

Why couldn't she take it for what it was, and simply enjoy it? And maybe she could have done. If only he would phone.

It was nearly a week before she heard from him and when she picked up the receiver and heard his drawled and sexy Italian accent, her instinct was to slam it right down again or demand to know why he had taken so long, though she suppressed it.

Instinct could be a very dangerous thing.

And besides, hadn't just the sound of his voice sent her heart racing into overdrive?

'Eve?'

'Hello, Luca.'

So cool, he thought admiringly. She had been on his mind a lot. She knew his number, both at home and at the office and he had given her his mobile— but she had not contacted him, nor sent him a text message, which women invariably did.

In a way it had been a kind of test to see if she needed him, and now that she had proved she did not, he wanted to see her.

'How are you?'

'Oh, you know. Busy. What about you?'

'I've been to Amalfi.'

'That's on the coast, isn't it?'

'Indeed it is. It's where I keep my boat.'

'And is it very beautiful?'

'What, the boat or the coast?'

Eve laughed. Damn him! Laughter could be just *so-o-o* seductive! 'Both.'

'Both are indeed *very* beautiful, just like you.' He paused. 'I've missed you.'

Not so much you couldn't pick the phone up, she thought, but the remark pleased her. 'Good,' she answered evenly. 'It's always nice to be missed.'

'And have you missed me, too?'

'Stop fishing for compliments!'

He laughed. 'So when am I going to see you?'

'That depends.'

'On what?'

'On whether we have corresponding free dates in our diaries.'

Even cooler! 'You mean you wouldn't cancel something if it meant seeing your Italian lover?' he murmured.

Oh, the arrogance! 'Certainly not,' said Eve. 'Would you?'

Curiously enough, he thought about jettisoning his proposed trip to the States, but for no more than a moment.

'Probably not,' he agreed, and then paused. 'So when?'

'Suggest some dates and I'll see if I'm free.'

'I have to go to New York next weekend—how about the weekend after that?'

'Okay,' she agreed. 'Where? In London?'

'Why don't you fly out to Rome?' he suggested casually.

Eve had never been to Rome before, and a city was never more beautiful than when you saw it through the eyes of someone who actually lived there. Luca on his home territory.

His penthouse apartment was on the Viale Trinita dei Monti, close to the Spanish Steps and it was to-die-for. Minimalist and modern—all stainless steel and frosted glass. The floors were mahogany and there was Carrara marble in the bathrooms. The rooms were almost all white, but the lights could be adjusted to create different colours and moods and the floor-to-ceiling windows showed the most amazing views over the city.

Outside was a terrace with tall terracotta pots with lemon trees growing and smaller ones with rosemary, sage and lavender plants—so that the warm air was scented with their fragrance.

It was, thought Eve as she stood and looked at Rome, the apartment of a man with no ties, nor room for any.

He showed her colonnades and palaces and churches until she was dizzy with the splendour of it all and so he drove her out of the city to the picturesque town of Tivoli, perched on a steep slope amid pretty woods and streams.

'This is just so beautiful,' she murmured as she gazed across at the twisted silvery olive trees of the Sabine Hills.

He touched her hair. 'So are you,' he said softly, and took her back to his apartment, where he spent the rest of the afternoon making long, slow love to her.

That evening, in a restaurant off one of the narrow, cobbled streets of Trastevere, they ate the simple, delicious *tonnarelli cacio e pepe* by candlelight, and drank wine as rich as garnets.

They lingered over coffee and Eve felt utterly relaxed. 'Tell me about your childhood,' she said lazily. 'Where were you born?'

'I am a Roman,' he said simply. 'I was born here.'

'And you never wanted to live anywhere else?'

He gave her a slightly mystified look and a very Latin shrug of his shoulders. 'Why should I? Everything I want is here.'

It gave her an insight into his fierce love for his country, his city.

'And your family? Where are they?'

'My sister lives in Rome also. My parents are both dead.'

Eve dropped a lump of sugar into her espresso. 'Mine are, too,' she said, though she noticed he hadn't asked.

'Then we have much in common,' he murmured, and his eyes glittered a sensual message all of their own. 'Apart from the very obvious.'

It was a blatant, sexual boast and she supposed it should have pleased her, but oddly enough it made her feel insecure. Because surely sexual attraction was a very ephemeral thing?

'Come, Eve.' He signed the bill which the waiter had placed in front of him, and looked at her. 'I think it is time to go home now, don't you?'

But once they were back in the apartment, Luca rubbed a finger at the tiny crease between her brows. 'Frowning, always frowning—ever since we left the restaurant! You know what happens when you frown?' he teased. 'Lines appear and there they stay, and no woman likes lines on her face.'

For some reason, the remark rankled. 'And when lines do appear, then we magic them away with surgery, isn't that right?' she questioned acidly. 'For while lines on a man's face denote experience—on a woman's they damn her with age!'

'*Cara, cara*—that is your judgment, not mine. You work in an industry which is defined by age.' He kissed the tip of her nose. 'And I am certainly not advocating the use of surgery!'

She thought that he wouldn't have to. She turned to look out over the glittering lights of the city. Men like Luca prized beauty, and wasn't youth synonymous with beauty? He would always have his pick of young, firm and unlined flesh.

'Eve?'

His voice was deep and low and beguiling and she closed her eyes as he began to rub his fingertips over her shoulders, pulling her back into the hard, lean contours of his body. Why spoil this? she thought as his hands moved round to cup her breasts? 'Mmm?'

'You are angry now? Fiery?'

She laughed and turned to him, smoothing her hand down over the chiselled outline of his jaw. 'Not angry, no, but fiery, yes.' Her eyes glittered him a teasing provocation. 'Always fiery.'

'Then come here and show me,' he breathed as he saw her mouth curve in a look of hunger. 'Show me.'

'Oh, I'll show you all right,' she said unsteadily as she began to unbutton his shirt.

That night she played the dominant role, undressing him and teasing him until he groaned for mercy. She kept her stockings on and straddled him as her hair flailed about her shoulders and she thought that she had never felt quite so uninhibited with a man.

And afterwards he lay there in silence for a little while, before eventually opening his eyes and giving her a rueful look.

'Wow,' he breathed.

She felt flushed and brimming over with confidence and with life. 'You liked that?'

He gave a lazy smile. Caught a lock of her hair and pulled her head down so that their lips were a whisper apart. 'Oh, *sì, cara*. I liked it. I liked the way you were so wild and so free.' He slipped his hand between her legs and she gasped. 'And you like that?' he murmured.

She began to squirm with pleasure. 'Oh, God— yes. Yes! Please don't stop.'

The smile became a growl of a laugh, like a lion.

'Stop? Let me tell you, *cara mia*, that I haven't even started yet.'

But the weekend came to an end all too quickly and at the airport he kissed her with a passionate goodbye which left her reeling.

'Stay an extra day,' he murmured into her ear.

The temptation almost overwhelmed her. Reluctantly, she withdrew a body which felt as though it could quite happily stay glued to his for ever.

'I can't,' she said regretfully. 'I have an early studio call in the morning.'

He nodded, dropped a kiss on the top of her head. 'I am away in the States for a month,' he said. 'And I will call you. Very soon.'

'Do.' She squeezed his hand and walked away, clutching her overnight bag.

Was that the irony of life? he wondered as he watched her sashaying towards the departure lounge with just a careless wave and a smile as she disappeared. That you always wanted what you couldn't have? If she had been living in the same city, there was no way he would have asked her to stay an extra day! Protectively, he would have wanted and guarded his own space.

He turned and began to walk away, oblivious to the women who watched him as his mobile phone began to ring and he slid it from his pocket and began to speak.

Eve arrived home in time to run herself a bath before bedtime, which she enjoyed by candlelight, dreamily and rather sentimentally listening to some Italian opera as she soaked in the lavender-scented suds.

And she was as bright as a button the next morning, despite a weekend of very little sleep, handling a sulky teenage pop star with aplomb and cleverly questioning the local Member of Parliament about why so little was being done about local traffic congestion.

In fact, she was on cloud nine, not really living in the real world but existing instead in the perfect world of the imagination, where life was like that weekend all the time. Until she reminded herself that life was never that good. It couldn't be, could it? Because it wasn't real.

Maybe it was because when you took a lover, he dominated your normal routine and drove everything else into the shadows. Especially when it was someone like Luca.

Was that because he lived so far away, and therefore the bits of him she got were the exciting, glamorous bits, with none of the everyday drudge bits in between, which usually made you view a relationship much more realistically?

If he were living up the road in the same village and they had settled into a grinding routine, then would she still feel this crazy floating-on-air feeling?

It was a couple of weeks later that she happened to glance up at the calendar on the kitchen and her eyes stayed fixed on it with a mounting sense of disbelief, her heart missing a beat of very real fear.

She was late.

Very late.

She carried on preparing her stir-fry, even though her hands were trembling, but when the fragrant rice and prawns were served out on a pretty plate decorated with sunflowers, she pushed it away, her appetite gone.

She was never late. Never, ever, ever. Not once in her life—why, she could have set her clock by it. Was that why she hadn't noticed it before, because she took it so much for granted? Or was it because her thoughts and her senses had been so full of Luca?

But she couldn't be pregnant. They had used condoms and they had been careful.

She tried to ignore it, but couldn't, clicking onto the search engine of her computer, to discover that there was a three percent chance the contraception could have failed. She felt sick, until she told herself that the odds were still hugely in her favour.

For a while longer she allowed herself to hope, but it was a hope which became increasingly forlorn.

The days became a series of long, agonised minutes while she waited and waited for something to happen which stubbornly refused to happen.

Luca rang and she tried to chat normally, but inside her head was screaming with the terrible reality of her situation. They hadn't even made a definite arrangement of when to meet, but where last week that would have bothered her, this week it barely even registered.

Seeing Luca was the furthest thing from her mind. She just wanted the confirmation that this was nothing but a hiccup, a bad and scary dream and that she wasn't pregnant.

But she was an intelligent woman who could not hide from the truth, however unpalatable. Fearful of discovery and wagging tongues, she drove out of the village to the nearest large, anonymous chemist to

buy herself a pregnancy kit, and by the end of the
day uncertainty became fact.

She stared at herself in the mirror as if expecting
to see some outward sign that she had changed, but
there was nothing. Her cheeks were still tinged with
roses, her eyes bright and shining. Perhaps a little
too bright and shining.

Didn't they always say that pregnant women
looked the picture of health?

And that was her. Healthy and yet terrified out of
her tiny mind, because she was pregnant with Luca
Cardelli's baby.

CHAPTER SEVEN

EVE tugged at the crisply clean duvet cover with a little more vigour than was necessary and then looked round at her bedroom, checking the room like a chambermaid. Luca was coming to stay and she had felt honour-bound to go through the motions of welcoming him.

Clean linen, fresh flowers and scented candles waiting to be lit. Would it resemble some kind of over-the-top boudoir?

She sank down onto the bed and promptly creased the cover. She didn't care. In fact, she didn't care about anything. How could she, when she was privy to a piece of news which was about to change the whole course of her life?

Listlessly, she glanced at her watch. Luca would be here within the hour and she had better get her act together. She was going to have to tell him, she decided, and sooner rather than later. And besides, she doubted whether she would be able to keep it secret from him. How could she look into his eyes and pretend that nothing had changed?

It was such a big secret that it seemed to have taken over her life—she had half expected people at work to stop her in the corridor and congratulate her, because she felt so obviously pregnant.

But if people *did* know—then they were hardly going to congratulate her, were they? A woman who found herself unexpectedly pregnant, without a steady, loving partner, tended to find herself an object of sympathy—even in these enlightened times. Oh, women made the best of it, and there was no reason why she shouldn't make her life—and the life of her child—a wonderful, glittering success. But there was no doubt that at the beginning, at least, it wasn't exactly news to send champagne corks flying.

How the hell was she going to tell Luca? Should she blurt it out straight away, or wait for the 'right' moment? And if such a moment existed, it would soon disappear, for she could predict what his reaction would be.

He was going to be furious. What man wouldn't? To find that they were going to become a father to the child of a woman who was 'nearly a stranger'?

She heard the sound of a car approaching, of a door slamming and murmured words carried on the wind. Through the antique lace of her bedroom curtain, she saw the tall, dark figure as he paid the taxi driver.

He was here. She should have been excited but her heart felt numb, with fear and dread the only emotions she was capable of feeling.

Luca glanced up at the cottage, his eyes narrowing. Had that been Eve up there, watching him? And if so, why hadn't she pulled back the curtain and waved?

His mouth hardened. You met a woman you thought was sexy and intelligent and uncomplicated and suddenly she started playing the diva. She had sounded strained on the telephone, the way a woman sounded if you forgot her birthday. Was she sulking already? And if so, why?

He lifted his hand and banged on the brass knocker. He was here now. He thought of her slender, tight body, the way she had ridden him to heaven and back, and felt the corresponding throb of desire. Who cared if she was sulking? He would kiss away her pique and make her sigh with pleasure for two whole days. And after that?

Almost imperceptibly, he shrugged.

The door opened and Eve fixed her brightest smile onto her face. 'Luca!' And flung her arms around him, mainly so that her eyes would give nothing away. Not yet. Not yet.

He smiled against her hair and dropped his bag to the floor. Better. Much better. 'Have you missed me, then, *cara mia*?'

Act as you usually would, she told herself as she drew her head away, a small smile playing at the corners of her mouth. '*Missed* you? I'm a very busy woman, Luca Cardelli—I don't have time to miss anyone!'

It was what he would have once deemed a textbook answer. A woman who did not make him centre of her universe. A woman with a life of her own. Perfect. But oddly, it did not please him. He *wanted* her to tell him that she had missed him. Break through her cool patina of sophistication. To conquer her, he realised, with a grim kind of shock. He liked to conquer his women. And once he had conquered them, he moved on.

'Come in. What would you like to do first? I could make us some tea and then we could go for a stroll down by the sea—' But her words were blotted out by his kiss, the seeking splendour of his lips, and she froze, like a block of ice in his arms.

Not yet. She couldn't. Not yet.

'Luca!' She pulled away. 'Anyone would think that you had come here with only one thing in mind,' she teased remonstratingly, her heart pounding, still with that terrible constricting fear.

'You don't want to take me straight upstairs and make love?' he demanded. 'You want *tea*?'

'Well, don't you? You've been travelling all day! Come on, I'll put the kettle on!' As she marched towards the kitchen she was acutely aware that she was coming over like a cross between a domestic drudge and a schoolmarm.

He followed her into the kitchen, his eyes narrowed with irritation. What kind of a greeting was this? Did she think that he had flown all the way here to be marched into her kitchen like a hungry schoolboy?

'You know, an Italian woman would never treat her lover so,' he observed, on a sultry note of caution.

Slowly, Eve turned around. 'Then I suggest you find yourself an Italian lover, instead of an English one.'

'Tell me, do you give all your men such a careless greeting?'

His silky question made it sound as though she had a line of lovers stretching as far back as the eye could see! Eve felt sick and the sickness reminded her of the secret—such a tiny secret at the moment— which was growing inside her belly.

And suddenly she realised that her instinct had been correct all along and that there wasn't any such thing as a 'right time' to tell him. To wait would be to perpetuate the deception and to let him make love to her first would be unthinkable. And much too poignant. Tell him when he was naked and she was vulnerable? She couldn't.

'Sit down, Luca,' she said heavily.

Luca's eyes narrowed. Something did not add up. He had been given an inkling that something was not right from the moment he had arrived, but he had put it down to nerves, even though there had been no nerves during that deliciously enjoyable weekend in Rome. She wasn't the kind of woman to be shy at showing him her home—for a start, he had already seen some of it and she wasn't insecure enough to need *his* approval about where she lived.

So what was it?

Silently, he pulled out a chair and sat down, stretching out his long legs, his expression poker-faced and shuttered.

Eve's nerve suddenly failed her. 'I'll just finish making the tea,' she blustered

Still he watched and waited.

Eve tipped boiling water in the teapot, making a drink that she knew neither of them would touch, but it seemed important to be going through the motions of doing *something*. And why didn't he *say* something? Why was he just sitting there, like a brooding dark and golden statue? Why wasn't he asking her what was wrong and then she could have blurted it out, instead of having to say it cold, searching for words to cushion it and knowing deep down that there were none.

'I'm pregnant.'

For a long, tense moment, Luca thought that he was dreaming, or in the middle of a nightmare.

'Turn around and look at me,' he said softly. 'And say that again.'

Her hands gripping onto the sink as if for support, Eve sucked in a hot, painful breath and turned around to face him. She had expected to see anger, fury, disbelief, but there was none of these things. His eyes were as cold and as forbidding as black ice and his face was like that of a stranger. She looked at him and felt as though she hardly knew him, and she didn't, she supposed, not really.

And yet, even now his child was growing inside her.

'I'm pregnant.'

His eyes roved to her belly, looking for a tell-tale swell, but the sweater she wore told him nothing.

He nodded. 'That is why you didn't want to make love.'

Something in the calmness of his voice washed over her like a balm and for the first time since she'd found out she felt a small degree of comfort. He was an intelligent and perceptive man—he had obviously realised that no earthly use would be gained from anger.

'That's right. I just felt that it would be *inappropriate* in the circumstances.'

He gave a low, contemptuous laugh. 'Inappropriate? For whom? For you, or for your baby—or for the poor fool who fathered it?'

She had thought that anger could only be expressed in a loud and furious storm, but Eve realised at that moment that there was another, different kind of anger. A quiet and scornful kind of anger which was far more deadly. She stared at him, her eyes full of consternation, not quite understanding—for if blame could be apportioned, then it was equal blame, surely? If fault was to be found, then they were both at fault.

'Luca—'

His icy words cut across her as if she hadn't spoken. 'Were you already pregnant the night you slept with me?' he hissed. 'Or was there just a chance that you might be?' He gave a low, bitter laugh, barely able to believe that he had been so sucked in by her offhand attitude that he had pursued her like a schoolboy!

His black eyes bored into her like daggers. 'Won't this complicate things for you?' he questioned sardonically. 'I should not think that the father will offer support if he finds out that you have been intimate with another!' Another low, bitter laugh. 'Well, do not worry, *cara*. He will not hear it from me! I will take it to the grave with me.'

His eyes were cold, she thought. So cold.

'And I hope to God that I never set eyes on you again as long as I live,' he finished woundingly.

As if she were a spectator watching a play, Eve watched him get up from the chair, her lips parting in disbelief. It was as if she were watching him in slow motion and something had taken away her powers of speech, for he was almost at the door when she managed to bite the words out.

'But you…you're the father, Luca!'

This time the silence seemed to go on for ever. He felt rooted to the spot, as if he had just been turned to ice, yet the blood which roared around his veins was as hot as the fires of hell.

'What?'

It was a single word, shot out like a threat, as if

daring her to repeat her statement again, but she had to. She *had* to.

'You're the father.'

He turned round and laughed. 'I am not the father!'

And something in his arrogance and contempt brought the real Eve back to life. The real, strong Eve, though a very different woman now. She had to be, nature had decreed it. How dared he? She thought of the life within her, created by accident and now denied by its biological father, and a slow fury began to simmer inside her.

She held her head up proudly. 'I can assure you that you are.'

His heart pounded. 'Prove it.'

Now it was her turn to look at him witheringly. 'I have no intention of "proving" it. And besides, I don't need proof, Luca—I know.'

'How?'

'Because I haven't slept with another man for two years!'

'You expect me to believe this?'

'I expect *nothing*!' she retorted. 'I am telling you simply because I believe it is your right to know— though, God knows, I wish I hadn't bothered now!'

He was nodding his head, as if a blindingly simple solution had just appeared before him. 'Of course,' he said. 'Of course.'

Eve sucked in a deep breath. Calm down, she told herself. It isn't good for you and it isn't good for the baby. He was bound to be shocked at first and go off at the deep end—who wouldn't after a momentous piece of news like that? She looked at him hopefully. 'Of course, what?'

He nodded once more. 'I understand perfectly now.'

'You do?'

'Sure. It's all coming back to me. That night in London, when you told me you wanted children. I remember you saying it, it struck me at the time. And you're a career woman, aren't you, Eve? A woman with a high profile and a demanding job. So who needs a man around? A baby is what you wanted, isn't it? A designer baby—women do it all the time, these days. And who better to father your baby than one of the richest men in Italy? Well, clever, clever, *cara.*'

He stared at her as if she were a particularly unappealing creature who had just landed from outer space. 'But I'm interested to know how you did it. Perhaps you deliberately scratched your pretty pink fingernails through the condom when you were putting it on? If so, it was an ingenious plan.'

She felt as though he had slapped her. 'Get out,' she said. 'Get out of here before I call the police and have you thrown out!'

But he didn't move. 'How much do you want?' he asked insultingly. 'A one-off payment, is that what you had planned?' He looked around at her pretty, cottagey kitchen and his lips curved into a disdainful smile. 'I expect you earn pretty good money, don't you, Eve? But my kind of wealth is way out of your league. With my money you can afford all the things you really want—the best nanny, a bigger house, a fancy car, holidays. Isn't that right, *cara*?'

'Don't *ever* call me that again!' she spat out. 'I'm giving you one last chance to leave, Luca, and if you don't, then God help me, but I *will* call the police!'

He glanced at the clenched fists by her sides. His temper was on such a knife-edge that he knew he had to get away. For all their sakes. And the fact was the she carried his child, and, though the method she had used was unforgivable, that fact remained.

'I am leaving,' he said coldly.

'And don't come back! I never want to see you again!'

He plucked a wallet from his jacket pocket, and for one awful moment Eve thought that he was going to throw some money down in front of her. But instead he extracted an expensive-looking business card and placed it on the table with calm and steady fingers.

'That's the address of my lawyer,' he said carefully. 'I'll let him know that you'll be in contact.'

And with those damning and insulting words ringing in her ears, Eve listened in disbelief as his footsteps echoed down the corridor and the front door slammed shut behind him.

This was getting to be something of a habit, she thought tiredly. But once he had gone, she felt oddly lighter—as though a great weight had been lifted from her shoulders, and until it had gone she hadn't realised just how much she had been dreading telling Luca.

His reaction had been even worse than her worst imaginings, but at least now it was over. The obstacle had been faced and overcome. Whatever happened now, nothing could be as bad as that had been, surely.

And then she remembered the cold anger on his beautiful face and she bit her lip, tears threatening to well up in her eyes, but she swallowed them down.

There was no point in thinking about it, or him. It was over.

She heard a protesting rumble in her stomach, and for the first time since she had found out the news, she felt hungry.

You've got a baby to feed, Eve Peters, she told herself sternly as she opened the fridge door.

CHAPTER EIGHT

'THERE has been no phone call?'

The lawyer shook his head. 'Nothing, *signore*.'

'And you telephoned her, as I instructed?'

'I have attempted to telephone Signorina Peters on four occasions, and on each occasion she has steadfastly refused to take my call.'

Beneath his breath, Luca swore. He turned to the window, his mind turning over the facts in his cool, clear-headed way.

But for once, he was perplexed.

This had been the last thing he had expected. Her words of protest he had naturally assumed to be false, her declaration that she never wished to see him again he had thought was the defiant words of a woman who meant no such thing but was simply playing a clever game. He hadn't been sure what it was she had wanted—him or his money, or both—but he had been certain that he would find out soon enough.

But indeed it seemed that she *had* severed all contact.

He continued to stare unseeing as the midday sun illuminated the magnificent spectacle of Roman rooftops, and then his heart clenched in fear.

Unless…unless there was a very good reason why she *hadn't* contacted him. Inside the pockets of his trousers, his fingers clenched themselves into tight fists.

What if…what if there was no longer any reason for her to do so? What if the pregnancy no longer existed?

For a moment Luca felt physically sick, and, for a man who had rarely known a day's sickness in his life, it was an unwelcome sensation. But then, he was getting quite used to those.

'Signor Cardelli?'

Luca turned around, surprising the look of concern on the face of his lawyer.

'You are sick, *signore*?'

Resolve returned to fill his blood with the fire of determination and Luca shook his head. 'No, my friend. Not sick at all,' he said grimly. It was time to take matters into his own hands. Something that he should have done weeks ago.

Eve cheerily said goodbye to the crew, but once she was headed for her car and her driver her smile faded. It was hard work trying to pretend that nothing was wrong, and she didn't know how much longer she would be able to keep it up.

Sooner or later she was going to have to tell Clare, her editor, and it had better be sooner rather than later, before she, or someone else on the show, guessed her secret. And it wouldn't take a member of the regional crime squad to do that.

Twice this morning she had had to leave the set, trying not to rush out to the bathroom, where she had been violently sick. She had stood before the mirror, trembling, before rubbing some blusher into her cheeks and hoping she looked halfway decent. She wasn't going to be much use as a breakfast presenter if she spent all her time throwing up.

But even if, as the doctor had suggested, the sickness passed—and, infuriatingly, by the end of the show all the nausea *had* passed—the fact remained that she was soon going to become very obviously pregnant.

No. She was going to have to make an appointment to speak to Clare.

She walked out into the bracing air, glad of the welcoming coolness after the stifling atmosphere of the studio, and as she looked around for her car her heart missed a beat.

For there, leaning against an unfamiliar silver car, stood a figure, as still and as all-seeing as if he had been hewn from a deep, dark marble. He was dressed all in black, and it made his hair and eyes look like the night. For one wild and crazy moment she thought about running inside, like a woman seeking refuge from the storm, but she knew that she could not.

She had to face him.

He studied her almost obsessively, searching for signs. Any signs. But the thick, sheepskin coat she wore enveloped her like a big, warm cloud and all he could see was her pale face and the green-grey eyes which glittered so warily at him.

He began to walk towards her.

'Hello, Eve.'

'I don't want to talk to you.' Desperately, she looked around the car park, deserted save for the swish silver car he had been standing beside. Where the hell was her driver? He was *never* late.

'I think we need to talk,' he said steadily. Last time he had been caught off guard in all kinds of ways. He had flown off the handle and raged in a manner which was guaranteed to achieve nothing. And Luca had always been an achiever.

She turned to him, unprepared for the effect he had on her. The way her heart crashed against her ribcage. The way her legs felt weak. She should feel nothing but contempt for him, the same as he so obviously did for her—so why wasn't it that easy? Why did she still feel outrageously attracted to him? But that was purely physical, she reminded herself. And she was more than just a physical person. Much more.

'I don't think you understand, Luca,' she said quietly. 'In a minute my driver will be here and I will get in the car and go home. Without you.'

'I am afraid that is where you are wrong.'

She stared at him uncomprehendingly.

'Your driver has gone. I sent him away.'

'You *sent him away*?' she repeated disbelievingly.

He pointed to the long, low silver machine. 'I have a car and I will take you anywhere you want to go, but I need to talk to you and I *will* talk to you. You owe me that.'

She hugged her coat tighter around her. 'I owe you nothing after the despicable things you accused me of.'

Again, he nodded, sucking in a deep, dry breath. 'I had no right to make those accusations, but I was…'

Her eyes were curious. 'What?'

He sighed. 'I felt as though my whole world had been detonated.'

'So the thought of fatherhood didn't appeal?' she said flippantly, because that seemed the only sure-fire way to hide her hurt. She shrugged. 'Then there's nothing left to say, really, is there?'

He froze. 'Are you telling me that there is no baby?'

It took a moment for the meaning of his words to dawn on her and, when they did, it was once again like being hit by a hammer-blow. Did he think…did he really think…?

'God, Luca,' she gasped, as if he really had struck her. 'Could your opinion of me get any lower?'

'What am I supposed to think?' he demanded heatedly. 'When you refused to take my calls!'

'Your lawyer's calls,' she corrected him. 'Because I didn't want to do *business*, that's why I didn't take them.'

'So?'

'Yes, there is still a baby,' she said slowly. 'But don't worry your head about it—it's *my* baby and it won't have anything to do with you.'

He could see her teeth beginning to chatter. 'Get in the car,' he said.

'No.'

'Please.'

The voice was deceptively soft and Eve felt so weak from the flurry of emotions he had provoked and simply from the impact of seeing him again that she could not have possibly refused. 'Oh, damn you,' she said indistinctly, but she did not walk away.

He opened the passenger door, but she shook off his arm as he attempted to guide her into the seat.

'I am *not* an invalid! Just pregnant!' And then, terrified that someone from the crew might be lurking around, she cast her eyes around anxiously, but there was no one except for them, and she expelled a sigh of relief.

He noted her reaction and it told him a great deal. So no one knew; of that he was certain. She had kept the pregnancy hidden. Why?

He started the engine. 'Where do you want to go?'

'Home.' She leaned her head back against the rest and closed her eyes, daring him to talk to her, to accuse her and harangue her, but to her surprise he didn't. The warmth and movement of the car lulled her, reminding her of just how tired she was. But tiredness came in great strong and powerful waves these days.

He glanced over at her, watching as her breathing became deeper and steadier. She was asleep. Around the steering wheel of the car, his leather-covered hands relaxed a little.

The sheepskin coat had fallen open, and her thighs were indolently apart and relaxed in sleep and he felt an unexpected and unwelcome shaft of arousal. Damn her! he thought. Damn her and her unstudied sensuality. He fixed his eyes on the road ahead.

The car drew to a halt and Eve snapped her eyes open, momentarily disorientated. She was outside her cottage, with Luca in the driving seat beside her.

She fumbled for the handle. 'Thank you for the lift.'

'I'm coming in.'

'No, you're—' But she heard the note of determination in his voice and knew that she was fighting a losing battle. And besides, had she really thought that he would come all this way, drop her off and then just go off again with a little wave goodbye? She would hear what he had to say, and then he could go.

The cottage felt cold. Stiffly, Eve took her coat off and didn't protest when he took it from her fingers and hung it up in the hall. She shivered. 'I'm going to light a fire.'

'Let me do it.'

She raised her eyebrows. 'Do you know how?'

He actually laughed. 'Of course I do. There are many things you do not know about me, *cara*.'

'I'm going to make some tea,' she said. Anything to get away from his presence, which, in the small, dim hall, seemed to overwhelm her.

When she returned with the tray he had managed to produce a roaring blaze. She put the tray down on a small table and watched him. 'I wouldn't have thought there would be much cause for fire-making in your fancy apartment.'

'No,' he agreed as he threw a final log on. 'But we had a place out in the country where we used to holiday when I was a little boy. Very basic. That's where I learned.'

It was odd to think of this assured, arrogant man as a little boy. Would she have a boy, she wondered, and, if she did, would he look like Luca? A beautifully handsome little boy, a permanent reminder of passion and its folly.

He moved from the fire to the tea-tray and poured them both a cup, and while part of her felt slightly resentful that he had walked into her house and now seemed to be taking over, the other part was so tired that she was glad to let him.

But it was dangerous to be passive. He had told her quite clearly what he thought of her and she could not and should not forget that. 'You'd better say what it is that you want to say, and then go—I'm very tired.'

Yes, he could see that for himself. Beneath her fine grey-green eyes were the blue-dark traces of shadows.

'Are you sleeping?'

'In fits and starts. And, of course, I have to get up very early.'

His mouth thinned. She should have handed her notice in immediately! 'You didn't contact my lawyer,' he observed slowly.

'Did you really expect me to?'

What would she say if he told her yes, of course he had expected her to. A lifetime of experience had made him cynical. His vast wealth had set him apart from the moment he had attained it. And that he would have considered it perfectly normal for her to have attempted to make a huge claim on his fortune. She, above all others, was surely entitled to?

'Yes,' he said simply. 'I did.'

'Well, rest assured—I didn't and I don't intend to. Your money is safe. Was there anything else?'

She was being so cold, so distant, as if ice were running through her veins instead of blood. And could that be good for the baby?

'I want you to have everything you need, Eve.'

'But I do! I have a house and I have a job, a good job.'

He remembered the way she had looked around her, as if worried her words would be overheard. He was pretty certain that her pregnancy was still a secret and his killer instinct moved in; he couldn't help himself. 'But for how long?'

She stared at him. 'Excuse me?'

'Have you told them you're pregnant?'

'That's none of your business.'

'I think it is.' A spark spat in the grate with all the force of a gunshot. 'You may not be employable as a pregnant woman.'

She gave a little laugh. 'There are laws governing that kind of discrimination,' she returned. 'So please don't worry on my account.'

This was going neither the way that Luca wanted, nor had expected. He had expected a little...what? Gratitude? That the past few weeks might have given her time to calm down and see sense. Surely she must realise that his money could make all the difference to her life as a mother?

'I do not want you to struggle for money—not when I have enough, more than enough.'

'But it isn't going to *be* a struggle. I'll manage—'

'I don't want you to *manage*, I want you to be comfortable!'

'What you want is not really what counts, Luca! It is what I say that does!'

'But it is my baby, too,' he pointed out.

'Oh?' She feigned surprise. 'So you're no longer disputing paternity? What happened? Did you have someone run a DNA test on me, while I was asleep?'

'Eve!' Proud, stubborn woman! 'Let me help you,' he said suddenly.

She was still hurting from the things he had said; it was hard to imagine a time when she would not. 'You think your money can buy you anything, don't you?'

His black eyes glittered. 'Would you deny me my child, then, Eve?' he questioned simply.

And something in the way he said it cut through all her defences.

Up until that very moment she had been able to think of the baby almost as an abstract concept—as if it hadn't been real and, even if it had been, it was nothing now to do with Luca. But she was fast discovering that she had been very naïve. By telling him she had involved him, and someone like Luca wouldn't take that involvement lightly.

Oh, why hadn't she kept it secret? He had never intended theirs to be anything other than a short-term love affair. He wasn't the kind of man who would ever settle down, he just wasn't. The affair would have burnt out after a few heady weeks, or months— he would have moved on to the next conquest, the way that men like this always did.

But could she honestly have kept it secret from him? Wasn't it his right to know that his seed had borne fruit? She bit her lip at the irony of it. Because he had never meant it to.

'What do you want?' she asked cautiously.

'I don't know,' he said, and it was the first time in all his charmed and powerful life that he had ever made such an admission. He sat down on the sofa and studied her, the dark eyes narrowed in question. 'You haven't even told me how far advanced you are.'

'Nearly five months.'

Five months! 'Already?' he asked, slightly unsteadily.

'Yes, my bump's hardly showing yet.' She met his eyes, and despaired, for their inky allure still touched a part of her she had decided had to be out of bounds. If he had stayed away—even for a bit longer—she might have become immune to him. But she wasn't—and that didn't help matters. 'Time flies when you're having fun,' she said sarcastically.

Had it really been that long? She must have got pregnant the very first time—before Rome, before he had gone to the States. He remembered with a sinking heart the way he had been incautious, the way he had wanted to make love to her straight after the first time. And she had stopped him.

He frowned. How had so much time passed, almost unnoticed? He had thrown himself into his work since she had first told him—perhaps, he recognised now, using it as a kind of denial therapy. And all the time he had been waiting for the financial demands he was certain would come his way. He had set her a test, he recognised, just as he had right at the beginning when he had waited for her to contact him. And wasn't that what he always did, in his professional as well as his personal life—set impossibly high standards and wait for people to fail to meet them?

Only Eve had not failed.

'Anyway.' She forced herself to be businesslike, because surely that was what it all boiled down to. 'If it's just the finance thing you're worried about, then don't, because I will be fine.' She gave him a bright smile. 'Unless there was anything else?'

He stared at her incredulously. 'You think this is simply about *money*? You expect me to walk out of that door without a backward glance and have no interest in this child of mine?'

This child of mine. Powerful words. Daunting words. But then Luca was a powerful and daunting man.

'I have no expectations whatsoever. I never did have,' she added deliberately and at least he had the decency to flinch. 'You'd better tell me what yours are. Some kind of contact, I suppose?'

'Contact!' he repeated furiously. 'What an ugly word that is!'

'Well, it may be ugly, but it happens to be the relevant word!' she retorted, stung. 'All in all it's a pretty ugly business, isn't it?'

He rose to his feet then, came over to where she sat and crouched down beside her. If it had been any other woman, in any other situation, he would have taken her in his arms, to comfort her and to soothe her. But her frozen stance told him not to try.

All his life, Luca had been able to seduce any woman he wanted, to persuade her round to his way of thinking, but now he suddenly recognised that Eve was not so malleable.

His eyes travelled to the perfect fingernails, painted a coral-pink today, and he remembered his outrageous accusation.

'So what is it to be?' continued Eve remorselessly. 'Every other weekend, with some of the holidays? Alternate Christmases? That's how it works, isn't it?'

'I don't give a damn how it works!' He reached out and caught her face in the palm of his hand and tipped it up to look at him, and to his surprise she didn't stop him. 'There is only one sensible choice which lies ahead of us,' he said, and his perfect English suddenly became a little more broken. And in a way, maybe this was how it was supposed to be. All his life he had run from commitment, but he could run no longer. 'You will marry me, Eve,' he said fiercely.

She looked at him. 'Marry you?' she said incredulously.

CHAPTER NINE

'AND those are the facts,' finished Luca, with a shrug.

'Wow!' said his sister softly, and handed him the sleeping baby.

Luca raised his eyebrows sardonically as his hands tightened automatically around the warm little bundle. 'What's this?' he questioned drily. 'Aversion therapy?'

'Nonsense! You are brilliant with your nephew—you always have been. You're a natural with babies, Luca.'

The baby stirred and sighed and Luca glanced down at him, his hard, handsome features softening. 'Just that it seems I won't get much practice with my own.'

'Oh, Luca—for heaven's sake! It isn't like you to be such a defeatist!'

'I am not being defeatist, Sophia!' he snapped, but the baby made a squeak of protest, so he lowered his voice. 'I am merely being practical. She lives in England and I live in Rome—and we are not together. The facts speak for themselves.'

'Well, why don't you *be* together?' demanded his sister. 'For heaven's sake, Luca, you can't spend your whole life as a commitment-phobe, searching for the impossibly perfect woman. You'll just have to marry her—I can't think of a better reason for breaking your long-term bachelorhood than a baby! People do it all the time!'

Thoughtfully, Luca stroked a tender finger across the glossy raven hair of his nephew and then looked up at his older sister, with an expression in his eyes he could see surprised her.

'I have asked her to marry me,' he said.

'You *did*?'

He nodded.

'And?'

'And she said no.'

There was a moment of shocked, stunned silence, and then, to his astonishment, his sister tipped her head back and burst out laughing, causing her son to squirm in Luca's arms and he handed him back, a stern look on his face.

'I see no cause for laughing,' he said icily.

Sophia wiped the corner of her eyes. 'You don't? Well, I think it's priceless! A woman has turned the great Luca Cardelli down! Do you know, I think I like this woman!'

'It is *not* funny!'

'No,' she said slowly. 'No, I suppose it's not. Well, you're going to have to do something, Luca.'

'I know I am,' he said grimly.

The red studio light went off and there was a burst of spontaneous clapping and Eve looked round and smiled as she saw the executive producer walking into the studio, a sheaf of papers in his hand.

'It went well?'

'Eve, it was absolutely *brilliant*!' He waved the papers like a winner's medal. 'I have here the viewer figures, my dear, and I can say, without fear of contradiction, that we have a hit on our hands.'

She knew they did. It was indefinable, that feeling, but she had worked in television long enough to know success when she encountered it. She had been pretty optimistic from day one, but you never really knew for sure, not until the figures came in.

'We've had a sack-load of letters and emails, the phone hasn't stopped ringing all week and the duty log is full of praise.'

It had all worked out perfectly, so perfectly that she sometimes felt she ought to pinch herself.

She hadn't even had to tell Clare about her pregnancy—the editor had guessed it for herself, and so it seemed had most of the crew. Leaving the set regularly in order to be sick had kind of given the game away.

Her early-morning sickness had shown no sign of abating. And that was when the idea had come up for Eve to be taken off the breakfast show and given her own daily slot just before midday. As someone had remarked, it wasn't exactly a loss to the world of television if they used the show to replace the endless reruns of a comedy which had been made two decades earlier.

Eve In The Morning! was to be modelled on the classic audience-participation theme, but with an added twist. As well as the usual studio discussions on the lines of: 'Too Fat To Enjoy Sex!' or 'My Husband Doesn't Know I'm A Stripper!', there was to be a special five-minute slot every week which would keep the viewers up to date with her pregnancy. Viewers liked to be involved, and what better way to involve them?

'That's fantastic.' Eve smiled broadly at the executive producer, some of the tension leaving her, and she placed her hand over her swollen belly as the baby gave a kick as if to say, Concentrate on *me*, now! Time to go home for a well-earned rest. She picked up her handbag, switched on her phone and it began ringing immediately.

Number unknown.

'Hello?'

'Eve?' The voice was so frosty that Eve was surprised it didn't freeze her slim little mobile phone.

The baby kicked again. It's your daddy, she thought to herself and her initial feeling was one of relief. She had not heard a single word from him since the day she had refused his offer of marriage, which had left her wondering whether Luca Cardelli had washed his hands of his baby. But it seemed he had not.

'Hello, Luca,' she said steadily, and licked her suddenly dry lips. 'Er, I can't really talk now.'

'Why not?'

'Because I'm in the studio and there are a lot of people around—'

'Then find somewhere where there are not!'

There was some note of implacable determination which made her do just that, and she quickly walked out until she found an empty dressing room.

'How are you?' she asked.

He ignored that, drawing in a deep breath in order to keep his temper in check. 'More importantly, *cara*,' he said silkily, 'how are *you* and, more importantly, how is my baby?'

Inexplicably, his possessive statement didn't ruffle her one little bit. Indeed, there was a mad, stabbing maternal pride that he chose to acknowledge his child like that. She sighed. Sometimes you just couldn't argue with nature.

'I'm fine. Well, I am now. They took me off the breakfast show because I was being so sick—and they've given me my own show—'

'I know they have,' he interrupted coldly.

'You do?' Eve frowned in confusion. 'But we don't transmit to Italy!' she said, rather stupidly.

'I am not in Italy.'

'Then wh-where are you?' she asked, but even as she asked it she knew what the answer would be.

'I'm in the Hamble.'

A nameless dread crept over her. 'What are you doing there?'

'We'll discuss that later,' he clipped out. 'I think we'd better meet for lunch, don't you, Eve?'

It was one of his questions which wasn't really a question at all, and Eve knew that there was only one answer which was acceptable to them both. For him, because he demanded it and she knew that he had the right to, and for her because her curiosity was roused. 'Okay, I'll meet you,' she said slowly. 'Where?'

'I'll meet you at the Fish Inn at one forty-five.'

'One forty-five,' she echoed.

The journey back seemed to take for ever, and Eve glanced at her watch. There wasn't time to go home first, and besides—what would she go home for? It wasn't like a normal lunch date with a normal man. She was pregnant and about to see the reluctant father. Not a lot of point prettying herself up. And suddenly Eve felt a pang. Luca was a formidable man.

So why the hell was he here?

The Fish Inn was the best restaurant in the village. Simply furnished, serving fresh food and with a stunning view over the harbour—people flocked from miles around to eat there. It was usually impossible to get a table at this short notice, but Luca had somehow managed.

He was already seated when she arrived and his tall, lean body unmistakable. His black hair was ruffled and he wore some beautiful cashmere sweater, the colour of soft, grey clouds, and her heart turned over at the sight of him.

And that is enough, she told herself. More than enough.

He stood up as soon as he saw her, his face looking brooding and shuttered and the dreamy feeling fled, leaving her with a faint feeling of unease.

From behind the lashed curtain of his narrowed eyes, he watched her approach as if his life depended on it. Her face was blooming, he noted with approval, and her eyes were shining with life and with health. She wore dark trousers and a big, soft oatmeal-coloured sweater. Big as a man's sweater, he thought viciously, and felt a stab of anger. But, big as it was, it could not disguise the definite swell of her belly and the anger transmuted into fierce and atavistic pride as he realised that the swell was part of him. His child in her belly. And, to his horror and shock, he felt the early, aching throb of desire.

'Eve,' he said.

He spoke pleasantly, but as he would to some casual acquaintance. It was as if they were oceans apart. There was no kiss on either cheek, no guiding of the arm to her seat. Nothing to treat her in any way as special. In fact, he seemed almost to recoil from her and she wasn't quite sure why that should hurt as much as it did.

'Luca,' she said evenly, and sat down.

'How formal we are with each other,' he mocked softly. 'Why, we speak as strangers, Eve. Who would know, to look at us—that we have made such beautiful love together, and that we have created a child which grows beneath your heart?'

His words were like weapons. *The child beneath her heart.* Didn't that phrase mock her with the tantalising image of what it *could* have been like, if theirs were a normal, loving relationship? And, at the same time, didn't it manage to emphasise just what little there was, or ever had been between them?

Was he trying to wound her, to pay her back?

How calm he looked today, light years away from the man who had stared at her in complete and utter disbelief when she had refused his offer to marry her.

'I don't want to marry you!' she had declared. 'You just want to use marriage to acquire me, and to acquire rights over our baby! Just as you would a business deal!'

He had neither denied nor confirmed it. Just given her a long, considering look and said flatly, 'And that is your decision?'

'It is.'

'Then there is nothing more to be said, is there?'

And the finality of that statement had left her wondering why she hadn't said the most sensible thing, such as: I'd like to think about it, or I'm not ruling anything out. Instead, she was aware that she had burnt her boats, until she reminded herself that her first assessment had been the correct one. She didn't want to marry a man who didn't love her.

With trembling fingers she shook out her linen napkin and laid it carefully over her knees, doubting that she would be able to eat a thing, not with those brilliant black eyes burning into her. But the action composed her, so that she was able to look up at him with a calm expression on her face.

'So,' she said equably. 'You were going to tell me why you were here.'

Did nothing touch her? he wondered furiously. He could be some business acquaintance she was meeting for the first time for all the reaction on her face. What was going on in her mind? In her heart?

For a moment he wished that he had arranged to meet her down by the water, where the foam-flecked grey waters would have drowned his angry words. But he must temper his anger. She carried his child, and although it would have made him feel better to have stormed his rage like the strongest tempest, he must not.

'I saw you on television this morning,' he said unexpectedly.

It was the last thing she had imagined he would say.

'Oh?' she questioned warily.

The waitress came up with her pad, but he waved her away with an impatient hand, then leaned across the table, so close that she could feel the warmth of his breath and see the darkened irises of his eyes which made him look like the devil incarnate.

'You are, as they say, very…telegenic, *cara*,' he drawled.

He made it sound like an insult.

'The camera loves you, doesn't it, Eve?' he continued softly. 'It throws intriguing shadows off those high cheekbones and makes your face look as though it is composed of nothing but those grey-green eyes, like an ocean that a man could drown in.'

The words were like poetry, but he delivered them like a man who didn't want to believe them. 'If that was supposed to be a compliment, then I'll pass on any others,' she said shakily and caught the waitress's eye, gave her a beseeching smile and, thank heavens, she came over.

'I'd like the sole with new potatoes and green beans,' she said steadily. 'And just water to drink. Luca? What would you like?'

If looks could kill, she thought, with a momentary satisfaction.

'I'll have the same,' he said shortly, but inside he was fuming. He was used to a woman letting *him* do the ordering!

Had she done that to demonstrate superiority or equality? A pulse began to beat at his temple and for just one wild, crazy moment he wondered what she would do if he went round to her side of the table and hauled her to her feet and began to kiss her. Would she press her body so eagerly to his, and wind her arms around his neck with the passion she had displayed in such abundance?

'Luca? Are you all right?'

The erotic, frustrating fantasy evaporated and hard on its heels came the sense of burning injustice.

'No, Eve, I am not "all right". In fact, I am angry, very, very angry—probably angrier than I have ever been in my life, but I am doing my best to control it.'

Was he trying to intimidate her? Because he would soon find that she would not be. 'And managing very admirably,' she said sweetly.

'I will not be managing very admirably unless you wipe that smug little smile from your mouth and tell me exactly why you have taken on this new *show*.' The word slid sarcastically from between his lips.

'*Eve in the Morning!*?' she questioned helpfully.

'Eve,' he said warningly. 'I would like some kind of explanation.'

She decided to stop playing games. She was a free agent. He might have claims on the baby, but none on *her* and she was perfectly entitled to live her life as she saw fit.

'I was too sick in the mornings to manage the other ones... Luca, what on earth is the matter?'

'Sick?' he demanded hoarsely. 'You did not tell me you were sick!'

'Of course I didn't—it's quite normal for a pregnant woman to be sick.'

'And the baby?'

Eve softened, because for a moment his face looked so ravaged that she couldn't help it. 'The baby is just fine,' she said gently. 'Honestly. I've seen the doctor and she says that I am as strong as an ox and as fit as a flea and whatever else it is they say about pregnant women!'

And, to his horror, the overriding thought which dominated his mind was his gratitude that she had chosen a woman doctor! If he was not able to watch her naked, growing belly, then he did not want any other man—doctor or not—to be able to.

'So they created this brand-new show, just for me,' she continued.

'So that the whole country is able to participate in your pregnancy! No one is excluded—except, of course, the father!'

'It's regional, Luca—not national—not the *whole* country at all!'

'You are deliberately missing the point,' he said furiously.

Their meals were put down in front of them.

'The point being, what?'

He sighed. To have to admit to feelings he would prefer not to have was something he had never had to do. But Eve was a strong woman, he recognised that. As well as fiercely proud and independent. And stubborn, too. It came as a bolt out of the blue to realise that she did not need him!

'Who knows that I am the father?' he asked suddenly.

Eve didn't answer for a moment.

'Eve?'

Their eyes met. 'I have told only Lizzy,' she admitted. 'Not even Michael—though I expect Lizzy will have done by now.'

She remembered Lizzy's reaction. Her friend had been shocked, but not surprised. 'Can't say I blame you,' she murmured, and then looked at Eve expectantly. 'And?'

Pointless to pretend that she didn't know what that simple one-word question meant. 'It's over,' she said quietly.

Lizzy wasn't able to hide her disappointment. 'And you're happy with that?'

Happy? 'Perfectly happy,' she said brightly.

'Oh, well, that's nice. Very modern!' Then Lizzy leaned forward slightly. 'It's probably all for the best, isn't it? I mean, Michael says that he's well known in the Italian press. Quite a reputation. Though that's hardly surprising, is it? Bad type of man to lose your heart to, Eve!'

'Very bad,' agreed Eve gravely. Please keep telling me these things, Lizzy, she remembered thinking to herself. For these are the things I need to hear.

Luca was staring at her. So she had not announced who the father was! He had expected it to be common knowledge, by now. 'You mean you are ashamed of the child's parentage?' he growled.

'Don't be ridiculous!'

'Then what?'

She put her fork down with a clang. 'Because I wasn't sure if you were going to be around or not and I thought that if you weren't then it would be better for everyone not to know, especially those who didn't need to. I didn't want everyone to be pointing the finger and making value judgements about me.'

He thought how a marriage would have easily solved all such problems, but she had steadfastly refused that.

'You should tell them,' he said. 'Tell everyone or no one, but evade the issue no longer. The child will know, so best that everyone else does.'

'It isn't as easy as that,' she said quietly and met the question in his eyes. 'Because of the job I do, everything in my personal life is considered relevant. That's why I've just said a terse ''no comment'' when people have asked who the father is.'

He swore quietly beneath his breath. 'And you are happy with this?'

Eve shrugged. 'It's the way things are.'

But surely he had the power to change them? He

saw the faint lines of strain around her eyes and decided that now was not the time. 'Eat your lunch!' he instructed gently, and then frowned. 'Have you been eating well, Eve? Properly?'

'Why?'

He frowned. 'You do not look very…pregnant.'

'No. Some women don't—it's the way I carry, apparently.' She thought how seasoned she sounded, as if she had done this a million times before instead of for the first time. And she also thought how *comforting* it was to be able to discuss this kind of thing with someone who cared—and if Luca didn't particularly care for her, he certainly seemed to be making up for it where the baby was concerned.

'So you are eating?' he persisted.

It was also, she discovered, rather nice to have someone who asked her this kind of thing. It was different from when the doctor asked her—that was professional, while this was personal.

She picked up her fork and speared fish and beans and chewed them like an obedient child. 'I am eating like a horse—see! Fish, fruit, vegetables and brown rice—with the occasional portion of cherry ice cream thrown in for good measure!' She gave him a small smile. 'Does that satisfy you?'

He poured some water. Satisfy him? He couldn't ever remember being quite so dissatisfied, both physically and emotionally.

Eve watched him as he lifted his eyes to her, and in them was an expression of respect, though made slightly acid by the wry smile which had curved the kissable lips. He looked so irresistible that she felt a sudden desire to be almost *biddable*…to tell him that it was all going to be all right.

But she didn't know that, and neither could she do it. She was having to fight down the urge to ask him if they couldn't just forget all the events which had brought them to this confusing place and this confusing time and start all over again.

But she couldn't do that either. Too much had happened, and there was a baby on the way. She needed to protect herself against hurt—not just for her sake, but for her baby's sake. A heartbroken mother would not be able to do her job properly.

Yet she wanted to teach her child—their child—all the things which were important, and surely one of the most fundamental was honesty.

'You haven't told me what you feel about this baby, not really,' she said quietly. 'Apart from the anger, of course.'

He remembered how it had devoured him, like a great, burning flame. 'The anger has gone. I should not have reacted so.'

'I guess it was a natural response.' Her eyes were very clear. 'What has replaced it?'

This was difficult for him. He was not a man to put feelings into words, but then this seemed far too important not to, and surely he owed her that. 'Pride,' he said simply. 'And excitement.'

Eve stared at him.

'You look surprised,' he observed.

'That's because I am.' She felt a warm and little protective glow deep within her and she realised how much she valued his pride and his excitement. For the baby's sake.

'And what about you, Eve?' he questioned suddenly. 'What were *your* feelings?' This felt like an uncharted domain. Asking a woman a question like that and actually *caring* what her answer would be.

'I feel excited, too. Yes, very.' And more than a little bit scared, too—if the truth were known. But she would not tell him that. She was a grown woman who had to take responsibility for herself. She was not going to start leaning on Luca.

He nodded, but there was something else he needed to know. 'But not angry?'

She shook her head. 'No. Not anger—I think it expresses itself differently for women. I felt stupid. Trapped.'

'I don't want you to feel trapped.'

'Just what is it that you *do* want, Luca?'

She had asked him this question once before and he had surprised himself by not knowing the answer. This time he did. 'I want to be part of your pregnancy,' he said. 'When you see the doctor, I would like to be there, too. When you have your scans, I want to see my baby's little heart beating.'

Suddenly very emotional, she put her fork down, and stared at her meal, his words making her feel almost unbearably poignant. It took a minute for her to compose herself, and when she looked up again she hoped that he didn't notice that her eyes were bright. He didn't mean it how it sounded. It was intimate, yes, but not truly intimate.

She put on her best, practical voice. 'But how on earth are you going to do that? We live miles apart. I suppose I could send you scans, email you—that kind of thing.'

But he shook his head. 'No, not second hand,' he said firmly.

'How?' she questioned simply.

'Give me enough notice and I can fly over for your appointments.'

'What about your job?'

He looked at her, realising that she had no idea about the nature of his work, but then why would she have? Intellectually, she might be aware that he owned a bank, but she did not live in Italy, she would not know the extent of his power and influence. And since she seemed to have no intention of making any claims on him, he saw no reason not to tell her. It was a curiously liberating feeling not to have to play it down.

'I am rich enough never to have to work again, Eve,' he said softly. 'And certainly in a position to take it easy for a while. I can come and go as I please. I can be there. For the baby.'

And Eve wasn't at all sure how she felt about that.

CHAPTER TEN

LUCA walked into the scanning room and the first things he noticed were the lights. He frowned, his eyes narrowing as they accustomed themselves to the brightness, but the frown deepened as he took in the rest of the small room.

There was Eve, lying on a trolley, with a white-coated technician smearing some thick kind of jelly all over her swollen belly—while a man dressed entirely in denim was swinging a little meter close by.

In one corner, a youngish woman with jangly earrings was in earnest conversation with another man—*another*—who was holding a hand-held camera.

They all looked up as he walked in, and the woman with the jangly earrings smiled and, before Eve could stop her, said, 'I'm sorry—but we're filming in here.'

There was a short, tense silence.

'And what *precisely*,' said Luca, in a voice of dangerous silk, 'do you think you're filming?'

The woman with the jangly earrings stared at him. 'We're doing a feature for a television show, and it's really very crowded in here—so if you wouldn't mind leaving.'

It was exactly like a bomb going off, thought Eve. A deadly little stealth bomb. 'I am not going anywhere,' he grated. 'But I'm afraid that you are. Get out.'

'I'm sorry?'

'You are not, repeat *not*, filming Eve having a scan. Now are you going to leave or do I have to pick up the damn cameras myself and throw them out?'

Jangly earrings looked at Eve. 'Eve?'

She should have been mortified, outraged, and furious with Luca marching in here and single-handedly managing to put her livelihood in jeopardy. But she was none of those things. In theory, the filming of her scan for the show had seemed like a great idea, but the reality was that it had felt intrusive.

And she had never been so glad to see someone in her life.

'Just who *is* this man, Eve?'

'He's...'

'I'm the baby's father,' interjected Luca icily. 'And I want to see the scan of my baby. In *private*.'

There was something about his face and something about the tone of his voice which dared anyone to defy him and the news crew were clearly not going to be the exception.

With much mumbling and clicking of tongues, they packed up their equipment and left, but not before the woman with the jangly earrings had turned to Eve.

'Perhaps you could call me later?'

It took Luca a moment or two to control his breathing, and the white-coated technician was blinking in bemusement.

'And here was me thinking I was going to be on television!' she joked.

Steadying his breathing, Luca shot Eve a look which said 'I will talk to you afterwards' and she felt exactly like a schoolgirl who had been summoned to see the headmaster.

But Luca's rage was temporarily forgotten when the technician began to slide the scanner over the bump and what had looked like a blur of grey and black gradually began to seem real.

'There we are,' said the technician. 'Two arms and two legs—perfect. And there's the heart—can you see it beating?'

There was silence, only this time a breathless, excited kind of silence.

'Oh, look!' said the technician, as if she hadn't said this a thousand times before. 'He's sucking his thumb!'

'He?' shot out Luca.

'Oh, sorry! We always say "he". Habit, really, I know I shouldn't. Would you like to know your baby's sex?' she asked casually.

At exactly the same time, Eve and Luca looked up.

'No,' they said together, their eyes meeting and in that meeting was a moment of shared and delicious collusion.

But when the technician had wiped off the conducting jelly and told her to get dressed, Eve began to feel slightly uneasy. Luca's face was a study in brooding displeasure. She reached for her trousers.

'I'd better get dressed.'

'I'll wait outside,' said Luca shortly.

As she pulled on her clothes Eve told herself that she was *not* going to be intimidated by him. She was *not*. She could tell that he was mad—hopping mad—but he had no right to tell her how to run her life.

She sighed as she slithered into a pair of trousers

with difficulty. Things had been going so swimmingly, too. He had behaved like a perfect angel on trips to see the doctor, shamelessly charming her so that the medic had billed and cooed at him with what Eve had thought was quite unprofessional abandon. He flew in at the drop of a hat, as if he were merely travelling from one part of the South Coast to another, and not from another country.

But then he travelled a lot. She knew that because he had told her, in one of his increasingly frequent telephone calls to see how she was.

She had begun to look forward to them. In a way, it was easier talking to him on the phone—then she didn't have to look at his gorgeous dark face or cope with the very real awareness of him as a man, and how her feelings towards him hadn't changed.

Or rather, they had. The attraction she felt for him hadn't, but getting to know him had made her realise what she had always feared, deep down—what she had thought the moment she'd seen him on the other side of the room at Michael and Lizzy's party.

That he was 'the one'.

But that was strictly a one-way street and there was absolutely no point going down there.

He was waiting for her outside in Reception and his face was like thunder.

'Did you bring the car?'

She nodded.

'Give me the keys.'

She handed them over and wondered if she was becoming one of those frightful women who secretly wanted to be dominated. But she reasoned that maybe it was just nice to have someone take over for a change. She yawned.

He didn't say a word when they got in the car, and when they were headed out towards the Hamble he still maintained a simmering silence.

'Luca?'

'Not now, Eve,' he said quietly. 'I am trying very hard to concentrate on driving and if we have this conversation then I am very afraid I won't be able to.'

He waited until they were back in her cottage and then he let rip.

'Are you going to explain what all that was about?'

'You mean the film crew?'

'Please don't play games with me, Eve. You are an intelligent woman—you know exactly what I mean.'

She sat down in one of the armchairs and looked up at him defiantly. 'It's for the programme.'

'Yes, I gathered that much.'

'They wanted to film the scan, that's all.'

'That's *all*?'

She shot a glance at him. 'I don't see what the problem is.'

He gave an angry laugh. 'You don't see what the problem is?' he repeated incredulously. 'What, for half the nation to be staring at your naked stomach!'

'It isn't half the nation,' she began automatically, and then stopped when she saw his face. 'It's supposed to help women see how easy it is,' she tried placatingly.

'And what about the labour itself?' he demanded, hotly. 'Are you going to let a film crew of men film *that*, so that the viewers can see how "easy" it is?'

'No, of course not!'

'Are you sure?'

'Quite sure.' In fact, the idea had actually been mooted at one of the production meetings, but Eve had turned the idea down flat.

'I suppose you think I'm being very old-fashioned.'

'Very.' But wasn't it also protective, and wasn't there some stupid side of her which thrilled to that? It must be the hormones making her react like that.

'I don't want the viewers seeing what is essentially a very private moment. It should be for the mother and father, Eve—for us.'

Except that there was no 'us'. Overwhelmed by an aching sense of longing for what could never be, Eve closed her eyes.

He looked at her. She was pale, he thought, and again a slow, simmering anger began to bubble up. What the hell was she doing, lying there being filmed, her stomach heavy with his child? How had he allowed this to happen? 'I'm going to make some tea,' he said shortly.

She could hear him clattering around in the kitchen, and when he came back in with the tray he was frowning. 'Why were you having a scan at this stage anyway?'

She shrugged listlessly. 'Just routine.'

'Sure?'

She nodded.

He sat down, and picked up her hand, began to stroke it, almost thoughtfully, and Eve's eyes flew open. It was such a little thing. Such a tiny, little thing and yet it felt like heaven. Her body craved comfort and human contact. She met his eyes, wanting above all else for him to take her into his arms, to hold her and to stroke her, but he did not and the dark eyes were thoughtful, watchful, wary.

'For how much longer are you contracted to do this show?' Idly, he circled a finger over her hand.

She swallowed. Don't stop touching me, she thought. 'It finishes on the third.'

'That's next week.'

She nodded.

'And then?'

'Then I'm on maternity leave. I'll look at other options when…when I've had the baby.'

'Eve.' He paused. 'Are you happy with what you're doing?'

'You mean the show?'

'That is part of it. But your life here. What you see for the future. Just what *do* you see for the future, *cara mia*?'

It was a long time since he had called her that, and it made her want to weep with longing. For what it might have been. For what it was not.

'It's like I jumped onto a merry-go-round and I can't get off,' she admitted slowly, and at that moment she didn't care if she sounded vulnerable. She *felt* vulnerable—and pregnant women were allowed to, weren't they? She was fed up with being brave and strong and coping. She *did* want to lean on Luca, if not emotionally, then at least practically. Just for a little. To pretend that he would really always be there for her…

'As for the future—well, it isn't something that I gave much thought to before. But now…' Her voice tailed off.

'Now?' he prompted.

'I realise that I have to. And I just don't know any

more. Oh, Luca!' And to her horror, tears began to slide from her eyes. She bit her lip and tried to stop them, but she could not and it was as though she had been teetering on a knife-edge of control as she began to cry.

An expression of pain crossed his face. Had he pushed her so far to cause her this? He pulled her into his arms and began to smooth his hand down over the silken mane of her hair, over and over again in a soothing and comforting rhythm. 'Shh. Don't cry, Eve. Don't cry, *cara mia*. No need for tears. Everything is going to be fine, I promise you.'

Her tear-wet cheek was buried in his neck. She could smell the raw maleness of him and feel the warmth which radiated from him. His arms were tight and strong and protective. Nothing could hurt her here. At least, no outside forces could—her ache in her heart was the most dangerous thing she had to fear.

She drew away from him, wiping her cheeks with the back of her hand. 'I'm sorry,' she sniffed.

'Don't be sorry.' He touched away a last stray tear with the tip of his finger. How shocked would she be if he told her that a part of him liked seeing her weak, like this? For her weakness meant that his own strength could come to the fore, and wasn't that the way he liked it best? 'What would happen if you told them you didn't want to go back to work? At least for the foreseeable future?'

'It would probably be the end of my career. Viewers have very short memories and even shorter loyalties.'

'Yes, your career. *Your damned career*,' he said softly. 'What's going to happen when the baby is born, Eve? Who will look after our son or our daughter when that car whisks you away to the studio every day?'

She looked at him. He was still so close, close enough to kiss, but she did not dare. 'I don't know anything any more,' she whispered. 'I don't even know how much I care about my career.' Her eyes glittered defiantly. 'I suppose you think that's a shocking admission?'

It was the best thing he had heard her say in a long time, but he was clever enough not to say so. 'Why should it be?'

She shrugged, thinking that the woman he had been attracted to was the smart, able career woman. 'I guess I think that my job defines me.'

'No job should define a person. And you haven't answered my question,' he persisted. 'What's going to happen when the baby is born?'

'I don't have a choice. I have to work.'

'But that's just the point, Eve—you *do* have a choice. You can come back to Italy with me. As my wife.'

There was a long, breathless silence.

'You don't mean that.'

'I never say anything I don't mean. But believe me when I tell you that I will not ask you again.'

She sat back against the cushions. 'Why? I mean—really?'

'Truthfully?' He rubbed his finger along the shadowed line of his chin. 'I would like the child to be born in Italy, and I want to see that child grow up.'

At least he hadn't told her lies. Told her that he loved her and couldn't live without her. 'You think those are good enough reasons for getting married?'

she asked, and her voice was trembling in a way that didn't sound like her at all.

'I can't think of any better,' he said simply. 'What is the alternative? That you bring up the baby here, alone.' His eyes darkened. 'Or maybe not alone. Think what you like of me, Eve—but the thought of another man bringing up my child as his own sickens me to the stomach.'

She nodded. Oh, yes, she could see that. They were qualities of possessiveness and ownership, certainly, but at least he had had the guts to admit it. He wasn't to know that the situation would never arise and she wasn't going to tell him that no man would feature in her life, not after him. For who could hold a candle to Luca Cardelli?

And the flip-side to his not being able to stand the thought of another man was the spectre of Luca being with another woman. Could she bear that? Imagine if Luca married someone else, and she had to send the child to stay with them, weekends and holidays and, worse, alternate Christmases? Another woman being a stepmother to her child. If there were qualities of ownership and possession, then Eve was just discovering that Luca didn't have a monopoly on them.

Shouldn't she give what they had—however precarious—a chance? Rather than risk time and distance making them grow further and further apart, so that it didn't become a case of *if* he got another woman, but *when*.

She thought of what he was offering her. 'It's more than just marriage, though,' she pointed out thoughtfully. 'It's a whole new life in a whole new country.'

'An adventure! A beautiful country, and a beautiful city.' His eyes glittered and his voice softened to rich velvet. 'I could so easily make you fall in love with my city, Eve.'

She didn't doubt it for a moment. He had managed to make her fall in love with *him* without even trying. But Luca was a passionate man, and there was an aspect to marriage he hadn't even touched. The aspect which had turned everything upside down, including their lives.

'When you say…marriage…'

He saw the way she bit her lip. 'You are afraid that I am going to start demanding my "rights"?' he mocked softly.

'Well, are you?' It should have been a teasing response and if it had been then who knew how he might have reacted? But, as it was, it came out more like a sulky little question and hung on the air like an accusation.

A pulse began to beat at his temple. 'I will demand nothing of you, Eve,' he retorted silkily. 'If that's what you're worried about.'

Could it be any more complicated than it was? she wondered. What had happened had put up barriers between them, of course it had. Luca had shown no sign of wanting to make love to her ever since she had first told him that she was pregnant. At first she had put it down to his anger, but now that the anger had gone he still hadn't gone near her. Which could mean that he no longer found her physically attractive.

Yet there were times when she caught him looking at her with a hot and hungry look in his eyes which made her think that perhaps he did. Though it was different for men, she knew that. They responded automatically to a woman sometimes—though, considering her current state of swollen ankles and swollen belly, she might simply have imagined it.

And now he said he would demand nothing of her. Did that mean that he expected *her* to make the first move? And how could she—so lumberingly and unattractively pregnant—make an overture towards him which he might then reject? Or maybe he wouldn't demand because he didn't want her in that way, not any more.

'You're having second thoughts?' he mused.

'I haven't even got through the first ones yet.'

He laughed then and it was the laugh that did it. To have the ability to make a man like Luca laugh surely meant something. She loved him and she was expecting his baby and he had offered to marry her. What was not to accept? What was to make her cling onto what she had here—a job which had become increasingly unimportant when compared to the enormity of bringing new life into the world?

She smiled. 'What type of wedding did you have in mind?'

CHAPTER ELEVEN

As IT was, with all the arrangements to be made, it was close onto a month before the wedding could take place, and by then she was almost up to the limit of when it was safe to fly.

There was a licence to be obtained, a dress to buy and a simple reception to be organised.

Though her choice of wedding dress was strictly limited by her physical dimensions.

'You look lovely,' sighed Lizzy.

'Liar! I look like a whale!'

'Well, you don't, and even if you did—who cares, when you're getting married to Luca?' sighed Lizzy. 'He obviously loves you whatever you look like!'

Eve didn't like to disillusion her. What would have been the point? She had taken Lizzy up to London with her, where, armed with a ridiculous amount of money, she had persuaded a hot, up-and-coming young fashion designer to try to work magic with her appearance. The result was a coat-dress, cleverly cut to disguise the bump, in fine cashmere of the softest, palest ivory. An outrageous hat had been made to match. 'It'll naturally draw the eye to your face,' said the designer. 'Which is just *glowing* with pregnancy!'

A bouquet which was luscious and extravagant enough to cover the bump completed the ensemble. In fact, the whole outfit was an illusory one, thought Eve as she twirled in front of the floor-length mirror.

Something made to look like something it wasn't—and maybe an accurate reflection of the marriage itself.

Still, she had agreed to go through with it, and she would do so with all her heart.

The day after she had accepted Luca's proposal she had gone into work and told them. And unfortunately someone had phoned the local press.

EVE IS THE APPLE OF ITALIAN'S EYE! reported the South Hampshire daily.

'In a way, I admire you,' Clare told her, a touch enviously. 'Giving all this up for love. And marriage.'

And Eve didn't have the heart to disillusion her, either.

On her final broadcast, she explained that she was getting married and moving to Rome.

'Why, you looked positively wistful when you said that, *cara*,' drawled Luca, who had watched the show. 'So was that genuine, or just good acting?'

Did he think of her as an actress, then? Able to hide her emotions behind a veneer of professionalism? And if so, wasn't that a skill which might prove useful in the ensuing months?

The wedding took place in the Hamble, in the yacht club where she had first seen Luca. A girl of about the same age as Eve had served them champagne and Dublin Bay prawns and Eve thought how heartbreakingly young she looked.

It was a small affair with Lizzy and Michael, and Kesi as bridesmaid, and Luca's sister Sophia had flown over, leaving her husband with her baby back at home. Eve had felt nervous about meeting her, but she was strung out with nerves anyway, and thought how faraway her voice sounded during the ceremony.

She felt strange, as if it were all happening to someone else, as if she were in a bubble which protected her from the rest of the world. And although her heart ached with love and longing, the vows they exchanged seemed to have no real meaning because they didn't really mean *anything*. Certainly not to Luca.

It was ironic in a way that she, who had always considered herself a very modern woman, should be entering into a very old-fashioned marriage of convenience.

Luca took her in his arms afterwards, briefly brushing his lips over hers in a kiss which didn't mean anything either, for there was no promise in it. Not for them the usual passion of the newly-weds, only restrained by social niceties, just a perfunctory kiss to make it look as everyone thought it should look.

'You look very beautiful,' he murmured.

But what bride could possibly feel beautiful at such an advanced state of pregnancy?

Yet Sophia had hugged Eve like a sister, and run her hand over the bump in a delighted way which spoke of pride, rather than something to be ashamed of. 'Stand up to him,' she had said, when rose petals and rice had flown off on the wind towards the water. 'He has had too much of his own way for all his life. And I'll see you in Rome, once you are settled, *si*?'

Settled?

Eve wasn't sure that she would ever feel settled again, and when they arrived at the front of Luca's apartment she felt the very opposite as he turned to her, his dark eyes glittering.

'Shall I carry you over the threshold, Eve?'

'Is that an Italian custom, as well as an English one?' she said breathlessly.

He smiled. 'It is indeed. Come.'

And he scooped her up in his arms and carried her into the apartment.

'Put me down, I'm too heavy,' she protested.

'Not for me,' he demurred.

No. He was a strong man and Eve wondered if he could feel or hear the thundering of her heart. It was, she realised, the closest they had been for a long time. With one hand beneath her knees and the other locked around her expanded waistline and her leaning against his chest. She could smell the raw, feral masculine scent of him, feel his hard body as it tensed beneath her weight.

If this had been a real wedding, he would carry her straight into the bedroom and lay her down and slowly undress her and make love until the morning light came up.

But it was not, and he did not. Instead, he put her carefully down in the centre of the vast, spacious sitting room as if she were some delicate and precious container, which was exactly, she guessed, how he saw her. For she carried within her his child, and nothing could be more precious than that to the man who had everything else.

The undrawn curtains framed the stunning beauty of the night lights of Rome, though she was blind to it. All she could see and sense was him. He was still wearing the dark and elegant suit he had worn for the wedding, though she had insisted on changing from her wedding finery for the journey home.

'It's more comfortable this way,' she had explained in answer to his silent look of query as she'd appeared in a trousers and a pink silk tunic, which by no stretch of the imagination could be classified as a 'going-away' suit. But it was more than that. She hadn't thought she could bear to go through the charade of people congratulating her, them—making a fuss of her on the flight, behaving as if they really were a pair of exquisitely happy newly-weds, when nothing could have been further from the truth.

His eyes had narrowed. 'So be it, *cara*,' he had said softly. 'Comfort is, of course, essential.'

And now they were here, and she was ready to begin her new life and she didn't even know what the sleeping arrangements would be.

He saw the wary look on her face. Like a cornered animal, he thought grimly. Was she afraid that he would drag her to the bedroom—insist on consummating this strange marriage of theirs?

'Would you like to see your room?'

Well, that told her. 'I'd love to!' she said brightly. 'I'm so tired I think I could sleep for a whole century!'

'A whole century?' he echoed drily.

In any other time or in any other situation, Eve would have exclaimed with delight at the bedroom he took her to. It was perfect. A room full of light, furnished in creams and softest peach.

But Eve had seen *his* bedroom. Had shared that vast bed of his, where tonight he would sleep alone. For one brief and impetuous moment she almost turned to him, to put her hand on his arm and say shyly that she would prefer to spend the night with him. But he had moved away to draw the blinds, and part of her was relieved, knowing that if they made love it would change everything—it would shatter what equilibrium she had and make her vulnerable in a way she simply couldn't afford to be. And there were far too many other things going on to risk that.

He turned back from the blinds, and the blocked-out night made the light in the room dim, throwing his tall, lean figure into relief so that he looked dark and shadowy, like an unknown man in an unknown room in an unknown city.

And that, she thought painfully, was exactly the way it was.

'Goodnight, Eve,' he said softly.

'Goodnight, Luca.'

'Do you have everything you need?'

No. 'Yes. Thank you.'

She stood exactly where she was, listening to the sounds of Luca moving around, until at last she heard the sound of his bedroom door closing quietly, and it was like a sad little signal.

Sighing as she looked at her brand-new, shiny wedding ring, she began to get undressed.

But when she woke up in the morning and drew open the blinds, she sucked in a breath of excitement at the sight of the city which lay beneath her, and it changed and lifted her mood. It couldn't fail to. It was like a picture-postcard view, she thought. And there was so much to discover.

She showered and dressed and wandered into the kitchen to find the tantalising aroma of good coffee and Luca squeezing oranges, a basket of newly baked bread on the table.

He gave her a slightly rueful look. 'I hope this is okay?'

She sat down, suddenly hungry. 'It looks wonderful.' She remembered the time when she had stayed with him, exclaiming that his fridge had been completely bare, save for two bottles of champagne and a tin of caviare. And he had taken her out to a nearby café for breakfast, explaining that he never ate in.

'You've taken to eating breakfast at home now, then?' she questioned as she poured her coffee.

'I shopped for these first thing,' he said, feeling like a man who had accomplished a mission impossible! 'I guess things are going to have to change around here.'

Automatically, her hand crept to her stomach. 'Well, er, yes,' she said drily.

He laughed. 'Homes have food, so I guess I'm going to have to learn how to shop. And cook.'

Eve laughed. He wore the expression of a man who had just announced his intention to wade through a pit of snakes. 'If you shop—I'm happy to cook.'

'You cook?'

She gave him a look of mock reprimand. 'Of course I cook! I love cooking.' She risked it. 'I could teach you, if you like.'

A woman teaching him!

'You might not be able to stand taking orders from a woman, of course,' she said shrewdly.

He met her eyes. 'Oh, I think I could bear taking orders from you, Eve.'

She hastily broke the warm, fragrant bread. She was going to have to watch herself, if some simple, throwaway comment like that was going to have her heart racing with some completely disproportionate pleasure, as if he had just offered her the moon and the stars.

He sat down opposite her, feeling oddly relaxed. It felt strange to be eating breakfast with a woman in his own home and not covertly glancing at his watch and wondering how soon he could get his own space back.

'I've made you an appointment to see an obstetrician tomorrow morning,' he said, and then added, 'He's the best in the city.'

She supposed that went without saying. Everything that was the best would now be hers for the taking, and she must try to appreciate it. Not get bogged down with wanting everything to be perfect, because nothing ever was, everyone knew that.

'And I think we might arrange a small party—that way you can get to meet everyone at once—what do you think?'

It was her first real entrée into his life. A whole circle of Luca's smart and sophisticated friends—how were *they* going to accept her? She hadn't even put that into part of the equation. 'What will they think?'

He raised his eyebrows in faintly insolent query. 'That you're my wife and that you're expecting my baby—what else is there for them to think?'

He was right. Even if it had been a conventional love marriage, he would not have gone around telling his friends so. They would just have made the assumption. Would they notice that he didn't touch her? That they behaved as benignly as two flatmates? She stirred her coffee. 'Luca.'

He let his eyes drift over her. Her hair was loose

and the morning light was spilling over it. He had never seen so many different hues in a head of hair and it looked like molasses and honey with warm hints of amber. Her green-grey eyes were bright and clear, their lashes long and curling even though she wasn't wearing a scrap of make-up. She looked wholesome and clean and healthy, he thought, and that, surprisingly, was incredibly sexy. He hadn't slept a wink last night, imagining her in the bed next door to his. What, he wondered, was she wearing in bed at the moment? Did pregnant women feel the need to cover up? He shifted slightly. 'Mmm?'

'I'd like to learn Italian, please. And as soon as possible.'

He heard the determination in her voice. It didn't surprise him, but it pleased him. 'All my friends speak English,' he commented. 'Spanish, too.'

'Yes. Yes, I sort of somehow imagined that they would.'

'And the baby is going to take a while to learn how to speak!' he teased.

'Yes, I know that, too! But I don't want to be one of those women who move to another country and lets her...her...husband do all the talking for her.' The word sounded strange on her lips. As if she were a fraud for saying it.

'I can't imagine you letting *anyone* do the talking for you, Eve,' he said drily. 'But, of course, I will arrange for a tutor for you. That might be better than going out to a class, particularly at the moment, don't you think?'

She nodded. How easy it was to arrange and talk about practical things. And how easy to suppress feelings and emotions. To put them on the back-boiler so that they didn't disturb the status quo.

'It seems strange to think of our baby talking,' he said slowly.

'Too…too far in the future to imagine?' she questioned tentatively.

'A little. But I was just thinking that his or her first language will be English, won't it? The mother tongue.' He thought then of the reality of what her being here meant. Or rather, what it would have been like if she had stayed in England. He wouldn't have got a look-in, not really. It would have been false and unreal and ultimately frustrating and unrewarding. Suddenly, he understood some of the sacrifice it must have taken for her to have come here—to start all over in a territory which was completely unknown to her.

'We'll need to think about decorating a room,' he mused.

'Pink, or blue?' She searched his face. What if secretly he was so macho that he would only be satisfied with a son—and what if she didn't produce one, what then? 'Which would you prefer, a boy or a girl?'

He frowned, as if the question had surprised him.

'I don't care which; there is only one thing I care about.'

'Yes.' Their eyes met and she smiled. 'A healthy baby. It's what every parent prays for.' She looked at him. 'So it's yellow?'

'Yellow? *Sì. Giallo.*' A smile creased the corners of his eyes. 'Say it after me.'

She felt giddy with the careless innocence of it. *'Gi-allo.'*

'So, there is your first Italian lesson!' He leaned back indolently in his chair and studied the lush breasts through narrowed eyes. 'What would you like to do today? The Grand Tour of the city?'

She thought about it. What she wanted and craved more than anything was some kind of normality, for there had been precious little of it in her life of late. And even if such a thing were too much to hope for, she needed to start living life as she—or rather, they—meant to go on.

'Will you show me round the immediate vicinity?' she asked. Would something like that sound prosaic to such an urbane and cosmopolitan man? 'Show me where the nearest shops are. Where I can buy a newspaper, that kind of thing. We could—if you meant it—go and buy some stuff for supper? Is there somewhere close by?'

He nodded. 'There is the *al mercato di Campo de Fiori* and there are shops. Sounds good.'

She hesitated. She knew something of his lifestyle—the man with nothing in the fridge who rarely ate in, who travelled the world and went to fancy places. 'Luca?'

'Eve?' he said gravely.

She drew a breath. 'Listen, I know you're usually out—probably every night for all I know. You mustn't stay in just because of me.'

'You mean you want to go out at night?'

'Like this?' She shook her head, and laughed. 'I'm far too big and lumbering to contemplate hitting on Rome's top night-spots!'

He frowned. 'You mean you want me to go out without you?'

'If you want to. I just want you to know that I

don't intend to cramp your style. You mustn't feel tied—because of the baby.'

He stared at her. Did she have a degree in psychology, or just a witch's instinct for knowing how to handle a man? That by offering him his freedom, he now had no desire to take it!

'I am no longer a boy,' he said gravely. 'And "top night-spots" kind of lost their allure for me a long time ago. So I'll stay in. With you.'

'Sure you won't be bored?'

'Let's wait and see.'

Her voice was wry. 'That seems to be a recurrent theme with us, doesn't it?'

'Indeed.' Their eyes met. He admired her mind, he realised, and her sense of humour, too. The baby was going to be a lucky baby to have her as a mother, he thought suddenly. 'I'm glad you're here, Eve,' he said.

She put her coffee-cup down with a hand which was trembling. But he was merely being courteous, and he should be offered the same in return. She smiled. 'And so am I.'

CHAPTER TWELVE

'WE'RE not going to cook every night,' said Luca suddenly, one morning.

Eve didn't answer for a moment. The baby's foot was sliding across the front of her belly and she sat and watched it, then lifted her head. 'You mean last night was a disaster?'

He shook his head. The simple meal they had eaten on the terrace beneath the stars had been almost perfect. Almost. She was engaging and stimulating company and, because sex was off limits, all the focus had been on the conversation and this was new territory for him.

Luca wasn't averse to talking to women but he usually regarded conversation with them as purely functional. You might talk to a woman if you were dealing with her at work. Or if you were flirting with her, or making pleasant small talk before taking her to bed, or chatting to the wives of friends. They were easier to talk to, in a way, because they had no expectations of you as a potential partner, which all other women did.

But he was a man's man—he rarely had conversation with a woman for conversation's sake. With Eve he had to—and last night he had realised why she had been so successful at her job. He had persuaded her to talk about her work, something she was normally reluctant to do.

He had understood for the first time that working

in television was not easy and that the skill lay in making it *look* easy. Not many people could cope with live and unpredictable interviews, while at the same time having the studio crew sending frantic instructions into your earpiece.

'Will you ever want to go back to it?' he had persisted.

In Italy? With a baby? Who knew *what* she would want—and did people ever get what they truly wanted? Protected still by the bubble of pregnancy which surrounded her, Eve had smiled. 'We'll see.'

Luca stared at her, watching the dreamy way that she observed the baby's movements. 'No, Eve, it was not a disaster.'

Disaster was too strong a word. Crazy was better.

It seemed crazy that they should part at the end of the evening and go off to sleep in their separate beds. Or rather, for him to toss and turn and think about how pregnancy could make a woman seem so intensely beautiful. Like a ripe and juicy peach.

He wanted to lie with her. Not to make love— something deep within him told him that it would be entirely inappropriate to consummate their marriage when she was heavy with his child. But he would have liked to have held her. To have wrapped her in his arms and smoothed the silken splendour of her hair. To have run his fingertips with possessive and wondrous freedom over the great curve of her belly.

'It is just that your freedom, and mine—will be restricted by a baby.'

'Only a few weeks now,' she observed serenely.

'Exactly! Time to make the most of what we have, while we still have it! We shall play the tourist.'

'I suppose when you put it *that* way,' Eve murmured. Maybe they should get out more. Heaven only knew, it was difficult enough to be this close to him and not close enough to him. Itching for him to touch her, to kiss her—anything which might give her some inkling of whether or not he still found her sexually attractive, or whether that had died a death a long time ago.

He showed her a different side of Rome. Took her to all the secret places of his boyhood, the dark, hidden crevices and sunlit corners.

'We aren't really playing the tourist at all, are we?' she asked him as they strolled slowly around a hidden garden, soft with the scent of roses. 'No tourist would ever find places as hidden away as these are.'

'Ah, but this is the true Rome. For Romans.'

Eve felt a brief, momentary pang of isolation. Their child would grow up and learn this secret Rome, with a native's knowledge which would always elude her.

'Eve?' said Luca softly. 'What is it?'

I'm frightened of what the future holds, she wanted to say to him. But she wouldn't. She had to learn to cope and deal with her own fears—not project them onto Luca. 'Nothing,' she said softly.

They dined with Patricio, Luca's oldest friend and his wife, Livvy, who went out of their way to make her feel comfortable. Livvy had a toddler about the same age as Kesi and Eve was glad that all Luca's friends weren't childless.

Gradually, she began to relax.

And then, one starlit evening, they were walking home after having late-night coffee and pastries and Eve suddenly stopped, drawing in a gasp as a terrible sharp spasm constricted across her middle. 'Ouch!'

Luca caught her by the arm. 'What is it?'

She could see the paling of his face and shook her head. 'It was nothing. It must have been the cake that… Oh, Luca…Luca—it hurts!'

'*Madre de Dio!*' he swore and steadied her. 'I *said* we should get a taxi!' He held up his hand and a taxi screeched to do his bidding as if it had been lurking round the corner, just waiting for his command.

Eve's Italian was still pretty non-existent, but even she understood the word '*ospedale*'. 'Luca, I am *not* going to hospital!'

'*Sì, cara,*' he contradicted grimly. 'You are!'

She stared him out. 'No,' she said stubbornly. 'And anyway, the baby isn't due for another two weeks. I want to go home!'

His impotent fury that she could not and would not be persuaded—he could tell that from the stubborn set of her mouth—was softened slightly by her instinctive use of the word 'home'. He nodded. 'Very well,' he agreed softly. 'We will go home. But the doctor will visit, and he will decide.' He saw her open her mouth to protest. '*He will decide, Eve,*' he said, in a voice which broached no argument.

'It's a waste of his time!'

But Eve was wrong and Luca and the doctor were right. It was not a false alarm. The baby was on the way.

Everything became a fast and frantic blur, punctuated only by sharp bursts of pain which became increasingly unbearable.

'I want an epidural!' she gasped as they wheeled her into the delivery room.

But it was too late for an epidural, too late for anything. She was having her baby and the midwife was saying something to her frantically, something she didn't understand.

'*Spinga, signora! Spinga, ora!*'

'*Luca*! I'm so scared! What is she saying?'

'She is saying, push, *cara*. And you must not be scared. Trust me, I am here with you.'

'Oh! Ow!'

She gripped his hands, her fingernails tearing into his flesh, but he scarcely noticed. 'You're doing fine,' he coaxed. 'Just fine.' He snapped something rapid in Italian at the midwife, who immediately began speaking in slow, fractured English.

'One more push, *signora*. One more. Take a deep breath and...'

'Now, *cara*!' urged Luca softly as he saw something in her face begin to change. '*Now!*'

Eve pulled her hand away from his, her head falling back as she made one last, frantic little cry and Luca moved just in time to see his baby being born.

'Here's your baby,' said the midwife and she deftly caught the infant.

He stared. A little wet black head and a long, slithery body. The world seemed to stand still as the midwife sprang into action, cutting the cord, wiping a plug of mucus from the little nose.

Eve half sat up in bed, her damp hair plastered all over her face, watching the midwife as if nothing else on the planet existed right then.

For one long and breathless moment, there was silence, and then the infant opened its lungs and let out a baleful and lusty cry and Eve burst into tears of relief as the midwife held it up triumphantly.

'You have a son, *signore, signora*!' and she swaddled him in a blanket and placed him straight on Eve's breast.

Luca turned away, feeling the unfamiliar taste of tears at the back of his throat, but Eve needed strength now, not weakness. He sucked in a deep breath as he tried to compose himself. He had watched her suffer, had heard her cry out in pain and seen the fear on her face as the overwhelming spasms had brought the baby from her body. For the first time in his life he had been helpless, the experience of it all making everything else he had seen in his life somehow insignificant, but that should not really surprise him. For this was a miracle. Truly, a miracle.

Joyfully, Eve stared down at the baby as it suckled from her breast and she glanced over at Luca, but he was staring out of the window. She needed him right now, but her needs were no longer paramount. And suddenly nothing else seemed to matter. Motherhood had kicked in.

She studied the tiny creature intently. 'Hello, baby,' she said softly. 'Hello, Oliviero. Oliviero Patricio.' Funny how the name they had chosen seemed to suit him perfectly. She put her finger out and a tiny little fist curled round it. Maybe because everything about him was perfect.

Luca turned round, still shaken, and stared at the tableau the two of them made. The child suckled at her breast and she was making soft little cooing sounds. She looked like a Madonna, he thought—as if the two of them had created their own magic circle, excluding the world and all others.

Didn't men sometimes say that they felt excluded when a baby was born? And that was when the re-lationship was as it should be. His mouth tightened, and he felt bitterly ashamed at the selfishness of his thoughts. Eve had given birth to a beautiful son, he thought. His son. And his heart turned over.

Eve saw him watching her, and felt suddenly shy, unsure how to deal with these big, new emotions. 'Would you...would you like to hold him?' she asked.

'He's not still hungry?'

The midwife laughed. 'A child of this size will always be hungry! Hold him, *signore*—let him know who his father is!'

Luca had always held his nephew with a kind of confident ease, but this felt completely different. He bent down and Eve carefully deposited the precious bundle into his arms.

She watched the two of them, transfixed by the sight of the strong, powerful man held in thrall to the tiny baby.

Luca looked down and his son opened his eyes and stared up at him, and in that moment his heart and his soul connected. 'I will die for him,' he said fiercely, hardly aware that he had spoken aloud. 'My little Oliviero Patricio.'

Eve lay back on the pillows, and the enormity of what had happened slammed home to her in a way it hadn't before. She had been protected by the slight sense of unreality which pregnancy gave you, which made you sometimes feel you weren't part of the outside world.

Hadn't part of her always thought that if it didn't work out, they would quietly divorce and she could slip back to England? But now she knew that would never happen. The possessive pride which had softened Luca's hard, handsome face told her that. He would die for him, he had said, and he would fight for him, too. She knew that. Whichever way she looked at it—as a gilded prison, or a marriage of convenience—she had better make the best of it, because she was here now for the duration.

She closed her eyes. She was weary now.

They took Oliviero home six days later, to a flat where Luca had clearly been busy. There were flowers everywhere—roses and lilies and tulips—colourful and scented, and more than a little overwhelming. The yellow nursery was filled with balloons, and there was a pile of cards, waiting, and gifts wrapped exquisitely in blue and silver and blue and gold. It looked as if a Hollywood film star were about to pay a visit and Eve found it all a little overwhelming.

And the lift journey up to the penthouse only served to remind her that this was essentially a bachelor's flat. She thought of the pristine white walls and the frosted glass and shuddered as her mind tried to make the connection with a rampaging toddler.

Luca carried the baby in and placed the carry-cot on the coffee-table, smiling at him tenderly before looking up at Eve.

'He sleeps well,' he observed softly. 'You feed him well, Eve.'

Stupidly, she found herself blushing and turned away. It seemed such an intimate thing for him to say, and yet what could be more intimate than the fact he had witnessed the birth? He had seen her at her most naked and vulnerable, stripped and defenceless and in a way that was scary.

Luca noted the way she wouldn't look at him, and his eyes narrowed. So be it. If distance was what she wanted, then distance was what she would get.

'Are you hungry?' he questioned.

Her instinct was to say no, but she knew she had to eat. She nodded. 'I think I might have a bath first.'

'That's fine,' he said coolly. 'Sit down, and I'll run one for you.'

She had offended him and she didn't know why. 'No, honestly—'

'Eve, sit down,' he repeated, rather grimly. 'You have been through a lot.'

Rather gingerly, she sat down, gazing at Oliviero as he lay sleeping so peacefully, listening to the sound of water rushing into the bath.

'It's ready.'

She looked up. Luca was standing there, silhouetted by the door, looking dark and edgy and somehow formidable. It would have been strange fitting into these new roles of mother and father whatever the circumstances, but the distance between them only seemed to make them stranger. A distance she didn't quite know how, or if, she could ever breach.

Slowly, she got to her feet. Still at that new-mother-scared stage of not wanting to let him out of her sight, she fixed him with an anxious look. 'You'll keep an eye on Oliviero?'

His eyes hardened. What did she think he was going to do? Take a stroll around the piazza and leave him? 'Sure,' he said shortly.

She couldn't remember ever seeing him quite so keyed up. Maybe it was the birth of a baby. It was a stressful time for a man, too—she mustn't forget that.

But the bath made her feel a million times better and so did the hair-wash. Through the soapy and bubbly water she looked down at her stomach, which seemed amazingly flat. Of course, it wasn't flat at all compared to its normal state, but it wasn't too bad, considering. The midwife had told her that she was going to be one of those lucky few who would be back in her jeans within the month, and Eve hoped so.

She had eaten healthily and carefully throughout the pregnancy and she didn't want to let herself go. For her sake, but also because of the sophisticated and sylph-like women in Luca's circle of friends.

And for Luca's sake? prompted a little voice in her head. Don't you want t keep your body looking good for him? She let the water out and stepped out of the bath, the droplets drying on her skin.

She stared at her face in the mirror. What happened now? Would Luca attempt to make her his wife in the most fundamental way now that there was no baby inside her? Not tonight, that was for sure—but in the days to come?

She pulled on some velvet trousers and hid their elasticated waist with a long, silky shirt in a shade of deep green which brought out the natural green in her eyes. She blasted her hair with the dryer and fussed around with it and stood back from the mirror, quite pleased with her reflection.

And when she came out from the bathroom it was to see that Luca had set the table and she blinked in surprise to see that it was lit by candlelight. There was salad and pasta and a dish of figs and white peaches.

And a bottle of champagne cooling.

Her mouth feeling suddenly dry with nerves, Eve sat down.

'That looks…very nice,' she said weakly.

He glanced up from tearing the foil from the bottle. He saw her eyes stray nervously to the wine. Did she think he was trying to lull her into letting her guard down?

His mouth hardened as he poured the champagne into two goblets and he handed her one.

'What shall we drink to?' said Eve. To love? she thought ironically as she saw the cynical curve of his mouth. To happy ever after?

'To our son. To Oliviero.'

Of course. 'To Oliviero.' She raised her goblet to mirror his and as their glasses touched she thought she had never heard a colder sound.

'It is good to be home?' he said carefully.

Eve took a huge mouthful as she looked around the room which had his beautiful and rather austere taste stamped all over it, wondering if it would ever truly feel like *her* home, as well as his. Wistfully, she remembered that glorious weekend she had spent here, when they had been unencumbered by anything except the sheer pleasure of the moment. It seemed like another lifetime ago, but in a way she supposed that it was.

She wondered how many different women had sat here, just where she was sitting now. Drinking champagne as a precursor to going to that vast bed of his and being made love to for the rest of the night.

But she would go off alone to her creamy, peachy bedroom and he would go off alone to his.

And the irony was that she was his wife!

She took the question at face value. 'It's good to be out of hospital,' she said carefully.

'That good, huh?' he mocked.

'I didn't mean it how it sounded.'

'Don't worry about it, Eve,' he said. 'It's bound to be strange.'

Frustratedly, she took another sip of the champagne. It was cold and dry and delicious and it seemed to dull some of the empty, aching feeling inside her. Dangerous to drink on an empty stomach. Alcohol loosened the inhibitions and who knew what she might then blurt out? She put the glass down and reached for the food instead.

She wished that he wouldn't just sit there like that, watching her from the narrowed dark eyes as if she were some kind of specimen in a test-tube, some new and undiscovered species. Maybe that was it. Maybe he just wasn't sure how to treat the woman who had just had his baby who was his wife, but in name only. Come to think of it, she thought slightly giddily— she couldn't blame him. There certainly wasn't a rule-book he could look up for guidelines on how to cope with such a situation.

'When will you have to go back to work?' she asked him.

'Whenever I please. I want to make sure that you're happy and settled before I do.'

Happy and settled. If only he knew. She wondered what had happened to the old Eve—who could chat and banter and tease him and feel like an equal to him. Had she been left on the shores of her native land, been cast off with her life as a single mother? 'That's very sweet of you.'

Luca had been described in many ways by women during his life, but 'sweet' had never been one of them. He did not want to be 'sweet'. He made an impatient little noise as he got up from the table and drew something from the back pocket of his jeans, a slim, navy leather box, and he put it on the table in front of Eve, as casually as he would a deck of cards.

Her heart was beating very fast. Everyone knew what came in boxes which looked like that.

'Wh-what's this?'

'Why not open it, and see?'

She flipped the lid off and drew in a breath of disbelief to see a bracelet glittering against the navy velvet. A band of iridescent, sparkling diamonds, each one as big as a fingernail. She stared at it, then looked up at him in genuine horror.

'Luca, I can't possibly accept this.'

'Of course you can. You're my wife and you have given me a beautiful son. Here, let me put it on.'

He bent his head to fasten the clasp around her wrist and Eve closed her eyes as his fingertips brushed against her skin, so warm and beguiling in contrast to the heavy, cold jewellery. Damn the bracelet, she thought. Throw it across the room and just touch me properly.

But he did not. He held her hand up and the brilliant circlet of jewels glittered, as if it were a trophy. Eve looked at it. It must have cost a fortune, and there were women who would have drawn blood for it, but she was not one of them.

'It's very beautiful,' she said dutifully.

The baby gave a little squawk and Luca almost seemed to expel a sigh of relief. 'I'll bring him to you.'

She watched him go to the carry-cot, her eyes drifting over the broad shoulders, the long, powerful legs and the way his dark hair curled slightly at the nape of his neck. The jeans stretched over the high, firm curve of his buttocks as he bent to lift the baby and she shivered with a hungry kind of longing. She hadn't exactly been immune to him before, but she had been preoccupied with the baby-to-be and with adjusting to life in a new city.

But now… Now all she wanted was to touch him. To rediscover the hard, strong lines of his face with her fingertips. To stroke them slowly over the silken flesh of his body.

She swallowed and turned appealing eyes up at him as Oliviero was placed warm and securely in her arms. 'You mustn't keep spoiling me like this. Honestly, Luca.'

'But I like doing it,' he said. And did it not simplify things? It had been so black and white when she had been pregnant. Thinking of her as a woman not yet recovered from the birth made it easier not to concentrate on the fact that no barrier now existed, and that they were just a man and a woman, living together. But not together.

Their eyes locked for long, confusing seconds and Eve felt a sudden tension which crackled through the room like electricity. Were they just going to ignore it, or endure it? And would it simply go away, or grow stronger and stronger?

'Luca—'

The baby wriggled restlessly and Luca knew he had to get away before he went back on everything he had vowed he would not do. 'Feed him,' he said shortly, and he didn't need to see the brief darkening of her eyes to know that he had hurt her.

CHAPTER THIRTEEN

THE soft, dark greens of the cypress trees painted umbrellas against the blue of the sky and the ancient stone walls passed by in a blur.

Eve leaned comfortably back in her seat and looked out at the countryside.

'All roads lead to Rome,' she said dreamily.

Luca gave a brief, satisfied smile. When had the change happened, he wondered, and when had he first started to notice it? He had watched her bloom and blossom, almost like watching a flower grow. And he had discovered that, just as a flower took time to blossom, change took time. You could not hurry it. Everything had its own rhythm. For a man used to clicking his fingers and getting exactly what he wanted, when he wanted, it had been a pretty major lesson in life.

'And all roads lead out of Rome, of course,' he murmured. 'As that's where we're headed!'

'Ha, ha!' She turned round and looked at Oliviero, who was peacefully asleep in his baby-seat. He was wearing a teeny little sailor-suit today—all crisp white cotton and embroidered anchors. Not quite what she would have chosen, but she had quickly discovered the Italian love of dressing their babies up, and she and Luca were driving out for a lunch party at Patricio and Livvy's country home and they had bought the outfit. 'He looks sweet, doesn't he?'

'He does indeed,' he said indulgently. *'Abbastanza buon mangiare.'*

'Which means?'

'Try and work it out.'

Eve frowned. She hadn't been learning Italian for long, but her progress had been remarkable, which she put down to Luca's tendencies as a slave-driver. *'Buon* means good.'

'Sì.'

The frown deepened. 'And I think *mangiare* is to eat.'

'It means, "good enough to eat".' He smiled and gave an exaggerated and very Latin shrug. 'You see? I can teach you nothing, Eve!'

But immediately she felt tension creep into the atmosphere and she didn't know whether she welcomed or cursed it. She was sure that there was plenty he could teach her, and she certainly wasn't thinking of the Italian language. So should she regard it as achievement or failure that she and Luca had managed to live together in relative harmony? As man and woman, if not man and wife.

How was it possible for them to communicate as friends and loving parents, and yet leave a great yawning hole in their communication about where their relationship was heading? And how long could it continue?

She stole a glance at Luca, who was swearing softly in Italian as a goat almost blundered into the road. He was just so gorgeous. He hated air-conditioning in cars, so had left his window half open and the warm, fragrant air blew in and ruffled his black hair. His shirt-sleeves were rolled up, showing the tiny dark hairs which sprinkled the strong arms, and the faded jeans emphasised the long, muscular definition of his thighs.

He was a hot-blooded and passionate man. She knew that for herself. She'd just had her six-week check-up following Oliviero's birth, and yet Luca had made no move towards her. How long could he continue to lead a life which was celibate? And it was one of those strange things—the longer it went on, the harder it would become to confront it.

Almost as if facing it would risk shattering the tentative trust and friendship they had built up together. And surely it was not her place to come out and say something? Was she living in fear that she might be rejected, or did it go deeper than that? For wasn't part of her terrified of the masquerade of having sex with Luca and pretending that it was just sex, when she had grown to love him so much and wanted nothing but his love in return?

And that was asking too much.

Luca turned his head, and smiled. 'Looking forward to lunch?'

She shifted slightly on her seat, afraid that he might be able to read the progression of her thoughts, half tempted to tell him to stop the car and then to hurl herself into his arms and see where *that* led them!

'Mmm. I like Patricio. And Livvy. I like all your friends.'

'Your friends too, now.'

'Yes.' But as friendships they were conditional, she knew that. They relied solely on her relationship with Luca and her position as his wife and sooner or later she was terrified that someone was going to discover just what a sham it all was. And then what?

Luca slowed the car down as it gingerly made its way down the bumpy lane, leading to a long, low farmhouse, sitting like a bird's egg in a glorious nest of green. Hens were scratching around by a barn door and, somewhere in the distance, Eve could hear a dove cooing.

Luca switched the engine off, his eyes roving over her as she undid her seat belt. She wore the simplest of outfits—a slim-fitting white denim skirt and a little T-shirt in jade green—and yet she managed to look like sex on legs. Thought maybe, he thought, subduing the familiar, dull ache—maybe that was more to do with his current state of heightened awareness. If she had worn a piece of all-enveloping sackcloth, he suspected that the end result of his thoughts would have been the same.

'You have got your figure back, *cara*,' he said softly. 'The outfit you wear looks lovely.'

Now why say something like *that*, just before they were due to go into lunch, or had that been the whole point? Pay her a compliment and make her aware of herself and leave her simmering and discontented throughout lunch? What the hell was he playing at?

'What, these old things?' she joked. 'Now, are you going to carry your son in, or shall I?'

The velvet-dark eyes glittered. 'Want to fight me for the pleasure?' he challenged softly.

Eve put her hand on the door-handle, afraid that he would see that it was shaking. Was he deliberately making everything he said absolutely *drip* with suggestive innuendo, or was that simply her interpretation of it?

'You can carry him,' she said quickly.

Everyone else had already arrived and were all

gathered beneath a vine-covered canopy. The adults were sitting down at a large, wooden trestle-table and various toddlers were waddling around on the terrace. It looked quite idyllic and perfect.

'Oh, doesn't it look peaceful?' sighed Eve longingly.

He looked at her profile, at the way her mouth had softened, and he nodded. 'The kind of way you thought Italy always should be?' he guessed softly.

She turned her head to look up at him. 'Kind of,' she admitted, but then voices were raised in welcome and there was no chance to say anything more.

Eve gave a wide smile, even though she couldn't really take in all the faces at first. But there was Patricio, and Livvy was getting to her feet and smiling a great smile of welcome.

'Eve! Luca! And Oliviero!'

Which gave the cue for everyone to scramble to their feet and coo over her darling baby, though Eve was acutely aware that the language switched immediately from Italian to English. And while she was working hard on it and knew that she couldn't possibly expect to become fluent overnight, she sometimes despaired of ever mastering the tongue with the careless ease which Luca and his friends had. But she would need to.

She didn't want to become one of those exiled mothers in a foreign land who never quite fitted in because they had never bothered to integrate. Or to have children who spoke a tongue which remained faintly foreign to her.

But thinking of the future like that scared her and so she forcefully put it out of her mind.

'Eve, come and sit down and have a drink,' said

Livvy. 'There are a few people here you don't know—let me introduce you.'

Eve accepted a glass of white wine and chewed on a salted almond as she was introduced to people with their impossibly romantic-sounding names— Claudio and Rosa, Caterina and Giacomo, Allessandro and Raimonda.

One woman in particular was just so beautiful that even the women seemed barely able to tear their eyes from her. Her name was Chiara, and she was younger than everyone else and with a man Eve hadn't seen before, either.

'Who is that woman?' she asked Luca softly as he positioned Oliviero in a quiet and shady spot.

Luca barely glanced over in the woman's direction. 'Her name is Chiara,' he said, in an odd kind of voice. 'And the man she is with is one of Italy's most famous film directors. She's an actress.'

Yes, she looked like an actress, Eve decided. She had met enough of them in her time. She had that way of holding herself which spoke of supreme confidence—but then who wouldn't be confident if they looked like that? Her glossy raven hair was knotted back in a French plait woven with ribbon and hung almost to the tiniest waist Eve had ever seen. She wore a simple dress in some kind of pinky-grey colour, but it moulded itself so closely to her body that no one could be in any doubt about what slender perfection lay beneath.

Eve helped herself to some salads and meats and began to falteringly attempt to speak a little Italian to Patricio, who laughed and teased her remorselessly. She drank wine and watched her husband as he kicked a ball to one of the little boys.

'Oh, Luca is just a frustrated footballer at heart,' shouted Patricio, and at that moment Luca looked up and met Eve's eyes and something inside her melted.

He wasn't just a frustrated footballer, but a frustrated lover, too, she thought. And so was she. And she wanted him. Desperately. All-consumingly. Someone had to put a stop to all this craziness and it might as well be her.

What could be the worst thing that could happen? That he would turn her down? No. That would not happen. She had seen the way he looked at her sometimes—he still wanted her, of that she was as certain as it was possible to be without actually testing it out.

So what was she really afraid of? That her love for him would grow deeper and deeper and never be reciprocated? And if so, wasn't that a pretty selfish way to view it?

Whatever. She wasn't going to hide from it any more. She was going to confront it, no matter how hurtful or painful. No matter what the outcome would be.

Livvy brought out a large chocolate cake to cheers from the men and greedy moans from the women, and only Chiara passed on the dessert.

'Go on—have a little,' tempted Livvy, but Chiara shook her head.

'But I have to wear tiny clothes.' She pouted and shrugged her tiny shoulders. 'It's how I earn my living!'

Eve had once read somewhere that men liked to see a woman eat—that it didn't matter what she did if they weren't around. Something about associating sex with hunger and that if a woman enjoyed her food, she would enjoy her body. If I were Chiara I would have taken a slice and played around with it, she thought. Until she remembered that she of all people was not in a position to hand out advice to anyone.

'Who wants to come and see my new horse?' asked Patricio.

'Oh, you men go and do your macho stuff,' said Livvy indulgently. 'We'll all just sit here and talk about you!'

'But we already know how wonderful we are!' swaggered her husband, and when she threw a cherry at him he caught it, and put it between his lips, biting on it, his eyes on his wife's mouth as he licked his tongue around the fruit and then slowly and deliberately threw the stone onto the grass.

Eve had to look away. How long since she had been intimate like that—*really* intimate? And if the truth were known, their sexual relationship had been so brief and intense that they had never slipped into that blissful state of being really comfortable with intimacy. She watched Luca go with a feeling of longing and suddenly she couldn't wait for the lunch to end.

'No more wine, thanks.' She shook her head. The unaccustomed alcohol and the warmth of the day had made her feel a little sleepy. Any minute now and she would doze off.

But then Oliviero woke and began to cry and Eve blinked and went over to pick him up. The little darling was damp with heat, despite the shade. She dropped a kiss on his head.

'Okay if I go inside and feed and change him?' she asked. 'It's cooler in there.'

'Sure.' Livvy smiled. 'I'll show you where.'

Eve settled herself in a shuttered and deliciously dark room. She fed Oliviero, then changed him, still marvelling at the size of his tiny little feet as she stroked her finger up and down the rosy soles.

She was just about to go back and join the others when Chiara came in.

'Hi!' Eve looked up and smiled. 'Too hot for you out there?'

Chiara smiled and shook her head as she ran a palm across her cool, sleek cheek. 'The sun doesn't touch me. I guess I'm used to it.'

Eve waited for Chiara to ask to hold the baby, but Chiara did not. Instead, she subjected Eve to a long and faintly puzzled scrutiny.

'You're English, aren't you?'

These were not good vibes, but Eve could cope— she had coped with enough women in the entertainment business to know how to handle women like Chiara.

'It's pretty obvious, isn't it?' She laughed politely but Chiara did not laugh back.

'You know,' Chiara said thoughtfully, 'you aren't really what we all expected—not at all the kind of woman we thought Luca would marry.'

Eve felt her heart begin to race. Suddenly her supposed ability to cope dissolved into a mass of insecurity. Keep it light-hearted, she told herself. Don't let her know it hurts.

'I think he rather surprised himself,' she said, but deep down she knew that this was vaguely dishonest. How triumphant would Chiara be if she knew the truth about their 'marriage'.

'You were pregnant, weren't you?'

Here it came. Just brazen it out. 'Yes, I was.'

Chiara nodded. 'It's a method which wouldn't work with a lot of men, but, of course, Luca was the perfect choice in more ways than one. He is far too much of a traditionalist to ever allow a child of his to be born out of wedlock.'

'I don't think this really is any of your business, do you?' asked Eve shakily, and hugged Oliviero to her, trying to concentrate on his sweet, baby smell and not the glitter of maliciousness in the actress's eyes.

But Chiara showed no signs of shutting up. 'I thought of trying it myself, if the truth be known.' She turned her huge chocolate-brown eyes up at Eve. 'But I left it too late and, by then, you had stepped in.'

'What are you talking about?'

Chiara smiled, as if she was enjoying herself immensely.

'Oh, didn't you know that I used to be Luca's lover?'

Eve's first reaction was to feel sick, until she told herself to grow up. He was bound to have had lots of lovers and they were bound to have been as beautiful as Chiara.

'No. No, I didn't.'

'In fact...' Chiara's manicured fingernails delved into her slim, neat handbag, and she pulled out a piece of newspaper '...this was the last photograph taken of us together. Would you like to see it?'

No, Eve would not like to see it, but she was not going to appear to be a totally-lacking-in-confidence kind of wife. She even managed a shrug. 'Why not?'

Because Eve was still holding the baby, Chiara

leaned over with the clipping and held it in front of her and Eve could smell the seductive musk of her fragrance.

'Here it is!'

If it had been any other couple, it would have been a pretty unremarkable photo, but it was not any other couple—it was Luca and Chiara. The beautiful people, thought Eve, slightly wistfully—with their jet-dark hair and olive skin and clothes which shrieked of wealth and success. Luca's eyes were narrowed at the camera. She knew that look—caught unawares and irritated. But Chiara was giving it everything she had—her hair tossed back and that big, mega-watt smile showing her perfect white teeth.

And then she noticed the date and her heart missed a beat.

It was the day...

It was the day after Lizzy's birthday.

The very same day that he had come round to Eve's house and tried to make love to her and she had very nearly let him. Dear God, he must have flown straight from her and into Chiara's arms!

In a way, she thanked God that she was holding onto Oliviero, for who knew what her reaction might have been otherwise? She guessed that she must have shown her horror and shock—she could feel all the blood draining from her face and she felt very slightly giddy.

But she somehow managed an equable smile.

'You make a lovely couple,' she said blandly.

It was clearly not the reaction that Chiara had expected, nor wanted. She put the clipping back in her bag.

'Yes,' she said, in an odd kind of voice. 'That's

what everyone said.' She sighed. 'It was a *wonderful* night. But then it was a wonderful relationship.'

Somehow Eve got through the rest of the afternoon, but she did it only by avoiding Luca's eyes wherever possible. She played with the children and she chatted animatedly with the adults, making sure that she was never on her own for him to come and speak to her, and making sure that her face bore a smile of enjoyment at all times.

Even in the car it was easy to maintain the masquerade. She didn't want a scene when he was driving, not with their son strapped in the back.

Luca frowned. 'Are you okay?'

Eve shut her eyes. 'I'm fine,' she said faintly. 'Just had a little too much sun and wine, I think.'

'Go to sleep, then,' he murmured. The powerful car purred along the rural roads and his eyes hardened as he stared ahead. Why the hell had Patricio invited Chiara? Her eyes had been following him round like some beaten puppy and he had felt sorry for the man who had been her companion.

Eve didn't sleep, just lay there, her mind going over and over it. There she had been, marvelling at Luca's restraint. Wondering why a man with such an overpowering sensuality had been able to suppress it.

Well, maybe he hadn't! Maybe that had all just been a ruse. What about the times when he had to slip out—to the shops or to his bank—was that all he was doing? Or was there some luscious lovely like Chiara, all too willing to give him what his wife was not?

Back at the apartment, she went through the motions of bathing and changing—refusing all Luca's offers of help—and she fed Oliviero in a simmering kind of silence.

Luca watched her, his antennae alerted to something, he didn't know what—but there was something about Eve's body language which told him that something was not right.

He waited until she had put the baby to bed, and then he looked up, noted the barely restrained fury on her face.

'So are you going to tell me what the problem is?'

'I should have thought that was perfectly obvious.'

'I am not going to conduct an entire conversation in riddles, Eve!' he snapped.

'Well, then.' She stared at him defiantly, hoping he wouldn't see the great oceans of despair in her eyes. '*I* am clearly the problem.'

He didn't react.

'Go on.'

It all came tumbling out then—all the hurt and longing and the feeling that she was here only because she had trapped him and that, in a way, she had trapped herself, and not just by having a baby. For she had come to learn that the love she felt was not returned, and how could she ever be happy knowing that? And that this might be the cleanest way to end it.

'You slept with Chiara the very day I refused to make love to you!' she accused. 'What happened, Luca? Did you get so stirred up that you had to do it with someone, anyone—that you had to do it with *her*!'

CHAPTER FOURTEEN

LUCA'S voice was like cold, deadly ice. 'Is that the opinion you have formed of me, then, Eve? A man so governed by his hormones that he is unable to control his sexual appetite? And surely if that were the case, then your theory contradicts itself—or no doubt I would have made more than one attempt to seduce you since you have been living here?'

Eve stared at him, her face warm with anger and confusion. Where was the remorse? The shame? The denial? 'What other explanation can there be?'

'Oh, I wonder,' he mocked sardonically.

Amid the hot fires of jealousy and the aching awareness that he had not so much as laid a finger on her since long before their marriage, Luca's look of disdain slowly began to seep into her fuddled brain and to make some kind of sense. She had judged him and found him wanting, choosing to believe the word of a woman she didn't know, without even giving him a chance to defend himself.

'So...you...you didn't?' Her voice sounded tiny, and the world seemed to hang on his answer.

He looked at her, and saw all the insecurity and fears written on her face. Had he been blind to them before? Or had he just chosen not to see? 'Of course I didn't,' he said softly. But he might have done, he supposed. A man less fastidious might have done. Or a man less blown away by an unknown woman in England who had turned him down...

'I guess I was angry that you wouldn't make love to me,' he admitted quietly. His arrogant sexual pride had suffered a wounding blow, but maybe it had needed to. 'Maybe even angrier with myself for having come on so strong.' He gave a half-smile. 'It's not my usual style, Eve.'

No, she couldn't imagine that he needed to.

He remembered back to what now seemed like a lifetime ago, but, of course, it was. 'I told myself that you meant nothing and so, yes, I agreed to see Chiara that night. I suspect that she tipped off the photographers, because when we came out of the restaurant the paparazzi were there. But nothing happened. I dropped her off and I went home. Alone.'

'So why did she say those things?'

'Because she wants me. Because she's jealous of you.'

'Of *me*?' said Eve, in an empty little voice. If only she realised what little there was to be jealous of. 'She said you'd had a wonderful relationship.'

'We had a brief affair—that was all.'

'Which is what ours should have been,' she pointed out painfully. 'Shouldn't it?'

He stared at her, realising how important his next words were. Realising that the truth could hurt, but that didn't mean you should avoid it. 'Who knows?' he said softly. 'No one can see into the future and no one can change the past. But that wasn't the way it turned out, was it, Eve? Things happened. Fate stepped in. We had a baby—'

'And we got married,' she finished. 'A...farce of a marriage.'

'Is that what you think it is?'

'Well, isn't it?'

'It isn't the marriage I want it to be, no,' he said carefully.

'You mean you want us to start having sex?'

He gave a bitter laugh. 'Are you trying to shock me, *cara*? Or anger me? Do you want to enrage me with your bold, flip comments so that I come over there and kiss you and take your clothes off and pull you to the floor and make love to you?' He saw the sudden dull flush which darkened her cheeks and he felt an answering ache which almost tore him in two. 'Oh,' he said softly. 'So you do.'

'Luca,' she said huskily and her tongue snaked out to circle her lips, like a hungry little animal. 'Yes. Yes, of course I want that. Don't you?'

He felt so close to acting out his words that he had to resist the desire with every ounce of self-restraint he possessed.

'No! No, I don't!'

She stared at him in hurt and confusion. This was the rejection she had always feared, but maybe it had been a long time coming. And maybe she needed to know. You couldn't keep hiding from your feelings just because you were afraid they might hurt you. Being mature meant having the courage to confront the real issues.

She stared at him, her voice shaking, willing herself not to cry. 'What, then? What is it that you want, Luca?'

He could talk around it for hours. Quantify and justify and explain it, but in the end there was only one thing he needed to tell her. 'I need to tell you that I love you, Eve,' he said huskily. '*Ti amo*. I love you so very much.'

Eve bit her lip. 'Please don't say that.'

'Why?' His voice was gentle. 'Don't you want me to love you?'

What had she just thought about having courage? 'Yes.'

It was such a soft whisper of a word that he barely heard it. 'Say that again, Eve.'

'Yes. Yes.' She turned her eyes up to him. 'Yes, of course I want you to love me as I love you, but I've wanted it for so long that I'm scared you don't mean it.'

'Oh, I mean it,' he said. 'But this is all new stuff to me, Eve. I have never said it before. Never felt it before.'

For a moment she saw vulnerability written on his face. 'What, never?'

He shook his head and now the aching within him became more than physical. For the first time in his life he felt a great, gaping emotional hole which only Eve could fill. '*Tesora*—'

The haunting, heartfelt term of endearment broke through every last barrier and she crossed the distance between them, only a little distance really, but it felt like the divide between the old life and the new.

'Luca. Dear, darling, sweetest Luca.'

He pulled her into his arms, kissed the top of her head and then tipped her face up to look at his and her green-grey eyes were huge. He saw the tears on her cheeks and he brushed them away with his lips.

'Never cry, *tesora*,' he whispered against her skin. 'Promise me you will never cry again.'

She shook her head. 'I can't promise you that,' she said shakily. 'We might have rows—fierce, terrible rows—and you might make me cry—'

'And will you make me cry, too?' he teased softly.

'You? A big man like you. *Crying?*' But her words faded to nothing when she saw the brightness in his dark eyes and in that moment she saw his vulnerability too and her hug became fierce and she was overwhelmed with love for him. 'Luca,' she whispered. 'Oh, Luca, *please.*'

He knew what she wanted and what he wanted, too. He had waited too long and he could wait no longer. Without another word he picked her up into his arms and carried her into his bedroom.

'I want to see you naked,' he said shakily. He unbuttoned the white skirt and let it fall to her feet. *'Cielo dolce,'* he murmured indistinctly. 'For too many nights have I dreamed of you like this.'

She felt his warm hands on her hips and she felt so dizzy with desire she thought that she might faint. 'I...I know. I've dreamed of it, too.'

'Undress me,' he urged as he slid a delicate little pair of panties down her legs, his fingertips brushing against the silkenness of her thighs and feeling her shiver beneath them.

'I...I...can't,' she breathed helplessly. 'I can barely think, nor breathe, nor feel...' But he took her hand and guided it to his heart.

'Can you feel that?'

The strong, powerful thunder of his blood. Her head fell to his shoulder. 'Yes.' She shuddered against him. 'Oh, yes.'

'That is for you, *cara mia*. All and only for you. Now lift your arms,' he instructed gently, as he would a child, and obediently she did as he said, so that he pulled the T-shirt off and tossed it away, snapping the clasp of her bra open so that her breasts fell free and unfettered. He wanted to take one into his mouth, to suckle and to tease it, but a need even stronger drove him on.

Ruthlessly, he stripped the clothes from his body until they were both naked and then he drew her down onto the bed, smoothing the hair away from her face, looking deep into her eyes.

Luca sighed. 'I want you. So very much.'

There was a split-second silence. 'Then kiss me.'

'I will kiss you until you beg me to kiss you no more,' he promised. But still he gazed at her, as if wanting to prolong this moment, this mind-shattering realisation of all that she had come to mean to him.

Eve lifted her mouth. 'Don't make me wait any more,' she moaned.

He kissed her back, feeling her fingers slide with abandon over his skin as if she was relearning his body by touch alone. 'Greedy woman,' he laughed, with soft delight.

He felt as though there were a million new nerve endings in his body. She could thrill him by the soft whisper of her lips, make him tremble with the wet touch of her tongue. He shuddered, helpless beneath her and then he moved above her and made his mouth move along the moist, erotic pathways of her skin until she cried out.

And when he entered her, he said her name and it was as if he had never made love before—the way people spoke of, but he had never believed could happen. Not to him. A complete communion, he thought dazedly. Afterwards he lay back and stared at the ceiling with eyes which felt new and reborn. 'Oh, Eve,' was all he said.

Eve kissed his elbow. It was a particularly gorgeous elbow. Then she clambered on top of him, her hair spilling untidily all over, some of it on his face, so that he laughed and blew it away.

'Luca?'

'Mmm?'

'How long have you loved me for?'

He picked up another errant strand and thoughtfully twirled it around his finger. 'Honestly?'

'Honestly.'

'If you want me to give you a time and a date, then I cannot,' he admitted. 'It kind of crept up on me. Like being out in the rain. A little drop at first, here and there, so faint that you thought you might have imagined it. And then a little more, and then more still—until suddenly I was standing in a deluge without quite realising how I'd got there!'

She pretended to pout. 'So I'm like a storm?'

'Mmm. Wild and strong and overwhelming.'

'But you knew that I loved you?'

He smiled. It had happened to him too often in his life not to. And as always the realisation had scared him, but this time for very different reasons—not because he wanted to run away from her love, but because he had to be sure he was worthy of it. It would have been easier to have been impetuous, but, caught up in these new and strange emotions, he had used caution. 'Yes, *cara*,' he said softly. 'I knew.'

'And when were you going to get around to telling me you loved me back?' she persisted. 'How long would you have waited? What if we hadn't had that row today—then I would never have known.'

'Oh, yes, you would. I suppose I was waiting for the right moment only, when it happened, it was a wrong moment, really. Not champagne and flowers but a misunderstanding over a jealous woman.'

Eve wriggled luxuriously against him. 'But it brought things to a head.' She yawned.

'Mmm.' He idly put her little finger in his mouth and sucked on it. 'You see, we have done everything the wrong way round, *cara*. At first there was passion and only passion, but before we knew it there was a baby, too.'

'And anger,' she ventured.

He nodded. 'And anger. But no getting to know you. No old-fashioned courtship. No getting to know each other. No trust built nor friendship established. I wanted that and you deserved no less than that— we needed that if we were to share our future.'

It was, she realised, a very matter-of-fact way of looking at it, but she didn't mind. And really—when you thought about it—it made sense. For marriage was a contract as well as a love affair.

'So this,' she said as a glorious thought occurred to her. 'This is really our honeymoon?'

'It sure is.' He smoothed the flat of his hand over her bottom.

'And…and how long will it last?'

'How does for ever sound?' he questioned huskily as his mouth moved down to cover hers.

EPILOGUE

THE afternoon sun was soft and so was the warm breeze which ruffled the hair of the two women as they sat watching the children play.

'Oh, Eve,' sighed Lizzy. 'This is just so-o-o beautiful.'

Eve looked around her, trying to see it through her friend's eyes, recalling her gasp of joy when Luca had first brought her here.

The house in Viale Monte Pincio was up in the mountains outside Rome and only an hour-and-a-half drive away from the city, but it was like being in another world. The entrance to the garden was through a tall, wrought-iron gate and there was an abundance of pine trees and bay bushes and many fruits growing there. Blackcurrant, raspberries, lemon and cherries.

'Yes,' she agreed quietly. 'So very beautiful.'

On the grass, among the daisies, Kesi played with Oliviero. Luca and Michael had gone to find some cool drinks while Eve and Lizzy were sitting idly watching them, listening to the buzz of the bees and the call of the birds.

'You're so happy,' Lizzy observed.

'How could I not be?' said Eve simply. 'I feel like I've come home.'

She and Luca had both come round to the way of thinking that maybe the apartment wasn't the best place for Oliviero to grow up in. They had decided to buy a house in the city itself, but more and more they came here, to this quiet, rural retreat. For the first time in his life Luca was taking time out to smell the roses. And the coffee. And proving to be the most hands-on father that Eve could ever have wished or hoped for.

'And Luca doesn't miss his apartment?'

'Not at all.' Eve shook her head. 'Actually, he was the one who brought up the subject about moving. We talked about it and decided that, lovely as it is, it wasn't really a family home.'

Lizzy sat up, which wasn't easy as she was pregnant and lying in a deckchair. 'You don't mean you're having another baby?' she questioned excitedly.

Eve giggled. 'No. Not yet. Maybe not for a while yet.' She and Luca adored their son with all their hearts but knew that another pregnancy would bring about another change and felt that they had had quite enough change for the time being! They were enjoying their life, their son and their love. They were content to wait. And see.

'And you don't miss working?' Lizzy questioned.

Eve shook her head. 'Not a bit. Luca has friends in the television industry over here and, now that my Italian is quite passable, it wasn't inconceivable that I could get a job in the business again—maybe editing or producing. *Grazie, il mio uomo piccolo*!' This to Oliviero who had just tottered up and planted a battered daisy in his mother's lap, before tottering off again. 'But I didn't want to,' she finished. 'Luca is around a lot and I...well, I love motherhood. I love being a wife. Luca's wife. Who could ask for anything more?'

'Not even a drink, *il mio angelo*?' questioned the deep silken voice behind her which always had the power to make her shiver with longing.

She smiled up at him. 'Oh, I think I could probably manage a drink!'

Michael flopped down on a deckchair and Luca put the tray down before sinking to the grass, leaning his head lazily against Eve's knees, and she ruffled his hair as she so loved to.

'It seems a long way from the Hamble,' observed Lizzy sleepily.

'A long way from anywhere. It's just so peaceful,' yawned her husband. 'Well, you're both very lucky, I must say.'

Luca glanced up at Eve and their eyes met in a long, precious moment. Yes, they were lucky enough to have the money to buy them houses in Italy, and to keep Eve's on back in England, too. But the luckiest thing was to have found each other. It didn't matter where they lived—they could make anywhere their home, just as long as they were together.

For they had both discovered that a relationship didn't have to have a perfect beginning to have the perfect ending.

THE ITALIAN'S
TOKEN WIFE

by

Julia James

Julia James lives in England with her family. Mills & Boon® were the first 'grown up' books she read as a teenager, alongside Georgette Heyer and Daphne du Maurier, and she's been reading them ever since. Julia adores the English and Celtic countryside, in all its seasons, and is fascinated by all things historical, from castles to cottages. She also has a special love for the Mediterranean – 'The most perfect landscape after England'! – and she considers both ideal settings for romance stories. In between writing she enjoys walking, gardening, needlework, baking extremely gooey cakes and trying to stay fit!

Look out for Julia James's exciting new novel *Greek Tycoon, Waitress Wife* out in September 2008 from Mills & Boon® Modern™.

CHAPTER ONE

'WHAT the hell do you mean, you won't sign?'

Rafaello di Viscenti glared down at the woman in his bed. She was a voluptuous blonde with flowing locks and celestial blue eyes, her naked body scantily covered by the duvet.

Amanda Bonham slid one slim, exposed thigh over the other, and widened her eyes.

'It's so *sordid*, darling—signing a pre-nup,' she said purringly.

Rafaello's sculpted mouth tightened.

'You agreed to all the terms in the pre-nup. Your lawyer went through it with me. Why are you balking at it now?'

Amanda pouted up at him. 'Raf, darling, we don't need a pre-nup! Wasn't last night good for you?' Her voice had gone husky, and she let a little smile play around her generous mouth. 'I can make it that good—every night.'

She nestled back into the pillows invitingly and slid her legs again, simultaneously letting the duvet slip to reveal one delectable breast.

'I can make it that good right now,' she went on, her eyes lingering over her lover's lean, honed body, with her sensual gaze openly stripping him of his extremely expensive hand-made suit of such superbly elegant tailoring that it screamed a top designer name.

Rafaello slashed an impatient hand through the air. He was immune to Amanda's plentiful bedroom charms—he'd had his fill of them for most of the night, and enough was enough.

'I don't have time for this, Amanda. Just sign the damn

document, as you said you would—' In his obvious anger his Italian accent was pronounced.

The inviting look vanished from the blue eyes, which were suddenly as hard as jewels.

'No,' said Amanda, yanking the duvet over her breast with a sharp motion. 'You want to marry me—you do it without a ridiculous pre-nuptial contract.'

Her lush mouth set in an obstinate line.

Rafaello swore beneath his breath, drawing on his extensive range of native Italian vocabulary unfit for polite society. He really, really could do without this.

His obsidian eyes bored into his bride-to-be.

'Amanda, *cara*,' he said with heavy patience, 'I have explained this to you already. I want a temporary bride only—you've gone into this with your eyes open; I have never attempted to deceive you. I want a bride for six months and then a swift, painless divorce. In exchange you get living expenses—very generous ones—for half a year, following one brief…very brief…visit to Italy, and you leave the marriage with a lavish pay-off. A pre-agreed lavish pay-off. *Capisce?*'

'Oh, I *capisce* all right!' Amanda's voice sounded hard. 'And now you can *capisce* me! The only pre-nup I'll sign is one with twice the pay-off!'

Rafaello stilled. So that was the way it was. She was upping the ante. He should have seen it coming. Amanda Bonham might be the ultimate airhead, but she had a homing instinct for money.

But no one, *no one* manipulated him—not this avaricious bimbo, not his *perdittione* father. *No one.*

A shutter came down over his face, and his olive-toned features became expressionless.

'Too bad.' His voice was implacable. Anyone who had ever done business with him would have known at that point to back off and give in if they still wanted to do a deal with Rafaello di Viscenti. Amanda was not so wise. Her blue eyes flashed.

'Seems to me you don't have a choice, Rafaello, *cara*,' she said bitingly. 'You need a wife in a hurry—well, that's fine by me—but I won't be hemmed in by a stupid pre-nup!'

He answered with a careless shrug as he made to turn away. 'Your choice.' He glanced back at her. 'I'll phone for a taxi for you.'

He walked across to the pier table set against the wall of the bedroom and picked up his mobile. Amanda scrambled out of bed.

'Now, wait just a minute—' she began.

Unperturbed, Rafaello went on punching numbers into the phone.

'Deal's off, *cara*. Better get your clothes on.'

A hand clawed over the fine suiting of his sleeve.

'You can't do this. You need me.'

He brushed her off as though she were a pesky fly.

'Wrong.' There was adamantine beneath the accent. 'Joe?' His voice changed. 'Call a cab, will you? About ten minutes.'

He glanced back to where the naked blonde stood quivering in outrage in his bedroom. Casually he slipped the phone inside his breast pocket.

'You can cool down under a shower—but make it quick.'

He turned to head to the double doors that led out into the rest of the apartment.

'And just *what* do you think you're going to do for a precious bride, huh?'

The voice behind him was taunting, and vicious. He didn't even bother to turn round.

'I'm going to marry the first woman I see,' he answered silkily, and was gone.

Magda flexed her tired fingers in the rubber gloves and set to work in the lavish marble-walled bathroom, wishing she didn't feel like death warmed up. Benji had been awake for two hours in the night—his sleep patterns were hopeless—but at least, she thought, smothering a yawn and brushing back a rogue wisp of hair from her forehead with the back of her wrist as she paused in rubbing at the porcelain with her cleaning sponge, it meant he was sleeping now.

A frown furrowed her brow. She wasn't going to be able to keep going with this job for much longer, she knew. While Benji had been younger it had been simple enough to carry him round with her, propping him up in his folding lightweight baby chair while she cleaned other people's luxury apartments, but now he was toddling he hated being strapped in and confined. He wanted to be out exploring—but in apartments like this, where everything from the carpets to the saucepans was excruciatingly expensive, that was just impossible.

She squirted cleaning fluid under the rim and sighed again. What kind of job could you do with a toddler in tow? Leaving him with a minder while she worked was pointless—what she earned would go to pay for the childcare. If she had any kind of decent accommodation she could be a childminder herself, and make some money by looking after other people's children as well as her own little boy, but what mother would want to park her child in the dump she lived in? Even she hated Benji being in the drab, dingy bedsit, and took him out and about as much as she could. She'd grown adept at making the hours pass in places like libraries, parks and supermarkets—anywhere that was free.

A smile softened her tired face. Benji—the light of her life, the joy of her heart. Her dearest, dearest son...

He was worth everything, *everything* to her, and there was nothing she would not do, she vowed, for his sake.

Rafaello strode angrily across the wide landing towards the open-tread staircase that led down to the reception level of the duplex apartment. Damn Amanda for trying to hold him to ransom. And damn his father for putting him in this impossible position in the first place.

His jaw tightened. Why couldn't his father accept there was no way he was going to be forced to marry his cousin Lucia and provide the rich husband she craved? Oh, she had looks, all right, but she was vain and avaricious and her temper was vicious—though she veiled it successfully enough from his father, who was now convinced she would make the perfect bride for his recalcitrant son. When orders and lamentations hadn't worked, his father had stooped to the final threat—selling Viscenti AG from under his son's nose. *Dio*, Lucia knew every weak spot a man had—from his father's obsession with getting the next-generation Viscenti heir to his own determination to keep Viscenti AG in the family. She'd played on both like a maestro.

His father's parting words rang in Rafaello's ears. 'I want you married or I sell up. And don't think I won't. But—' the older man's voice had turned cunning '—present your bride to me before your thirtieth birthday and I make the company over to you the same day.'

Well, thought Rafaello grimly, he would, indeed, present his bride to his father on his thirtieth birthday. But not the bride his parent had in mind…

A bride that would meet the letter of his father's ultimatum, but nothing more.

Anger spurted through him again. Amanda Bonham would have been the perfect bride to parade in front of his father—a fitting punishment for forcing his son to this pass. She'd have sent the old man's blood pressure sky-high. A born bimbo, with hair longer than her skirts and nothing between her ears except conceit in her own appearance and a total devotion to spending her innumerable lovers' money.

And now she'd blown it and he was back to square one.

Looking for a bride who would infuriate his father and wipe the smirk off Lucia's face. A frown crossed his brow. It had been all very well calling Amanda's bluff just now, but getting hold of a bride in a handful of weeks was going to be a challenge—even for him.

He walked down the stairs with a lithe, rapid step, a closed, brooding look on his face—and stopped dead.

There was a baby asleep in the middle of the hallway.

Magda gave a final wipe to the pedestal, and reached into her cleaning box for the bottle of toilet freshener. At least bathrooms in luxury apartments were a joy to clean. All the fittings were new and gleaming—and top quality, of course. On the other hand, in luxury apartments there were always an awful lot of bathrooms—one per bedroom plus a guest WC like this one, tucked discreetly off the huge entrance hall.

For a moment she wondered what it must be like to live in an apartment like this. To be so rich you could have a two-storeyed flat as big as a house, overlooking the River Thames, with a terrace as big as a garden. The rich, Magda thought wryly, really were different.

Not that she ever saw the inhabitants. Cleaners were only allowed into the apartments when the owners were absent.

She flicked open the cap of the toilet freshener bottle and upended it, ready to squirt the contents generously into the bowl.

'What are you doing here?'

The deep, displeased voice behind her came out of the blue, and made her jump out of her skin. The reflex action made her squeeze the bottle prematurely, and turquoise fluid spurted out of the bottle onto the marble floor.

With a cry of dismay Magda fell on the blue puddle and mopped it furiously with her cleaning sponge.

'I spoke to you—answer me!'

The voice behind her sounded even more displeased. Hurriedly Magda swivelled round, and stared up.

A man stood in the doorway of the bathroom, looking down at her. Magda stared back, blinking blindly. Her dismay deepened into horror. The apartment was supposed to be empty. The caretaker had told her so. Yet here, obviously, was someone who definitely did *not* use service lifts.

And he was quite plainly furious. With dismay etched on every feature, she just went on kneeling beside the toilet pedestal, cleaning sponge in her hand.

'I'm very sorry, sir,' she managed to croak, knowing she had to sound servile for someone like this, even though it was not her fault that she was where she apparently should not have been. 'I was told it was all right to clean in here this morning.'

The man's mouth tightened.

'There is a baby in the hall,' he informed her.

With one part of her brain Magda registered that the man could not be English. Not only was his skin tone too olive-hued, but his voice was definitely accented. Spanish? Italian? Too pale to be Middle-Eastern, he must definitely be Mediterranean, she decided.

'Well?' The interrogative demand came again.

Clumsily Magda scrambled to her feet. She could not go on kneeling on the floor indefinitely.

'He's mine,' she blurted.

Something that might have been a flash of irritation showed in the man's dark eyes.

'So I had assumed. What is it doing there? This is no place for a baby!'

A child that age should be at home, not being dragged around at this hour of the day? What kind of mother was this girl? Irresponsible, obviously!

'I'm very sorry,' she said again, swallowing, hoping some more abject servility would soften his annoyance at finding her cleaning when he was in residence. Clearly he

was furious his pristine apartment was being cluttered up
by something as messy as a baby. She bent to pick up her
cleaning box, cast a swift glance around the bathroom to
make sure it was decent, and said, as meekly as she could
manage, 'I'll go now, sir. I'm very sorry for having disturbed you.'

She made for the door and he stood aside to let her pass.
It was uncomfortable passing him so close. He was so immaculately attired, obviously freshly washed and showered,
and she had just spent several hours cleaning. She was dirty
and sweaty, and she had a horrible feeling she smelt as bad
as she felt. She hurried out to Benji, who, blessedly, was
still asleep, and made to scoop up his chair.

'Wait!'

The order was imperative, and Magda halted instinctively, Benji a heavy weight on her arm. Hesitantly she
turned round.

The man was looking at her. Staring at her.

Magda froze, as if she were a rabbit caught in headlights.
Or rather an antelope realising a leopard had just come out
of the undergrowth.

Oh, help, she thought silently. Now what?

Rafaello let his gaze rest on the girl. She was slightly built,
drab in the extreme, with hair the colour of mud and unmemorable features. She also—his nose wrinkled in disdain—smelt of sweat and cleaning fluids. There was a smut
of dirt on her cheek. She looked about twenty or so.

He found himself glancing at her hands. They were covered by yellow rubber gloves. He frowned. His gaze went
back to her face. She was looking at him with a look of
deepest apprehension.

'You don't have to bolt like a frightened rabbit,' he said.
Deliberately he made his voice less brusque, though it
didn't seem to alter her expression a jot. She still stood

there, poised for flight, baby in one hand, cleaning materials in the other.

Rafaello took a couple of steps towards her.

'Tell me—are you married?'

The brusqueness was back in his voice. He didn't mean it to be, but it was. It was because part of his mind was telling him that he was completely mad, thinking what he was thinking. But he was thinking it all the same...

A blank look came into the girl's eyes, as if he had asked her an unintelligible question.

'Well?' demanded Rafaello. The woman seemed beyond answering him.

Jerkily, the woman shook her head, her eyes still with that fixed, blank look to them. Rafaello's gaze focussed on her more intently. So, she wasn't married—he hadn't thought so, even without being able to see if she wore a wedding ring. And despite the baby.

His eyes glanced across to the sleeping infant. He wasn't any good at telling the ages of babies, but this one looked quite big. Too big for that chair, in fact. It was dark-haired, head lolling forward, totally out for the count.

But a baby was good—however irresponsible the mother! A baby was very good, he mused consideringly. So was the rest of her. Once again his eyes flickered over her, taking in the full drabness of her appearance, and he thought he could see her wince.

'Boyfriend?'

Her eyes widened and then went even blanker. With the same jerky movement she shook her head. She also, Rafaello spotted, edged very slightly closer to the front door. He frowned. Why was she being so jumpy?

'I have a business proposition to put to you.' His voice was clipped as he banked down the anger at his predicament that still roiled within him like an injured tiger.

A noise came from her that might have been a whimper, but that seemed unlikely since there was no reason for such a sound. Rafaello walked to the door leading into the kitchen and held it open with the flat of his hand.

'In here.' He gestured.

The strangled croaking noise came again, and this time the woman definitely shrank back towards the door.

'I have to go!' Her voice came out high and squawky. 'I'm very sorry!'

Rafaello frowned again. Just then a door slammed on the upper floor. The next moment Amanda was descending as fast as her four-inch heels and very tight short skirt would permit. As she saw the tableau below her face lit up with a vicious smile.

'Why, Raf, darling,' she purred venomously, 'how galling for you. ''The first woman I see''.' She gave a bad imitation of his Italian accent. 'And that's what you get. Bad luck.'

The man's accented voice answered the woman. He was purring, too, but it was the purr of a big cat, and it made the hairs stand up on the nape of Magda's neck.

'Yes, indeed, Amanda, *cara*, and she is just perfect for me.'

The look that crossed the other woman's face was a picture. Fury mingled with disbelief.

'You're joking. You have to be.'

For his answer, Rafaello simply lifted one darkly arched eyebrow and gave the woman a mocking look.

'Your taxi will be waiting downstairs, *cara*. Time to go.'

For a moment the woman just stood there, fizzing with fury. Then with a tightening of her face she marched to the front door, shoved Magda aside, and flung it open.

'Wait!' squawked Magda, and tried to rush after her. What possible reason could the apartment owner have for wanting to know if she were married or had a boyfriend? No good ones she could think of—and plenty that were bad. She'd heard enough stories from other cleaners about men who liked forcing their attentions on vulnerable women in lowly jobs.

'Get away from me, you disgusting creature,' snapped the other woman. She stormed off. Desperately Magda tried to catch the front door, but it was taken from her abruptly.

'I said I had a business proposition for you. Have the courtesy to hear me out.' The accented voice dropped into a sardonic range. 'It could be to your financial advantage.'

Magda flung him a terrified look. Oh, God, she was right. He was about to make some kind of obscene proposition. 'No, thank you—I don't do that sort of thing.'

The man frowned again. 'You do not know what I am about to ask you,' he countered brusquely.

'Whatever it is, I don't do it. I'm just a cleaner. It's all I do.' Her voice was a squawk again. 'Please, let me go—please. I do the cleaning. That's all.'

The man's expression changed suddenly, as if he finally realised the reason for her near panic.

'You misunderstand me.' His voice was arctic. 'The business proposition I want you to consider has nothing to do with sex.'

Magda stared at him, taking in his expensive male gorgeousness. Reality came back with a vengeance. Of course a man like him would not sexually proposition a woman like her. Seeing herself through those disdainful eyes, suddenly she felt as if she were two inches high. Mortification flooded through her.

Abruptly, she felt the weight of her cleaning box taken from her.

'Come into the kitchen,' said the man, 'and I will explain.'

Magda sat, completely frozen, on one of the high stools set against the kitchen bar. Benji miraculously slept on, snug in his baby chair on the floor.

'Say…say that again?' she asked faintly.

'I will pay you the sum of one hundred thousand pounds,' the man spelt out in clipped, accented tones, 'for you to be married to me—quite legally—for six months, at the end of which period we shall file for divorce by mutual consent. You will need to accompany me to Italy for…legal reasons. Then you will return here, and your living expenses will be paid by me. On our divorce you will receive one hundred thousand pounds, no more. Do you understand?'

No, thought Magda. I don't understand. All I understand is that you're nuts.

But it seemed unwise to point this out to the man sitting on the other side of the bar from her. She was acutely, utterly uncomfortable being here. And not just because the man was making such an absurd proposition to her.

It was also because he was, quite simply, the most devastating male she had ever seen—inside or outside the covers of a glossy magazine. He had lean, slim looks, very Italian, but with an edge about him that kept his heart-stoppingly handsome face from looking soft. He had beauty, all right, but it was male beauty, honed and planed, and the long eyelashes swept past obsidian eyes that had an incredibly dangerous appeal to them.

'You don't believe me, do you?'

The question caught her on the hop, interrupting her rapt, if surreptitious gazing at him, and all she could do was open her mouth and then close it again.

A tight, humourless smile twisted at his mouth, changing the angles of his face. Something detonated deep inside Magda, but she had no time to pay any attention to it. He was speaking again.

'I would be the first to concede the situation is…bizarre. But, nevertheless—' he spread his hands above the bar, and Magda noticed how beautiful they were, long and slender, with a steely strength to them despite their immaculate manicure '—I do, as it happens, require a wife at very short notice, for a very particular purpose. Perhaps I should point out,' he went on, in a voice that made her feel ashamed of her own lack of physical appeal in the presence of a man with such a super-abundance of it, 'that the marriage will be in name only. Tell me, do you have a passport?'

Magda shook her head. A look of irritation crossed the man's face, then he moved his right hand dismissively. 'No matter. These things can be arranged in time. Now, what about your child's father? Is he still on the scene?'

Magda tried to think what on earth to say, but failed miserably.

'I thought not.' The expression of unconcealed disdain for her child's fatherless state silenced her even more than her inability to provide an answer under such circumstances. 'But that is all to the good,' he swept on. 'He will not interfere.'

A dark glance swept over her, as if he were making some kind of final internal decision. 'So, altogether, I can see no obstacles to what I propose—you are clearly extremely suitable.'

Panic struck Magda. He was sweeping ahead, dragging her along as if she were nothing more than a tin can rattling on a piece of string behind a racing car. She had to stop all this right now. It was too absurd for words.

'Please,' she cut in, 'I'm not suitable at all, really. And I'm sorry, but I have to go now. I have other apartments to clean and I'm running late—'

She didn't, this was the last one, but there was no need to let him know that.

His voice came silkily.

'If you accept my proposition you will never clean another apartment in your life. For a woman of your background you will live in comfortable circumstances—if you are financially prudent—for several years simply on what I shall pay you for six months of your life.'

Emotions warred inside Magda. Uppermost was umbrage

at the way he had said so disdainfully 'a woman of your background', as though she came from a different species of humanity. But beneath that, forcing its way to the surface, was something more powerful.

Temptation.

Comfortable circumstances...

The phrase jumped out at her. What on earth had the man said—something about a hundred thousand pounds? It couldn't be true. The thought of so much money was beyond her. With a hundred thousand pounds she could move out of London, buy a flat, even a little house, stop having to depend on state income support, stop work, look after Benji properly...plan for the future.

For a moment, so intense that it hurt, she had a vision of herself and Benji in a nice little house somewhere, with a little garden, on a nice road, and nice families all around. Nothing spectacular, just normal and ordinary and...nice. Somewhere decent to bring him up. Somewhere that was a real home.

She saw herself in the kitchen, baking cakes, while she watched Benji tricycle round a little paved patio, with a swing-set on the lawn beyond, a cat snoozing on the windowsill, washing hanging on the line. With next-door neighbours who had children, and hung up their washing, and baked cakes. Who lived normal, ordinary lives.

An ache of longing so deep inside it made her feel weak swept through her.

Across the bar, Rafaello's dark eyes narrowed. She was taking the bait; he could see. It had been hard work to get her to this point—far harder than he had envisaged. But at last she was responding.

And the more time and effort he put into persuading her, the more he was convinced she was perfect for the job.

Dio, but his father would be apoplectic! His son presenting him with a bride who had a fatherless kid in tow and who cleaned toilets for a living. Who looked as drab and plain as the back end of a bus. That would teach him to try and force his hand—

Magda saw the gleam of triumph in the obsidian eyes and quailed. She must be insane even to *think* of thinking about what he had offered her! A hundred thousand pounds—it was ridiculous. It was absurd. Almost as absurd as the notion of a female like her marrying a man like that…for whatever lunatic reason.

'I really do have to go,' she said with a rush, and got to her feet. As she did so she must have jogged Benji's chair, because he gave a sudden start and woke up. Immediately he gave out a little wail. Magda stooped down and cupped his cheek. 'It's OK, Benji. Mum's here.'

The wail stopped, and Benji reached out one of his little hands and patted her face. Then, promptly, he started wriggling mightily, trying to free himself from his bonds.

'It's all right, muffin, we're just going.' She hefted him up onto her arm, shifting her leg to balance the weight. She picked up her cleaning box with her other hand.

'I'll…er…let myself out…' she said awkwardly to the man who had just asked her to marry him, and who was still sitting on the other side of the bar, watching her through assessing eyes.

'A hundred thousand pounds. No more cleaning. No more having to take your son around like this. It's no life for him.'

His words fell like stones into her conscience—pricking it and destroying it at the same time.

'This isn't real,' she said suddenly, her voice sounding harsh. 'It can't be. It's just nuts, the whole thing!'

The thin, humourless smile twisted his mouth again. 'If it's any comfort, I feel the same way. But—' he took a deep, sharply inhaled breath '—if I don't turn up next month with a wife, everything I have worked for will be wasted. And I will not permit that.'

There was a chill in his words as he finished that made her shiver. But what could she say?

Nothing. She could only go. At her side, Benji wriggled and started to whimper.

'I'm sorry,' she said helplessly, but whether to Benji or this unbelievable man with his unbelievable proposition, she didn't know.

Then she got out of the apartment like a bat out of hell.

Music thumped through the thin walls of the bedsit, pounding through Magda's head. She'd had a headache all day, ever since finally making her escape from that madman's apartment.

But what he had said to her was driving her mad as well. She kept hearing it in her head—a hundred thousand pounds, a hundred thousand pounds. It drummed like the bass shuddering through from next door, tolled like a bell condemning her to a life of dreary, grinding, no-hope poverty.

Would she ever get a decent home of her own? The council waiting list was endless, and in the meantime she was stuck here, in this bleak, grimy bedsit. When Benji had been a baby it hadn't been so bad. But now that he was getting older his horizons were broadening—he needed more space; he needed a proper home. This wasn't a home—it never could be—it was barely a roof over their heads.

Not that she was ungrateful. Dear God, single mothers in other parts of the world could die in a gutter with their children without anyone caring. At least here, the state system, however imperfect, provided an umbrella for her. Not that she hadn't been pressed to give Benji up for adoption.

'Life as a single mother is very hard, Miss Jones,' the social worker had said to her. 'Even with state support. You will have a much better chance to make something of yourself without such an encumbrance.'

Encumbrance. That was the word that had done it. Made her stand up, newborn baby in her arms, and say tightly, 'Benji stays with me!'

Encumbrances. She knew all about them.

She'd been one herself. An encumbrance so great that the woman who had given birth to her had left her to die in an alley.

Well, no one, *no one*—neither man nor God—was going to take Benji from her!

Through the wall the music pounded, far too loud. None of the residents dared complain. The man with the ghetto-blaster was on drugs, everyone knew that, and could turn ugly at the drop of a pin. Eventually he would turn it off, but often not till the early hours. No wonder Benji had broken sleep patterns.

Knowing there was no way she could get him to sleep, even though it was gone eight in the evening, Magda let him play. He was sitting beside her on the lumpy bed, quite happily posting shapes through the holes in a plastic tower and gurgling with pleasure every time he got it right. It was a good toy, and Magda had been pleased to find it in a charity shop. All Benji's toys and clothes—and her own clothes and possessions—came from charity shops and jumble sales.

As she played with him, trying to ignore the pounding music, her mind went round and round, thinking about that extraordinary encounter this morning.

Had it actually happened? Had a man who looked like every woman's fantasy Latin millionaire really suggested she marry him for six months and thereby earn a hundred thousand pounds? It was so insane surely it couldn't have happened.

The knock on her door made her start. On the bed, Benji looked round interrogatively. The knock came again.

'Miss Jones?'

The voice was muffled and she could hardly hear it

through the racket coming from next door. Was it the land-lord? He turned up from time to time to check up on his property, from which he made a substantial living by letting it out to those on state benefits. Cautiously she went to the door. She'd fitted a chain herself, not feeling in the slightest secure with neighbours like hers.

Bracing her weight against the back of the door, ready to slam it shut, she opened it a crack.

'Yes?'

'It's Rafaello di Viscenti. We spoke this morning. Please be so good as to admit me.'

CHAPTER TWO

TOTAL astonishment made her obey. As she opened the door to him Rafaello experienced a momentary qualm. Could he really go through with this? Marry this…this… what was the English word for it…? Skivvy? Even for the reasons he had. Seeing her again brought home just how dire she was. She was wearing a saggy sweatshirt and baggy trousers, her stringy, mud-coloured hair was scraped back, and her face was gaunt, with hollows under her eyes. She was, he could safely say, the most physically repellent female he'd ever set eyes on.

But that is what makes her so perfect. OK, so she was the antithesis of Amanda, his first choice, but now, instead of a sexy, airhead bimbo he could take home this plain-as-sin, single mother! It would work just as well—if not better.

Besides—the thought came to him with a stab of dis-comfort as his quick glance took in the dump she lived in and finally settled on the baby sitting on the bed, staring at him with big, chocolate eyes—she could certainly do with the money more than Amanda could…

'What…what are you doing here? How…how did you find me?'

The girl was stammering, clearly in a state of shock. Rafaello stepped inside and shut the door behind him. She shrank back, getting between him and the baby.

Rafaello frowned. *Dio*, did she think he was going to harm her child?

'There is no need to panic,' he said in a dry voice. 'I found you, Miss Jones, through the cleaning agency you work for, that is all. And I have been waiting to speak to

23

you again all day. You have only just been reported back here. Where have you been?'

He made it sound as if she'd been absent without leave.

'Out,' said Magda faintly, backing away to the bed so she could snatch up Benji in a moment if she had to. 'I don't spend much time here.'

Her visitor made a derisive noise in his throat. 'That I can understand. Where is that music coming from?' he demanded, glaring around.

'The room next door. He likes it loud.'

'It is intolerable!' announced Rafaello.

Yes, agreed Magda, but all the same I have to tolerate it, and so does everyone else in the house. She was still in a state of shock, she knew. She had almost persuaded herself that the unbelievable events of the morning had never happened. Now, like something out of a dream, the man was standing in front of her again.

Rafaello di Viscenti… The name rolled around her brain like a verbal caress. The name suited him absolutely, she realised, perfectly complementing the image he presented of the luxury-class Italian male.

She blinked, realising she was staring at him gormlessly. He crossed to the table in the room, which served as dining table and general work surface, and placed an elegant leather document case down upon it, from which he proceeded to withdraw a wad of documents.

'I have had the requisite papers drawn up,' he informed her. 'Please read them before you sign them.'

Magda swallowed. 'Er…I'm not signing anything, Mr Viscenti.'

'Di Viscenti,' he said. 'You will be Signora di Viscenti. You must learn the correct form of address.'

Magda rubbed the suddenly damp palms of her hands surreptitiously on her trousers. 'Um…Mr di Viscenti, I…er…I…er…don't think I can help you. Really. It's all a bit too…er…*weird* for me…'

She cast around in her mind desperately, trying to find a tactful way of saying that the whole thing was so flaky she wouldn't touch it with a bargepole.

His arched eyebrows rose. 'Weird?' he echoed. Then, brusquely, he nodded. 'Yes, it is weird, Miss Jones. But, as I explained to you this morning, I have no choice—it is a matter of who controls our family business, Viscenti AG, the details of which need not trouble you. But it is sufficient reason for me to require a very temporary marriage, under very controlled circumstances, to meet certain…conditions…that amount to nothing more than an empty legality. It is a mere formal exercise for which, unfortunately, my marriage—even though a temporary one—is necessary.'

'But why to me?' she burst out. 'A man like you could pick any woman to marry.'

Rafaello accepted the ingenuous compliment as nothing more than the obvious. 'Think of my proposition not as a marriage, but as a job, Miss Jones. A very temporary job.' His voice became dry. 'That was something the previous…candidate…found difficult to accept.' He made a very Italian gesture with his hand. 'The woman you encountered this morning?' he prompted.

'You were going to marry *her*?'

'Yes. Unfortunately she…withdrew at the last moment. Hence,' he went on with heavy civility, 'my urgent need for a replacement. I must marry as soon as possible.'

'But why *me*?' Magda persisted. It still seemed so totally absurd. However, she had to admit that the knowledge that he had been on the point of entering into this weird marriage he wanted with that underdressed cow who had stormed out of his apartment this morning did make what he was proposing more credible. But it still left his choice of herself as a replacement incredible. After all, surely a man like that would know women like that first one by the score.

'Because there is one essential difference between you…and women like her. Amanda *wanted* the money I was going to pay her. You…' He paused and looked at her, and his eyes suddenly seemed to see right into the heart of her. 'You *need* the money. That makes you more… reliable.'

Magda stilled.

Remorselessly he went on.

'You do need the money, Miss Jones. You need it desperately. You need it to save you—and your child.' His dark eyes held hers, holding her as if he were the devil himself. Tempting her beyond endurance. 'You can't go on living here—you know you can't. You have to get out— you know that. My money will let you do that. It's a life-raft for you—and your child. Take it—take the money I'm offering you.'

Her face had paled. He could see the emotions working. Ruthlessly, as if he were driving yet another hard-nosed business deal, he pressed his advantage. The thump of the music vibrated in every stick of furniture in the shabby bedsit.

'I hold the key to a new life for you—a new future—in exchange for four weeks of your life now. That's all I ask of you in exchange. A month in my company—and then you are free. Free—with enough money to get you out of here for ever…'

His eyes were boring into hers. She couldn't think, couldn't feel. Could hardly breathe.

'I…I don't know who you are… You could be anyone…' Her voice was faint.

His chin tilted with an inborn arrogance that had been bred into his genes. She could see that.

'I am Rafaello di Viscenti. The di Viscentis are a family of the utmost respectability and antiquity. I am chief executive of Viscenti AG. It is a company valued at well over four hundred million euros. I do not usually—' there was a distinct bite in his voice '—have to present my credentials.'

Magda swallowed. 'Yes, well,' she mumbled, 'I don't exactly move in those circles…'

'And the offer I have made you,' he went on, with that same edge of hauteur in his voice, 'is exactly what I have outlined to you. There are no hidden clauses, no tricks to deceive you. You may talk everything through with my lawyers if you wish. What is in those papers—' he gestured with his hand to the documents on the table '—is what you will get. Now, tell me, if you please, what is stopping you from signing them?'

You, she wanted to shout. It's *you*. She stared at him wildly. I can't marry a man who looks like you, who's as rich as you, who's as gorgeous as you—I can't marry a man, no matter what for, or how temporarily, who looks as if he's stepped out of a celebrity mag. It's absurd. It's nuts. It's…

A wail distracted her. Benji, bored with posting shapes, had knocked over the tower and started to howl. Automatically Magda collapsed back on the bed and lifted him up to her knees, hugging his firm little body. The sobs ceased, and Benji twisted round in her lap to pay some attention to the stranger in the middle of the room. Magda's arms wrapped round him, and she felt his little heart beat against hers.

'A hundred thousand pounds,' said Rafaello softly. 'Think…*think*…what you could do with it…'

Magda's body started to rock… Go away, she thought desperately, *go away*. Take your designer suit and your expensive briefcase and go…go before I give in, before you tempt me like Lucifer himself…

'You wouldn't be doing it for yourself. You'd be doing it for your baby.'

She shut her eyes, trying to block out that soft, seductive voice.

'If I walk out now—never to come back—how will you live with yourself? Knowing you turned down the chance to get your baby out of here, for ever?'

She went on rocking, her arms wrapped so closely around Benji that he began to protest.

'Four weeks—no more than that—in my family home in Italy, which is very respectable, Miss Jones, I do assure you—and then you're free.'

'Benji comes with me.' Her voice was high-pitched.

Rafaello spread his hands. 'Of course the baby comes with you—that is essential.' It wasn't necessary to spell out to her just why his bride should arrive accoutred with a fatherless child. 'You just have to sign the papers, that's all you have to do…' He slid his hand inside his breast pocket, taking out a gold fountain pen, slipping off the top, proffering it to her. 'Come—'

There was an imperiousness in his voice she could not resist. Slowly, as if she was sleepwalking, she slid Benji from her lap back on to the bed, ignoring his wail of protest. Slowly, very slowly, she got to her feet. It wasn't real. None of this was real. She'd wake up in a moment and find it had all been a dream.

He held the pen out to her. Numbly she took it. Numbly she looked down at the table, to where he was turning the documents to the last page and placing one long, lean finger where she should sign.

The ink flowed from the gold pen in smooth, lustrous curves, despite the halting jerkiness of her signature. In the evening light it seemed blood-coloured. As she handed it back to him, standing at her side like a dark, infernal presence, she felt a wave of weakness go through her.

What have I done? Oh, dear God, what have I done?

But whatever it was, it was too late to go back.

Magda sat, staring out of the porthole, at the sunlit cloud-scape beyond. Benji was on her lap, asleep. He'd had a bad takeoff, even with sucking on the bottle of juice to ease the pressure on his little eardrums, but now, after half an hour of grizzling, he'd finally fallen asleep.

She glanced covertly across the aisle to where Rafaello di Visenti was sitting. He was working through a pile of papers laid out on the table in front of him, and so far as he was concerned, she could tell, he might as well have been alone on the plane.

There were no passengers apart from themselves on the luxurious executive jet winging its way across Europe. For Magda, who had never flown in her life, it was an experience she could hardly believe was happening.

But then her whole life since she had signed her name at Rafaello di Visenti's arrogant bidding had been completely unbelievable. She knew that if she had thought too much about what she was doing she could not have gone through with it. So she'd just let herself be swept along, let herself be that tin can racing along behind Rafaello di Visenti's powerful, unstoppable car taking her into an undreamed-of future.

Not that she'd seen him between that evening and today. Ironically, it had been his total indifference to her once he had got her to agree to marry him that had reassured her most. It was indeed, in his eyes, just a job, and she was nothing more than a junior employee. He had despatched one of his other junior employees to ensure the correct documents for their marriage were in place, to accompany her to register the marriage, and to arrange passports for her and Benji.

This morning she had been collected from her bedsit and driven to her local register office. The ceremony uniting them in matrimony had passed in a complete haze. She must have said the right things at the right time, but all she could remember now, as she sat and stared out at the sun-drenched cloudscape, was an overwhelming impression of a tall presence beside her, a deeply accented voice interspersing with hers and the registrar's, and that was that.

Only one moment stood out—when the tall presence beside her had lifted her hand and slid a gold wedding ring on her finger. Something had prickled through her like electricity. It must have been the coolness of his brief touch, nothing more. A moment later she'd been required to perform the same office for him, and to her own astonishment had realised she could hardly do so—her hand had trembled so violently.

She'd managed it somehow, all the same, and then, distracting her completely, she had heard Benji, kept back in the outer room with some more of Rafaello di Viscenti's minions, give out a mournful wail. From that moment on her sole thought had been to get back to him, and the rest of the ceremony had been lost to her.

As soon as she could she had hurried out, back to Benji, and scooped him into her arms. Then Rafaello had been beside her, taking her elbow and saying smoothly, but completely impersonally, 'If you are ready, we must go.'

A limo had whisked them to Heathrow and, apart from asking her in that same impersonal manner if she were comfortable and had everything she required, that was all her new husband had said to her. He'd seemed, Magda vaguely registered, to be quite abstracted during the whole procedure—as abstracted as she was.

The haze around her brain deepened. *Go with the flow,* she told herself, and smoothed Benji's silky hair, gazing again out of the porthole. Shock was keeping her going, she knew. Yet beneath the numbness she could feel a thread of excitement stirring. However bizarre the circumstances, she was going abroad for the first time in her life.

Italy. Could she really be going there? In the time since she had given in to Rafaello di Viscenti's imperious will she had got out as many library books as she could on the country. Reading had always been her solace, ever since

she had discovered it was a way of blotting out reality—
the reality of being brought up in care—taking her away to
magical lands, with wonderful people, a world away from
the disturbed, unhappy children that surrounded her, the
cast-off jetsam of adults too dysfunctional to be responsible
parents themselves, making their unwanted children pay the
price for their own emotional shortfalls.

As she stared out over the radiant cloudscape—another
mystical land up here, so far above the earth—her memory
fled back to Kaz. Her face clouded. Although she might
feel the desolation of a child utterly abandoned by its parents, at least Magda knew she had come off lucky compared with Kaz. Kaz had had the bruises, the badly mended
bones, the haunted eyes. Taken into care to be safe from
an abusive stepfather and alcoholic mother, Kaz had been
almost as withdrawn as Magda. Perhaps it was natural the
two of them had drawn together, to form, for perhaps the
first time in either of their lives, a real friendship, a real
emotional bond.

Sorrow pierced her. She gazed out over the fleecy, sunlit
surface of the clouds. Are you out there somewhere, Kaz?
she wondered.

In her arms, Benji stirred. Gently Magda bent to kiss his
fine dark hair, her heart swelling with love. She lifted her
eyes again and stared out of the window. She had done the
right thing in agreeing to this bizarre marriage; she knew
she had. However weird this was, she was doing the right
thing for the right reason.

For Benji.

For the first time since Rafaello di Viscenti had turned
her world upside down, she felt at peace with herself for
what she had done.

The peace lasted until the plane landed. Then, in the confusion of a busy Italian airport, hanging on to a wailing
Benji, whose ears had set off again during the descent into

Pisa, Magda once more felt like that tin can rattling along a motorway.

A hand pressed, not roughly, but insistently, into the small of her back.

'This way,' said Rafaello di Viscenti, the man she had married a handful of hours ago, and guided her forward. They made their way out of the airport to where a large limousine hummed at the kerb. Within moments they were inside, luggage in the boot, and the chauffeur was drawing out into the traffic.

The journey took well over an hour, and the latter part, away from the *autostrada*, was by far the most fascinating. Magda stared out of the window, drinking in the Tuscan landscape, a world away from the rainy South London streets she had left that morning. As the car purred along she pointed things out to Benji, whose baby seat was closest to the window. She leant over him, glad of the opportunity to put as much distance between herself and the man occupying the far corner of the huge car. Since he seemed to be preoccupied with his work still, tapping away at a laptop on his knees, she assumed he preferred to be left alone.

That suited her completely. Having to make stilted conversation with him would have been much worse. Right now, she just wanted to savour being in Italy.

Talking softly to Benji, she drank it all in. Road signs in Italian, driving on the wrong side of the road, houses, cars and people—all Italian. They were steadily climbing, she realised, heading up into the hills. Summer sunlight drenched the rolling landscape, etching the cypresses like ink. She stared, entranced. Stone farmhouses and picturesque stone-built towns, olive groves and vineyards, goats and sheep grazing, and, as the road grew steeper and narrower, old men with donkeys, old women covered in black from headscarf to heavy shoes.

Finally, as the roads grew narrower and the traffic more and more sparse, the limo slowed and turned in through large ironwork gates that opened at a buzz from the chauffeur. She heard Rafaello click off his laptop and close it up.

'We are here,' he announced.

She glanced briefly across at him. His face was expressionless and, it seemed to her, particularly tense. Automatically she tensed as well. It dawned on her that the flight and car journey had been nothing more than an interlude. Now, right now, in front of others, she was about to take on the role of Signora di Viscenti.

As if reading her attack of nerves, Rafaello spoke suddenly.

'Be calm,' he instructed. 'There is nothing for you to be anxious about. For you, this is simply a job. Please remember that.'

Was she imagining it, or had a grimmer note entered his tense voice? His dark gaze flicked over her again, and something in it sent a chill through her. Instinctively, Magda felt the chill was not directed at her. But there was anger deep down in there somewhere, she knew. Anger at having been required to marry at all.

Well, she thought resolutely, that was his business, not hers. She was simply doing what he was—to put it bluntly—paying her to do. She had gone through a wedding ceremony but it was nothing more than a legal formality. She was Signora di Viscenti in nothing more than name—and she would never be anything else.

For a moment so brief it hardly existed a longing struck her, so intense it pierced like pain, that somehow, if fairytales were real, this might be one—she really was sweeping along the driveway to her new home, with a husband beside her to die for…

But fairytales weren't real. They were just…fairytales.

Nothing to do with her.

The car drew up in front of a castellated villa that made Magda's eyes widen in wonder. It was ancient—and beautiful. The old stone was weathered, the huge wooden door studded, and the grounds stretched all the way to the woods and hills beyond.

Carefully she extracted Benji, who had been lulled off to sleep some time ago, by the rocking motion of the car, and clambered out with him. She held him on her hip and gazed around. The warmth of the late afternoon after the limo's air-conditioning struck her like a blessing, warming her through the thin material of the cotton dress she was wearing. It was the best she possessed, though it had cost under five pounds in a charity shop and was a size too large for her. Its low-waisted, button-fronted style, she knew, would probably have suited a matron of fifty better than herself. But what did it matter? If Rafaello di Viscenti had objected to it he would have got one of his minions to arrange an alternative.

'Come—' The man she had married that morning slipped a hand under her elbow. There was a tension in his grip that communicated itself to her and to Benji, who gave a little grizzle.

Magda suffered a swift glance at Rafaello's face. Its expression was closed and shuttered, and looked, she thought, very remote. Instinctively she realised that she and Benji were the last things on his mind.

As they approached the front door it swung open suddenly, and a man came out. He was elderly, dressed in shirtsleeves and a waistcoat, and she realised he must be some sort of butler. He greeted Rafaello, and though she could understand not a word she could tell he had definitely not been expecting his arrival.

And certainly not hers.

More rapid Italian followed, and Magda was sure she was not imagining the strong disapproval in the man's reaction—nor the shocked expression when he took in not just her, but Benji, too. Rafaello, she could tell, was simply terse and uncommunicative—and definitely not pleased by something the man had said to him.

Then they were indoors and Rafaello was turning to her.

'You and the child must be tired. I am sure you would like to rest a while. Come.' His voice was impersonal.

They proceeded up a grand staircase, and Magda could not help staring bug-eyed around her. The inside of the house was as beautiful as the outside, with white plain plaster walls hung with tapestries and oil paintings, and a marble staircase edged with scrolling wrought-iron banisters. Everything looked incredibly antique and expensive, a world away from the modern luxury apartments she cleaned.

Disbelief welled through her again—she was going to live *here* for the next few weeks? This was definitely a fairytale!

Rafaello took her into a large room leading off the broad upper landing. Again she just gazed around, wide-eyed. A vast carved wooden bed dominated the room, which was filled with huge pieces of furniture but, such was the size of the room, there was no sense of being cramped at all. A fabulous Persian carpet spread out beneath her feet, and heavy drapes cascaded to the floor either side of the pair of shuttered windows. A huge stone fireplace faced the bed.

'The *en suite* bathroom is through that door,' Rafaello informed her in the same terse, blank tone. 'Do you have all that you need for yourself and the child? Giuseppe will obtain anything you ask him for.'

She managed to nod, feeling incredibly awkward. The butler-type—Giuseppe, she presumed—had followed them up, and now came in, carrying her suitcase from the limo. Its shabbiness looked as out of place here as she did.

'Good,' said Rafaello. He glanced at his watch. 'Refresh yourself, and the child. Would you like some coffee?'

She nodded. 'Th-thank you,' she stammered faintly.

'Good,' he said again. 'Giuseppe will show you downstairs in a while, when you are rested. Oh…' He paused, and his eyes flicked over her again, unreadably. 'There is no need for you to change.'

Then he was gone, and Giuseppe with him.

Alone, Magda gazed around again. It was obvious that she was simply being stashed away until required, but she could hardly complain about her storage conditions. The room was exquisite. Her only worry was that everything in it was far too precious for her and Benji.

Benji, however, was eager to be mobile. She put him down and he promptly tottered off, eagerly exploring this new environment. She watched him head for the huge bed. She would not have to ask for a cot—the bed was easily big enough for her and Benji.

And her husband?

She pushed the thought away. Rafaello di Viscenti was her husband by nothing more than a legal sleight-of-hand. Where he slept had nothing to do with her.

Rafaello walked back down the staircase, his expression tight. He did not look forward to the imminent confrontation, but it was both inevitable and essential. He had to teach his father, once and for all, that he was not a puppet with strings to be pulled.

For his father Viscenti AG, founded over a hundred years ago to restore the ailing fortunes of a landed family, was simply a business, yielding a more than comfortable living for the di Viscentis.

Rafaello knew better. The world had shifted—globalisation was the name of the game. The only game. Viscenti AG had to move into the twenty-first century, and the only way to do that was to become major league on a global stage. The euro was seeing to that, if nothing else—Europe was wide open, and the blast of competition blew with a chillier wind than ever. Cosy family businesses just wouldn't survive.

Up till now Rafaello had had to fight for his strategy of taking Viscenti AG global every inch of the way with his father. He might be chief executive, but his father was chairman, and owned the majority shareholding. He had looked with grudging disapproval upon all Rafaello's endless labours in opening up the European market to the company, and, even though turnover and profits were soaring, Rafaello knew his father wished Viscenti AG had stayed the native enterprise it always had been.

But Rafaello had worked his backside off for the company he had so dramatically expanded, and he was not, *not* about to see his efforts wasted—or the family company sold off to strangers.

To prevent that he would do anything—whatever it took.

As he had proved that morning.

He strode across the marble-floored hallway and into the book-lined library he used as an office. Crossing to the window that overlooked the ornamental pool with its trickling fountain, Rafaello pushed back the sides of his suit jacket and splayed his fingers along his hips, looking out moodily. Typical of his father not to be here when he wanted him to be. Giuseppe had informed him, when he'd arrived, that both his father and cousin had gone out for lunch and were not expected back until late afternoon. He'd then promptly gone on to try and discover who the young female with the baby was.

Rafaello had cut him off, refusing to be drawn. The girl's identity was going to be a surprise for everyone. Oh, yes, certainly a surprise. He gave a grim smile. She was, just as he had anticipated, ideal. She'd stared around openmouthed as he'd taken her upstairs, as though she'd landed on an alien planet, her child hitched on her hip, her cheap, wrong-sized, unflattering dress hanging on her skinny body, her complexion pasty and her mud-coloured hair scraped back.

His smile tightened. His father would be incandescent

with rage—not just at having been outmanoeuvred, but at having the name of di Viscenti so totally insulted by his own son presenting him with such a female for a daughter-in-law.

A momentary frown creased his brow, then it cleared. The girl could have no idea of what made her so ideal for his purposes—and, besides, she was being paid what was for her a vast sum of money, had entered into the arrangement of her own free will. So far she had done exactly what he wanted—which was, predominantly, to do what she was told, ask no questions and keep out of the way until required.

He turned away from the window and sat himself down at his desk. He might as well get some work done while he was waiting. It might distract him from the coming confrontation.

Why did it have to be like this? he wondered, his expression drawn. Why this unnecessary, painful showdown with his father? Why couldn't he simply talk to him—communicate instead of confront?

He sighed. He'd had more communication in the last fifteen years with Giuseppe and his wife Maria. It had been they who'd seen him through from adolescence to adulthood—Giuseppe, who'd doused his morning-after head before his father saw him; Maria, who'd refused to hand him the keys of his first sports car when he'd been too angry to drive after another explosive head-to-head with his father. And it had been Giuseppe who'd listened to him when he'd expounded his dreams of making Viscenti AG a global name, Maria who'd rung a peal over him for leaving a trail of besotted girls behind him, making him wise up and stick to society women.

He knew his father considered him dissolute—hence his determination to force him into matrimony. His mouth tightened. If there had been *any* real hope of communication with his father he would not have had to do what he had done this morning. A shadow crossed his eyes. It was his mother's death in a road accident when he was fifteen that had caused the rift between father and son. They had both grieved—but not together. His father, mourning his adored wife, had withdrawn, cutting off his son. And Rafaello knew, with the hindsight of his thirty years, that the wild behaviour he had plunged into as a teenager—the fast cars, the partying, the girls—had been his cry for attention, for help—for love from a father who had turned away from him just when he needed him more than ever.

And now it was too late. The wall between them that had been laid, brick by brick, in Rafaello's adolescence was too solid to break through. His father had hardened, and so had he. Now there was only challenge—and strife.

With the latest round just about to start.

The sound of a car approaching along the drive made him look up from his work. He could recognise the note of the pricey little roadster that his cousin Lucia drove. It was always important to her to be seen in the right car, wearing the latest clothes by the best designers, and socialising with the right people. Hence her burning desire for a rich husband.

When he could hear voices out in the hallway he strolled out, forcing himself to appear relaxed.

'Rafaello?' His father stopped short.

'Papà.' Rafaello strolled forward.

'When did you get here?' demanded Enrico di Viscenti, visibly taken aback by his son's arrival.

'This afternoon,' replied his son laconically, and proceeded to cross to where his cousin was standing, stock still.

'Lucia,' he said dutifully, and bent to kiss her on either cheek. She smelt of too much perfume, and her face was too made up, but she was a handsome female for all that—as she well knew.

'Rafaello,' she murmured. 'Such a surprise.' Her voice

was neutral, her eyes assessing. Rafaello returned her look blandly.

'As you see, the prodigal returns,' he observed laconically. 'Have you had a pleasant day?'

'Very,' returned Lucia. 'Tio Enrico accompanied me to the launch of an art exhibition in Firenze. A new artist I enjoy.'

A polite smile grazed Rafaello's mouth. 'And does he enjoy *you*, too?' he murmured.

Lucia's face stiffened immediately. 'You offend, Rafaello!' she snapped.

He shrugged elegantly. He shouldn't bait her, he knew— but he was well aware that Lucia Foscesca took her lovers mostly from artistic circles. Young men who were likely to put up with her in exchange for the influence she could bring to bear on their careers. It was one of the—many— reasons that Rafaello refused to gratify his parent's insistence on the suitability of marriage between the cousins. Call him old-fashioned—and Lucia frequently did, with a taunting laugh that could not quite hide her annoyance— but he would prefer his bride to be less well acquainted with the opposite sex.

He stilled. The word 'bride' pulled him up short. The idea that upstairs a scrawny, unlovely, sexually undiscriminating twenty-one-year-old English girl, with a nameless, fatherless child in her arms, was actually, in the eyes of the law, his *bride* of less than twelve hours struck him as completely unbelievable. Had he really gone through with it? What he had done still felt completely unreal. Insane. Then he hardened his resolve.

Yes, he had done it—put his name and hers on a wedding certificate. He had had no other option. His hand had been forced. Angry resentment seethed through him, but he banked it down. He'd get his revenge for what his stubborn, pig-headed father had made him do—get it right now.

His father was speaking again.

'And to what, may I ask—' his father's voice sounded biting '—do we owe this unexpected honour?'

Rafaello's dark eyes glinted. 'Why, Papà, tomorrow is my thirtieth birthday. Surely you knew I would come?'

Enrico di Viscenti's eyes narrowed. 'Did I?' he countered.

His son smiled. 'And here I am—as dutiful as ever. Come,' he went on, 'join me on the terrace—I believe a little…celebration…is in order.'

He was aware of Lucia's piercing scrutiny and sudden, riveted attention, and his gaze moved from his father to meet her assessing gaze. He smiled blandly, his eyes glinting just as his father's had done.

'Lucia—you will join us, of course.'

His voice was urbane, but it signalled volumes. He watched as a slow expression of satisfaction, swiftly veiled, passed over her handsome features.

'Good,' said Rafaello, and smiled again. But beneath the smile a hard, tight band seemed to be lashing itself around his heart.

CHAPTER THREE

'WELL?' demanded Enrico, taking his seat at the ornate ironwork table at the shady end of the terrace outside the formal drawing room of the villa. 'Can it be that you have come to your senses at last?' His voice was sharp, and the gaze he rested on his son even sharper.

The hard, tight rope around Rafaello's chest lashed the knot around his chest tighter.

'Did you doubt that I would, Papà?' he replied, his voice level.

His father made a sound in his throat between a growl and a rasp. 'I know you are more obstinate and self-willed than any father deserves. It was always the way with you!'

'Well,' said Rafaello, with a temporising air, 'for once I am being the model son—'

If there was a bite in his voice, no one heard it. He went on, 'But first I would like, Papà, to confirm that if I do what you want, and marry by my thirtieth birthday, you will give me undisputed control of the company. Is that right?' Rafaello addressed his father directly, keeping his voice brisk and businesslike.

'Hah!' exclaimed his father. 'You know perfectly well it is so.'

'And you give me your word on that?'

'Of course.' He sounded affronted that he had even been asked.

Rafaello smiled inexpressively. 'In which case, Papà,' he went smoothly on, his voice bland, 'you may wish me happy—and keep to your side of the agreement.'

His father stilled, his hands gripping the arms of his

42

chair, unable to speak for the moment. Not so Lucia. With a breathless little laugh, she spoke.

'Rafaello, you are the most abominable man.' Her voice was full of flirtatious exasperation. 'Proposing to me in such a fashion.' She gave her tinkling laugh again. 'But I shall punish you for your lack of gallantry, be sure of that.' She turned to her prospective father-in-law. 'Tell me, Enrico,' she said with coy feminine teasing, 'how shall I punish this boorish son of yours for depriving me of my rightful wooing?'

She gave another little laugh, coquettish now, and let her gaze slip back to her husband-to-be.

There was a curious look on his face. Half-shuttered, half-revealing. He held up a hand.

'Before we go any further, I think it is time for champagne, no?'

On cue, Giuseppe appeared, bearing the requisite beverage, and as he placed the tray on the table between them Rafaello murmured something to him. The man nodded, and retired. Rafaello busied himself opening the bottle and liberally filling up the glasses and spreading them around.

Lucia gave a click of irritation. 'Giuseppe has brought one glass too many,' she said acidly. 'It is high time he took his pension!'

Rafaello presented her with her foaming narrow glass. 'When you are mistress here, you may tell him so,' he said lightly.

A small but distinct smirk of satisfaction—and anticipation—curled at her scarlet mouth. Rafaello watched it, his face still quite unreadable.

His father picked up his glass and got to his feet. 'A toast.' Satisfaction rang in his voice. He was well pleased with his son's decision to finally see reason, as was his niece. 'A toast to the new Signora di Viscenti—'

Rafaello lifted his glass. 'How kind,' he murmured. There was a slight sound in the doorway to the drawing room and he tilted his head towards it. 'And how very timely.'

The girl stood there, Giuseppe just behind her. Fierce gratification surged through Rafaello. The girl made exactly the picture he had intended. As the others at the table turned to stare at her she stood there, atrociously dressed, her hair drawn back off her plain face with an elastic band, and— best of all—an open-mouthed baby on her hip. Her expression was completely blank.

Rafaello got to his feet and drew her forward. She was as stiff and unyielding as a board, and almost stumbled. He took her hand, making sure the wedding ring was visible.

'Allow me to present,' he said, in a voice that was as bland as milk, 'my wife, Signora di Viscenti.'

For a moment, as Magda stood completely immobile, wanting the earth to swallow her, there was complete silence. Then, a second later, there was uproar.

It was the old man's voice that was the loudest. It was like a lion roaring. She could understand not a word, but the rage in it was like a hurricane pouring over her. At her side Rafaello di Viscenti, the man to whom she had been legally joined in matrimony, gripped her left hand in a vice.

Her breath was frozen in her chest. The old man—who just had to be Rafaello di Viscenti's father, for the arrogance of his head and the similarity of the features argued nothing else—was still roaring. The butler-type was looking as if he'd been hit over the head by a heavy object— and the woman sitting next to the older Signor di Viscenti was simply looking totally and completely incredulous.

For one long, timeless instant there was nothing except the roaring Italian rage of the old man, and then, in absolute terror, Benji started to howl.

Magda jerked her hand free and used it to cradle her son up against her breast, turning away, back into the lavishly elegant drawing room.

What on earth was going on? A new voice had interrupted the roaring—Rafaello's. His voice was sharper, far more biting, but just as angry. Desperately Magda got as far away as she could, clutching the sobbing Benji to her while she tried to calm him—an impossible task, given the human racket going on out on the terrace.

Suddenly her sleeve was seized. There was an overpowering smell of heavy perfume, and a voice was hissing something at her in Italian. The venom in the words, incomprehensible though they were, made Magda flinch.

'Please—' she said jerkily. 'I...I don't understand.'

The woman caught breath. Her eyes narrowed. *'Inglese?'* Then she shook Magda's arm again. 'Who are you? What are you playing at? Pretending to be Rafaello's bride.' The woman tried to seize her ring finger, as if to check its authenticity, but Magda fielded her off, turning so that her body was between the woman and Benji. He was still howling fearfully.

She tore herself away and headed for the door. Stumbling, Benji still wailing in terror, she rushed across the marble hall and hurled herself up the staircase as quickly as she could, heading back to the sanctuary of the bedroom. Only when she was safely within did she pause to draw breath.

Her first thought was for Benji. He was all but hysterical now, and calming him down took for ever. But gradually, as she sat on the bed with him on her lap, rocking gently and soothingly, his anguished sobs died away. A thumb slipped into his mouth and he began to relax at last.

Magda felt shaken to the core. She might not have understood a word of that roaring anger, but the fury had been unmistakable.

Oh, dear God, what have I let myself in for? Please, please, let me wake up and find myself at home...

But it was no dream. She was indeed here, in a Tuscan villa, married to a man whose family had gone apoplectic at the news.

If she listened, she could still hear the storm raging downstairs. It seemed to have moved in from the terrace, but it was still in full flood. Magda shrank back, clutching Benji. He felt her distress and discomfort, and started whimpering again.

Footsteps, hard and angry-sounding, echoed across the marble hall. Doors slammed several times. What sounded like paternal denunciation rang up through the floorboards. Finally, in a last flurry of raised voices, there was a heavier door slamming. It reverberated right through the house, it seemed to Magda, and then everything went quiet. A moment later there came the throaty roar of a powerful internal combustion engine, gunning fiercely and then roaring away.

Silence reined. Total silence. It was almost as unnerving as the noise.

Knowing, instinctively, that the only thing she could do was keep her head tucked well down beneath the parapet, Magda kept to her room. Gradually Benji cheered up, but it was not long before another need made itself increasingly urgently felt. He was hungry.

She rifled through her hand baggage, extracting an apple and some rusks. Benji wolfed them down, still hungry when they were all gone. For the next forty-five minutes Magda tried to mollify him, but in vain. Even juice could not sate him. He needed proper food, and milk. There was nothing for it. She would have to go and find some.

With her heart in her mouth she gingerly opened the door of her bedroom. It was dusky outside on the landing. Cautiously she went down the grand marble staircase into the deserted hall. Hoping to find Giuseppe, she went through what must be a service door into a stone-flagged corridor. A door stood ajar at the end, and she entered reluctantly. If it were just herself she'd go to bed hungry, but she could not starve poor Benji. Surely someone would take pity on him?

As she entered, she realised she was in a vast, old-fashioned kitchen. A cavernous fireplace at the far end was filled with a huge cooking range. Dominating the centre of the room, however, was an endless long wooden table. To the side, beneath an old-fashioned window, an elderly woman was vigorously scrubbing a huge copper saucepan at a stone sink.

As Magda hovered hesitantly in the doorway the woman turned to stare at her.

'*Si?*' she demanded, in an unfriendly tone. Her face was strong-boned, and her expression was anything but welcoming. She glared at Magda.

Magda swallowed. '*Mi dispiace,*' she ventured haltingly, hoping she was pronouncing it right from the Italian phrasebook she had bought. '*Ma…este possible….?*'

'I speak English,' the woman snapped at her. 'What is it you want?'

Almost, Magda turned and ran. Then, as Benji huddled in closer to her, sensing her unease, she swallowed again. 'I am so sorry—' her voice was almost a whisper '—but would it be possible, please…a little food…and some milk…for my baby…?'

Fierce black eyes from beneath beetling greying brows bored into her. She felt her throat tighten with tension. Surely the woman would not refuse sustenance for a little child, however angry she was at having been disturbed—as she so clearly was—by such an unwelcome person as the female whom Rafaello di Viscenti had brought here to cause uproar.

The eyes were scanning her, taking in her shabby clothes, her thin, drab figure, the baby clutching her, and then going back to Magda's strained, nervous face. Suddenly the woman's expression changed. She threw up her hands, exclaiming something vociferously in her native language, and bustled forward.

'Come—come—come…' she announced. 'Sit—' She propelled Magda with surprisingly strong arms, considering her age, and plumped her down at one of the chairs at the long table. 'You are hungry, yes? Foolish girl—why did you not ring from your room?'

'I…I…didn't want to be a nuisance…' Magda stammered.

The woman made a tch-ing noise in her throat. 'A baby must not wait for his food,' she announced. 'Nor the mother.'

She bustled off to the far end of the kitchen, this time to the cooking range. There were various pots on it, and out of one she proceeded to scoop up, with the aid of a huge wooden implement like a spoon, with horizontal prongs, a generous serving of spaghetti. On top of this she ladled spoonfuls of tomato sauce. She carried the dish back to Magda, placed it on the table, and deftly tied a huge teatowel around Benji's neck to protect his clothes from the sauce.

Benji's little mouth was already wide open, and Magda had scarcely time to check the pasta was not too hot before he had seized her wrist and was guiding the forkful towards him.

He made a hearty meal, and as soon as he had finished another, even larger bowl of pasta and sauce was placed in front of Magda.

'Eat,' the woman instructed, taking Benji from her. Balancing him expertly on her own hip, she turned to fill a cup with some water, and gave it to him to drink from with equal expertise. Surprisingly, Benji seemed perfectly happy with this, and started to gurgle.

The woman beamed, and addressed him in voluble Italian of which Magda caught only one word—*bambino*. Then, extracting a wooden stirrer from a large earthenware pot on the window ledge, the woman presented it to Benji—who grabbed it eagerly—and sat herself down opposite Magda.

'Eat,' she repeated, as Magda paused in her own consumption of pasta. It was totally delicious, and she was wolfing it down as eagerly as Benji had.

'Thank you,' she murmured, still feeling intensely awkward as well as grateful.

The woman let her finish, amusing herself by entertaining Benji, who was in no way dismayed to be addressed in a foreign language. Magda watched covertly, between mouthfuls. The woman was obviously very experienced with children, and knew exactly what Benji found entertaining—which was largely banging the wooden stirrer on the table and trying to knock over the pepperpot.

Magda scraped the last of the tomato sauce with her spoon and gave a satisfied sigh. The woman looked across at her.

'So,' she announced. 'Now we talk.' She hefted Benji from one side of her lap to the other. 'You tell me,' she said in her heavily accented English. 'Is Rafaello the father?'

A look of total stupefaction filled Magda's face. Her mouth fell open in shock. Her reaction seemed to please the woman.

'Well, that is one relief at least,' she announced. The snap was back in her voice, and Magda, finally overwrought by all the events of the day, found her throat tightening.

'So,' went on the woman relentlessly, 'he has married simply to make his father angry. *Idiota!*'

Magda stared helplessly. She didn't know what to say. Didn't know what she *could* say. She had had no idea that she would be walking into such a volatile situation. But evidently it did not surprise the housekeeper—or so she assumed this woman must be.

'Is he mad, finally to do this to his father?' the woman exclaimed. 'Always the same—always. Always they fight like…like the men of sheep…their heads—so!' She slid one hand past Benji and made a fist, together with the other, and clashed the knuckles together, like rams' horns impacting. 'But this—this is the worst.'

'I…I'm sorry,' said Magda. It seemed the only thing to say.

The woman said something in Italian. 'Well, well,' she went on in English. 'It is done now. So, if Rafaello is not the father of your child, why do you marry him?'

The bluntness of the question took Magda aback.

'Um—Signor di Viscenti said he needed to be married for legal reasons by his thirtieth birthday. I…I agreed because…'

She felt silent. Suddenly it seemed shameful to admit that she had married a complete stranger for financial gain.

The woman's eyes took on a shrewd expression.

'He offers you money, yes?'

Colour stained Magda's cheekbones. She looked down. 'With…with the money Signor di Viscenti has promised me I can buy a little house for my son.'

The tch-ing noise came again. 'And the father of your *bambino*? No, no, do not tell me.' The voice sounded old and tired. 'He has gone, no? It is always the same—the men do not care and the girls are foolish.'

She started to clear away the empty pasta dishes, handing Benji back to Magda. 'Well, well, there is nothing to be done. But I tell you—' a dark, warning look came Magda's way '—after this his father will never forgive Rafaello.'

Sunlight pressing on Rafaello's eyes made him groan. Slowly, he roused to an unwelcome consciousness, and then wished himself still in oblivion. He'd stormed out of the villa yesterday evening, his father's curses still ringing in his ears. Tearing down the valley in his high-powered sports car, he'd replayed every ugly word that had been exchanged. His father's incandescent rage and his own vicious taunting, telling him that thanks to his insistence on his son marrying he now had a daughter-in-law who came complete with a fatherless baby and who cleaned toilets for a living.

For ten seconds he'd thought Enrico would have a cardiac arrest on the spot—until his temper had burst out again and he'd rained down verbal abuse on his son for shaming the family name. As for Lucia, she'd been wearing an expression like Lucretia Borgia on a bad hair day—looking for someone to poison that could only be him.

He'd ended the night working his way through a bottle of grappa and damning the whole world.

A punishing shower brought him back to a semblance of half-life. It was nearly noon, a glance at his watch told him. Noon on his thirtieth birthday. He didn't feel like celebrating. He crossed to the window of his bedroom and stared out balefully. Below, the vista of the gardens brought him no comfort. He tried to focus on important things. He must go to Rome and call a board meeting to confirm him as the new chairman, then start implementing the strategy for global expansion into the USA and Australia for Viscenti AG that he'd been planning for so long.

A movement to the side of his field of vision caught his eye. The girl and her little boy were rounding the side of the house. She was going very slowly, holding his hand as he toddled unsteadily along the gravelled path. *Dio*, he'd all but forgotten about her. He watched her stoop swiftly to catch the child as he stumbled momentarily and then set him back on course.

What the hell was he going to do about her? She'd served her purpose—provided him with the wife he required to confront his father. He didn't need her any more, but he could not risk giving rise to public speculation that his was a fraudulent marriage by sending her back to England straight away. He gave a shrug and turned away. He would tell Maria to keep her out of his hair and she could enjoy a free holiday at the villa while he was in Rome.

He was just about to turn away when another figure came into view, stalking out from the house.

Lucia.

She was clearly on course to the girl, and in a raging temper.

Out in the gardens, Magda came to a halt. That woman, whoever she was, who had been as furious at Rafaello's announcement as his father had been, was heading purposefully towards her. Magda waited apprehensively. The woman's high heels scrunched noisily on the path.

She came to a stop in front of her. Yesterday Magda had been in too much shock to take in anything about the woman. Now she could see she was an immaculately coiffed, flashing-eyed brunette, wearing a tight-fitting designer outfit.

Her eyes were narrowed with blazing hostility. Magda's hand tightened over Benji, who was crouching down to inspect the gravel.

Whatever the woman was going to say to her remained unsaid. More crunching footsteps sounded, heavier and rapid, and Rafaello appeared around the corner of the house. He was wearing, this summer morning, a lightweight suit in pale grey, and he looked, as Magda stared helplessly, completely breathtaking.

He launched into rapid Italian directed at Lucia.

'You should leave, Lucia. There is nothing for you here—there never was. You should have known I would never marry you.'

Lucia's eyes flashed angrily. Her face contorted. 'So you married this *putana* instead of me! Look at her. She's like some scrawny chicken.'

The contempt in the woman's eyes as she raked Magda's face made Rafaello's jaw tighten.

'*Basta.*' He cast a rapid glance at the girl. She was looking ashen suddenly, and for a moment Rafaello hoped she didn't have the wit to realise what Lucia had called her. But doubtless she could hear the hostility in his cousin's voice, whatever language she spoke. He took a sharp breath.

'I think, Lucia, it would be best if you returned to your apartment in Firenze. You have done my father no favours in making him think of you as a prospective daughter-in-law.'

An ugly look flashed in the woman's dark eyes. 'And you think you have done him a favour bringing him home that…that girl?' she spat angrily. 'I hope you are proud of what you have done, Rafaello.'

She turned on her stilettos and stalked off. Slowly, Magda let out her breath, unaware till now that she'd been holding it. Benji was clinging to her hand, huddled close, clearly frightened by the anger all around him.

'It's all right, muffin,' she whispered comfortingly into his hair, as she scooped him up into her arms.

But it wasn't all right. It was all wrong. Everything here in this beautiful place was as wrong as it could be. Her throat tightened.

'You should have told me.'

Where the words came from she did not know. Where the courage to say them came from she certainly didn't know. But she had said them, and now she was looking at the man she had thought she was marrying simply for a matter of legal detail in reasons of business.

But this was surely nothing to do with Viscenti AG—it couldn't be! The anger and fury that had erupted since she had stepped out on to the terrace yesterday could not possibly be about something as impersonal as business.

This was family. Ugly, emotional, volatile, bitter family.

'Told you what?'

Rafaello's voice was sharper than he meant. His unpleasant exchange with Lucia made it sound harsher.

'Told me that I was walking into a human minefield,' Magda said tightly. 'Everyone is furious that you married me. Your father, that woman—whoever she is—even the housekeeper and your butler. I didn't know everyone here would be angry with me.' There was a tremor in her voice she tried desperately to conceal.

'They are not angry with you,' Rafaello answered flatly. 'They are angry with me. And the only person I am angry with,' he continued, even more flatly, 'is my father. You might as well know…' He took a heavy breath. 'He wanted me to marry Lucia—she is my cousin, and would like to be Signora di Viscenti and have my money to spend. She worked on him to persuade him she would be the ideal wife for me—and the ideal mother of the grandchildren he is obsessed with having. He sought to force my compliance by threatening to sell his controlling share of the family company. That I will not permit—I have worked too hard for the last ten years to throw away all my efforts just to ensure I am not manipulated into marriage with a woman I do not wish to marry. So I outmanoeuvred him. I arrived the day before my thirtieth birthday already—already married.'

'To a *putana*.' Her voice was even flatter than his.

Rafaello stiffened. Could she possibly know what that word meant? As if she could read his thoughts, she said thinly, 'A whore—isn't that the right translation, Mr di Viscenti?'

She started to walk past him. She just wanted to get away. The ugliness around her was choking her.

He caught her arm. 'You must take no notice of Lucia. She is bitter and angry. She lashed out at you. That is all.'

'Thank you—but I prefer not to be lashed out at in the

first place. You and your cousin know nothing of me or my circumstances—or my son's.'

His face darkened at her retort. 'I know that a young girl with a baby and no man to support it means that you were, at the very least, careless about who you chose to sleep with.'

Her expression stiffened. 'I think I was more careless, Mr di Viscenti, about whom I chose to marry yesterday morning. I definitely should have checked out your charming relations.'

She shook her arm free and walked rapidly away from him. Behind her, Rafaello swore. Then, quickening his step, he caught up with her.

'I regret that you were exposed to such a scene,' he said tightly. 'But I would suggest you remember that you are being paid a substantial amount of money to undertake what you have done.'

She stopped, deflating instantly at his blunt reminder. She stared down at his polished shoes. He was right—and she must not forget it, however economical with the truth he had been about his reasons for marrying her.

'I've done my best, Mr di Viscenti,' she answered with quiet dignity, lifting her eyes to him. 'I've done what you wanted me to do, when you wanted me to do it. But I really didn't appreciate that one of my duties would be to serve as a punch-bag for those of your household who are displeased by your marriage.'

Rafaello's lip curled. 'Are you asking for more money?'

Her face seemed to whiten under his question. 'No, Mr di Viscenti, I am not asking for more money. I am asking merely not to be subject to the anger and insults of members of your household. If nothing else, it is upsetting for Benji. And now, if you please, if you would be so kind as to give me my instructions for the day I shall carry them out to the best of my ability. Do you wish me to return to my room?'

'You may do whatever you please.' A spurt of quite unnatural anger at her response shot through him. 'The house and grounds are at your disposal. I am not an ogre—and I have expressed my regret for my cousin's behaviour. She will be leaving shortly, as shall I. Please make yourself at home.'

He walked away, leaving Magda feeling impotently angry. Slowly the feeling drained away. What was the point of her making a fuss like that? The rich were heedlessly indifferent to others; she knew that well enough. To Rafaello di Viscenti she was nothing more than a tool to be used—hired and paid for. When she was of no use to him she should stay quiet and not make a fuss—whatever uproar was going on around her.

She let Benji slip down to the ground again, and silently watched him busying himself scooping up handfuls of gravel and throwing them down again with a satisfied air. When, finally, he was bored, she took his hand.

'Come on, let's go back indoors.'

She made her way around the side of the villa, back to the servants' entrance at the rear. At least here she felt more at ease. The housekeeper—whose name, she had been informed over breakfast, when she had tentatively made her way down to the kitchen once Benji had surfaced, was Maria—at least seemed to have decided to tolerate her. She was being kind enough, in a sort of rough-edged way that Magda suspected was her customary manner, hiding a very soft heart.

'Milk,' pronounced Maria now, as Magda entered the huge kitchen, 'for the *bambino*.'

Benji toddled cheerfully over to her, expressing confidence in being welcomed by this new person in his life that was amply repaid. Chatting away to him in Italian, Maria sat him on the table and presented him with a mug of creamy milk.

'*Latte,*' she informed the infant as he gulped down the contents greedily, and repeated the word several times.

'La',' replied Benji, and beamed at her expectantly. 'Mo'?'

'He means more,' said Magda diffidently. 'Um—*piu?*' she ventured, racking her brain for what she had read in her Italian phrasebook.

'*Ancora,*' corrected Maria, refilling Benji's mug. She looked at Magda. 'He is a good boy. Even with no father.' Her black eyes rested on Magda, and then softened. 'But you love your *bambino*, that I can see. And that makes you a good woman.'

Unaccountably, the rough kindness made Magda's eyes prick with tears. The housekeeper made her tch-ing sound, and placed another mug of creamy milk in front of her, as well as refilling Benji's.

'Drink,' she said again, to both of them.

To her surprise, Magda found the rest of the day actually enjoyable. Maria took her under her wing, managing to find time to make a great fuss of Benji, which he openly adored. Fetching his toys from her room, Magda settled in the vast kitchen at one end of the table while Maria got on with the task of serving lunch—presumably for Rafaello's father. Lucia had, according to a terse announcement by Giuseppe as he looked into the kitchen at some point, departed. Judging from the way she was spoken about, Magda gathered that Rafaello's cousin was no favourite below stairs. Rafaello, too, had gone, roaring off in his car, the noise of his departure causing Maria's lips to tighten ominously. Magda, however, could only be relieved.

It was much easier being here in the servants' quarters. After all, she reasoned, it was where she naturally belonged.

After lunch came a real treat. Maria took her and Benji out to the swimming pool. Set in a sheltered walled garden, the water shimmered invitingly in the sunshine. Benji, who adored swimming, tottered eagerly towards it.

'Won't Signor di Viscenti mind?' Magda asked diffidently.

Maria's mouth tightened. 'You are Signora di Viscenti. No, no, do not tell me that it is in name only. He has married you. You are his wife. If you wish to swim— swim.'

Magda could not resist. Although the water was still a little chilly, Benji splashed so vigorously and enthusiastically in the rubber ring and water wings that Magda had no fears he would take cold. In the peaceful sunshine, with the pool to themselves, the time flashed by.

Afterwards, exhausted by his exertions, Benji fell fast asleep on a lounger beneath the shade of a large umbrella that Giuseppe had opened for them at the poolside. At his side, Magda sunned herself.

Whatever the storms raging around her, one thing was for sure: she would never again in her life get the chance to enjoy such idyllic surroundings. She would make the most of what was happening to her, she resolved, and let everything else wash over her head. Rafaello di Viscenti's quarrels were nothing to do with her.

She spent a quiet evening with Benji, keeping Maria and Giuseppe company in the kitchen. No one sent for her, and Rafaello did not return to the villa.

'He has gone to Rome,' said Maria. She sounded disapproving. Magda simply felt relieved.

Later, with Benji asleep in the huge bed, she sat beside him, sipping the coffee Maria brought up, reading for an hour or two. Just before she turned in herself she sat by the open window, drinking in the soft sounds of the Italian night.

My second night in Italy. It seemed hardly possible, yet it was so. As she looked out into the velvet darkness, the noise and tatty raucousness of South London seemed a universe away.

I am fortunate beyond my dreams, she said softly to herself. *Simply to have this experience is more than I ever thought I could have.*

A face swam into her vision. Dark-eyed, olive-skinned, high cheekbones, sculpted mouth…male beauty in its ultimate form. She felt her heart give a crazy, unstoppable little skip. Oh, he was indeed the kind of man you could feel weak at the knees over.

Weak in the heart over!

But Rafaello di Viscenti was as remote from her as if he were a portrait by Titian hanging on a *palazzo* wall.

Her lips pressed together and she stared out, eyes wide and painful, into the Tuscan night, where the wind winnowed softly in the cypress trees and the scent of flowers exhaled like the sweet breath of the sleeping earth.

Slowly, she got to her feet and went to bed.

CHAPTER FOUR

RAFAELLO gunned his sports car and overtook a hopelessly slow tourist hire-car travelling along the Pisa-Firenze autostrada well below the maximum speed limit. He should be in a good mood. Viscenti AG was his completely, all confining paternal strings cut. But he was not. He did not want another encounter with his father—still less with the girl he had made his bride.

She made him feel uncomfortable.

There was no reason for it, he told himself impatiently, gunning the engine again. He was setting her up financially for life. She had nothing to complain of.

Except being dumped in a strange place with not a word of the language and having everyone yelling their heads off all around her...

His mouth tightened, and he changed gears more roughly than the superb engine warranted.

And you walking out on her and leaving her to it.

He overtook another car and cruised back into his lane. Well, of course he'd not hung around pointlessly at the villa! How could he have? The whole purpose of this total farce was to call his father's bluff so he could get Lucia off his case and not lose his life's work at Viscenti AG. He wasn't there to nursemaid one of life's waifs and strays just because he'd happened to marry her the day before. She knew what she was doing when she signed the papers.

No, she didn't...

The irritating voice in his head nagged at him again, making him blast his horn at a car hogging the outside lane.

Just like she told you—she didn't know she was going to

60

detonate an explosion of family fury. She walked into it and hadn't a clue.

Yes, well, he thought grimly, there was still no reason for him to feel bad about it. She was just some not-too-bright London girl who'd probably got pregnant on purpose to live on social security—she couldn't have understood a word of what was being yelled about yesterday. And today she'd had the run of a millionaire's villa—a free holiday in the sun. His father wouldn't go near her, he knew—he would simply lock himself in the library and fume—Lucia had been sent off-pitch, and he'd made sure that Giuseppe and Maria would keep an eye on the girl and her kid.

Ruthlessly he quashed any riposte to this final analysis of the situation and put his foot down hard on the accelerator. The powerful car shot forward and Rafaello felt a rush of familiar exhilaration.

Speed always put his troubles far behind him.

They caught up with him again, though, when he drew to a halt in front of the garage at the rear of the villa some half an hour later. A familiar car met his eyes. Wonderful, he thought grimly. Reinforcements had been summoned.

He should not have been surprised. His father always turned to his sister when he wanted to complain about his son. Well, Tia Elizavetta could say what she liked on this one—and she would too; she had a sharp tongue in her head—but it was too late for recriminations. He had out-manoeuvred his father and that was that.

Giuseppe intercepted him the moment he stepped inside the hallway. He was looking poker-faced and Rafaello knew he was not pleased—the moment the man opened his mouth he knew who he wasn't pleased with.

It was 'Signor' this and 'Signor' that, uttered in such stiff accents that Rafaello got the message loud and clear. He was in the doghouse with both Giuseppe and the formidable Maria.

'My aunt and uncle are here, I see,' he said, doing his best to ignore the glacial attitude of this man who knew him better than his own father.

'*Si, signor.* They arrived an hour ago. They are with your father.'

There was a wealth of meaning in his words. Rafaello nodded. 'Well, I might as well get it over and done with,' he remarked. 'Are they in the library?'

Giuseppe indicated that they were.

'Right,' said Rafaello, and started to head towards the double doors leading through to the library.

A reproving cough came from behind him. He halted, and turned his head questioningly.

'Signora di Viscenti is in the gardens with her little boy,' Giuseppe informed him, his face studiedly expressionless. 'Perhaps you would like to greet her before seeing your aunt and uncle?'

Rafaello stilled. 'Later,' was all he said, and headed into the library. Behind him, Giuseppe's disapproval was tangible.

As he walked into the long room he could tell instantly that his father had been enumerating his son's crimes and misdemeanours in graphic detail. His aunt had her older-sister look about her, and his uncle had the familiar glazed look that meant his mind was miles away from yet another family furore.

'So! You deign to return at last,' was his father's opening salvo as his son approached. 'First you destroy me, and then you desert me. But what other treatment should I expect from you, hah?'

Rafaello felt the familiar surge of tense exasperation fill him. 'I needed to go to Rome, Papà. I had to call a board meeting as soon as possible to confirm the new chairmanship.'

A hiss that sounded like a steam train escaped his father's mouth. 'Already. Already you discard me. Well, when you leave the family company in ruins with your reckless over-ambition remember that you took it from me by treachery.'

'You gave me your word, Papà, to let me run the company if I were married by my thirtieth birthday. That condition I have met. That is all.' Rafaello spoke with iron control, and watched the colour mount dangerously in his father's face. His own darkened, and his control slipped fatally. 'I am not a schoolboy any longer. What you attempted to do was unforgivable. This is my life—you have no right to play with it like a toy.'

His voice had risen, and so had his temper.

His aunt stepped forward, holding up her hands between them.

'Rafaello, enough. And you, too, Enrico. Can you at least try for civility if nothing else?'

'*Civility?*' Enrico spat. 'You ask for civility, Elizavetta? After what he has done?'

His sister gave a heavy sigh. 'It astonishes me, Enrico, that after all these years you still do not know Rafaello is as stubborn as you. Good God, where else does he get it from but you? You tried to force his hand—and he retaliated. What did you expect him to do, with your blood in him? I warned you not to pursue your stubborn course! If he had wanted to marry Lucia he would have done so without your help.'

Her brother looked mutinous at this criticism, but his sister gave him no chance to respond. She turned her attention to her nephew.

'And thank heaven you had more sense than to marry Lucia. One day, I hope—' her voice had a reproving note for Rafaello '—you will make a marriage based on love. But first you have to disentangle yourself from this ridiculous misalliance you have tied yourself up with. I do not approve of what you have done, Rafaello, I tell you that straight. However,' she went on imperiously, 'I still have hopes that you might yet prove yourself something more than a business brain and a handsome face.' Her voice became sharper than ever. 'You might even bring yourself to greet your aunt.'

She held her arms out commandingly, and Rafaello crossed to bestow the customary kiss and greeting on either cheek.

'Yes,' she said tartly to him. 'That is better.'

She held his eye a moment. For all her sharp tongue he got on well with his outspoken aunt. 'You and I will talk, young man,' she told him. 'And I will contrive, not for the first time and no doubt not for the last,' she said wearily, 'to see if I can sort out this latest disaster.' She let him go and stood back. 'But first I should like to refresh myself. The journey from Bologna was tiring. Your uncle has been working too hard—his lecture tour was arduous and he has papers to write. You should time these tempests better. Bernardo—come.'

Sweeping her husband with her, barely giving him time to exchange hurried greetings with his nephew by marriage, she headed for the door. For a moment Rafaello stood uncertainly, looking across at his father, still smouldering like a keg of dynamite threatening to explode. Why? he thought bitterly. Why is it always, always, *always* such a battle?

A wave of depression swept over him. His father was a stranger. An angry stranger.

A fierce light sparked in Enrico's eyes as he saw his son looking at him. 'And you—you can get out, too. Get out of my sight.'

Rafaello did not need telling twice. He turned on his heel and left.

A swim, he thought. That was what he needed. The weather was warming up, and the physical exertion would do him good. Drain off some of that hard, angry emotion roiling around inside him like bilgewater in a rotting hull. But when, clad in his swimming trunks, towel over his shoulder, he strode through the stone archway that led into the walled pool area, he stopped dead.

There was someone in the pool already. In fact, he realised instantly, two people. His bride and her son.

He watched them for a moment, half hidden by some cascading climbing roses. She was playing with the child, standing in the shallow end, legs apart, throwing the infant up into the air with a whooshing noise and catching him as he plunged back down into the water. She was laughing, and so was the child—uproariously. Evidently this experience was of enormous pleasure to him, for the little boy gave a shout of glee as he went up into the air before descending yet again for a mighty splash.

Rafaello stepped forward and immediately Magda halted in mid-lift, seeing him enter the pool area. She froze, indifferent to the abrupt wail of the baby as his fun was interrupted.

She was staring at him—horror-struck, so it seemed to Rafaello, and he felt an immediate burst of irritation. There was no need to look at him as if he were Dracula. But she was already wading to the semicircle of steps that led out of the water as fast as she could, wielding the protesting baby in front of her like a shield. She started to climb out hastily.

'I'm very sorry. I didn't realise I should not be swimming now,' she said apologetically, and Rafaello experienced another stab of exasperation. He felt like Frankenstein's monster as well as Dracula.

'There is no need to get out,' he informed her, dropping his towel down on to one of the loungers. 'I only require one lane. Continue with the child.'

But she was getting out of the pool all the same. 'No, no—we've finished.'

Judging by the wail that the child let out at that point, he, for one, considered his swim far from finished.

'Stay in the water.'

His voice came out harsher than he meant it to. It was just that there was no reason for the girl to be looking at him like that. As if he were an ogre.

'No, really…' the girl mumbled. She'd stopped staring at him. Her gaze seemed awkward now instead, and she started to sidle towards the lounger her things were on, holding the protesting baby under his armpits. His legs kicked out furiously. His wet body started to slip through her hands, and for a moment Rafaello thought he would slide through them. He lunged forward just as the girl, at the same time, bent her knees to lower the child from a safer height to the ground.

For the barest second his eyes met hers, before he backed away, realising his assistance was unnecessary. What he saw in their expression shocked him. She looked absolutely terrified.

He straightened up. 'I thought he was going to fall,' he said.

She straightened as well, keeping hold of the baby's hand, though he was tugging as hard as he could in the direction of the water.

'His name is Benji,' she said suddenly, and just as quickly she wasn't looking terrified at all. She was looking fierce. 'Just because he doesn't have a father doesn't mean he doesn't have a name.'

Rafaello's mouth tightened. She was a pint-sized thing, he thought. The swimsuit she was wearing should have been thrown away long ago. Thinking about it, it probably had been. It was a size too large for her, for a start, and its elasticity was completely gone. It was crinkling around her abdomen and hips, bunching over her squashed, unappealing breasts. It was also a hideous shade of purple and green, in a spectacularly unlovely pattern.

As he looked at it in disgust he realised her expression had changed again. It was one he recognised. She'd worn a similar expression the time he'd looked her over in his flat, deciding that she was ideal for his purposes. This time he recognised it.

Mortification.

He also recognised his own reaction to it—that same sense of discomfort he'd felt on the drive back from the airport this evening. OK, he admitted, so it wasn't the poor girl's fault she looked about as appealing as a plucked chicken. And she certainly didn't have any spare cash to splash out on a decent swimsuit that might actually do something *for* her body instead of *against* it. In fact, that restriction must apply to her whole wardrobe, which was certainly the most appalling he'd ever encountered.

A sudden image of Lucia flashed into his mind, curved and poured into her endless designer numbers, worn a bare handful of times before being discarded.

The comparison was unkind. The girl in front of him might have come from a different planet.

He frowned. Another memory flashed in his mind— Lucia calling her a *putana*.

The stab of discomfort came again, stronger this time. What the hell business had Lucia to call her that? The idea was ludicrous.

More than ludicrous.

It was offensive.

His eyes flicked to the child again, still desperate to get back into the pool. OK, so there was no father around— but accusing her of being feckless, as she obviously had been, was hardly the same as accusing her of prostitution.

You know nothing of me or my circumstances...

Her accusation of the morning bit into his mind. And she'd understood what Lucia had called her. She shouldn't have, but she had.

The feeling of discomfort mounted.

She was dragging the wailing boy towards the lounger, speaking to him sternly, and had managed to get a towel around his little body. He promptly threw it off with an even louder wail. But the girl wrapped him up in it yet again, and just as swiftly wrapped herself as well, knotting the towel around her like a sarong. She straightened up.

Maybe it was because the towel veiled from his eyes the hideous swimsuit, or maybe it was the lowering sun casting an amber glow over the pool area, reflecting warm light on to her, but suddenly he thought she looked quite graceful, with her slender limbs and sunlit skin. She had long hair, he noticed with mild surprise. It wasn't loose, though, it was tied back in a long stringy ponytail. He hadn't even realised she did have long hair—she'd always had it clamped on the back of her head by some kind of clip in a totally style-less way.

He watched her pick up the kiddie, hoist him on to her hip. His wails had died away now, and he was staring at Rafaello instead, with his big dark eyes. What had she said his name was? Benji? He'd try and remember next time. It might stop her correcting him in that snippy way.

She cleared up her stuff and left, muttering a defiant 'Excuse me' as she moved past with all her clutter. The child—*Benji*, he reprimanded himself—was clutching his inflatable ring as if it were golden treasure.

A mixture of exasperation and discomfort filled Rafaello. The girl had obviously been enjoying herself with her baby—*Benji*, he reminded himself—and now they were hurrying away. It was quite unnecessary. They wouldn't have bothered him, provided they stayed out of his swimming lane.

Well, too late now. She'd insisted on going. It was hardly his fault, he told himself, feeling irritated. He took up a position by the edge of the pool and executed a perfect racing dive, ploughing down to the far end twenty metres away in a punishing, rapid freestyle.

Forty minutes and two kilometres later he hauled himself out, tired but in a markedly better mood. The sun had gone now, and dusk was settling in, but the air was still pleasantly warm. He walked down the length of the pool, picked up his towel and rubbed his hair, before wrapping the towel over his body.

Hunger nipped at him. He'd shower, change and take an aperitif. His aunt would pounce on him, he knew, and give him an earful, but his mood after exercise was good enough to put up with it. He was glad she'd turned up. She always managed to calm his father down—she'd been doing it all her life.

And having his aunt and uncle present would certainly help to make dinner less of an ordeal. They would help to keep things civil. He'd try and get Bernardo started on whatever his current research was—his uncle didn't speak much, except when it was on his favourite scholarly topic. Then he could expound for ever if he found a willing victim.

A smile curved Rafaello's mouth as he headed back indoors. He had a lot of time for Bernardo—there was a whole lot of good sense in there, and a tempering disposition that went well with his aunt's acid-tongued approach to life—and family. They'd never had children, and Rafaello had fond memories of both his aunt and uncle making a huge fuss of him when he'd been little, arriving for family celebrations and holidays up in the cool Tuscan hills.

Right on cue, some twenty minutes later, as he sipped his chilled beer, sitting out on the terrace overlooking the gardens stretching away all around the villa, the cypress trees framing the vista of the valley below, he heard the businesslike tread of his aunt approaching. He stood up as she came to him, and helped her take a seat.

'So,' she began, with a martial light in her eye, 'now we talk.'

Upstairs, Magda was giving Benji his bath. It was hardly necessary—he was as clean as a whistle from the pool—

but it seemed compensation for him after having been dragged away from the water. She didn't feel too bad about it, however—it hadn't been their first dip. They'd already swum twice earlier in the day, which had been spent, like yesterday, in blissful ease.

She'd swum, had lunch with Maria and Giuseppe, swum again, napped with Benji and then explored the beautiful gardens and grounds of the villa—a skilful mix of formality and cultivated wildness—even venturing further up the hill behind into the lower slopes of the plentiful chestnut woods that stretched behind the villa. Hearing from Maria on their return that Rafaello's aunt and uncle had arrived, she'd hidden herself and Benji in the pool area again for a final swim.

She cringed inwardly with memory. Oh, why hadn't she left the pool ten minutes earlier instead of being caught by Rafaello? If embarrassment was fatal she'd have been dead on the spot! For the millionth time his image burned into her retinas—six feet of honed, smooth, tanned muscle, total physical male perfection...

Thank God she hadn't blushed. That would have been the ultimate mortification—letting him see that she couldn't take her eyes from him. As it was she had simply had the familiar mortification—if more intense this time—of having him look at her as if she were covered in slime.

She sat back on her heels, letting Benji scoop up a handful of foam and plaster it to the tiles beside the bath with a gurgling laugh. She pushed back a strand of unruly hair that had got loose, and as she twisted her head slightly she caught sight of herself in the wall-length mirror inset opposite the bath.

Oh, God, she looked so awful. Her T-shirt was totally shapeless and faded. Not that anything could have flattered her, she knew. Her face was unremarkable, her hair dull and mousy, besides being stringy and overlong. She tried

o remember the last time she'd had it cut and failed—long
hair was cheaper than short hair.

She was a mess, repellent to any man—let alone a man
so blessed with gorgeousness as Rafaello di Viscenti. The
memory of him staring disparagingly at her, his long-lashed
eyes sweeping condemningly over her every unpleasing
feature, made her feel ashamed.

She knew such a feeling was illogical. It was not her
fault she was plain, nor Rafaello's that he was male beauty
incarnate. Nor, she added punishingly, was it his fault that
any woman who caught his eye would have to be a stunning beauty for him to appreciate her.

A dab of flying foam caught her on the chin, distracting
her. Benji chuckled wickedly. Magda's frown lightened,
and deliberately she put aside all painful thoughts. Benji
could not care less what she looked like—all he wanted
was her love. And that—she smiled down lovingly at him,
and paddled more foam in his direction—he had for ever
and ever.

Afterwards—bathroom tidied and Benji changed into a
clean nappy and his second-hand pyjamas—she sat him in
the middle of the bed, propped up against the pillows with
his scruffy but adored little teddy bear, and settled down to
read his favourite bedtime picture book. He was tired tonight, and would soon be asleep, she could see. When he
was she would sneak down to the kitchen and beg a sand-
wich for her own supper—with guests in the house she did
not want to be a nuisance to Maria and Giuseppe. And she
would feel much safer tucked up away in her bedroom, out
of sight of any of Rafaello's family—and especially
Rafaello.

It would be what he wanted, too, she knew.

Rafaello had not expected to enjoy his aunt's lecture, and
he did not. But at least she could see his side of things as
well—unlike his father—even though she told him roundly

that the pair of them deserved everything they handed out
to each other.

'You are impossible, the pair of you!' she finished. Then,
taking another breath, she said, 'Very well, now that I have
made that plain to you, you had best go and fetch this bride
of yours.'

Rafaello stalled in the act of lifting his beer glass to his
mouth. He'd been nursing it all the way through the lecture
and he was now in need of its reviving contents. He stared
at his aunt.

'Well, there is no point hiding her any longer. I might
as well see for myself,' his aunt told him.

'She is in her room,' Rafaello said stiffly.

'Well, go and fetch her. She can't stay up there all night.'

Rafaello set down his glass with a distinct click. 'She is
looking after her child,' he said remotely.

His aunt waved her hand in an Italian fashion. 'One of
the maids can sit with the infant. You had better go and
see if she is ready to come down to dine yet. You know
your father cannot abide tardiness.'

Rafaello's jaw tightened. 'You do not quite understand
Tia—' he began, but his aunt cut him short.

'What I understand, Rafaello,' she said, and there was a
definite snap in her voice, 'is that you deserted the poor
girl the moment you brought her here. Haring off to Rome
if you please, simply because you are obsessed with that
wretched company. But I tell you this: however pressing
your business affairs—however eager you are to take over
from Enrico—you do *not* abandon your bride in your own
home. It is insupportable. And I do not care *how* much of
a marriage of convenience it is to you, or how much of a
misalliance. There are decencies to be observed and this is
one of them. Whoever the girl is, however utterly unsuit-
able she is to be Signora di Viscenti, you have married her
and that is that. She is your wife.'

Rafaello lips pressed together. This was not something

he had anticipated at all! He stood up abruptly, looking down into his aunt's militant expression.

'Very well,' he said bitingly, and then suddenly found himself continuing, 'But I must ask you to…to go easy on her.'

It was that stab of discomfort again, pricking at him. His aunt was a formidable woman—she would make mincemeat of that hapless creature upstairs in her bedroom. And suddenly he found that the thought of the girl ripped to shreds by his aunt's sharp tongue was painful.

But as he spoke he found his aunt was looking at him with a strange light in her eye. As if he had surprised her.

'I shall take into account her…unfortunate circumstances,' she answered dryly. 'Despite my brother's histrionics as to her morals and background, from what Maria tells me—yes, I have had a talk with her as well, and very enlightening it was, too!—the girl is nothing more than a misfortunate single mother, of which a large number abound these days. She certainly seems to have convinced Maria she is nothing worse, and that is no easy task. I admit I am curious to see her for myself. Well, be off with you. Go and fetch your wife.'

His wife. As Rafaello strode away at his aunt's imperious bidding, the words tolled in his brain. This was not supposed to be happening. The girl was not supposed to intrude into his life in this way—simply marrying her had been intrusion enough. And now here was his aunt, demanding that he fetch her as if she were his wife for real.

But she is your wife—you married her.

But I didn't intend to get landed with her, he thought balefully as he took the stairs two at a time. He reached the door of her bedroom and rapped sharply.

Magda started. She'd been half dozing, watching the foolish moths fly in through the open window and head, unerringly and fatally, towards the bedside lamp she'd set carefully down on the floor so it gave enough light for her to read by but did not shine in Benji's eyes as he slept beside her. As she watched, trying ineffectually to shoo them away from the lethal lure, she felt a frightening sympathy with them. Rafaello di Viscenti was like that light—beautiful, irresistible, and quite deadly. She could so easily let herself be like one of the moths...

The rap came again, and, casting a nervous glance at Benji lest he wake, she scrambled off the bed and went to open the door.

Her jaw fell open.

Rafaello was standing there, looking breathtakingly attractive in charcoal trousers and a dark blue shirt whose open collar in no way made him look casual but instead gave him an air of Latin cool that made her breath catch helplessly in her throat.

'May I come in?' He stepped inside even as he spoke, his glance taking in the sleeping baby. 'Do I disturb you?'

Yes, screamed Magda inside her own head. You absolutely terrify me. You walk in here, looking like every woman's fantasy, and you ask if you disturb me.

Belatedly she summoned her scattered wits. 'No,' she gulped. 'Not at all.'

He nodded. The diffused light from the lamp on the floor turned his hair to sable and threw the planes of his face into edged relief. She felt her breath catch all over again.

'Dinner will be served shortly. Can you be ready in time?'

She stared gormlessly.

'One of the maids is coming to sit with the ch—' he caught himself, and amended his words. 'To sit with Benji. She will fetch you if he wakes.'

'He usually sleeps through until after midnight,' Magda said faintly, scarcely taking in what he had just said. 'Then he wakes, usually.' Except that last night, and the night before, Benji had slept soundly all night—exhausted, she fancied, after all the exertions and new experiences, as well as the silence of the Tuscan countryside. It had given her the first good sleep she'd had since he'd been born, and it had done her good, she knew. She was feeling far more rested than she usually did. Of course, she thought wryly, she was also living a life of total leisure at the moment. That helped as well…

'Good.' Rafaello was speaking again, and she forced herself to listen. 'Then I will leave you to change. Please be as quick as you can.'

His gaze flitted over her saggy T-shirt disparagingly.

She acknowledged him faintly and, nodding briefly, he took his leave.

Downstairs, he joined his aunt and uncle in the drawing room, to be greeted by the news from a poker-faced Giuseppe that his father had declared he was too ill to eat and retired to his bedroom. Rafaello's mouth tightened, but he said nothing about his father's obvious refusal to sit at the same table as his unwanted daughter-in-law.

His aunt was less forbearing.

'Impossible man!' exclaimed his aunt. 'I just hope this bride of yours has a thick skin, Rafaello.'

Her nephew's face shuttered. The familiar stab came again. A thick skin? She had needed that from the moment he had looked her over and decided she was the perfect vehicle of his revenge…

The sound of the door opening made him turn suddenly. As if his thoughts had summoned her, she was there, standing uncertainly in the doorway.

She looked like a mouse, he found himself thinking. She was wearing that atrocity of a frock, the same one she had married him in, with its hem hanging unevenly around her calves, no waist and a most unflattering sagging neckline, and her hair was tightly brushed back and knotted punishingly on the back of her head. The best that could be said about her was that she looked neat and clean-scrubbed.

'Good evening,' she said in a strangled voice that was scarcely audible.

For a moment the tableau held, and then, as he saw the colour—what there was of it—start to drain out of her face, Rafaello stepped forward and went up to her.

CHAPTER FIVE

'COME and meet my aunt and uncle.'

He took her elbow and drew her forward. She was as tense as a board under his touch, and she almost stumbled as she walked into the room until he let her go. Even then, as he stood by her side, he could see she was stiff as wood.

'Tia Elizavetta—this is Magda. Magda—my aunt, Elizavetta Calvi. And this is my uncle, *il professore* Bernardo Calvi.'

Magda felt her breath solidify in her lungs. Shock rippled through her. Rafaello di Viscenti had called her by her name.

Up till now it had been pointedly—painfully—obvious that he never addressed her by name, simply spoke directly to her. And this evening—her eyes widened in realisation— he had called Benji by his name as well! She could hardly believe it.

Nor could she believe that he was actually introducing her to his aunt and uncle. When she had walked in and seen them present she had steeled herself for another explosion like the one that had greeted her first presentation to Rafaello's family. But now, instead, the elegant woman in her discreetly stylish clothes who was his aunt was merely looking her over with gimlet eyes. She stood still, letting the woman inspect her. True, the woman's mouth had tightened as she perused her, but she hadn't gone apoplectic. Then, suddenly, the woman smiled at her. Not a huge smile, nor a very warm one, but a civil, social smile, and a smile for all that. She received a smile from the woman's husband as well, the professor, this time more warm if a little vague.

77

'Unfortunately,' Rafaello was saying in a remote voice, 'my father finds himself indisposed tonight. I hope you will excuse him.'

Magda bit her lip. It was perfectly obvious that Rafaello's father was avoiding her as if she had the plague. Well, she thought thinly, from his point of view I do. I'm hardly his ideal daughter-in-law. Oh, why on earth hadn't Rafaello realised that he should have chosen a woman from his own world if he'd wanted to avoid marrying his cousin? Instead he'd just rashly married the first woman he'd seen—she could recall that posh blonde's words with punishing clarity—and now look at the mess he was in. He should have thought a bit more about what his father's reaction was going to be to a wife who worked as a cleaner. *And* had a baby with her to boot. Didn't Rafaello care that that only made things worse?

Her chin lifted. Well, that was between Rafaello and his father. For herself, she couldn't care less if she earned her living cleaning the homes of rich people—or if Benji had no father. Benji was her life, Kaz's most precious gift to her—a final gift.

Giuseppe was clearing his throat and informing them that dinner was ready to be served. Rafaello moved closer to her and took her elbow once more. She tensed all over again. She knew it was nothing but show, but she wished he would stand about half a kilometre away from her. Then she forced herself to untense. She might as well be a block of wood as living flesh. She had not missed his disparaging look at her appearance, however swiftly it had been veiled.

Soon they were in the dining room, and Magda's eyes were shooting around the silk-hung room with its antique furniture. She was grateful to sit down at the gleamingly polished table.

Giuseppe and a pair of maids busied themselves serving the first course—delicate folds of Parma ham with sliced fresh pears, accompanied by a delicately flavoured white wine. Magda waited until the others had started eating, and then reached for whatever implements they had selected. As she took the first mouthful she paused, savouring the rich saltiness of the ham combined with the fresh nuttiness of the fruit.

'Is it to your taste?' Rafaello's aunt asked. Her English, though accented, was as impeccable as her nephew's.

'It's delicious.' Magda found herself answering spontaneously.

Signora Calvi smiled benignly. 'The pears are imported, alas, of which I do not approve—I, like most Italians, prefer to eat the fruits that are in season, and it is too early still for pears. But the ham is excellent. It is Parma ham—from a city perhaps better known in England for its cheese— parmesan.'

She was clearly going out of her way to make her feel comfortable, Magda realised. The kindness was appreciated, even if the explanation had been unnecessary. Parma ham was a familiar, if expensive item in British supermarkets these days, though doubtless quite inferior to what she was eating now.

'But there are many Tuscan specialities you will enjoy as well, I am sure,' Signora Calvi sailed on, placing an emphasis on Tuscan. 'Tuscany is famed for its simple cuisine, for dishes such as *bistecca alla fiorentina*, which is steak charred on coals, as well as duck and boar.'

Her husband held up a hand as he drank some of his wine. 'Do not be so harsh on poor Parma, my dear—after all, it shares a link with Tuscany, does it not?'

It was the first time Magda had heard Rafaello's uncle speak, apart from his quiet greeting to her, and he, like the rest of the family, spoke fluent English. His voice was a little dry, but good-humoured all the same. He glanced at her now, his face expectant, as though she were one of his students he was quizzing.

'This is Magda's first visit to Italy, Bernardo, she is unlikely to know your reference—' Rafaello's interjection was swift.

'The Duchess of Parma.' Magda spoke almost simultaneously as she remembered what her guidebook had told her. 'Marie-Louise, the Duchess of Parma and Napoleon's widow, was also the Duchess of Lucca.'

'Very good.' Professor Calvi beamed approvingly. 'You must be sure to visit Lucca very soon—it is a jewel of Tuscany.'

'I've read a little about it in the book I brought with me,' Magda replied. 'It is famous for its walls, I believe?'

'Yes, indeed. They were built at the end of the fifteenth century to repel the Spanish. Lucca succeeded in retaining its independence, and at one point was the only independent civic polity in Italy other than Venice—until Napoleon bestowed Lucca on his sister, Elisa, whom he also made Duchess of Tuscany.'

Magda frowned uncertainly. 'Was she the sister who was Queen of Naples?'

'No, that was Caroline, wife of his general, Murat. They, of course, replaced the deposed Bourbon monarchs of Naples, whose queen, also Caroline, has a rather romantic link with England.'

He paused again, clearly awaiting her answer. Magda cast about for the reference.

'She was friends with Lady Hamilton!' she remembered. 'That's where Emma Hamilton met Lord Nelson—in Naples.'

'Very good!' The approving beam came again.

'My husband is a historian, as you must already suspect,' his wife interjected dryly, having subjected Magda to a highly assessing and, she surmised, surprised look. 'Bernardo.' She turned to her husband. 'You must not be a bore.'

Magda smiled diffidently. 'History can never be boring—especially not in a country like Italy—there is just so much.'

She had said the right thing by the professor.

'And here in Tuscany is the richest history—even the name Tuscany hints at the earliest great Italian civilisation.'

'The Etruscans?' ventured Magda.

'The Etruscans,' confirmed the professor, and he was away, expansively expounding on the mysterious pre-Roman civilisation that had dominated the region long before Rome was mighty.

Magda was fascinated. All she knew came out of books, but here, across the table from her, was a native and an expert. She sat and listened, quite rapt, as Rafaello's uncle explained about the major Etruscan sites, their mysterious origins, strange religion and even stranger language that still remained undeciphered.

'I have always approved of the Etruscans,' put in his wife at one point. 'Their women were astonishingly liberated—they ate with the men and owned property, and were quite outspoken.'

Magda hid her smile. She could quite see why the formidable Signora Calvi should approve of such a state of affairs. She found she had glanced towards the head of the table, to see if Rafaello found his aunt's comment amusingly revealing, but when she looked at his face she stilled.

He was staring at her—simply staring at her—as if she'd sprouted extra arms and heads. She blinked, puzzled. Had she done something wrong? She looked away again, feeling her heart beating faster than it should. Was she behaving inappropriately? Was that it? Shouldn't she be putting herself forward and joining in the conversation, asking his uncle questions or presuming to answer them?

Then, across the table, she heard the professor say to Rafaello, 'Your wife will keep you busy for quite some time, my boy—you must take her on a tour. She has everything to see.'

She bit her lip again. The last thing Rafaello would want would be to be landed with taking her sightseeing.

'Oh, no,' she put in hurriedly, 'that would not be possible—my little boy…'

'I am sure your son will be quite content to be looked after by Maria and myself,' Signora Calvi replied calmly. 'This is ideal weather for touring.'

'Oh, no,' said Magda, disconcerted. 'Please—really— I couldn't leave Benji.'

'It will be good for him to develop the ability to be happy without your constant attendance,' pronounced Rafaello's aunt. 'You need have no anxiety about leaving him with us. Maria is extremely experienced with children, and she tells me he is a very good, well-brought up child, well advanced for his age. He is a credit to you, she tells me.'

She gave her benign smile, and Magda felt her colour rise. Her throat went tight. She stared down at her plate. Suddenly she felt a light touch on her hand.

'It has been hard for you, I think, no?' said Rafaello's aunt quietly. 'People will often make harsh judgements.'

She threw a deliberate look at Rafaello, who tightened his mouth. Then, with a deliberate change of subject, she said, 'Ring for Giuseppe, Rafaello. He may serve the next course.'

The remainder of the meal passed with relative ease. The professor, having discovered an eager listener in his nephew's bride, required very little prompting to continue his discourse, which ranged extensively over the history of Tuscany and that of Italy as a whole. Apart from a nagging worry over whether Benji was all right—even though she knew perfectly well that the smiling maid Gina was babysitting him—Magda found herself feeling less and less uncomfortable. It helped, too, that Rafaello said almost nothing, and that both his aunt and uncle seemed quite happy to let him remain as silent as he did.

It was not until Signora Calvi informed Giuseppe that

they would take coffee in the drawing room, and they got up from the table, that Rafaello was able to ask the question that had been infuriating him all evening.

As they stood back to let the professor and his wife leave the dining room, Magda felt her arm gripped.

'Perhaps you would like to tell me why,' demanded Rafaello, with a grim note in his voice that made her feel alarmed, 'given that you are quite evidently an educated woman, you earn your living in such a menial occupation.'

Magda stared up at him. He was too close to her again, but this time that was not the sole reason for her startled reaction.

'Educated?' she echoed.

'You have an excellent knowledge of history, for a start!' elucidated Rafaello bitingly. 'And you are obviously intelligent. So why do you work as a cleaner?'

Her face cleared. She was able to answer his question. 'I have no qualifications—I've always loved reading, but that's all. School was…difficult.' No need to bore him with the difficulty of being a child from a care home at a school where that was a cause for derision and mockery by more fortunate pupils. 'Although I did manage to get some GCSEs—they're the basic school leaving exams—I wasn't able to study any further.'

No need to tell him that that was the period when Kaz had first been diagnosed. 'But one of the things I would like to do, and you have made it possible—' she swallowed '—is to pursue further studies so that when Benji starts school I may be able to get some qualifications and get a better job eventually. I wouldn't work full time, of course, just during school hours. So I am always there for him.'

'Rafaello.' His aunt's voice came imperiously. 'Allow the poor child to have her coffee.'

Her arm was released and she was ushered with polite courtesy through to the drawing room.

'Come and sit beside me,' commanded Elizavetta Calvi,

having cast a shrewd look at her nephew and his wife, and she patted a space on the exquisite silk-upholstered sofa. 'Rafaello—Bernardo would like a cigar, but he is not to smoke in here. Be off with you both to the terrace, if you please.'

Subtlety clearly wasn't her strong point, thought Magda, and once again caught herself glancing at Rafaello. This time he met her eye, and for the barest second only amusement glimmered in them. And something else, too. A question. His aunt caught it, too.

'Magda will be perfectly safe,' she said caustically. 'She need tell me nothing she does not wish to.'

Personally, Magda had severe doubts about that, but the time she had spent over dinner had convinced her that, overbearing and autocratic as Elizavetta Calvi was, she was fundamentally well-meaning. There was no hostility directed at her.

And so it proved. Over two cups of coffee Rafaello's aunt proceeded to grill her comprehensively about her life, her job, her child and her reasons for marrying Rafaello di Viscenti. Only on one aspect did she hold back, to Magda's surprise—Benji's parentage.

'Such things happen,' she said bluntly. 'They always have and they always will. But I tell you, frankly I admire your courage in deciding to keep your child—it would have been so easy to have given him away.'

Never! The word leapt in Magda's throat, filling her with horror. More horror came on its heels—the knowledge that her own unknown birth mother had not even bothered to try and give her away. Simply left her to die in an alleyway. But she had survived, and with Benji would go on doing so.

Through the French windows she saw the silhouette of the man she had married for a hundred thousand pounds. Something kicked inside her, hard and painful. She looked away. No. That was pointless. Immature fantasy. Stupid and pathetic. He was not for her. Not even in her dreams.

She was awakened next morning by a maid bringing in a tray of coffee.

'*Buon giorno, signora,*' the girl said smilingly, cooing in Italian over Benji. He was still asleep, and Magda wondered at that as she sipped her fragrant coffee, looking out through the window to the tops of the cypress trees beyond, all bathed in morning sunlight.

She felt a wave of wellbeing go through her. All my life I'll remember this, she thought—how beautiful this place is. She felt sadness pricking at her that her time here was to be so short, before telling herself sternly that she was fortunate beyond belief to be here at all.

Her mind went back to the evening before, filling her with strange emotions. Rafaello's aunt and uncle had been so nice to her—and Rafaello had been so polite and civil, too! Signora Calvi hadn't even seemed to mind that she had married her nephew for money.

'Of course it is wrong,' she had said, in that unarguable fashion of hers, 'but it is quite understandable. I do not blame *you*, child.'

Magda frowned. Did that mean she blamed her nephew?

Heaviness filled her. Although she had walked into this minefield unwittingly, it was a still a horrible position to be in—everyone wishing you were a million miles away…

Benji's waking was a welcome diversion. He always woke in a playful, affectionate mood which could melt her even on days when she was half-dead with tiredness, let alone now, when her days were easy and her nights undisturbed.

Later, with both of them dressed, she picked up the coffee tray carefully with one hand, took Benji's small fingers with the other and set off for the kitchen and breakfast. But as she closed the bedroom door behind her she heard footsteps coming along from the far end of the wide landing.

Rafaello's father was walking towards her. When he saw her, he stopped dead. Magda froze. Although she'd seen him only briefly that hideous afternoon three days ago, she knew it was Enrico di Viscenti immediately. He was far too much like Rafaello some thirty-odd years on.

His face hardened. Magda didn't know what to do. Say good morning? Say nothing? Go back into her bedroom?

Benji, sensing the atmosphere, wrapped his arms around her leg as she stood there, coffee tray in her hand, not having a clue what to do.

'So,' said Enrico di Viscenti in a harsh voice, 'you are still here.'

Magda said nothing. She didn't know what to say.

'Do you imagine you will make yourself a home here?' Enrico threw at her in that same harsh voice. 'Do you imagine yourself as a great lady now—you and your *bastardo*?'

She tensed all the way through her body.

Rafaello's father took a menacing step towards her. His dark eyes bored into hers, filled with fury and disgust.

'Then know this! My benighted son chose you to insult me. He threw it in my face that he defied my wishes so much he deliberately brought home a bride who is the lowest of the low. He chose you because you are the worst wife he could find—plain, ignorant, common, amoral. From the slums of London, cleaning toilets for a living. He chose you to disgust me.'

She thought she would faint. She could hear the blood drumming in her ears. Around her leg, Benji buried his face in the worn material of her cotton trousers and whimpered. He could not understand the words—but he could understand the anger, the raw hatred that came through. The contempt.

Her vision blurred. Rafaello's father strode past her, and she heard him descend the marble stairs to the hall below.

She felt the tray shaking in her hands and knew that if she did not put it down it would fall from her nerveless fingers and crash to the ground. But she couldn't stop her hands shaking.

Then, suddenly, the tray was taken from her.

'In here—'

She felt herself propelled back through the bedroom door—open again somehow—felt Benji lifted away, heard his protest, and then she was sitting on the bed, Benji in her arms. She just sat there clutching him, *clutching* him, not seeing anything, not feeling anything, just hunched there, holding Benji, who was whimpering in her arms.

Someone was standing in front of her. Tall and dark, blocking out the light. She knew who it was. Rafaello di Viscenti. Who had chosen her for his bride not because she was convenient and malleable but because she would disgust his father. She was the 'lowest of the low'—his father's hideous words rang like blows in her head—the perfect insult to throw in his father's face.

'Magda…'

His voice came low.

She went on clutching Benji to her and staring blindly down at the carpet, trying not to think, not to feel…

'You must not—must not believe what my father said. It is me he is angry with.' The words grated from him.

Her hand curved round Benji's head, his hair satin-smooth. She could say nothing. Nothing at all.

Rafaello watched the gesture. He wanted to find the words but he couldn't. There were none to find. His father had said them all. But he had to try, all the same.

'Magda, I—'

Her head lifted and her eyes met his. Hers were quite, quite blank.

'You don't have to say anything. It's quite unnecessary.' If her voice had a crack in it, she ignored it. Refused to acknowledge it. She would not feel anything; she *would* not. She stood up, settling Benji on to her hip. Another half-cracked breath seared from her. 'Please tell me where I should go for breakfast this morning—or would you prefer that I stayed here in my room?' Her voice was controlled, but it was thin—thin like wire pulled so taut it must surely break any instant.

Rafaello's mouth thinned.

'In summer the family has breakfast on the terrace. Come—'

He held out his hand to her. She ignored it, and walked to the door instead. Rafaello was there before her, opening it and letting her go through with a courtesy he would have afforded a duchess. Instead, she thought, with the peculiar blankness that seemed to have closed down over her, he's wasting it on *me*.

He chose you for that very reason, deliberately and calculatedly, to knowingly insult his father by his choice of bride. He'd known exactly how his father would react all along—he hadn't been thoughtless at all. He'd been coldbloodedly set on using her to insult his father.

Family breakfast on the terrace was the very last thing that she wanted to endure, but the blankness would make it bearable after all. When she walked out with Rafaello she saw that his aunt and uncle were already there, as was his father.

Seeing Magda, the professor got to his feet and bade her good morning. She barely managed a nod in reply. With a scrape of iron on stone, Rafaello's father got to his feet, too. He picked up his full cup of coffee.

'I shall be in the library. I have matters to attend to.'

He walked away, making it obvious he refused to share her company.

The lowest of the low.

The words hit her again, and again.

Magda sat down, not where Rafaello was holding a chair for her, but at the farthest end of the table. She wanted to die, to sink through the floor. Her heart was in a vice, crushed with a pain she would not acknowledge.

'So,' said Elizavetta Calvi, her voice a little too loud, a little too determined, 'this is your little boy. And you said his name is—?'

'Benji,' said Rafaello, sitting down opposite Magda and flicking open his napkin. His voice was strained and Magda wondered why. Maybe it was the effort of giving her fatherless child his name.

She busied herself settling Benji on her lap, not meeting anyone's eyes, and one of the maids came out, bringing some warmed milk in Benji's feeding mug, which he gripped with delight and proceeded to imbibe gustily. For herself, she had no appetite. She seemed to be very far away, sitting behind a sort of glass wall that separated her from the others at the table, even when they spoke to her and she made brief, low-voiced, withdrawn replies. There was none of the drawing out or stimulating conversation of the night before.

'You are tired,' observed Rafaello's aunt, in a manner that was more a statement than a question.

Magda nodded in docile agreement, not meeting her eyes, feeding Benji a soft roll. Everyone was still very far away—especially Rafaello. He seemed to be light years away from her.

But he was watching her, she could see. His face was unreadable, and there was something shuttered about his eyes. Presumably, she thought, with that same remote, distant feeling that seemed to be pervading her whole brain, he is thinking how low and common I look, polluting his ancestral home. Wishing he could just dump me out with the trash.

Why did it hurt so much that Rafaello di Viscenti, a complete stranger to her in every meaningful definition of the word, should have deliberately and calculatedly used her to insult his father? Why did it hurt so much that he *wanted* her to be the lowest of the low, that he *wanted* to throw her in his father's teeth precisely because she was plain and common, a feckless single mother from the slums of London who cleaned toilets for a living?

She knew, with her head, that none of his litany of accusations was her fault, that she had nothing, *nothing* to be ashamed of. Someone had to clean toilets—and everything else. Someone had to keep the rich and pampered clean and comfortable. Those who did it were not shameful. To look down on someone because they were poor—*that* was shameful.

But she could tell herself that all she liked—somewhere, deep inside it just hurt that Rafaello di Viscenti had looked her over and catalogued every fact and factor about her that might disgrace his rich, well-bred, cultured, respectable family…and relished finding them so he could throw them in his father's face.

A scraping of chairs roused her from her painful reverie. Signora Calvi was speaking to her—Magda forced herself to listen.

'My dear, let Benji come with me for a while. Maria tells me one of her great-nieces has brought along some playthings her own children have outgrown. I believe there is a tricycle, and some toys that I am sure your little boy will adore. No, do not disturb yourself—he will come with me very happily, I have no doubt.'

She lifted Benji off Magda's lap and stood him on the terrace.

'*Vene.*' She smiled down at the infant. 'Come and see some new toys.'

'Toys' was a word Benji was pretty clued up on, and he toddled off happily, Signora Calvi holding one tiny hand, her husband the other. Magda watched the little procession make its way along the terrace and disappear around the corner of the house. She still felt dull, and numbed, and very far away inside.

Rafaello watched her watching them. She seemed very small, very young sitting there, far too young to have responsibility for a child.

Far too young to have to bear the cruel accusations his father had thrown at her.

His hands clenched on his thighs. *Dio*, she was hurt; it was obvious. There was a bleak, wounded look in her eyes which made him feel terrible. She'd withdrawn inside herself, shut herself away—and he couldn't blame her for that.

The feeling of discomfort he'd come to be familiar with around her sharpened acutely. Sharpened into guilt. He found himself wishing, with all his might, that he could undo the ugly scene that had played out in front of her bedroom door, that he could have stopped his father throwing those harsh, unpalatable insults in her face.

But Rafaello blamed himself, too. He had deliberately presented her to his father that first afternoon with a furious, sarcastic flourish, delineating every single unappealing, unflattering, unsavoury aspect of the woman he'd just married in order to ram home the message to his machinating father: You force my hand, force me to marry—well, look—look at the bride I've brought back with me.

Oh, he'd never intended the girl to find out—she wouldn't have understood what he'd shouted at his father—and yet, all the same, he had used her quite deliberately, used her wretched appearance and circumstances for his own ends.

Guilt flushed through him. A rare, unpleasant feeling.

And something more than guilt. Something that had started to spark in him all though that painful breakfast as he had sat there, watching her, watching her closed face, the wounded look in her eyes.

Anger.

An emotion very familiar to him over these last months as his father had sought to reel him in, tighter and tighter, into Lucia's grasping clutches. He'd lived with anger, day in, day out, until it had soaked all the way through him, obliterating everything else except his absolute, total determination not to let his father play with his life as if it were a toy. Yes, anger was a familiar feeling.

But this time there was something different about it. This time it was directed at himself.

With an abrupt movement he got to his feet.

'Come.'

Magda's eyes snapped away from where Benji and the Calvis had just disappeared. Rafaello was standing there, looking tall and commanding. Haltingly she stood up, dusting breadcrumbs from her trousers. As she looked up she saw Rafaello studying them disdainfully.

Yes, she thought silently, they are cheap, and unflattering, and hopelessly unfashionable. I do not wear them from choice, but necessity. If I had your money I would not wear them—but I don't, so I do. Poverty is not a crime. And it is not a cause for shame. I will not, she told herself, bow my head in disgrace for my lack of wealth. Nor will I bow it because I do not know who my parents were!

'Today,' announced Rafaello in a tight voice, 'we are driving to Lucca.'

Magda's eyes widened. She had not in the slightest expected this. Then she realised that it must be something to do with dinner last night, when the professor had talked about Lucca and his wife had urged her nephew to take his bride touring.

'It is quite unnecessary,' she said. Her voice was low and blank.

'You will,' replied Rafaello, 'allow me to be the judge of that.'

She sensed anger in him beneath the clipped words. She could not be surprised. His aunt had chivvied him, in her imperious fashion, to take her sightseeing, and it was obvious he would not be too thrilled at the prospect of not only wasting a good day but wasting it in the company of a woman he had chosen for being the lowest of the low...

'I can't leave Benji,' she said. She couldn't meet his eyes, she found. Hers were focussing somewhere just below, where the smooth strong column of his throat rose out of the open-necked top of his polo shirt. She found that was not a good place to focus and shifted her gaze a little lower. But that meant her gaze was now eyeballing the broad expanse of his pectoral muscles, straining at the knitted fabric of the polo shirt, descending to the narrow leanness of his abdomen.

She flicked her gaze so that it was staring harmlessly over his shoulder instead, at a distant cypress tree edging the gardens.

'Benji will be fine,' Rafaello said, with the dismissiveness of a childless man for the neurotic anxieties of a mother. 'Between Maria and my aunt he will do very well, be assured—they are both very taken with him.' He glanced at his watch—a thin, expensive-looking circlet of gold on his strong wrist. 'I should like to set off in half an hour. Please be ready.'

He nodded at her and was gone, striding off indoors.

She sighed. What should she do? Dig her heels in and refuse to go with him? She certainly wanted to. The very thought of having to spend any time at all with him was anathema, let alone being dutifully carted around sightseeing by a man who wished her to perdition. What on earth was he doing this for? Surely he could have come up with some excuse about pressing matters of work to distract his aunt from her evident determination to pack them off together? And it didn't matter what he said—she did not like to leave Benji. She'd never spent any time away from him at all—ever.

Yet when she went off in search of him she found that he was not missing her at all. Maria and Rafaello's aunt were making a huge fuss of him, and he had an exciting push-along trike to ride. The housekeeper hurried over to her.

'Go,' she instructed her. 'The little one will be very happy. He does not notice you are not here. If he sees you he will want you. So go now. Yes, yes, if he is unhappy without you I shall phone Signor Rafaello on his mobile phone, and he will return you at once. He has promised me. But we shall take care of the boy as if he were ours. And I have cared for many, many children—go, go now.' She shooed Magda away and returned eagerly to Benji, volubly admiring his prowess on his vehicle.

Reluctantly she turned and left. She knew that it was sensible for Benji to start being happy away from her, for when she returned to England and bought a proper place of her own to live it would be time to start introducing Benji to playgroups and nursery school.

But it still pulled at her terribly as she went up to her room to tidy herself and change into something very slightly less shabby. She had a cotton skirt with her, khaki-coloured, which although it hung on her hips was at least a skirt. She put on a white cotton short-sleeved blouse with it, slipped an olive-green jumper into her capacious bag that seemed strangely empty without its usual complement of baby stuff, and then went downstairs again. She ached to go and check on Benji again, but knew it would be counter-productive.

She stood in the hall, wondering what to do, hoping that whatever happened she would not meet Rafaello's father. But with any luck he was in that room with closed double doors—she could hear opera wafting out of it. Verdi, by the sound of things. Though she owned no hi-fi, she had scraped enough money to buy a small portable cassette player and radio, and usually spent the evenings once Benji was asleep reading and listening to the wealth of current affairs, arts and science programmes available, as well as her favourite classical music stations.

Rapid footsteps on the stairs made her turn. Rafaello was descending—looking, she thought as her breath caught in her lungs, like some Roman god coming down to earth, all lithe power and grace in dark, immaculately cut chinos and his pale, open-necked polo shirt. A silk-lined jacket was hooked over his shoulder with his finger, and from the other hand dangled a pair of sunglasses. She stood, battered bag held in front of her with both hands, awaiting his bidding and trying to stop thinking that he was the most beautiful male object in the universe.

'You are ready? Good.' His tone was brisk, impersonal, the way it usually was when he was required to address her.

He headed for the front door, and reluctantly she went after him. Outside, the sun dazzled her, and she blinked, following his crunching footsteps over the gravel as he headed around to the back of the villa.

'Wait,' he instructed her, as they arrived at what was evidently a row of garages. Dutifully she did so, and he headed inside one of them. A moment later a loud, throaty roar sounded—like a dragon disturbed in its lair. A monstrous beast of an open-topped car emerged slowly, gleaming scarlet and bearing the easily recognisable insignia that marked it as a top-of-the-range sports car.

Rafaello nosed it round to position it beside Magda. Then he leaned across and opened the door.

'Get in—'

She did, very trepidatiously, and seemed to sink almost right down to the ground. Just as she was getting her bearings he leant across her, reaching for the seat belt.

She froze. He'd never been this physically close to her, and it was unnerving. She shrank back into the deep bucket leather seat, and tried not to feel that at any moment her breasts would brush his arm. Then, just as swiftly, he was gone again, sitting back in the driver's seat. He slipped his dark glasses over his eyes, put the car into gear, and roared off.

Magda hung on for dear life, as if she were on a roller-coaster, as they headed down towards the autostrada running along the valley of the River Arno.

She stared ahead, and around, as the Tuscan landscape shot by her, blurred by speed, and glanced at Rafaello's hands on the steering wheel. They curved around it, tensile and expert, tilting and twisting just enough to manoeuvre the awesomely powerful car-just the way he wanted it, dropping one hand repeatedly to the gearstick to change gears relentlessly up and down as the journey required.

He seemed, Magda thought, to be working something out of his system.

CHAPTER SIX

THE walls of Lucca were as spectacular as her guidebook had promised, girdling the ancient city and topped with plane trees to make, she could see, an elevated walkway.

But the walls were not Rafaello's destination, nor the medieval cathedral of San Martino, nor any of the city's host of churches within the ancient *centro storico*, nor the art museum, nor the Puccini museum which commemorated one of Lucca's most famous sons. Instead, Magda found herself being walked up to a narrow building with an elegant frontage, in one of the lanes that led off the fashionable Via Fillungo. She had been going along in a daze, her neck craning crazily as she took in all around her. Wherever she looked were the wonders of an ancient Tuscan city, drenched in history: the *palazzos* and the churches, the cafés and the restaurants, and she soaked up the architectural glory that was Italy.

'Come,' said Rafaello, and ushered her inside the doorway.

A brightly lit reception desk faced her, staffed by a chicly-dressed woman in her twenties. She looked up from an appointments book as they entered, and her face lit up.

'Rafaello.' She launched into voluble Italian, coming around from behind her desk and lavishing kisses on both his cheeks, openly hugging him. He said something to her with a laugh, clearly at ease with her. Then he began to talk.

Magda stood uncomfortably a little way away, aware from the expression on the woman's face, and the little glances she threw at her from time to time as she heard Rafaello out, interjecting a few questions of her own, that she was the object of their conversation. She clutched her bag awkwardly and felt the colour rising dully in her cheeks. She was just about to turn away and stare out through the window on to the narrow street outside when the woman gave a delighted laugh, clapped her hands, and turned to Magda.

'Come, come,' she said brightly in English, 'there is *so* much to do, and so little time. But, oh, the result will be *favoloso*!'

She beckoned to her smilingly. 'Rafaello we send away—he is quite useless here, and I have no wish for his opinions.' She glanced at him humorously. *'Vattene! Vattene! A piu tardi.'* She made shooing gestures with her hands.

Magda finally found her voice. 'Please—what is happening?'

The woman's dark eyes sparkled mischievously. 'A surprise!'

Magda looked anxiously at Rafaello, hands clenching each other over the worn strap of her bag. His face was unreadable, but abruptly he said something to the woman, who, giving an understanding nod, headed out through a door at the rear of the room. He looked at Magda a moment as she stood there, visibly anxious.

'There is nothing to worry about,' he said. His voice came more tersely than he had intended. 'Just place yourself in Olivia's hands and you will be fine.'

'I don't understand,' she said stiffly.

He looked down at her a moment longer. Then, as if finding the words difficult, he said, 'If I could undo what you heard my father say this morning I would do so. But I cannot. All I can do,' he finished, 'is disprove it.'

Her face stilled. It was like a mask sliding over her face—the way it had been when he had taken her back into her room, the way it had been at breakfast. Giving her a wall to hide behind—a wall to shield her from what she had heard his father tell her.

Only the eyes gave her away. He could see the hurt in them.

'But you can't disprove it,' she said quietly, her voice quite expressionless. 'Because it is the truth, isn't it? What your father said? I was…am…the perfect insult to throw at him. The total opposite of anything your family could possibly welcome as a bride. And that's why you married me. That's exactly why you married me and not someone from your own world. To insult your father.'

He made a noise in his throat as though he was going to speak, but she went on. 'I told you it didn't matter, and it doesn't. You are paying me a hundred thousand pounds, and for that I have no business to make a fuss.'

She spoke quite steadily, but all the same there was something not quite right with her voice.

Something twisted inside Rafaello like a knife in his gut. 'You say it is the truth, Magda—but it isn't. You've already proved it a lie to me—and to my aunt and uncle, and Maria and Giuseppe. Now I just want to finish the job.'

She stared at him. 'What part is a lie? Tell me? That Benji has no father? That I dress like something left on a rubbish dump? That I clean toilets for a living? That I am so far from being the sort of female who could be your wife that I might as well be a clod of earth underfoot? What part is a lie?'

A nerve started to tick in his cheek. She was looking at him quite expressionlessly, but he felt emotions surging inside him. One was anger, that same brand of anger that had driven him this morning. But there was more than anger.

Guilt. It burned him like acid.

He spelt out his repudiation to her. 'You are not the first woman to have a child outside marriage. It is no longer the stigma it once was—even here in Italy. And we have already discussed your situation—you obviously have the intelligence to be something far more, and one day, when you are freed from the drudgery of poverty, you shall be. Your origins are not your fault, any more than your son's are his. And as for your appearance—well, that is about to be dealt with.'

He turned his face away from her—he did not want to see her looking at him, hiding the hurt behind that shuttered mask she had put over her face. 'Olivia.' He spoke in Italian and the woman emerged, an enquiring look on her face.

'It is all explained?' she said in English. 'Good.' She smiled at Magda again. 'Now we begin.'

'I will return later,' said Rafaello to Magda, and walked out.

She stared after him helplessly. What should she do? Should she go after him and tell him…? Tell him what? Tell him she'd like to do something else—like go back to London and never lay eyes on him or his family or his precious Tuscan villa ever again? Well, she couldn't. She had signed papers—a contract, a wedding certificate—and there was nothing whatsoever she could do until Rafaello di Viscenti decided it was time to send her back to England without risking any possibility of the marriage being declared fraudulent and invalid and so play right into his father's hands again.

'Come this way,' said Olivia in her bright, smiling voice. With a dull, numb feeling of resignation, Magda followed her.

Rafaello sat at the café looking out over the piazza which had once been a Roman amphitheatre, two thousand years ago. Apart from making one single purchase, he'd cooled his heels for well over two hours now, spending the time moodily striding around the city, wandering in and out of the countless churches, ignoring, as he always did when he wasn't in a receptive mood, the more than frequent glances he received from tourist and Italian females alike.

It had been impulse—impulse and guilt—that had made him yank that poor scrawny creature out of the villa this morning and throw her into Olivia's clutches to improve upon nature somehow—anyhow. But maybe he had not done the girl any favours by letting Olivia loose on her. He frowned. Maybe the material Olivia had to work on was hopeless! Maybe he had only set her up for yet another round of humiliation at his hands…

Hadn't he already humiliated her enough?

He gestured for another cup of coffee and picked up his newspaper again. Perhaps the miseries of the world at large would take his mind off his guilt.

Some forty minutes later his mobile sounded. Reaching inside his jacket pocket, he flicked it on.

'*Pronto*—'

'Rafaello?' It was Olivia. 'We're all done. We'll meet you at the restaurant. See you there.'

He made his way to the restaurant where he'd reserved a table for lunch. Inside, he spotted Olivia immediately, by the crowded bar area. She saw him and gave a wave. He headed towards her, wondering what she'd done with Magda. Misgiving filled him again—perhaps Olivia had found it so impossible to make the girl presentable and had left her behind in the salon while she conveyed the bad tidings to him.

As he approached, a woman seated with her back to him at the bar caught his eye. There were a good many females in the place, but this one definitely caught his attention. His eyes flickered over her. She was sitting very straight, and very still. She was wearing a sleeveless shift in dark cinnamon raw silk. She was very slender, with a long, elegant back. Her hair, a delicate, unusual shade of light brown, skilfully coloured, he realised, with soft amber highlights, rested in a sleek wave over her shoulders, lightly flicked at the ends. Interesting, he found himself thinking. Something different. Intriguing. He wanted her to turn, so he could see if she looked as good from the front as the back.

Then, remembering this was hardly the occasion to be assessing the charms of other women, he dragged his eyes back to Olivia. She was watching him approach, his gaze clearly taken by the woman at the bar. He reached her and greeted her with the customary kiss on either cheek.

'Well—how did it go?' he asked in Italian. Mentally he prepared himself for the worst. He glanced around, but there was still no sign of Magda.

'See for yourself,' replied Olivia in a curious voice. If he hadn't known better he'd have said that she was trying not to burst out laughing. He glanced around, still not seeing the poor dab of a girl he'd thrust at Olivia that morning. Resolutely he ignored the intriguing woman with her back to him—he must not eye her up. She would just have to be one that got away, that was all.

'Magda—' said Olivia, and Rafaello saw her lips twitching as she watched him *not* looking at the woman seated at the bar. Clearly it amused her that he wanted to study another woman when his only concern should be what Olivia had managed to do with the one he'd handed over to her more than three hours ago.

Even so, as he glanced around for Magda, he couldn't help noticing from the corner of his eye that the woman at the bar had chosen that very moment to swivel slowly on her seat. He couldn't resist it. He turned to look at her.

For a moment he just stared, disbelieving. There was something wrong with his eyes—there had to be. The woman at the bar had Magda's face.

But it wasn't Magda's face—it was the face of a stunning female that was drawing more eyes than his.

'*Dio mio,*' he breathed. '*Non posso crederici!*'

Olivia gave a crow of delight, but Rafaello ignored her. He was still staring, still disbelieving. It was Magda, but it wasn't Magda. Her unprepossessing features had all been subtly rearranged, it seemed, and the effect was extraordinary. It wasn't just the make-up that Olivia had applied—skilful though that was—it was more. Her skin was not sallow and blemished, it was flawless. There was no pale pastiness but a beautiful, translucent glow about her. Her eyes were deeper, larger—quite beautiful. Her narrow face was delicate, framed by that fall of gleaming, polished hair, her cheekbones were sculpted, drawing attention to those beautiful eyes. And her mouth...

He felt a kick in his stomach. Her mouth simply made him want to slide his hand beneath that fall of hair and bring his own mouth down...

'You like?'

It was Olivia's deliberately arch, openly teasing voice that brought him back. But only momentarily. His eyes slid back to the woman he hardly recognised, moving from her face to drink in the rest of her. She was as slender from the front as the back—not scrawny. *Dio*, how could he have thought her scrawny? She was like a willow, pliant and graceful. The simple, superbly cut line of her shift delineated each breast, not full, but high and softly rounded...

He could not take his eyes off her.

And she was staring back at him. Staring with that same expression of stunned disbelief as his. He wondered why. Then he stopped wondering and went back to working his eyes down her slender body, right down her gazelle-like legs and then back up to her face again.

Absently he felt a slight kiss brush against his cheek, heard a soft, '*Ciao*, Rafaello—enjoy...' as Olivia slipped past him, but he paid no attention.

'Magda?' His voice husked, as if it were not working quite properly.

She bit her lip, and with that familiar gesture he suddenly accepted that this really, truly was the poor dab of a creature he'd so arrogantly made use of for his own self-obsessed ends and treated with total indifference as a god-sent tool, ideal for his single purpose—to confound his father.

Emotions warred within him. Some familiar, some completely new. Up to now, the best emotion he'd been able to come up with for her had been pity—a sort of careless, almost contemptuous pity for so unlovely and wretched a member of her sex. Pity shot with guilt that he'd exposed her to the vituperation of his father, his lashing out at her, forcing a knowledge upon her that had been vicious in its cruelty.

He had never meant her to realise why he had chosen her. Never meant her to have that cruel truth thrown at her.

The twist in his guts came again.

You thought that you could just pay her, and she'd put up and shut up.

Well, he knew better now. His father had held a mirror up to him, and the sight had not been pleasant. Hearing his own litany of condemnation echoed by his father had made him realise, horribly, for the first time, just how callous he had been.

But he intended to make it up to her. To prove his father wrong. To prove himself wrong!

And, *Dio*, how he was being proved wrong!

The emotions battled inside him. The guilt was becoming familiar now, but the second was completely new—and blew him away.

It was desire.

Magda was reeling. Reeling and whirling in a kind of white-out blur of emotions which were swirling inside her head so tempestuously she could scarce make sense of them. She caught at one, the easiest one to catch, and knew that it was shock, sheer shock and disbelief, that Rafaello di Viscenti—beautiful, arrogant, breathtakingly gorgeous Rafaello di Viscenti, who was as far removed from her as if he were one of the gods of old—was looking her over as if she were…as if she were a woman—a real, flesh-and-blood female with face and hair and breasts and limbs—all the accoutrements of a woman. A woman worthy of looking over.

It was as if she'd just snapped into existence for him. As if before, as she had known with a shame that only a plain, undesirable female could know, she had simply not existed as a female to him at all. All she had been to him was something it would not occur to him to look at, and when he had he'd left her feeling that she was covered in slime. Repulsive to him.

But now—now it was as if someone had truly sprinkled fairy dust over her and brought her to radiant life in his eyes. She was there, in front of him—a living, breathing woman. And he was looking her over. Very, very thoroughly.

And that lit the fuse for the second emotion that was sending her reeling. The impact of being inspected, head to toe, by Rafaello di Viscenti, as a fully paid-up member of the female sex worthy of his attention was just devastating—like being caught in a beam of high-power light that licked like flame all over her.

The moment seemed to go on for ever and ever, and then dimly Magda became aware that someone was standing beside them, deferentially proffering two large leather-bound menus. The man murmured something and Rafaello dragged his eyes from Magda and took the menus, replying distractedly.

'What would you like to eat?'

There still seemed to be a husk in his voice that Magda had never heard before, and it served to send a little tingle up her spine. But then her whole body was tingling.

And not just because she'd been caught in Rafaello di Viscenti's devastating eyeline. The three hours she'd spent in Olivia's clutches had been the most extraordinarily terrifying and exhilarating experience. She had simply yielded to the other woman's smiling enthusiasm and let herself be stripped naked, hair unpinned, inspected, tut-tutted over, before being worked on in a major, major way.

Magda hadn't known such beauty treatments existed! She'd been wrapped up in weird stuff, neck to toe, had her face slathered and unslathered; her body had been rubbed and polished and waxed and smoothed and creamed. Her hair had been washed and conditioned and coloured and cut and blown and styled. And then Olivia had approached with a treasure chest of make-up and proceeded to paint a face on her that she simply had not believed when she saw it reflected in the mirrors of the changing room where Olivia had selected from a range of beautiful clothes. She had stared, dumbstruck, as Olivia had slipped a cool, silky shift over her head, zipped it swiftly up the back and stood away.

'What did I tell you?' Olivia had said softly. 'That I would make you look *favoloso*. And I have.'

She had, too, and Magda was still walking on air, feeling like Cinderella must have felt when the fairy godmother had finished with her. She had stammered her thanks incoherently to the other woman, who had laughed, and said, 'Good—now we show you off to Rafaello and watch his jaw fall to the floor.'

And so it would have—if Rafaello di Viscenti had been capable of so inelegant a reaction. As it was, just seeing that look of stupefaction mingled with that tingle-inducing, shiver-making, blush-urging looking over had swept away all Magda's fears and misgivings that perhaps Olivia had got it totally, totally wrong…

She tensed. Rafaello was leaning towards her, his shoulder almost touching hers as he reached out a hand to run down her menu.

'Would you like me to translate?' he asked.

She wasn't capable of reciting the alphabet at this moment in time, let alone working out a menu written in Italian.

She swallowed. 'I...I'll just have something simple, please,' she managed to get out in a whispery sort of voice.

His glance flicked to hers and she suddenly saw the golden lights in his dark eyes, swept by those long, impossible lashes, caught the heady scent of his oh-so-masculine aftershave...and his own, even more masculine scent.

She felt faint, breathless.

He drew back. 'Very well.' He gave a smile, and the way his mouth indented, altering the planes of his face, made her feel faint again. She had seen him smile before— at his aunt last night, at Olivia this morning—but this time...this time the smile was for her. Faintness drummed at her again. This couldn't be happening. It was like a dream...

But if it was a dream, it was one that she didn't wake up from. Rafaello took her elbow, his hand burning on her skin, doing extraordinary things to her insides, which had a whole flock of butterflies soaring away invisibly, and led her through the restaurant out into a tiny cobbled courtyard at the back, decked with flowers and set with shaded tables.

She took her place, terrified she was going to stumble on her unaccustomed high heels, but there was no mishap, and she was sitting there, beneath the awning, with eyes for no one and nothing except Rafaello di Viscenti.

For a while, as he got on with the business of ordering food and wine, she was left in peace simply to drink him in, to tell herself that it could only be a dream, that she was not really sitting here, transformed by a magic wand, with the most beautiful man in the world. Then, ordering done, Rafaello turned back to her.

There was something in his eyes that made all the butterflies swoop upwards in one soaring flight.

'It is *incredibile*!' he said to her, and his eyes flickered over her face, her hair, her torso. 'I do not know what to say.' He spread his hands in a very Italian gesture.

Magda shifted uncomfortably. 'It's the make-up and everything.' Her voice was strained.

'Everything?' Rafaello echoed. 'Yes, everything. I have been blind—quite blind.' There was something curious about his voice, and her eyes met his. There was a strange expression in them that made her feel…feel what?

She could not put a name to it.

He was talking again.

'Blind to everything,' he said. 'And now I ask you…' his voice changed '…if you will forgive my blindness and accept a peace offering.' He slipped a hand inside his jacket pocket.

He extracted a little flat, circular packet, exquisitely wrapped in silvery tissue with a golden ribbon, the fruit of his shopping that morning, and placed it in front of her.

'Open it,' he said, in that same curious voice.

Uncertainly, but obediently, she did so. As the ribbon fell away so did the tissue, revealing, unmistakably, a blue velvet jewel case. With the butterflies jostling in her stomach, she lifted the lid.

Inside was a necklace, fine and delicate, made of intricately woven gold in a design that was as skilful as it was beautiful. She stared at it, blinking.

'Will you accept it as a token of my regret for my treatment of you?'

His voice was low, and there was still that note in it she could not identify. But she was in no state to analyse his tone of voice.

Her throat tightened. 'I can't take this,' she got out. 'Please—it is quite unnecessary. You are paying me so much money that—'

Her words were cut off. Rafaello's hand had snaked out and set down on hers.

'No,' he said, and there was a sharpness in his voice that

made her look at him almost fearfully. 'Of that we will not speak. Now…' his voice changed again '…if you like the necklace put it on. It will go well, I think, with what you are wearing.'

Yes, thought Magda desperately, that's how I must think of it—as nothing more than an accessory to the dress. And the dress, and everything else that Olivia did to me, is just part of what Rafaello wants. He's got fed up with having such an eyesore in his house, and he's done something about it. Don't, *don't* read anything more into it. You mustn't, you *mustn't*!

So, obediently, she picked up the necklace, which was light as a feather in her fingers, and made to put it on. Her fingers fumbled at the back of her neck, trying to fasten it. In a moment Rafaello was there, his hands sliding away her fall of hair and his fingers brushing hers as he took the necklace from her.

'Allow me…' he murmured, and started to fasten the necklace.

The butterflies inside her went crazy—and every drop of blood in her body dropped to her feet. She gasped as the nerve-endings in the delicate nape of her neck quivered with exquisite sensation.

If she could capture that moment for ever she would glimpse heaven, she thought, her eyes fluttering shut as she gave herself to the lightest, most blissful feeling.

Then it was gone, and so was Rafaello, back in his seat, viewing his handiwork.

And her.

'Today,' he said softly, and his eyes drank her in like a rare, vintage wine, 'we start again.'

The whole day was like a dream—and Rafaello was like a different person, Magda thought. As if he had never looked at her and seen nothing more than the last person his father would welcome as his son's bride. That Rafaello seemed to have vanished. Now there was only a man—the most beautiful man in the world to her—sitting opposite her and treating her as if she were a princess. It was a heady, heady feeling, and she had to try very hard to keep her feet on the ground, lest she soar upwards with the butterflies that stayed with her all through lunch, fluttering inside.

Over lunch, which seemed to last for ever and yet but a moment, he kept the conversation very impersonal. He told her about Lucca, and Tuscany, and Italy, and conversation ranged from the historical to the contemporary, as he regaled her with the mores and the customs of modern Italians.

Even though she felt awkward at first, and could only respond to his conversation in stilted phrases, gradually, as the wine in her glass went down, she slipped into the kind of enquiring questioning she'd given his uncle the evening before, and found herself relaxing and talking normally. She drank it all in, storing the time away as a precious memory, a dream that seemed, quite unbelievably, to be happening in real life. And all the time, as they talked, she was aware of a current running like electricity through her body, making it harder and harder to refrain from doing what she just ached to do—stare and stare at the homage to male beauty that was the perfection of Rafaello di Viscenti.

It was as lunch ended that another reality finally penetrated.

Benji.

With a pang of guilt she said, as Rafaello placed his credit card on the table for the waiter to collect, 'Please— would it be possible—may I phone Maria—to see if Benji is all right?'

'Of course.' He smiled his ready assent.

He extracted his mobile, dialled and spoke rapidly, then disconnected.

'Benji has had an excellent morning, eaten a hearty

lunch, and is now sleeping peacefully,' he reported. 'However, Maria suggests that it would be good if you were there when he wakes. In which case perhaps we shall leave a more extensive tour of the city for another occasion, and content ourselves with making nothing more than a short *passagiata* along a section of the walls. It is a very pleasant stroll to take.'

Under any circumstances the walk along the famous walls of Lucca would have been pleasant, but for Magda it was blissful. She worried a little that her feet would be pinched in the beautiful cinnamon-coloured high heels that Olivia had procured for her, but the leather was so soft, the fit so perfect, that there was no problem at all. Only, as she walked she was conscious of the effect of the high heels, how they lifted her hips and made her sway.

Self-consciously, as they moved out on to the bright sunlit pavement from the restaurant, she fished inside the stylish handbag that matched the shoes and extracted the pair of dark glasses that Olivia had bestowed upon her. It was much easier, wearing sunglasses, to look without being seen. And as they strolled along, Rafaello's hand attentively at her elbow, she realised with a kind of disbelieving shock that they were drawing attention. At first she thought it was just that women were looking at Rafaello, a highly understandable phenomenon, but then she became aware that she, too, was drawing eyes.

Men were looking at her, quite openly, quite obviously, as they walked past, or they looked across at her from the cafés. It was so blatant that she felt as if she had no clothes on, and found she had pressed closer, quite unconsciously, to Rafaello.

He glanced down at her, a wry smile indenting his mouth.

'In Italy we are not shy about admiring a beautiful woman. Do not worry—with me beside you they will do no more than look. But—' his voice became dry 'I do not advise that you tour on your own—you would be like a honeypot to every man around.'

She felt herself colouring—and heard Rafaello's words humming in her head.

He called me a beautiful woman!

In a daze, she walked on.

Along the walls it was easier. There were more tourists here, and she felt she drew less attention. She moved a little away from Rafaello again, and he let her be, simply strolling beside her, constraining his pace to hers.

It was a leisurely progress as Rafaello stopped to point out landmarks on both the city side of the walls and the outer sides.

'The wealthy Lucchesi in the sixteenth century built their summer villas in the countryside around the city, and several are open to view. Perhaps we shall go and visit one another day. There is so much to see in Tuscany you will be spoilt for choice.'

'Please,' said Magda, awkward suddenly, 'you do not have to take me around. I am perfectly happy staying in the villa—I am sure you must be very busy with work and so on.'

'There is nothing that needs my urgent attention,' Rafaello said dismissively. The board meeting to confirm him as chairman would not take place until the following week. The delay did not alarm him—his father would not, *could* not, for his pride's sake, renege on the unholy bargain he had struck with his son.

His mind flicked away. He did not want to think about his father right now. Too much anger roiled beneath the surface. A grim smile flickered on his mouth. When they returned he would force his father to acknowledge Magda—wipe out the ugly, cruel litany he had thrown at him, that was choking in his father's craw.

He glanced down at the silky head that barely reached to his shoulders. He could still not get over the transfor-

nation. It was, indeed, incredible. She walked along beside
him, high heels doing all sorts of miraculous things to her
posture, and the dress, blessedly simple—though he knew
the bill for anything that simple, that superbly cut, would
be astronomical—doing the most amazing things to her figure. As for the rest of her—well, it was a dream. Not
scrawny, but wand-slim. Not plain and pasty but…radiant.
That was the only word for her now.

She would grace any setting—and he would make his
father see that. Make him acknowledge her intelligence, her
education—self-taught, and all the more credit to her, he
thought soberly, given her grim financial circumstances.
Make him see that every cruel description of her had been
wrong—see even that it had been her devotion to her baby
that had made her stoop to such menial work as he had
found her in.

A frown flickered in his eyes.

Abruptly, without thinking, he spoke.

'Tell me about Benji's father.'

Magda halted in mid-step, then started walking again.
There had been a harshness in Rafaello's voice that took
her aback. Why did he want to know?

Slowly, she framed the words. 'It…it isn't easy to tell,'
she answered. 'You see,' she went on, looking ahead of
her, 'when I was in the home—'

'Home?'

'Children's home—care home. An orphanage—I don't
know what it would be in Italian.'

'Brefotrofio.' He frowned. What was this? She had been
an orfano? 'What happened to your parents?'

'I…I don't know.'

'Come?'

She risked a glance at him. He was frowning. It made
him look intimidating.

'How is it you do not know?' he pursued.

'I…I don't know who my parents were. I…I was found,

when I was a few hours old. The police tried, without success, to trace the woman…well, girl, really, I suppose—
most women who abandon their babies are very young; she
was probably a teenager, pregnant by mistake and terrified,
which is why…why she just wanted to get rid of me.' Her
voice was strained. 'It's very understandable.'

Her voice trailed off. Rafaello said nothing. She went on
walking. 'So, you see,' she continued in the same strained
voice, though she tried very hard to make it as normal-
sounding as possible, 'I don't know who my mother was,
and I have no idea at all about my father—well, the boy
who fathered me, presumably equally by mistake. Maybe
he didn't even know he'd got my mother pregnant. Or
maybe—' her voice tightened '—my mother didn't even
know which boy had got her pregnant. So, anyway…' She
took a breath. 'I was taken into care, and—'

Cold was running down Rafaello's spine. 'I knew nothing of this!'

His interruption made Magda flinch. The harshness was
back in his voice with a vengeance. Her feet slewed to a
halt. The fragile edifice of civility which had been built up
over lunch crashed down around her ears. She stole a look
at him. He had stopped, too, and stood looking down at
her. His eyes, veiled behind his dark glasses, were invisible
but his mouth was set in a tight, grim line.

Her heart plunged to the ground. It was like walking
headfirst into a blizzard after spring flowers had blossomed.
Oh, why didn't I just make some excuse and tell him nothing about Benji—or me? she thought in anguish. He's hor-
rified—appalled! She felt sick inside.

'I…I thought you knew,' she said in a small, shaky
voice. 'It was on my birth certificate. "Parents unknown."
And my time of birth was the closest estimate the hospital
could come up with. You wanted my birth certificate for
the marriage licence.'

'I did not see it,' he replied remotely.

Magda bit her lip. Of course. Why should Rafaello di
Viscenti bother himself with trivia like her birth certificate?

'You were telling me about Benji's father.' The voice
that prompted her was distant still. With a heavy, sinking
heart, Magda forced herself to continue her sorry tale.

'Um—it was in the care home—there was another in-
mate. Kaz. We sort of…stuck together… Then—well,
um—it gets…complicated.' She swallowed through her
tightening throat, forcing out words that brought back so
many agonising memories. 'We'd just left the home, let
loose on the world, and we were living together when Kaz
was diagnosed with cancer. At first the treatment worked,
for a couple of years, but then the cancer came back.
Terminal this time. Kaz…Kaz died just after Benji was
born….'

She couldn't go on. Just couldn't. She started walking
again, but she couldn't see anything. She was grateful for
her dark glasses because they kept the tears hidden. Her
steps were jerky.

Suddenly her arm was taken. Held in an iron grip. She
tried to pull away, but she could not. She felt tears seeping
from under the lower rim of the dark glasses, and lifted a
hand to try and wipe them away.

'I am ashamed,' came the low voice. 'I am ashamed of
everything I have ever thought or said about you.'

He turned her towards him, taking her other elbow in
that vice-like grip. She screwed up her eyes, trying to stop
the tears coming. Her throat was burning with the effort of
keeping herself from crying.

She felt one hand let her go, and then he was sliding her
dark glasses from her eyes.

'No tears—they will spoil your make-up.' There was a
careful humour in his voice—deliberate, she realised.

She gazed up at him, eyes swimming. His face was a
blur. With infinite gentleness he scooped his little finger
along the line of her lower lashes, catching the moisture on

each before it could run down her cheeks. As her vision cleared his eyes came into focus, looking down into hers.

It was as if she were suspended in time, suspended by the lightest strand of gossamer, the gossamer touch of his fingertip, yet she could no more move, no more breathe, than if she were held in bands of steel.

Everything stopped—her breathing, her heartbeat, so it seemed, and all the world everywhere—just stopped. All that existed was Rafaello, looking down at her, the strangest, most enigmatic expression in his dark, dark eyes.

Her lips parted as the softest exhalation of breath sighed from her.

Slowly Rafaello brushed the tips of his fingers into the fine tendrils of her hair.

'So lovely—'

His voice was a murmur and then his head was lowering to hers, and as Magda's eyes fluttered shut she gave herself to the exquisite wonder of Rafaello di Viscenti, the most beautiful man in the world, kissing her.

His mouth was soft and warm and oh-so-skilful, moving with delicacy, with exploring slowness, tasting her lips as if she were the sweetest dessert.

It went on for an eternity. Yet it was over too soon— achingly soon...

As he drew back from her she felt a loss that echoed through her whole body.

She gazed up at him, her emotions naked on her face.

With that enigmatic expression still in his eyes, Rafaello took her hand and tucked it into the crook of his arm, sliding her dark glasses back over her eyes.

'We must return to the car,' he told her.

She went with him as if she were in a complete daze— because she was. A sort of unreality was enveloping her and she could think no coherent thoughts. Not one.

The journey back to the villa was conducted mostly in silence. Rafaello drove with the speed and total concentra-

tion with which he had driven in the morning, but this time
there was no aura of anger coming from him. Instead he
seemed to be taking particular relish in driving the mega-
powerful car—and Magda spent the entire journey, head
turned towards Rafaello, holding her hair with one hand,
as it blew about wildly, and gazing openly at him in utter
wonder.

From time to time he glanced across at her, and she saw
a little smile playing around his mouth, as if he were
pleased, very pleased about something. She didn't know
what it was, only that when his mouth indented like that
her insides just dissolved all over again.

She wanted the journey never to end.

CHAPTER SEVEN

RAFAELLO was in a good mood. A very good mood. It was the first good mood he'd had for months—ever since his father had given him his impossible ultimatum: marriage or disinheritance.

It made him realise just how bad his sustained mood had been, and for how long.

But all that had changed. The world was smiling again, and he was smiling with it. It was a good, good feeling. A burden had been lifted from his shoulders.

Back at the villa, he received with mixed emotions the news from an expressionless Giuseppe that Enrico had departed for Rome and was not expected back any time soon. Uppermost was, he acknowledged ruefully, relief. In his new improved mood he did not relish any more confrontation, and if his father had decamped to the Rome apartment, well, that was his choice, thought Rafaello. He had better put in a few phone calls to other board members, just to ensure that Enrico was not up to anything so far as his plans for Viscenti AG were concerned, but he was confident enough that his father would not renege on him.

It was with a lighter heart that he turned to Magda.

'Giuseppe tells me my father has gone to stay in Rome—we have an apartment there. Now,' he breezed on, 'why do you not go and see to Benji, hmm?' He smiled at her, and again she felt the butterflies soar on magic wings. 'I must check my e-mails and make some phone calls, but I shall join you soon.'

He strolled off towards the library and Magda, informed by Giuseppe that Benji was asleep upstairs in her room, went upstairs, still in a complete daze.

She wanted desperately to think about what had happened, but Benji was far too pleased, waking from his afternoon nap, to allow time for reverie. His delight at seeing her made her forget everything else, at least for the moment, and she scooped him up and hugged him closely, thanking Gina for her care of him.

Refreshed from his slumber, Benji was ready for action again, and Magda headed downstairs with him.

Maria intercepted her in the hall.

Her eyes gleamed as she took in Magda's transformed appearance, but she said nothing about the new look, merely saying, 'I will bring coffee to the terrace—Signor and Signora Calvi are there.'

So, too, as Magda found, was Benji's new pride and joy—his sit-upon wooden trike on which he could easily push himself along. He fell on it with a cry of glee, and in a short while was racing up and down the paved terrace like a pro. As for Rafaello's aunt, she was decidedly more open about Magda's new appearance.

'Excellent! You look very lovely, my dear—and you will be pleased to hear that the rest of your new wardrobe has been delivered already.'

Magda looked surprised.

'Of course,' said Rafaello's aunt, smiling admonishingly at her expression. 'You cannot survive on one outfit alone. I have inspected the selection and they are all excellent. Gina has already hung them up. Now, come and have a cup of coffee and tell us what you thought of Lucca—and I shall tell you of all the antics of your extremely lively little boy this morning.'

Elizavetta was clearly in a very good humour, and when Rafaello emerged on to the terrace some thirty minutes later he was received in the same tone. But Magda was not blind to the rapid but scrutinising glance she subjected both of them to as he took his seat beside Magda. She felt herself colour slightly. Inside the butterflies set off again as she sipped her coffee, intensely aware of Rafaello's presence beside her as he chatted to his aunt and uncle.

The awareness heightened when, ten minutes later Rafaello turned to her and said suddenly, 'It is time to cool down—and I am sure Benji would enjoy a swim. Come—'

As he spoke he was aware of a degree of disingenuousness about his invitation. True, he would like to cool down and probably both mother and child would enjoy a swim but what he himself would enjoy most would be seeing what Magda looked like in a decent swimsuit.

His thoughts flew back to the previous afternoon, when he'd been surprised to see that, hideously saggy swimsuit apart, she really had a quite unexpectedly pleasing figure Now, after a morning in Olivia's expert hands, and wearing what he knew would be a beautifully styled piece of swimwear, the results would be, he anticipated, even more pleasing...

His expectations were rewarded. Magda did, indeed, look every bit as good in the sleek peach-coloured one-piece as he had hoped. Cut high in the leg, it emphasised the slenderness of her thighs and hips, her hand-span waist and most enticingly of all, the gentle swell of her breasts.

Her skin tone had ripened from the Tuscan sun to a warm honey, and with her lovely hair loose over her shoulders as she slowly and self-consciously walked into the pool area her little boy held by the hand, he could not take his eyes from her.

How had she been hiding all that natural loveliness all this time? He cursed himself for his own blindness—he'd been blinded by that muddy-coloured hair, scraped back her total lack of attention to her appearance and those atrocious, unspeakable clothes. And now—

Whatever the size of the bill Olivia presented to him, he would have paid it ten times over just for the pleasure of seeing Magda walk towards him now, with her shy, natural grace...

He came near to her. He was all ready for his swim, clad in nothing but his trunks, and he realised from the surge of blood he felt, as powerful as it was instinctive, he would need to get into the water pretty damn fast if those faint stains of colour on her cheeks were not to turn fiery red. Already he could tell she could not cope with his almost nudity—and if her gaze dragged downwards, from where it seemed to be fixated on his torso, then she would have cause to blush indeed!

With a lithe movement he launched himself into the water. The cold had the effect he wanted—for now, at any rate. Several strongly executed lengths later he surfaced to find Magda sitting nervously by the shallow flight of steps leading into the water, Benji already immersed, splashing away mightily. Rafaello hauled himself gracefully and effortlessly out of the water, and reached for Benji's inflatable ball.

'Catch!'

He tossed it towards the little boy, who gave a crow of delight and started to paddle towards the floating ball as fast as his chubby little legs and rubber ring would carry him. He batted at it, and it swirled away, and he chased after it. Magda laughed, and so did Rafaello. He lowered himself into the pool and started to play with the child.

It was, he discovered, extraordinarily easy to entertain an infant. All that was required was a complete lack of dignity and a willingness to engage in a highly repetitious game of throw the ball, throw it again, and again, and again…

'He won't get tired of it before you do,' warned Magda. She was still sitting there, feet in the water, knees pressed together, feeling incredibly, exposingly self-conscious.

Rafaello laughed, and she felt a warmth spreading through her. Her mind was still in a total daze. Could this really be Rafaello di Viscenti, who hadn't even wanted to call Benji by name, now playing with him with every sign of pleasure?

And could this really be Rafaello di Viscenti, who had previously looked at her with such disdain, who had looked at her just now, as she'd walked towards him, as if he were unable to take his eyes away from her for a single moment.

I can't take it in—I can't believe this is happening!

If this was nothing but a dream, it was one she never, ever, wanted to wake from.

'So—where would you like to go today?'

Rafaello's voice was inviting. And why not? He was relaxed—more relaxed than he'd been since he could remember, since before his father had started to be fixated upon the idea of him marrying Lucia. He felt, he realised, carefree, with nothing to do but enjoy himself and be pleasurably self-indulgent. Yes, the future of Viscenti AG lay in his hands, and he would take up his responsibilities in due course, but right now global expansion could wait—right now he had another project to pursue.

A very pleasurable one.

He cast a look at the object of his attention.

'Firenze? Pisa? Sienna?'

Magda bit her lip. Rafaello tried not to let his gaze focus on it. There would be time enough for what he intended, but for now the day stretched before them. He wanted to show Tuscany off to Magda—wanted to get her to himself again, truly to himself, without the watching chorus of not just his aunt and uncle but Maria and Giuseppe as well.

'Please,' she said, 'you don't have to show me around—really.'

'It is my pleasure,' he replied airily. 'You have but to choose your destination. How about Firenze? The most magnificent jewel in the crown of Tuscany—whatever the quieter charms of Lucca.'

She smiled, but still looked uncertain.

'Please—don't think me ungrateful, but I feel I cannot leave Benji here—it is not fair either to him, to Maria or your aunt.'

'Then we take him with us.' It was not what he particularly wanted to do, but he could see her point.

Her uncertainty persisted. 'A busy city is perhaps not the best place for him, let alone art museums and historical monuments.'

With a wave of his hand Rafaello disposed of this objection, too. 'The solution is obvious—we'll go to the beach.'

As if he had uttered a magic word, Magda's face lit up. 'Oh, can we really? Benji would adore a beach. He's never been—neither have I...'

Her voice was wistful. Something about it stabbed Rafaello. She had never been to the beach.

But then she had lived such a deprived life—not just in poverty, but with no family. A foundling—abandoned by her mother. Could such things happen? Anger shot through him. No wonder she had clung to this boy from the orphanage, this Kaz of hers. No wonder she had sought comfort in his arms—his bed.

A shadow crossed his eyes. And even that had been taken from her...

'Then it is decided,' he announced decisively. 'The beach it is.'

It was, thought Magda by the afternoon, the best day of her life! Even better than yesterday—for today she had with her both Benji and Rafaello. And Rafaello as she had never yet seen him—as gorgeous as ever, as bewilderingly attentive and approving as yesterday, but as playful as he had been with Benji in the pool at the villa.

And something more as well. She didn't know what the 'more' was, only that it set the blood singing in her veins—

a song that soared to the highest notes whenever she and Rafaello exchanged glances.

She knew she was living in a dream—knew that as she sat on the beach at Viareggio, Benji snug between her outstretched legs, Rafaello industriously rebuilding the sandcastle that Benji, without fail, would take exuberant pleasure in demolishing, sun glinting off his golden torso, bronzing his dark silky hair—knew that all she could do was make a memory of the moment.

And she knew, too, how dangerous was the tempting, impossible thought that was seeding itself against all reason, all reality, in the deepest part of her—the sweet, utterly unattainable fantasy that she could rewrite reality and be sitting here, not with a man who had married her solely to thwart and insult his father and safeguard his inheritance, but with her true husband, the father of her child…

But they were not a family—no such thing. Rafaello was being kind towards her, that was all. He was just trying to prove wrong the ugly words his father had thrown at her. She felt bad that he was moved to do so. It had hurt, knowing Rafaello had deliberately chosen her for her undesirability, both social and personal, but for herself she did not take shame in it. She was not responsible for her origins, and Benji was a gift from Kaz that she treasured beyond her own life, for whom she would do whatever it took to keep him safe and raise him well. Whether it was working as a cleaner or marrying a stranger who despised her for doing so…

Her eyes flickered to Rafaello again. But he was not despising her now! He was going to great lengths to be kind to her. She felt her heart squeeze.

He caught her gaze, pausing in the act of restoring—yet again—the sandcastle, and as his eyes held hers she felt colour stain her cheeks. He gave her a slow, intimate smile that deepened the colour along her cheekbones. For a long, timeless moment he held her gaze, and what flowed between them made her feel weak.

Benji, sensing distraction, launched himself forward and fell full-length on the castle, demolishing it utterly.

'Oh, Benji, you little monster!' cried Magda, laughing, breaking eye contact with half a sense of relief and half a yearning sense of loss. Rafaello was laughing, too. He climbed to his feet, taking Benji with him in a swinging arc.

'Come,' he told him with mock sternness, 'time to get you wet!' He held a hand down for Magda, and self-consciously she placed hers in his. His grip tightened and he pulled her to her feet. 'You, too!' he told her.

He ran them down to the sea's edge, lapping gently on the sand, and Benji clutched at his hair, infused with laughter. They all collapsed into the water in a splashing heap, and soon Magda was breathless with laughter as Rafaello whooshed Benji in and out of the water, breasting him through the tiny waves while the little boy shouted with pleasure.

Her heart turned over as she stood, legs apart, thigh-deep in water, watching them. Rafaello was so wonderful with Benji. She could not believe it.

Something tugged at her with an emotion that was almost pain. Again the dangerous, tempting thought flitted across her mind—what if this were real? What if they were what the other people on the beach clearly took them for—a family?

She pushed the thought away. Today—this wonderful, heavenly day—was just a memory in the making.

One which would have to last the rest of her life.

It was with a sense of sated happiness that they finally headed back inland at the end of the day. Dreamily she sat beside Benji in the back of the sleek saloon, lost in a haze of sweet contentment. Benji, exhausted and replete with *gelati*, nodded off in his child-seat.

As they wound eastwards along the autostrada, heading for the rolling hills, Magda thought how utterly different this journey was from the one she had made from the airport at the beginning of the week, only four days ago.

Was Rafaello really the same person now as he had been then? She remembered how he had sat, in his corner of the limo, totally absorbed in his work, paying no attention to her or Benji.

We didn't exist for him then, she thought. We were just objects to be used and moved the way he wanted—the way he paid for.

Her eyes shadowed. That last had not changed—he was still paying her. So how did that square with the way he was treating her now? She knew he was being kind to her, but today he really had seemed to be enjoying himself as much as she and Benji. Was that just being kind?

Again, she put the thought aside. There was no point in thinking about it. She would not spoil the sweetness of the day. She would simply sit here, as the powerful car purred along, continue to watch the man who drove, and store up memories.

By the time they reached the villa Magda, too, was nearly asleep. The sun and the sea air had tired her out. Sleepily she extracted Benji, who promptly surfaced with renewed vigour and demanded to be set down. She slid him to his feet and he toddled purposefully towards the door, opened by Giuseppe, who came down to say something to Rafaello and help with the baggage.

'My aunt and uncle have left,' Rafaello said to Magda as he extracted the beach bags from the boot of the car. 'They have gone to console my father in Rome, so Giuseppe tells me. We have the house to ourselves.'

He smiled at her—that same intimate smile he had smiled on the beach. A frisson went through Magda, and a sudden sense of panic as she realised that there would no longer be the reassuring presence of the Calvis over dinner. Last night they had served to dilute the intensity of her awareness of Rafaello, seated at the head of the table and dominating the meal by his presence alone.

Tonight there would be no such buffer. The realisation was alarming.

So when Rafaello said casually, as they went indoors, 'We have been invited out tonight—some friends want to wish me a happy birthday! There will be plenty of time for you to rest and prepare yourself, and put Benji to bed,' her first reaction was relief.

Then, straight away, the implications of what he had just said struck her.

'No, please—you do not have to take me. I will do perfectly well here—' she started.

Rafaello paused and looked at her. 'They also,' he went on, a touch of humour in his face, 'want to take a look at you—they are most curious.'

Magda bit her lip. 'Um—is that wise? I mean,' she went on hastily, 'won't that lead them to think that…that this is a real marriage?'

The words were hard to say, but she had to say them. A strange, unreadable look came into Rafaello's eyes for a moment. Then it cleared. In a bland voice he answered, 'But this *is* a real marriage, Magda—it is quite legal, and we need to behave accordingly. Besides—' a humorous, cajoling note entered his voice '—are you not eager to try out one of your new evening dresses?'

She made no answer, feeling awkward, but Rafaello simply went on smoothly, 'Now, why do you not refresh yourself? Then let Maria have some time with Benji and give him his supper. You can bath him and get him off to sleep, and then get ready for the evening, hmm? Oh…' He paused at the foot of the stairs. 'Maria suggested she root out my old cot—it must be in an attic somewhere—and put it beside your bed. She is anxious, she tells me, that you may roll onto Benji when you are asleep. I trust you do not mind?'

Magda shook her head. 'No—no, of course not. It is very kind of her.'

The cot was already in the bedroom when she went in some moments later with Benji. It was a magnificent affair, well worthy of a di Viscenti, carved and painted, and clearly freshly spring-cleaned by Maria. To her relief, Benji took to it immediately, sitting in it with every sign of complacent possession. Wryly, Magda wondered how fond he'd be of it once it dawned on him that with the wooden side raised and locked into position he would not be able to get out alone. But since it was right up against the high bed she was happy enough for him to try.

It certainly made life easier as she got ready for the evening. Knowing he was safely inside the cot, bathed and ready for sleep, having a last play with his toys, she could go about her ablutions with greater confidence, especially when it came to styling her hair. She had had to wash it after the day at the beach, and was worried she would not be able to recreate the chic style that Olivia's salon had so effortlessly produced. However, she followed the other woman's advice, moussing it a little and then gently blow-drying it with the hairdryer she found in her bedside cabinet.

The effect, when combined with the make-up Olivia had sent, which Magda applied to the best of her ability, was much better than she had hoped. As she stared at herself, at the gently waving mane of hair clouding her shoulders, her kohled eyes huge and her lipsticked mouth lush and vivid, she could not believe such a transformation really was possible.

As Benji, hugging his teddy bear, silky hair smoothed soothingly back from his forehead, sank into a deep sleep,

Magda extracted a long evening gown from the huge antique wardrobe and slipped it on.

It was black, cut on the bias and clung to her hips, and folding softly over her breasts, held up by tiny shoestring straps. She did not need a bra with it; any slight support she needed was built into the bodice. As the fine-grained material slid over her head and shimmered down her slender body she felt its magic begin to work. She walked to the mirror and stared, transfixed.

Wonderingly she touched her throat.

Is this really me?

It seemed impossible—but the reflection staring back at her could not lie. It showed a slender, graceful woman, exquisitely gowned, with her hair in a soft cloud and wide, luminous eyes.

She could not take her eyes from the reflection, staring in wonder at herself.

A soft knock on the door disturbed her reverie. It was Gina, taking over on babywatch.

'Signor di Viscenti is downstairs waiting for you, *signora*,' the girl said, casting an admiring look at Magda's appearance.

Magda picked up a black satin handbag with a discreet designer logo, slipped her feet into the strappy high-heeled shoes, and headed downstairs after bidding Gina goodnight.

As she gingerly descended the wide sweeping stairs, taking careful steps in her narrow long skirt and high, high heels, she realised Rafaello was staring up at her.

She stared back. Her breath caught.

If she had thought Rafaello superb in a business suit, casual clothes and beachwear, in a tuxedo he was, quite simply, breathtaking. The black cloth of the evening jacket stretched tautly across his shoulders, sheathing his torso and providing an ebony contrast to the white dress shirt. He was freshly shaven, freshly showered, his hair still slightly damp as it feathered over his brow. His cheekbones seemed higher than ever, thought Magda, dazzled, and the sculpted line of his mouth could have been hewn by Michelangelo himself...

She went on walking down, eyes fixed on him—and, conscious of him as she was, she was also burningly conscious of how his eyes were fixed on her in return.

As she reached the marble floor he came towards her. Before she could register what he was doing he had lifted her hand and raised it to his mouth.

The graze of his mouth on her knuckles made her want to faint. He straightened his head, but kept her hand in his.

'You look exquisite,' he breathed, his accent stronger than ever, and all she could do was stare up at him, her hand caught in his, her lips parted, her breath stilled.

'You require only one adornment—this.'

His words were accompanied by his slipping his left hand inside his tuxedo jacket and drawing out, not a jewellery case this time, but a sliver of white rainbow. As he opened the palm of his hand Magda could not stop herself giving a gasp.

The necklace was a river of diamonds, fantastic, unbelievable, and as she stared, incredulous, Rafaello simply let go her hand, turned her around, and draped the glittering necklace around her throat, brushing aside her hair to fasten it.

'I can't wear it!' she told him anguishedly. 'I'll lose it.'

He just laughed and turned her back towards him.

She clutched at it around her throat all the way in the car—which Rafaello drove at a pace that was almost sedate.

'I don't want to muss your hair,' he said, and smiled at her, and for a second his gaze held. 'I'm saving that for later,' he murmured, and then, as the road curved, he flicked his gaze back ahead.

Did he really say that...? Magda wondered, thinking she must have misheard. Another thought came to her.

'Rafaello—' it was still strange to say his name; it didn't

ome out naturally yet, for all that he was being so nice
nd kind to her '—what do I need to know about this eve-
ing?'

He glanced across at her again, one hand resting lightly
n the wheel, the other dipping expertly to change gear and
ev up the engine as they rounded a sharp bend in the road.

'Paolo and Sylvia have been married a couple of years—
hey have one little boy, and Sylvia is expecting her next.
've known Paolo for ever. He'll be curious to know how
ve ended up together, but don't worry.' He paused min-
tely to change gear. 'He knows why I've married so sud-
lenly. He's heard action replays of my battles with my
ather for years.'

Magda swallowed. 'So he knows,' she said awkwardly,
how you came to select me? And for what reasons?' she
dded bravely. 'Won't…won't he think it strange that you
re taking me with you this evening?'

'No,' he replied tightly.

A sudden new, hideous thought occurred to her. 'You're
ot…you're not taking me there tonight to…to tell every-
ne…where…where you found me, are you? Part of…part
f your…battle…with your father?'

There was fear in her voice, open and naked. Was that
vhat Rafaello was going to do tonight? Walk her into a
oom full of strangers and tell them all he'd married a
voman who cleaned toilets for a living?

Rafaello swore. Then, with a screech of tyre rubber, he
ulled the car over to the side of the road. He turned in his
eat.

She was looking at him, stricken, eyes wide, hands twist-
ng in her lap. Something gutted him. She'd looked like
hat when he'd come out on to the landing to hear his father
pill his poison all over her—poison that *he* had fed his
ather in the first place.

'No!' he said forcefully, then, more gently, 'No—no.
'his time—' there was irony in his voice, and self-

accusation '—this time I have no such intent. This time…'
His voice changed, and sent a slow quiver along the base
of her spine. 'This time I am taking you with me be
cause—'

His voice cut out. Then, with a twist of wry humour, he
continued, 'Because if I don't then Paolo and Sylvia will
simply turn up tomorrow at the villa to take a look at you.
I thought it would be easier if they met you in the middle
of a party—that way there will be more people around, and
we have the option of leaving whenever we want.'

She was still looking at him, her eyes huge and fearful
in the dim light.

'Don't look scared, *cara*, I will let no harm come to you,'
he told her softly. And then, to chase away that expression
to stop her looking at him as if she were terrified of the
hurt he could inflict on her—and, he admitted to himself
wryly, to do something he'd been wanting to do since she'd
first walked down the stairs looking so heartbreakingly
beautiful he had not been able to stop staring at her—he
leant across and kissed her.

It was a soft kiss, not passionate—not yet—but a prom
ise. A promise to her. A promise to himself.

His mouth touched hers and she melted into liquid
honey, her eyes fluttering shut as his lips softly moved.
Then he drew back. Her eyes opened again and he was
looking at her, holding her gaze.

'Don't be afraid, *cara*…'

He gunned the engine and pulled out into the road again
heading off into the dark, headlights cutting a vivid beam
of dazzling brightness through the dark Tuscan night.

The party, Magda discovered, proved no ordeal at all. Quite
the reverse. True, the square Renaissance villa was so op
ulent, and the driveway so packed with the most expensive
fantastic cars, that Magda's heart had hammered with

nerves. She couldn't go in! They would all know she wasn't one of them.

As she'd stiffened in fear, an arm had come around her shoulder.

'You look a million dollars—and I will take care of you.'

And he did. Rafaello did not leave her side for a moment, all evening. Not that she needed protection, Magda found. Paolo and Sylvia were welcoming and charming, with a real kindness behind their open curiosity about their friend's unexpected bride. But nothing awkward was asked or said by anyone; everyone simply seemed to accept her at face value.

There was only one tricky moment. About halfway through the evening Sylvia came hurrying over to Rafaello and murmured something urgently to him in Italian. Rafaello merely stilled a moment, then said something dismissive. Sylvia patted his arm approvingly, and disappeared again.

Rafaello turned to Magda. 'Lucia has turned up. Do not be alarmed. She will have no opportunity to insult you.'

But it seemed that insulting the female who had snatched her prospective husband from under her nose was not, after all, Lucia's intention. Instead she glided forward, wearing an excruciatingly figure-hugging gold tissue gown, and her dark eyes widened as she took in the unbelievable transformation of her cousin's wife.

'A Sonia Grasci gown, no less, and diamonds, too! Quite a tribute.'

Her voice was honeyed, but Magda stayed tense. Lucia gave a light laugh.

'Oh, don't look like that. What's done is done. And I don't hold grudges. Besides, it isn't me you have to win over, but Rafaello's father. He was set on me becoming his daughter-in-law.'

There wasn't anything Magda could say to this, and Rafaello simply replied, thought tightened lips, 'My father should have known better than to try and play with my life, Lucia. And now, if you will excuse me, we must circulate.'

He whisked Magda away and promptly introduced her to yet more friends who, like everyone else, seemed to see nothing exceptional about her—only that she had arrived so suddenly on the scene.

Only one was bold enough to comment on it—and on Lucia's disappointed expectations.

Rafaello merely smiled silkily. 'As you can see—' he pulled Magda a little more closely to him to make his point '—I was busy elsewhere.'

The other man grinned. 'So that's why you were forever disappearing to London!'

Rafaello's smile deepened. 'Who could blame me?' he murmured, as if confirming the other man's assumption that his acquaintance with his English bride was long standing.

Magda's breathlessness at being held so close to him precluded any possibility of her saying a word.

As they circulated yet again, Rafaello, who did not re- linquish his hold on her, with a continuing effect on Magda's ability to speak coherently, paused and looked down at her.

'Enjoying yourself?' he asked.

She nodded dumbly. Then managed to say, 'Everyone is very nice.'

He smiled indulgently. 'You are being much admired,' he went on.

Magda coloured. 'It's very kind of you to say so,' she answered quietly.

He gave a laugh. 'Kind? Is that what you think, *cara*? I can see I shall have to persuade you otherwise.'

He looked down at her, and there was something in his eyes that made her breath catch.

They did not stay much longer. Magda had no idea what time it was, but soon they were climbing into Rafaello's car, being bade farewell by Paolo and Sylvia. Both, she saw, had knowing smiles on their faces.

Rafaello caught her embarrassed expression as he started the engine.

'They know we are newly-weds,' he said. 'We are being permitted to leave early on that account.'

'Oh,' said Magda, and busied herself with her seat belt.

The journey back seemed to take no time at all. Perhaps, thought Magda, it was the result of the champagne singing in her bloodstream.

Back at the villa, as Rafaello helped Magda out of the car, her heel caught on the gravel slightly. The steadying arm that Rafaello put around her shoulder seemed to invite her to lean back into him, finding that she fitted very snugly against the smoothness of his tuxedo jacket. They walked indoors.

'Do you want to check on Benji?' Rafaello asked. 'I expect Gina will be glad to go off duty.'

'Oh—yes,' she answered. She headed upstairs, carefully gathering the narrow skirt of her dress in one hand, conscious of Rafaello's regard as she ascended.

In her room, having thanked and said goodnight to Gina, she went to gaze at Benji, fast asleep in his lordly cot. Gently she dropped a silent kiss on his forehead, her heart filled with love for him, then turned away, unfastening the diamonds at her throat.

A sadness seemed to fill her at knowing the evening was over. More than sadness—a restlessness she could not name. On impulse she pulled back the heavy curtains and opened the window. She leant against the sill, chin on the heels of her hands, gazing out, letting the warm night air sift over her face, scented with flowers.

She gave a little sigh. The shadowed garden, shot with a dim pool of light from her own window and one, she assumed, from Rafaello's, beyond hers, spread mysteriously below. The sounds of the night came soft to her ears.

She gave another little sigh. She had nothing to be sad about, she knew. Tonight had been magical and its memory would be treasured for ever, along with every other moment she had spent with Rafaello di Viscenti. Wanting him so much and knowing she would never have more of him than she had now. He was not for her, nor she for him, however beautiful he made her feel…

'That, I should inform you, *cara*, is a very dangerous position for you to be in.'

CHAPTER EIGHT

THE deep voice behind her was a drawl, shot with humour—and something more. Magda started, drawing back and straightening up, turning towards him.

'I...I won't fall out,' she protested.

Rafaello sauntered towards her, hands in his trouser pockets. He must have emerged from the bathroom, through the previously locked adjoining door. Though he still wore his tuxedo jacket he had loosened his tie, and it hung on either side of his undone top shirt button. Magda felt her insides turn over.

'That was not the danger I referred to,' he corrected her. 'It was this.'

He closed in on her. A hand slid around her back and spanned her derrière.

'It was projecting far too temptingly,' he murmured down at her.

There was a light in his eye that made her insides churn again.

'Rafaello—' she gasped faintly, trying to draw away from him. But that only made the warm, devastating pressure on her rear increase. As if unwilling to tolerate her escape, he simply pulled her closer against him, moving his hand upwards into the small of her back and curving his other hand beneath the cloud of her hair to hold the nape of her neck.

She had no breath in her. No breath to speak, to protest, to exclaim—or even to breathe.

Rafaello smiled down into her face.

'There is only one way,' he told her softly, 'to end an evening like this.'

His head lowered to hers, and closed over her breathlessly parted lips.

He started to kiss her.

It had happened so suddenly she had had no time, no
chance, to do or say anything. One moment she had been
gazing out of the window into the Tuscan night, thinking
the evening was over, and the next Rafaello had closed in
on her and was making love to her.

Because that was what he was doing—making love to
her mouth, his lips brushing over hers, moistening and laving, teasing them apart with his, sensually, devastatingly
to open her to him and take his fill of her.

She was lost, so completely lost that the roof could have
caved in and she would not have noticed. His fingers
speared into her hair, kneading at her scalp. His other hand
slipped down over the soft mound of her bottom, and did
likewise to the silk-covered flesh there.

Sensation shot through her body like fireworks. His
kisses were deepening, her mouth was fully open to him
now, and his tongue was meeting hers, tasting and mating.
The blood pounded in her veins, her ears, and of their own
volition her hands wrapped over his hard, lean spine and
held him close, crushing his torso against her breasts which
suddenly, extraordinarily, felt full and swollen.

He was murmuring something into her mouth, but she
could make no sense of it. Could make no sense of anything, only go on, and on, kissing and being kissed.

Then his arm was around her waist, his hand at her
shoulder, though his mouth never left hers, and he was
urging her forward.

'My bed,' she heard him say, and his voice was a husk.

She found her voice, dragged it up from the depths.

'Rafaello—please—I...I...'

'Hush,' he said into her mouth. 'Hush—it will be good—
this is right for us, *cara*—trust me. I want you so much...

His kiss deepened again and almost, almost she gave

herself to it totally, gave herself to everything he was offering, everything she had never dared even dream about.

But dreams were not real—and this was not reality. It could not be. It must not be.

She dragged her mouth away again, halting as he swept her forward.

'Rafaello—no. Please—please listen to me—you don't understand—'

He heard the plea in her voice and let her draw away, but only so far as he could still hold her in the circle of his arms. His dark eyes searched hers in the low light.

'Don't be afraid—I will not hurt you. I know it has been a long time for you, and that losing Benji's father so tragically was hard—unbearable. But you must move on, embrace life again.'

Her eyes had widened at his words and she seemed to be trying to speak, but he would not let her.

'You are a beautiful, desirable woman—a whole new life is opening to you now. The past is gone—remember Kaz for the son he gave you, but now embrace life again.'

There was consternation in her face now, and her mouth worked until words came.

'Kaz? No—you don't understand—Kaz wasn't Benji's father,' she said faintly.

He stilled, as if she had struck him. 'Then who—?' He frowned—what was happening?

She felt his arms around her slacken, and drew back.

'I...I don't know.'

His face darkened. *'Come?'*

She swallowed. 'I don't know who Benji's father is. You see—'

He stepped away. Tension was in every line of his body.

'You do not *know* who fathered him?'

There was a haunted look in her eyes, but he ignored it. Inside he felt a slow-burning fuse of anger ignite.

'You have been with so many men you do not know which one got you pregnant?'

The biting harshness of his words flayed her. He could see she looked stricken, appalled, but he struck again. 'So this Kaz you spoke of—this tragic loss—is just a sob story—to soften me?'

She took another step backwards. 'You don't understand,' she whispered.

His mouth twisted. 'Oh, I understand, all right. I understand the truth now. I thought to defend you—to prove that my insults were untrue! But however misfortunate your life there is no excuse—none—for indulging in promiscuity so great that you could not even be bothered to choose a single father for your child.' Disgust filled his face. 'Did you never stop to consider the effect of your total irresponsibility upon an innocent child? Are you yourself not living proof of the fruits of such irresponsibility? And yet you do it again, to your own son.'

'Benji has *me*!' she cried anguishedly. 'I will never leave him, *never*!'

His face stilled.

'A boy needs a father.'

There was something in his voice that was bleak.

'A boy needs a father,' he said again. 'And you have deliberately deprived your son of that right—he will not even know who his father was! Or will you lie to him and tell him this Kaz of yours fathered him? To shield him from the truth of what his mother was?'

His voice was scornful, condemning. Angrily he strode across the room, heading for the bathroom and his own room beyond. He felt gutted, as though something wonderful, something rare and surprising, had just turned to mildew in his hands.

As she watched him go Magda stood, reeling. From passion to fury in a few moments. She felt winded. But she also knew that she had to go after him.

She reached the communicating door just as he was about to shut it, and held her hand out to halt him.

'Rafaello,' she said, in a low, unsteady voice, 'I don't know who fathered Benji, it's true. And I know that depriving a child of its father is a terrible thing to do—but...but...please make allowances for Kaz.'

His face darkened.

'Kaz? You just said he was not Benji's father.'

Magda swallowed. 'It's true. Kaz wasn't Benji's father. Kaz...' She hesitated, then said it. 'Kaz was Benji's mother.'

He stared at her as if she had run mad. She forced herself to go on.

'Kaz was like a sister to me. We only ever had each other in all the world. When...when the cancer came back she went...a little mad, I think. She knew she was going to die before she had even begun to live. And she told me...she told me...' There was a tight steel band constricting her throat, making it impossible to breathe, to talk, but she forced herself on. 'She told me that if she couldn't live, if she was going to be wiped out as if she had never existed, then she wanted...wanted to prove that she *had* existed—that if *she* couldn't live she would leave a part of herself behind. Was it so wrong?' Her voice was a whisper. 'Was it so wrong for her to conceive a child any way she could, to leave something of herself behind? How could I tell her no? How *could* I, when I wasn't facing what she was facing? All I could do was promise to raise her child and be the mother she was not going to be allowed to be. She knew I would never abandon Benji—*never*—because I had been abandoned myself. She knew she could trust me with him. So she gave him to me, just before...just before she died.'

The tears were rolling down her cheeks now, unstoppable, as the memories of her friend came crowding back. She stood there, her hand against the door, and could say nothing more.

Then arms came around her, strong and protecting, and gathered her up, and the tears flowed and flowed. She could hear Italian being murmured, but all she could tell of it was the comfort in his voice as she clung to him.

It took a long while for the tears to stop. In the early months, when she had still been raw from Kaz's death, with Benji still so tiny, so bereaved, they had come often, in the loneliness of the night, but it had been a long, long time since she had cried—and never with anyone to comfort her.

At last there were no more tears. Rafaello slipped his arm around her shoulder and led her into his room. 'Sit,' he said, and there was a gentleness in his voice she'd never heard before. He lowered her down to an armchair beside the empty fireplace and hunkered down beside her. He took her hands.

'Forgive me for my anger at you—I spoke in ignorance.' His mouth twisted wryly. 'As I have done before about you.' He paused a moment. 'I have only one thing to say— that Benji is a fortunate child to have such devotion from you.'

'He is my son.' It was a cry from her heart.

Rafaello pressed her hands. 'He is your son,' he confirmed. 'And your love for him shines like a beacon in the dark. You have taken him into your heart, and he is there for ever now.'

He raised her hands to his lips. Something was singing inside him—something that sounded a sweet, clear note. He stood up, taking her with him, still holding her hands.

And then, in the dim light, he kissed her.

It was a light kiss, as soft as silk, but when he kissed her again, holding her hands against his chest so that she could feel the warmth of his body through the palms of her hand and the fine material of his shirt, his embrace deepened.

'I desire you very much,' he told her softly. 'Will you stay with me tonight?'

Her eyes were deep and dark.

'Rafaello—I…there is something you should know—'

He smiled. 'You have more secrets?' he chided. 'Tell me all!'

She felt herself colour slightly. 'A moment ago you thought me promiscuous and you were angry—'

He shook his head. 'My anger was at the thought of your irresponsibility in conceiving a child who could not name his father. But,' he acknowledged, 'as for promiscuity itself—well, I have known many women—perhaps I should not have, but…' he met her eyes with a rueful look '…it came easily to me. Do not think me too conceited, but a man with money is always attractive.'

'Especially if he looks like you,' Magda found herself answering with her own little tug of a smile.

'If I agree you will definitely think me conceited,' he answered, with a faint, wry smile. 'But, whatever the cause, I am therefore hardly in a position to criticise you if you are as experienced as I am.'

'Yes, but the thing is,' she replied, embarrassed, dipping her head so she wouldn't have to look him in the eye, however dim the light was, 'I'm not experienced at all.'

Her words fell into a pool of silence. Then, wordlessly, he put her away from him, letting slip her hands.

'That's why I said about Kaz not being Benji's father when you said I should not hold back for Kaz's sake,' she went on, feeling mortified now. 'I knew—I knew you would obviously assume that I had at least sufficient experience to have become pregnant, but in fact I…I don't have any experience. None. Never.'

Her voice trailed off and she wished, oh, just wished, she could disappear down a crack in the floor.

'You are a virgin?' There was something odd in his voice. She didn't know what it was, she just wanted that crack to widen, so she could slip away through it, boring, unexciting, inexperienced reject that she was. She should have remembered that Cinderella returned to her rags at midnight. Of no interest whatsoever to a sophisticated, worldly, experienced man like Rafaello di Viscenti.

'I'm sorry,' she said miserably.

'You are sorry?' There was that odd note in his voice again. She stared down at the floor, her fingers twisting in the fabric of her skirts.

Then, suddenly, he had stepped towards her again, and his long, cool fingers were sliding either side of her jaw, tilting her face up towards him.

'Don't you know,' he said softly, 'that there is only one thing to be done with a virgin?'

She gazed at him, her breath catching. He was just so perfect—his dark, beautiful eyes, his silky black hair, his sculpted, sensual mouth...

'Seduce her...' he breathed. 'Take her body...' His fingers slipped into the softness of her hair, teasing the delicate border between her cheek and the graceful fall of hair, touching, oh, so lightly, the lobes of her ears. 'Take her body touch by touch, by touch...' His fingers drifted along the line of her jaw, the length of her throat, with such feathering lightness she thought she must die of it. 'Kiss...by kiss...by kiss.' Each word was murmured against her eyes, fluttering shut, the corner of her mouth. 'Until you have taken her with you on that most perfect journey of all...'

His mouth grazed hers, and she lifted her face to him like a flower, drinking in his nectar.

'Will you come with me, cara, on that journey? Will you let me take you there?' He was kissing her as he spoke, light, seductive kisses that she could no more resist than a snowflake melting on a warm cheek. There were only two people in the entire world—herself and Rafaello di Viscenti, the most beautiful man she had ever seen. His hands were framing her face, his fingers teasing, his mouth caressing hers with exquisite, feathered lightness. But beneath the lightness a hunger was growing. She could feel it, building in her veins, her head, making her mouth answer his, taste him as he was tasting her, dissolving the world around her into nothing more than exquisite, honeyed sensation.

She wanted it never to stop, but for all that it was not enough—it was feeding its own hunger, its own yearning.

Her body pressed itself against his, a slender wand against his lean hardness, her palms caught between her breasts and his chest.

She gave a little moan, deep in her throat, as he teased open her mouth, releasing yet more and more sensation, until she felt flame flickering throughout her body. She felt her breasts quicken, swelling against him, and the sensation was as wondrous as it was arousing.

Time slipped away, lost in sensation. There was nothing, nothing but this. Nothing but the touch of his fingers at her shoulders, slipping the tiny shoestring straps over the cusp of each arm, and gently, oh, so gently, his hands warm on her flanks, sliding the silky material of her dress down the slender column of her body. He was kissing her all the while, but as the dress pooled at her feet he let her go and stepped back.

She stood there, the dark material spread on the floor, her body bathed in the soft light from the low lamps. Her instinct was to cover her breasts, but instinct was fighting with another impulse, yet more powerful—to stand quite still and let Rafaello's eyes drink in the sight of her as a thirsty man would drink purest spring water. So she stood, one slender silk-clad leg taking slightly more weight that the other, the tiny line of her wisp of panties around her narrow hips, her eyes huge and liquid as she displayed herself to him.

'*Bellissima…*' His voice was low, and husked. 'Beautiful—so beautiful…'

Her heart soared. To hear such a word on his lips was a pleasure so sweet, so melting she could not believe it.

'Am I?' Her words were a whisper.

'Do you doubt it?' His hand reached out and slowly, with infinite delicacy, his fingers traced around the swelling aureole of her breast. It flowered beneath his touch, and a shiver of pleasure went through her, a trembling in all her limbs. His fingers moved to her other breast and performed the same office there.

'*Bellissima,*' he said again. Then his hand slipped to hers and, folding her fingers in his own, he led her towards the bed.

It was a dream, thought Magda—it had to be a dream. Reality this wondrous, this magical, could never exist. Yet how could it be a dream? The touch of Rafaello's hands was upon her body, laying her down upon the cool sheets. Pausing only to swiftly shed his own clothes—making her first gaze in adoration at the lean, dark revelation of skin and sinew, muscle and smooth, smooth flesh, making her lashes wash blushingly down over her eyes as her gaze worked downwards from his torso—he came and half lay beside her, lowering his head to kiss, not her lips, but those swelling, aching orbs that yearned again for his arousing caress.

She felt her spine arch, lifting her breasts towards him, and her hands reached for him, her fingers stroking into his dark, silky hair. A sigh of bliss eased from her as his tongue and lips suckled her, laving her nipples, one after the other, again and again, until sweetness was flooding through her.

Yet for all the sweetness, all the bliss, she wanted more. Bliss was feeding bliss, arousing her yet more and more, and a strange, yearning aching was spreading through her body, through every vein, every nerve, making her strain towards him.

He lifted his head from her. His eyes were dark pools, pupils dilated.

'You must take this journey slowly, *cara mia*, the first time. It cannot be hurried, this first flowering of your body.

And the waiting…' a slow, sensual smile played over his parted lips as he dropped his voice '…is part of the journey.'

As he spoke he moved his fingers to the soft underside of her breasts, grazing them. Then he let them trail downwards, across the flat planes of her abdomen, smoothing along her flanks before drifting inwards to tease at the central dip of her belly button. But even as his forefinger circled there the spread of his hand spanned the vee of her legs, and all at once, instantly, achingly, she became aware, for the very first time in her life, of the low, insistent throb that had started up.

Did she give a little moan? She did not know, could not tell. Could only tell that now his forefinger was moving slowly, tantalisingly along the dark band of her panty waist, back and forth, while the throb between her legs intensified and the aching, yearning feeling became yet more and more insistent.

He cupped the mound at her vee, and the sudden pressure of the heel of his hand made her gasp, head rolling. He pressed again, and then his other hand was at her throat, spanning upwards to her jaw, holding her still while his body moved over hers.

As his mouth came down she opened to him eagerly, and the weight of his body seemed glorious and possessive. For a long, endless moment he kissed her passionately, his tongue forging deep within her, mating with hers, and she responded, excitement flaring within her like a hot crimson flame. Then, just as suddenly, he withdrew from her.

'Ah, Magda *mia*.' His voice was rueful. 'I betray my own promise and become greedy for you myself.'

As of itself, her mouth reached up for his. 'I don't mind,' she said huskily, and tried to catch his lips as her hands curled around his shoulders to draw him down to her again.

But he lifted his head further back and smiled crookedly. 'No. This first time is a dish to savour slowly—afterwards—ah, well…' his voice rasped '…then we shall see…' A deep, shuddering breath went through him as he steadied himself, and for the first time Magda registered that part of the hard, masculine weight resting on her was very, *very* masculine…

Her eyes widened in recognition of the fact, and as if he could read her thoughts that crooked, rueful smile came again. 'I must be gentle with you, *cara*, and feast upon you…slowly.'

His voice dropped on the last word and sent a shiver of anticipation through her. His smile became sensual, his eyes speaking.

'There are pleasures, my sweet one, in making love in many ways. As I will show you…'

As he spoke his hand, which had been holding her hip, gentled, and began to slide down her thigh. As it encountered the embroidered top of her stockings he gave a mock frown.

'What is this?' he demanded softly.

He did not wait for an answer. Instead he started to slide the silky fabric downwards, his fingers, as he did so, grazing deliciously along the tender flesh of her inner thigh. It was like having warm honey poured over her, she thought, and her mind dissolved into bliss. She felt her body relax into the bedclothes, lose the urgent tension of the past few moments, when it had been consumed by a need she could not name.

Now she needed nothing, nothing in all the world, except this most exquisite sensation of Rafaello's hands sliding her stocking down her leg. When he reached the end, and flicked it aside, he returned to pay attention to her other stocking. His fingers played with the embroidered top, and as they grazed along her inner thigh she felt her legs part a little, falling open slightly. The delicious, exquisite sensation of his taking the stocking off her came again, pouring warm honey over every millimetre of skin. She sank back into the deep, soft bedclothes, her eyes fluttering shut, giving herself to the sensation.

And then, as the second stocking was flicked aside, she felt his hands drifting back up her leg again. But this time when he reached the top of her leg his fingers went on, grazing along the tender flesh of her inner thigh, relaxed and open now, as she lay abandoned to him, and began to brush with tiny, insidious strokes closer and closer to the satin edge of her panties.

The sensation was exquisite—if she had thought his touch on her thighs exquisite she had known nothing, *nothing*! A soft little moan came from her throat as his forefinger came to rest on the plumped satin cupping the curling nest beneath. Warm honey melted through her again, and as his finger began its minute circling movements she realised that it was not just the sensation of melting honey that was flooding through her—her own body was responding to his intimate touch. She seemed liquid, molten, and as the sensation became almost unbearable he intensified it almost beyond endurance. His head lowered to her breast again, his tongue laving softly at the aureole, until her whole body felt like a warm, liquid flame.

Then his fingers were picking at the skimpy waistline of her panties, shushing them down over her hips, sliding them down her parted legs and casting them aside with her stockings.

And then they returned to where she ached for them to be.

It was bliss, bliss beyond imagining, beyond dreams. Her body moved beneath his hand, his mouth, and she felt that warmth flooding through her more sweetly yet, more yearningly still, until every fibre, every nerve ached with wanting.

With agonising slowness his fingers explored her silky folds, eliciting yet more and more pleasure, until she was faint with it.

'Rafaello…' Her voice was weak—weak with longing, weak with desire. She wanted, oh, she wanted… She did not know. But the desire, the need for it was all-consuming. The need for him…him…to join with her, possess her…

'Rafaello…' It was a plea, abject and full of desire. Her hands had found his body, sliding across his shoulders, his back, glorying in the muscled silk of his skin, wanting to draw him down upon her, to draw him into her…

She was flooding—flooding with moisture and desire. The flame of her body was twisting, aching, the sensations at her breast, her body's core, crescendoing, wanting.

'Rafaello—' she said again, and this time, this time his mouth came from her breast and plundered hers instead, kissing her deeply, oh, so deeply, that she gave another moan in her throat and fed upon him as he fed upon her. Then he was moving over her, his fingers loosing from her, steadying himself, his thighs warm and heavy on hers, holding himself above her as for one last, exquisitely tormenting moment his finger centred on the tiny, swollen bud, vibrating it until the warm flame that was her body suddenly, blissfully, seared into incandescence.

The sheet of liquid fire spread out from her ignited core and she gasped with delight and disbelief, for how could such bliss, such ecstasy be possible? And as she did her body opened to him and he was drawn into her, piercing and filling her as her convulsing muscles widened around him and took him into her.

There was pain, but it was fleeting, pushed out by the tide of ecstasy flooding through her, and she cried out, arms wrapping around him urgently.

He filled her absolutely, and as her virgin muscles stretched around him the waves of bliss seemed to intensify, and she cried out again, and again, into the warmth and hunger of his mouth.

'Yes,' he soothed her. 'Yes. Yes, my beautiful girl.'

She did not hear him, could not hear him. Could only

feel. Her whole body was sensation, wonderful, unutterable sensation, which went on and on, ceaseless and without end.

He took her every centimetre of the way, urging her on with subtle movements of his body, with the kisses of his mouth, the urging of his hands on her flanks as the tide of bliss took her on to the very end of her journey.

To leave her there, exhausted, sated, disbelieving, in the shelter of his arms.

He smoothed the hair from her face, smiling down at her, and she felt her heart melt as her body had done, into warm, honeyed flame. A sweetness she had never known filled her heart and soul.

'Rafaello…' Her voice slurred, but her eyes shone with a luminescence that drank him in.

'*Cara?*' he said, and kissed her softly.

Her heart was racing, and she could feel its pulse in her throat, her wrists.

'Thank you…' she breathed.

The smile came again. 'It was my pleasure,' he told her. 'And yours, I think.'

His long-lashed gaze washed over her. He knew exactly what she had felt, what she had experienced.

'Oh, yes!' she answered on a rapturous exhalation. 'Oh, yes…'

His mouth quirked. 'And tell me, my beautiful little virgin-no-more, would you like to feel that way again?'

Her eyes widened incredulously, and he laughed softly. 'Did you think such pleasure comes only once? For you…' his voice took on a rueful, envious tinge '…there is no limit. But for me—' his voice changed '—I can wait no longer—'

He began to move within her, and Magda, eyes widening in her ignorance of such matters, realised with a shock that he was still as full and strong within her as he had ever been. He registered her reaction and smiled again—but this time there was something wolfish in his smile.

'Do not be anxious, *bellissima mia*, you shall come with me, be assured.'

He was as good as his word. As he lifted himself to stroke within her she felt a surge of pleasure shaft through her. She caught her breath, astonished at her sated body's quick recovery. He moved within her, deeper yet, and when she felt the walls of her body resist, suddenly they yielded again.

She clutched him more tightly, clenching her muscles around him, simultaneously tightening her arms around his back.

He gave his wolfish smile again. 'More?'

The expression in her eyes gave him the answer he expected, and he obliged her yet again. But with every stroke she could see, though her body was starting to focus purely on its own renewed pleasure, that this was as good for him as it was for her.

He stroked again, and again, and again, and with each stroke the surge of excitement thrust through her. She clutched at his back, feeling the skin dampen as the pace of his lovemaking increased. There was an urgency to him now, and she joined him, as eager for him to find his pleasure as she was to find hers again. Their bodies moved in unison, her hips rising to meet his thrusts, her head thrown back, feeling with each urgent, pulsing stroke that she was coming nearer, nearer to something, something...

Something that crested like a deep ocean wave, crested and then thundered through her, shocking her with its intensity, a surging, powerful breaker that caught her and plunged her into a maelstrom of overpowering sensation, seeming to roll her over and over, tumbling her, limbs threshing, muscles convulsing, sensation bucking through her, carrying her on and on and on...

She lay in utter exhaustion, supine beneath him, and real-

sed dimly that his dead weight was pressing down upon
her, the full length of his body. His heaviness was total,
his limbs completely inert. For a long, timeless while they
lay together, still one but both cast away on the furthest
shore.

She was tired, infinitely tired. Slowly, heavily, her arms
fell from his back, collapsing on to the sheets. Her eyes
sank shut and she breathed in the scent of his body as sleep
took her.

CHAPTER NINE

SHE awoke, it seemed, an aeon later. As she eased into consciousness her first thoughts were confused. Where was she? Where was Benji? Why hadn't he woken her as he always did? Panicked, she hauled herself upright and blinked, even more disorientated as she stared around at the strange bedroom. And then total, absolute memory flooded through her, and at the same time she became aware of a dull, strained ache between her legs. But more pressing matters asserted themselves.

'Benji!' she cried out in alarm, and as if he had simply been waiting for her call at that moment Rafaello sauntered into his bedroom via the adjoining bathroom, carrying Benji. Seeing her, both broke into smiles, Benji immediately reaching out his arms for her. Rafaello—clad only, Magda became immediately aware, in a pair of jeans—crossed to the bed, bared torso very clearly on display, and lowered Benji down to her.

'Maria has given him his breakfast and got him clean and dressed.' His eyes swept down over her. 'You were tired, *cara*, and I let you sleep.'

Magda bent her head, feeling heat stealing into her cheeks, and busied herself embracing an enthusiastic Benji. But as soon as he had reassured himself of his mother's presence he climbed off her and started to burrow under the bedclothes. Magda wished she could do the same. Looking Rafaello in the eye right now was not something she felt she could do.

'Shy, *cara*?' he enquired softly, recognising her reaction.

He found it enchanting. Swiftly, Rafaello's mind worked back, trying to recall any similar instances of past partners

154

greeting him in the morning with a becoming flush, downcast eyes and a general air of shy confusion. There were none.

All his previous women had been highly sexually confident females, knowing full well their own attractions. He couldn't imagine any of them ever having been shy about going to bed with him—or anyone.

Magda was a million miles away from any of his previous women.

And not just because of her virginity. Or her shyness.

Just *what* it was about her that made her so different he couldn't work out yet.

But he'd find out.

He lowered himself to the bed, noting with inner humour how she automatically jerked her legs away from him beneath the bedclothes. Placing his hands on the mattress either side of her thighs, he leant forward.

'*Buon giorno*,' he said invitingly, his eyes gleaming softly.

She didn't seem to know what he wanted, so he showed her.

A soft kiss of greeting, just brushing her tender mouth and then withdrawing. As he drew back he saw her flush had mounted, and she still could not meet his eye.

He smiled, and saw her gaze flicker momentarily to his.

'There is no need for shyness, *cara*. You are a woman now.'

Yes, he thought, and I have made her so. An amazing feeling swept through him at the realisation. It was quite extraordinary. She was transformed from that poor, scrawny, unlovely creature whom no man would look at once, let alone twice, into something…someone….who would turn heads wherever she went.

A strange sensation moved inside him. He did not know what it was—it was something he had never felt before, and he wondered at it. His eyes swept over her again, looking at him so shyly, so uncertainly—and yet with a hunger in her eyes for him that he was sure she did not realise was blazing through her embarrassment. The hunger he recognised, for it mirrored his own. He started to lower his head to hers again. She looked so *good*, lying back against his pillows, even if the bedclothes were clutched up to her chin. He reached forward with a hand, meaning to draw them off her so that he could see her lovely, delicate body in the warm morning light. And more than see…

A head pushed itself out from under the bedclothes by his elbow and a tiny hand landed plumply on his, where it pressed into the mattress bearing the weight of his inclining torso. A gurgle of infant laughter burst out of Benji as he crowed at his achievement, emerging from his hiding place.

Rafaello sat back, wry resignation in his face. There would be no lovemaking this morning, he could tell. Immediately he started thinking how swiftly he could convey Benji into Maria's care, so that he could get Magda to himself again.

But not yet, it seemed. Benji wanted to play. Especially with this interesting new addition to morning playtime. He crawled across to Rafaello and deposited himself on his lap, chuckling and making jigging movements to encourage him.

'He wants you to bounce him on your knees,' said Magda, finding her voice at last. At least talking about Benji was possible—he was a safe, neutral subject, and nothing, nothing whatsoever to do with what Rafaello had been talking to her about—which, right now, she couldn't cope with—not at all, not in the slightest.

'Like this?' enquired Rafaello, and twisted round so that he was sitting at right angles, with his feet on the floor again.

'Yes. You hold him on and play "This is the way the lady rides",' explained Magda helpfully.

She ran through the game with him, explaining how the

ady rode very timidly, and the gentleman rode very sol-
mnly, but then the farmer rode with a huge and exagger-
ted bumpety-bump which reduced Benji to peals of laugh-
er.

And Rafaello, too. Magda watched him repeat the game
t least five times for Benji, and her heart simply turned
ver and over in her chest. He looked so *beautiful*, with
is smooth, lean torso, not an ounce of fat on him, his
trong arms holding Benji firmly but with such care, and
h, his face, his face, with its sculpted planes and laughing
nouth, and his dark, beautiful eyes crinkling at the corners,
nd his dark, silky hair flopping over his forehead...

Her heart went on turning and turning and turning...

She felt so happy she thought she must die.

But not so happy that she wasn't still filled to the brim
vith total, absolute shyness about what had happened.

Thank goodness Benji was there! After the fifth repeti-
ion she lifted him from Rafaello, taking great pains not to
ctually touch the man who had swept her to paradise last
ight, terrified that if she did it would immediately be ob-
ious to him that what she longed for right now was for
im to sweep her there all over again.

'That's quite enough, you little monster.' She nuzzled
ffectionately at Benji. 'It's time to get up.'

She was about to throw the bedclothes aside and stand
p when she realised with a flush that she had not a stitch
n. She froze.

Rafaello took pity on her. He got to his feet.

'I'll take Benji downstairs. We'll be on the terrace. Come
nd have your breakfast there with me.'

He scooped Benji from her, taking far less pains than
Magda against touching as he did so, and she felt her skin
uiver where his fingers brushed her bare arms as she trans-
erred Benji to him. Only when he had definitely left the
oom did she dare get out of bed and dart through into the
athroom.

She stopped short, seeing her reflection in the bathroom mirror.

It was her body—and yet not her body. She stood, gazing, seeing the fullness of her breasts which surely had not been there before. There was a curve to her hip, too, and—this she was definitely not imagining!—there were soft, lip-shaped discolorations on her throat and breasts. As if in answer to her own thoughts she became aware of the dull throbbing between her legs.

It really happened, she thought, her eyes gazing at her reflection in amazed wonder. It really happened...

That deep, quivering flush of happiness suffused her again, at its core a wonder and a piercing ache that made her feel her heart was opening. A slow, blissful smile lit her face. Whatever happened, whatever happened to her the rest of her life, she would have this moment—this wonderful, blissful, unbelievable moment—when the most beautiful man in the world had taken her to his bed and made a woman out of her.

Despite the residual soreness that remained from the physical experience of that transition, she showered and dressed on winged feet, filled with an overpowering longing to be in his company again. She did not know what the day would bring—what any part of the future would bring. She only knew that now, right now, she just wanted to be with Rafaello, feel his presence, and drink him in like a glass of golden champagne.

On the terrace Rafaello was waiting for her. As she approached his eyes lit with an assessing look, and she immediately became super-conscious of the way the beautifully cut pale blue sundress she had not been able to resist putting on from the huge selection that now crowded her wardrobe moulded her breasts and hips.

She took her place and occupied herself pouring out coffee. Benji glanced at her briefly from astride his new trike before zooming off along the terrace.

Rafaello leant towards her. His bare chest was like polished steel in the bright morning light.

'Well, *cara*, what would you like to do today, hmm?'

He might have been asking her as a tourist, but the expression in his eyes made it perfectly clear what he wanted
her answer to be. She felt the colour run up her cheeks
again.

'Um, whatever you like,' she answered confusedly. Then
went on hurriedly, 'But don't you have to go into the office
or something?'

Rafaello shook his head. 'I can think of nothing more
tedious,' he answered.

And it was true. The very thought of sitting at his desk,
expanding di Visconti AG into a global empire, was the
most boring idea in the world. No, his world today was
centred here—on this extraordinarily enticing woman.

Benji came roaring back in true Formula One style, and
as Rafaello glanced at him he felt himself still.

She had taken on another woman's son to raise as her
own. A dying woman had trusted Magda with her own
child...

He felt something constrict inside him. What did it take,
he thought, to do such a thing? It was a choice that had
cost her so much in material terms. For the sake of her
dying friend she had taken on a newborn baby, with no
support other than what the state provided—no family,
barely any money, not even a home of her own to raise
him in. But she had done it—turned herself into a drudge,
living in penury, because she would not turn her back on
a helpless baby who had no one else to look after him.

Emotion surged through him.

Thank God I found her!

He had taken her away from all that poverty-stricken
drudgery, brought her here and released her, like a bird
from her cage, to fly on iridescent wings in the summer's

warmth. Well-being flooded through him, and something more—something more...

A hand planted on his knee drew his attention. Benji wanted to climb up. He bent down and scooped him onto his lap, marvelling at the solid warmth of the infant, the way he trustingly snuggled up against him before turning his attention to the bread rolls on the table.

With a laugh, Rafaello fed him while Magda sipped her coffee.

'Another day at the beach,' he announced decisively. 'That's what we all need.'

Benji would be in seventh heaven, Magda would be happy and he—well, he would have another opportunity to admire her swimsuit...

'More coffee?'

Magda shook her head. Part of her wanted to say yes, because that would mean she could go on sitting at the table. Upstairs, Benji was fast asleep, exhausted by the pleasures of the seaside, and Rafaello had persuaded her to entrust his safety to a newly-purchased baby alarm monitor that even now relayed his deep, even breathing from its receiver beside her place.

They were still out on the terrace, even at this late hour, for the weather had turned even warmer and Magda was drinking in the glory of the Italian night sky. A scrape of metal on stone accompanied Rafaello's getting to his feet. He came around the table to her and held out his hand.

'Bedtime,' he said softly.

Her breath seemed to catch in her throat. She knew exactly what he wanted—and she knew with all her heart, with all her body, that she wanted it, too. She wanted to feel his arms around her again, feel that hard, lean body against hers, feel his hands, his mouth...his tongue... moving over her, taking her step by step back to that

wonderful, ecstatic, unbelievable, heavenly paradise he had
taken her to last night.

'I have waited all day,' he went on, looking down at her
with his dark, velvet wanting eyes. 'For countless, agonising hours…waiting for this moment, *cara*, when I would
take your hand and draw you to your feet, like this—' with
soft, insistent force he drew her up '—and wind my arms
round you, like this—' his arms folded her against him
—and lift your face to mine and taste, ah, taste again that
honey from your mouth—like this—'

His mouth lowered to hers, and with a little sigh she gave
her lips to his.

It was bliss, it was heaven, it was the stars moving in a
slow, insistent arc across the sable sky as his mouth moved
upon hers, opening her like a flower, to feast on the nectar
he sought.

'Come,' he said again, 'it is time for the night to begin…'

Could it really be, she thought, her mind a mist, her body
a soft velvet fire, as good again as it had been before? And
yet it was—and more. As he swept her inside his bedroom
he did not even go through to check on Benji— 'He is
fine, *cara*—listen, I have brought the monitor with me—he
sleeps like an angel.' Rafaello breathed into her mouth as
he kissed her again and again, and with each kiss, each
touch, lit flames in every portion of her body, peeling from
her the flimsy covering of her clothes until once again she
stood naked in his embrace.

He lowered her gently to the bed, parting her legs and
coming down, quite as naked as she, upon her.

'*Dio*, I will be as gentle as I can, but the waiting has
been hard—'

He arched over her, his lean body like a perfect bow,
eager to find its mark, his mouth plundering hers, then moving down to capture each peaking breast as his hands swept
down over her slender body. Hungrily he sought the rip-

ening core of her body, preparing it for himself—preparing
her for him. At his touch she moaned, incoherent with the
desire rushing through her.

His words echoed her own longing. 'I want you so
much—right now...'

She was like a pale flame beneath him, burning like a
lens, reflecting all her heat into him, his body.

'Rafaello—'

'Yes—say my name. I want to hear it—want to hear you
cry it out aloud, to me, now, right now—'

He held her poised beneath him and then, as if of their
own accord, her hips lifted to his, gyrating very slightly,
feeling his hard, powerful length ready to pierce her. He
needed no second invitation, and with a low growl he thrust
within her.

And then her body was welcoming him, remembering
him, moving around him, beneath him, clasping him to her
so that he groaned again and lifted his head from her.

'*Dio*—what are you doing to me? How can I hold back?
Cara—come with me—I must...'

He surged within her, and as if a match had been thrown
into driest tinder she scorched into flame around him. A
cry was wrenched from her throat, an answering cry from
his, and he thrust, and thrust again as she lifted her hips to
him, every muscle straining. Her head was thrown back,
her eyes closing tight shut as wave after wave of sensation
broke like an unstoppable tide through her.

His possession was total—as was hers of him. She
clasped him to her, her hands folding and unfolding on his
smooth, muscled back, her arms reaching across its broad-
ness as she held him to her and he surged to the very utmost
of her limits.

'Rafaello! Rafaello—'

It was a dying fall, a homage to him, to his beauty, to
his possession, to her desire for him—and his for her, which
seemed so wondrous she could not believe it was really

ue. And yet it was true. As the tide of sensation gave one
nal, blissful breaking through her convulsing body she
new, *knew* that the intensity of what she had felt had been
s strong for him as it had for her. He had wanted her,
esired her as she had desired him, and the wonder of it,
ie glory of it, made her weak.

For a long, timeless while they lay together, wound in
ach other's arms, no words left, no words possible. She
vanted nothing more in all the world.

She must hold this moment, hold it for ever—this sweet-
ess of bliss, this wonder of joy that was filling her and
ooding her.

I love you…

The words formed on her lips, welling out of her heart,
nd she felt their power and their glory. But they were
ilent words, breathed into his living skin, into her soul.

I love you…

A silent promise. A secret gift.

Rafaello! No. Someone might see!'

'Who? There is no one for miles.'

'Shepherds—farmers—people on holiday.'

He grinned, a wolfish parting of his teeth. 'There's not
soul around, *cara*, no one to save you from me.'

He rolled her over on the rug, spread beneath shady
hestnut trees in this most remote spot, a sheltered slope
vith no habitation for miles. One by one he spread her
ands above her head and arched his body over her.

'No one to save you from me,' he echoed, the smile on
is mouth, the expression on his eyes, all portending one
itention only.

She gazed helplessly back into his eyes.

'I don't want to be saved,' she breathed.

'*Bene*—the very words I want to hear,' he told her.
lowly, infinitely slowly, he kissed her, and she thought
he would die of it, it was such bliss. He drew back a little,

still arched over her, his palms pressed onto hers. Then h
kissed her again, his warm, wine-sweetened mouth movin
with leisurely exploration. She felt desire stir yet again, an
wondered at it.

They had spent all morning in bed together. She ha
woken to discover that once again Rafaello had woken be
fore her, and whisked Benji off to Maria. But this mornin
instead of bringing him back to Magda he had returne
alone, informing her that Maria was taking Benji to pla
with her infant great-nieces, and that he would be happ
and entertained and not miss her for a moment—which wa
highly convenient, as it happened, because right nov
Magda would have no time, no time at all, for paying at
tention to anyone else but him...

In the shuttered bedroom Rafaello had done what he ha
wanted to do the day before—kept Magda entirely and ab
solutely to himself, feasting and feeding on her withou
satiation, without end. It had been a sensual overload tha
had melted every fibre of her body, dissolving the hours i
endless, timeless bliss until at last Rafaello had risen fron
his bed and declared it was time, finally, to get up for th
day.

If that had been his intent it had been unwise, though
Magda, of him to have suggested that, since they were bot
in the bathroom at the same time, they might therefor
shower together...

It had been a long, long shower...

And now, after a luscious picnic in the most remote spc
Rafaello could find, she realised with a sigh of pleasure jus
what he had in mind.

To make love in the open air, beneath a bower of gree
leaves, the soft, warm breeze sighing in the grass, was t
be Adam and Eve, she thought, in the garden of paradis
As her needless fears of discovery melted in the irresistibl
solvent of desire she gave herself to him in the dapple

unlight, gave herself utterly and entirely, all her being, all
er heart and soul.

She loved him, she knew. Knew that it could not be
therwise, that she was helpless against its power. And
hilst the bliss and glory of it filled her, far below, in the
eep recesses of her being, she knew it was not for her.

Today and tomorrow she could have—whatever time
as to be allotted to her to have and to hold this most
eautiful of men, this most cherished of beings by her side,
n her arms. She did not know why he had chosen to change
owards her, had no answer for it beyond, perhaps, curi-
sity, whim, an impulse he had decided to indulge. But she
new, however, that it would not last—could not last—that
. was some kind of dream out of time, a brief, impermanent
isitation of bliss that would flame like marsh fire before
xtinguishing itself.

But she did not care. As she lay beneath him, her eyes
taring up at the mesh of chestnut leaves above them, his
ated body heavy on her, folded closely to her in her clasp-
ng arms, she knew that she did not care that it would not
ast—could not last—that the end would come, and that she
ould wake one morning to his final kiss, his last embrace.

She felt his weight lift from her as he levered himself up
rom her a little, shifting his weight onto one elbow. Her
yes flickered to his and she gazed at him, helpless with
er love for him.

She hoped he did not see it. Hoped it did not show.

Idly he plucked a long blade of grass and trailed it along
e side of her cheek. The slight tickling sensation after all
he had just felt made her smile.

'Why do you smile?' he asked softly, smiling back at
er as he spoke.

'Because I am happy,' she told him simply.

His smile deepened.

'So am I, *cara mia*, so am I.' He kissed her gently. 'Very
appy.'

For a long, close moment they just looked at each other. Looked deep into each other's eyes. After all they had just shared—the absolute union of their bodies, the journey they had taken together to the country of passion and desire, then the flow back to this, a gentler, less tempestuous union, but still a union—Magda knew with a deep, abiding certainty that was far closer than all that had gone before. As she gazed into his eyes, and he into hers, she felt a living bond flow between them…a wondrous, living bond…

And then, as a tiny, unknown bud of emotion began to unfurl deep within her—an emotion she dared not acknowledge, dared not give a name to—she saw his eyes veil. Withdrawing from her.

The moment was gone, and so was the emotion.

It had been hope, and it had just slipped away.

They took Benji with them on their next picnic, the following day, and although Rafaello had to forgo the pleasure of love in the open air in exchange for the pleasure of seeing Magda and her son enjoying themselves, he more than made up for it on their return to the villa, as the sun was lowering over the Tyrrhenian Sea.

With almost indecent haste he handed Benji over to Maria, who had come bustling out of her domain at their arrival, slipped his hand over Magda's and simply said, 'Vene,' heading with her to the staircase.

Quite unable to meet Maria's eye, merely able to pat Benji's head and tell him to be a good boy—'He is always good, signora,' Maria assured her, with approval in her voice—Magda let herself be led upstairs.

She had the feeling that Maria's approval was not just for Benji's behaviour, but for theirs. Ever since Rafaello had transformed her from an ugly duckling the housekeeper had radiated approval upon them both. Rafaello she fussed over like a boy on his birthday, and presented him with enough food at mealtimes to fatten him for Christmas—no at it ever made the slightest difference to his greyhound eanness, Magda thought, her eyes lingering on his smooth, ard torso as he slipped his shirt from his shoulders with lear intent. And as for her, Maria simply beamed at her whenever she looked at her, saying nothing—but her eyes were eloquent.

And Magda knew why. She knew Maria thought that omething *real* was happening here. That this strange, temporary marriage was becoming real.

But it wasn't. She knew that. Knew that deep, deep in er bones, in her heart, in her mind, in her soul. As he tepped towards her, the shuttered light in the bedroom naking his body bronze, she knew that Rafaello was merely intrigued by her, that he was still caught up in the nexpected pleasure of having turned her into, if not a wan, then at least a graceful songbird—a little street sparow he had touched with gold and taught to fly.

And she was flying now. Lifting on wings of passion as e stroked her sun-warmed skin and murmured soft Italian words to her, bent to taste the sweetness of her mouth and arry her to his bed as together they began to soar towards he all-consuming sun and burn within its fiery heart.

Afterwards he held her close, his arm around her, and he rested her head upon his chest. His fingers played idly with her hair. They said nothing, but in the silence Magda ound a peace she had never known before.

He took her out for dinner that evening, after Benji was sleep and Maria had been entrusted with the baby monior—not that she didn't cast it a jaundiced look, Magda oted with a smile—and they dined in a formidably elegant estaurant with a wonderful view over the valley beyond. Magda sat there feeling like a princess in her blue silk gown with diamonds around her neck.

But it was Rafaello who made her feel like a princess, ot the designer gown or the priceless diamonds—Rafaello. 'he man she loved. But because she knew that princesses

only lived in fairytales, not real life, she knew that althoug
she was not the ugly duckling any more, she was sti
Cinderella—and the hands of the clock were edging to
wards midnight.

She did not know when it would strike. Did not know
how long Rafaello would continue to be intrigued by her
diverted by his own unexpected magic trick of turning
drab, downtrodden char into a woman worthy of his atten
tion—worthy of his bed. She knew he would never be hars
to her, never discard her cruelly, but she knew, with a deep
terrible certainty, that one day the phone would ring, or a
e-mail would arrive, or his father would return, or he woul
simply remember that his real life had nothing to do wit
the woman he had hired to marry him so that he could ge
control of the company his father had threatened to se
under his nose.

And when it happened she would pack her bags, and pic
up Benji, and take one last, long look at the man who hel
her heart in his hands—a gift he had never asked for, woul
never even know he possessed—and go back to *her* rea
life, taking with her nothing but memories, every one c
them a priceless, precious jewel to treasure all her days.

'What is it?'

His voice was low, penetrating her thoughts.

She made herself smile, lifting her wine glass. 'Nothing
I was pitying people back in Britain. I saw an Englis
newspaper headline that said it was the wettest June fc
years.'

Rafaello gave an answering smile. 'Don't think abou
wet English summers—only glorious Tuscan ones!'

She set down her glass. 'I'll remember this summer a
my life—thank you, Rafaello. Thank you from the bottor
of my heart.' She met his eyes, pouring into her expressio
all her gratitude to him for granting her this magical fairy
tale to live in for a little while.

Something flickered in his eyes. She could not tell wha

t was. He gave a little bow of his head, an oddly formal
gesture.

'It was my pleasure, *cara*. And still is…' He reached
across the table and took her hand in his, lifted it to his
mouth. His kiss was soft—his eyes softer.

Magda felt her heart still, and just for a moment completely cease to beat. Then, as she gazed wordlessly at him,
t happened again. His expression was veiled and he set her
hand free.

'Tomorrow,' he announced, 'I show you Firenze.'

A weight pressed against Magda's heart as she continued
with her meal.

Florence was magnificent. The Italian Renaissance made
visible in stone and marble, oil and fresco, so rich with
treasures of art and architecture that it left Magda reeling.

And yet it oppressed her. Or something did. As she gazed
at the glories of the Uffizi she found herself longing again
or that magical day in Lucca, when Rafaello had waved
his magic wand over her and she had appeared to him for
the first, most wondrous time in all her life, pleasing as a
woman…

She did her best to hide her inner oppression. Not just
because she knew she had no right to make him feel uncomfortable about her in any way—he had never asked her
o fall in love with him, never wanted her to—but because
t would simply waste one of these most precious golden
days with him.

So she smiled, and feasted her eyes upon him, and rev-
elled at the closeness of his body to hers, the casual wrap
of his arm around her shoulder, the way he held her hand
as they gazed at the glories of the Renaissance masters.
And she crushed down the dull foreboding deep within her.

They were taking time out with a much needed coffee
in one of the *piazzas*—Magda half watching the world go
by, half watching the way the sinews of Rafaello's bare

forearm with its rolled back shirtsleeve combined such a miraculous artistry of strength and grace as his hand covered hers warmly—when someone approached them.

'Rafaello! *Ciao!*' A stream of Italian followed, and Magda saw that the chicly dressed female greeting Rafaello was Lucia. Hovering at her side was a louche young man with tight curls and full lips.

Rafaello returned the greeting civilly, and Lucia turned her attention to Magda.

'So, you have been enjoying Tuscany to the full?' Her voice was pleasant enough, and Magda nodded, making an appropriate reply.

Lucia's head tilted very slightly in Rafaello's direction.

'And all that Tuscany has to offer you, I expect—no?'

This time there was a clear alternative meaning to her words. Magda found herself slipping her hand away from under Rafaello's and managed merely to smile slightly, as if she did not understand what Lucia had been so obviously referring to. The woman shrugged slightly.

'Well, enjoy what you can while you can. Now, do please excuse me—Carlo is impatient to show me his latest masterpiece.'

She tucked her arm proprietorially into the young man's and with an elegant little wave took her leave.

Something that sounded like a dismissive rasp sounded in Rafaello's throat.

'*Dio*, to think she ever thought I would marry her!' He glanced contemptuously at the man at his cousin's side.

'She doesn't seem to be pining for you,' Magda agreed. Lucia was leaning into her lover now, making it clear that was exactly what he was.

Rafaello's eyes suddenly flicked to hers.

'And you, *cara*, would you pine for me?'

The question had come out of the blue. Magda froze. She dipped her head, unable to meet Rafaello's eyes.

'I...I don't think you'd want me to pine for you, would you?'

Her reply was low-voiced, but she tried hard to make it unemotional. As she finished speaking she made herself lift her eyes again, keeping her expression steady.

He was silent a moment, and for that instant he looked into her eyes and she could not read his expression. She felt frozen still.

Then, with a little shake of his head, he said, 'No, I wouldn't want you to pine for me.'

There was a note in his voice she did not know. It seemed to her to be a warning. She slipped her gaze past his, towards the medieval church on the far side of the busy *piazza*.

How much human happiness and sorrow its stones must have seen—and mine is just one more...

The thought should have brought her comfort.

But it did not.

She knew at once the next morning that something was wrong. When she woke Rafaello was standing by the window, looking out over the beautiful gardens of the villa, bathed in early sunlight. He had his back to her and he was wearing the same business suit he had worn the day he'd married her. It made him look dark, and forbidding.

As he heard her stir, he turned. His figure was outlined against the brightness of the day outside, and it came to her that it was earlier than they usually woke.

'Magda?' His voice was querying. Then, realising she was awake, he crossed to the bed. He looked taller, more austere as he looked down at her, freshly shaven and with his hair subdued into crisp businesslike neatness.

'I must go to Rome. The board meeting takes place today and I must be there.'

His voice was clipped, his tone impersonal. The Rafaello he had come to know and love so deeply seemed a million miles away. In his place was the man who had paid her to marry him, hired her for a job he could find no one else to do. Something chilled inside her. Oh, she knew he was not always this man—knew that the Rafaello who had made her a fairytale princess was there still—but not today. Not this morning. This Rafaello had put the other one aside—it was time to go back to his real life.

'Oh,' she heard herself say blankly, lifting herself clumsily onto her elbow, keeping the bedclothes around her. 'Of course.'

He went on looking down at her. There was something formidable about him standing there, looking like the rich powerful businessman he was, as remote and alien as when she had first laid eyes on him, cleaning his bathroom on her knees.

A frown creased between his eyes. He started to rotate the gold cufflink on his left wrist.

'When I come back,' he said abruptly, 'we must talk. You understand that, *cara*?'

She nodded. A lump had formed in her throat, hard and choking like an unswallowable stone.

'Yes—'

His mouth tightened. 'We have been living in a dream these days together...'

The stone swelled in her throat. 'Yes—'

She tried to hide her expression, desperate for him not to see what she was terrified must be there. He stood looking down at her, his expression troubled. Then, with a sudden softening of his eyes, he spoke, and for a moment it was Rafaello back again, the man who took her to paradise and held her in his arms.

'I will take care of you, *cara*—be assured.'

Then, twisting his wrist, he glanced at his watch and gave a rasp of displeasure.

'I have to go—'

He bent swiftly, leaning his arm against the wall, and dropped on her mouth one last, hurried kiss.

And was gone.

CHAPTER TEN

MAGDA was at the pool with Benji. Her heart was heavy. Rafaello couldn't have made it clearer that this golden magical time was over. Again and again she heard his words echoing in her head—*When I come back we must talk.*

They tolled like a funeral bell against all her happiness. She did not need to be clairvoyant to know what it was he wanted to talk to her about. Rafaello's real life had reclaimed him—the real life that consisted of him being a driven, powerful businessman, with important things to do in the world far beyond dallying with a woman he had never intended to dally with in the first place.

She had known it would happen eventually. Yet all the knowledge in the world about just how temporary her bliss could be did not make its impending loss any easier to bear. Her sense of oppression thickened, bowing her like a physical weight.

The sharp click of heels upon the stone path approaching the pool area made her turn her head. Her gaze froze as she saw Lucia approaching her. What was she doing here? Every instinct told Magda her arrival was not happy.

'Magda—I have bad news.' The other woman's voice was staccato, and for a second Magda bristled. Then, a second later, she realised Lucia was not being hostile—her face was stiff with shock.

'Enrico has had a heart attack!'

A gasp escaped Magda, and she stood up from the shaded lounger, sliding Benji to his feet.

The other woman ploughed on. 'He has been taken to

174

hospital. Rafaello is with him. They do not know if he can live—'

She broke off with a choke.

Magda stood there, not knowing what to say. Oh, poor, poor Rafaello, she thought—what agony for him.

'I'm so sorry,' she heard herself say in a whisper. She took a breath, feeling helpless as she said it, but knowing she must, 'Is there anything…anything I can do?'

Lucia looked at her. She nodded.

'This is difficult for me to say.' She paused, then went on, 'I do not say this in enmity, you must understand that—but…' She paused again, then continued, 'The best thing you can do now is go.'

For a moment Magda thought she meant go to Rome, to Rafaello, and then, as if a knife were suddenly slicing into her heart, she realised that was not what his cousin meant.

The expression on Lucia's face was troubled, and she seemed to find what she was saying uncomfortable.

'Enrico needs Rafaello—and Rafaello needs Enrico. I once thought…' She hesitated, then continued, 'I once thought that the way to bring them together again was through Rafaello marrying me. I was mistaken. Rafaello merely saw it as his father's ploy to control him—and he will not be controlled. You, of all people, know the ends he went to in order to escape being controlled by his father. But now—Enrico may die. He must make his peace with his son—and Rafaello with his father.' She looked Magda straight in the eyes. 'They cannot make their peace if you are still here. You must see that.'

The knife was still slicing through Magda's heart. But through the pain she heard the inescapable logic of what Lucia was telling her.

'I must be able to tell Enrico—if he still lives—that you are gone. Then he can make his peace with his son.'

The pain was so bad Magda did not know how she was

bearing it. As if it were visible in her face, Lucia spoke
again. Her voice was kinder this time.

'I know it will be hard for you. You have fallen in love
with my cousin. No, do not deny it—it was obvious from
the start that you would do so. How could you not? To you
Rafaello is like some prince out of a fairytale. But, though
you will not thank me for saying so, he should not have
awakened you with his kisses. While you were...as you
were when you first came here...you were safe from him.
But now...' She sighed. 'Oh, Rafaello does not understand—he never has. Girls have been falling in love with
him all his life. He does not mean to be cruel, but he just
does not see it happening.' She gave a little shrug. 'That
was why I thought a marriage between us might work—I
know him too well to fall in love with him, so he could
never have hurt me.'

She looked at Magda. Her dark eyes were not unsym-
pathetic. 'You did not believe it meant anything to him, did
you? You did not think that it could last, this brief affair?'

The pain was running down every limb of Magda's body.
She tried to fight it, desperate to deny what Lucia was saying to her despite the resonance it found so readily in her
own heart.

'I can't just go—without Rafaello's say-so. He may not
want me to go yet...'

Even as she spoke she knew she was deceiving herself.
Rafaello was not concerned with her now—he was concerned only, as he should be, with his father.

Lucia was taking something out of her handbag, something pale that fluttered as she held it out to Magda.

'He asked me to give you this.' Her voice was strained
and she would not quite meet Magda's eyes. As she took
the piece of paper and looked at it Magda knew why.

It was a cheque. It was made out to her—for ten thousand euros. As she stared, her heart crushed in a vice that

queezed the blood from every pore, Rafaello's strong,
black signature wavered in front of her eyes.

Lucia was speaking again.

Magda forced herself to listen, though inside herself she
could hear only a terrifying, deafening silence that just went
on and on without end.

'Rafaello said…' The woman hesitated again, as if only
too aware what Magda must be going through. 'Said that
he would be in touch later, to sort everything out. But that
right now his first duty is to his father. He hopes you will
understand…' Her voice trailed off. 'I'm sorry, my dear.
You see, he won't have realised what you have come to
feel for him. For him this marriage was always just
a…business transaction.'

Magda could say nothing—nothing except a dull, broken
assent. The crushing weight in her heart was agony.

Lucia was saying something again, glancing at her
watch.

'Forgive me, I do not mean to…upset you further, but I
have merely stopped here on my way to the airport. I am
catching the next flight to Rome, so that I can be with Tio
Enrico if…if he still lives.' There was a strain in her voice
Magda could not ignore. 'If it will not take you long to
pack, I can take you to the airport with me. Rafaello has
asked me to arrange your ticket and so forth.'

She looked pityingly at Magda, still standing there, Benji
at her side gazing uncomprehendingly, clinging to his
mother's leg.

'It would be best not to linger.' Her voice was as pitying
as her expression.

With feet of lead, Magda collected her things and headed
indoors.

It was raining. Rain pattered on the thin roof of the caravan,
splattered on the glass in the windows. Benji whined irri-
tably at Magda's knee.

'I know, muffin, it's horrid—all this rain. Perhaps tomorrow will be sunny.'

A gust of wind caught the caravan. It was old, shabby inside, and no one wanted to rent it on the beachside site. But that was what made it cheap—cheap enough to hire for a month in high season. Cheap enough to buy.

The enormity of what she was planning to do swept over Magda again, but she put her doubts aside. The south coast seaside just had to be a better place to raise Benji. There was nothing for her in London—her bedsit was gone, and so was her job.

There's nothing for me anywhere...

Angrily she pushed the despairing thought aside. That wasn't true; she still had Benji.

She stroked his head and opened up the jigsaw box, tipping out the pieces. Refusing to let the memories come back.

They came all the same, crowding in, impossible to push away.

Rafaello. So impossibly beautiful, so impossible not to adore. Rafaello holding her in his arms, smiling at her, laughing with her, kissing her. Making love to her.

It wasn't love. It was just an affair for him—a dalliance. She had known from the start it must end.

More memories rushed in, though she tried even harder to keep them out. But they pushed in, piercing her like knives.

One final memory, from the last time she had set eyes on him. He'd stood there, looking down at her, his face grave. *I shall take care of you—*

Well, he had. He had taken care of her. Made sure she had gone home with what she came for. Money.

That was why she'd married him. For money. Money to make a home for Benji. Not for love, for money.

She hadn't wanted to cash his cheque, had resisted for two weeks while she lived on the money she had got back

rom the airline company at Pisa airport after exchanging
Lucia's business class ticket for a humbler fare. She'd
anded at Gatwick, not Heathrow, and on impulse had taken
he train to the south coast, found a caravan camp which
till had vacancies this wet summer.

But now she needed Rafaello's pay-off to buy the cara-
an outright—make a home for herself and Benji, however
umble—and have a nest egg to tide her over for a while.
As for the rest of the money Rafaello had promised her—
he knew she could never take it.

Just as she had not been able to take the clothes he had
ought for her, nor the gold necklace he had given her.
Besides, they would hardly fit her lifestyle now.

She smiled, painful though it was to do so. At least she
ad her memories.

They would need to last a lifetime.

Across the shingle the grey tide churned the pebbles, pluck-
ng and knocking. Benji was crouched down, picking up
he shiny sea-wet stones. His feet were in wellingtons, his
ttle figure clad in a waterproof jacket. Rain swept in from
he west, slanting in chill, unrelenting strokes that stung her
heeks and blurred her vision.

Magda stared across the bleak, drear English Channel.
ar out to sea was an oil tanker, ploughing its slow way
astwards. There were no sailboats today, hardly anyone on
he beach. She had ventured out because she could stay
ndoors no longer. Benji was pettish, refusing to be enter-
ained by anything. She was restless, heart aching like an
gue in her bones.

Day by day the reality of it was sinking in. Rafaello had
one from her life. Gone completely. Gone as abruptly as
e had come.

Sternly she tried to pull herself together. She had no right
o mope like this. She was blessed with Benji, she had her
ealth, her strength—a home of her own. This would be a

good place to bring up Benji—fresh air, and the seaside on her doorstep....

And here, at least, she could stand in the rain and the wind blowing up the Channel and stare southwards, towards Italy, with a hopeless longing in her heart never to be fulfilled.

Her cheeks were wet. But not with rain.

Benji picked up one last stone, and threw it with all his tiny might into the sea. It landed with a plop that was quite inaudible in the noisy surf. Then, bored, he turned and tottered off.

Magda followed him, hugging her anorak around her, facing into the endless rain. Her booted feet crunched the shingle, slowing her down. Raindrops spat in her face. As she pushed back her wind-whipped hair, twisting her neck to try and refasten it into the clip it had escaped from, she stilled. And stared.

On the shingle shelf, above the high tide, a figure stood. Quite immobile.

She blinked. Something caught at her.

She reached for Benji's hand blindly, halting him. She went on staring landwards. The figure at the top of the beach started to walk towards her. A gust of wind buffeted her and she hung on to Benji's hand to steady him. And went on staring.

Time was slowing down. Slowing right, right down. The rain seemed to be stopping, slowing and stilling in mid flight. The wind dropped.

Silence drummed all around her. She felt Benji's fingers pressing into hers. Felt him tugging her. She was unresponsive. Her feet were leaden; she could not move.

Nor could she breathe. The air was solid in her lungs.

The figure kept on walking towards her.

His face resolved itself, through the rain, through the blurring of her vision.

She couldn't move. Couldn't breathe.

Then, suddenly, Benji's hand pulled free of hers. She saw him totter forwards, arms outstretched.

'Ra—' he said. 'Ra—pick up!'

Rafaello picked him up.

'Hello, Benji,' he said.

Then he looked at Magda. His dark eyes pierced her like a knife, cutting straight into her heart.

'Come home,' he said. He held out his free hand to her. 'Come home, *cara*.'

She didn't move, couldn't move.

'I don't understand.' Her words were a whisper, lost in the wind.

His mouth twisted. 'Nor did I. Not when I came back from Rome that night, to find you gone. Not when Maria took one look at me and threw up her hands, saying that you had set off after me that very morning. It made no sense. And then she said you'd had a lift—a lift from a very helpful visitor.' His face darkened. 'And when she told me who your visitor had been—then I understood.' His eyes shut, lashes sweeping long, before opening again. '*Dio!* When I heard that I understood, all right!'

She was swaying in the wind. It went right through her bones, scouring her heart.

'How—how is your father?'

'My father? Ah, yes, my father.' His voice was heavy. 'Making an excellent recovery, you will be glad to know— from his non-existent heart attack.'

She stared.

His mouth twisted again. 'My father has the constitution of an ox. Don't you see? Lucia lied to you.'

'Why?' Her voice was faint.

'*Why?* To get rid of you, of course!'

She swallowed. Her voice was painful. 'She could have waited another day, then. It would have saved her a journey.'

A frown darkened his brow. Carefully he set Benji down

again, and while the little boy fell with glee upon a gleaming shell he straightened and demanded, '*Non capisco?* What do you mean?'

Her voice didn't work properly, but she made the words come.

'You'd already warned me—that morning—that…that you were going to send me back.'

He stared. 'What is this you are saying?'

He seemed angry. She wondered why. 'You said…you said we would have to talk. I…I knew what you meant.'

There was nothing in his face. Nothing at all. Then, very carefully, he spoke.

'And what, *cara*, did I mean? Tell me.'

Her hands clenched in her pockets.

'Rafaello, please. I knew—I knew, I promise you. I knew that you were only being kind to me—that you had waved a magic wand over me and…and decided to be kind, let me have my little dream. I knew that was all it was—that it was not supposed to be more than that. I understood. I did—truly.' She swallowed, then went on. 'You gave me fair warning—that day in Florence. You warned me then that you would not want me to pine for you. I understood then.'

He looked at her. There was something strange about his face. She could not read it—but then all she wanted to do was gaze and drink him in. For this was heaven, a tiny, minuscule sliver of heaven, beamed down to her by special delivery to make another, final memory for her to keep and treasure all her days. One last joy.

She was drinking him in as a thirsty man would drink water in the desert. Drinking in his dark, beautiful eyes, his silken rain-wet hair, the beads of water on his lashes, the strong column of his nose, the planes of his face, the sculpted beauty of his mouth.

'You understood?' His voice was flat. Benji patted his knee, proffering the shell. Absently he took it, murmuring

something to the child. She watched him turn the shell over
in his fingers. His eyes went back to hers.

'You understood?' he said again. Then, with a savage
movement he hurled the shell far out into the sea. Benji
stared, open-mouthed with admiration at such might, and
tried to follow suit with a pebble.

His audience were not watching.

They were kissing.

Heaven. Heaven had swept over her again, drowning her.
As the shell had left his fist Rafaello had reached for her
and crushed her to him.

'Then understand *this*!' he rasped, and closed his mouth
over hers.

Magda's eyes fluttered shut. She was not standing on a
sodden English beach, lashed with rain. She was standing
beneath the Tuscan stars, with the scent of flowers all
around her, the sweet Italian air in her lungs, the warm
Italian night embracing her—and Rafaello—Rafaello kissing her.

She clung to him. Clung to him in desperation, in delir-
ium, because it must be a figment of her imagination. It
must be. There was no reason for him to kiss her. No reason
for him to crush her so close against his lean, hard body
that she felt herself fuse to him. No reason for his hands
to cup her rain-wet head as if it were precious alabaster.
No reason for him to speak into her mouth words she could
not believe—must not believe.

He let her go.

'*Now* do you understand?' His eyes blazed down at her.

'No,' she said faintly.

'*Per Dio!* Then come—come home with me, and I will
spend all my life trying to make you understand. I love you
so much.'

She heard, but could not believe. He saw it in her face.

'Your doubt shames me,' he said in a low voice. 'I
thought I had made it so clear to you—every night we were

together. But then…' His voice dropped even lower and he took her hands in his. 'Even I did not realise what name to give my feelings for you. They were so new to me—I could not recognise them. They confused me, made me question everything. But they grew in me and grew in me until I saw them for what they were—and realised I must turn a dream into reality. That is why I said I wouldn't want you to pine for me—because there would never be a reason for you to do so. I would turn the dream into reality for us both. *That* is why I was so solemn that last morning—I knew we must make our marriage a real one and that I would have to tell my father so. Tell him that even if he never spoke to me again—severed all ties, sold the company to the first passing stranger—you would stay my wife for ever—because I had fallen in love with you and could not live another day without you.'

She felt faint again, but it was bliss running through her, taking the breath from her body.

'Did you truly not see it?' he asked, looking down at her with disbelief in his eyes.

'How could I? How could I think such a miracle would happen to me?' There was wonder in her voice.

He smiled, and his smile was an embrace. 'You are my miracle, Magda. You and Benji. You crept into my heart, the pair of you, day by day, and now you are there for ever. My love for you was in my eyes, my touch.' His expression changed. 'Lucia saw it that day in Firenze—saw that we were in love with each other. And she knew she had found a way of revenging herself for my rejection of her. She determined to part us. So she came to you with that story of Enrico's collapse—oh, yes, I got the truth out of her, spitting and snarling though she was by the time I managed it. Lies, every word of it.'

'But…but the cheque? She gave me a cheque from you…'

A growl rasped from his throat. 'A forgery! She had gone

hrough my desk to find a chequebook before seeking you
ut. She knew it would convince you that I indeed wanted
ou to leave Italy right away.' His face shadowed. 'How
could you believe her lies, *cara*?'

'She played on my fears,' said Magda achingly.

His mouth thinned. 'Just as she played on my father's
obsession for a grandchild and my own obsession with the
company. Trying to manipulate us all. Well—' his voice
hardened '—that is over now. I have warned her that if she
ever tries to make trouble again I will press charges for
fraud. But,' he went on, his voice softening, 'that cheque
did give me the means of finding you at last.'

Magda stared, not understanding. He gave her a wry
smile. 'I stopped the cheque as a forgery, *cara*. My bank
informed me the moment it was presented for payment, and
at which bank. That's how I traced you.' His voice changed
again. 'You do not know what I have been through—every
day has been an eternity without you.'

He pressed her hands so tightly that the pressure should
have hurt. But she could feel no pain. Only a happiness so
deep, so absolute that it consumed her very being. How
could fairytales come true?

She looked at him, and all the love she had for him
blazed from her eyes.

He kissed her again, in sweet possession, and she folded
against him. As his arms wrapped around her, holding her
so close she could feel his heart beating next to hers, one
last doubt assailed her.

'Rafaello?' She lifted her face, eyes troubled.

He smoothed her hair. *'Si?'*

'Your father—?'

'—is perfectly well. I told you—Lucia lied to you.'

'No—I meant—I...I don't want to come between you.'

He brushed her brow with his lips.

'You have brought us together—finally, after so many
stupid, stubborn years.'

She looked at him questioningly.

'When he saw my despair when I could not find you, my grief at losing you, something broke between us—that cruel, hard wall that had separated us for so long. You see…' There was a catch in his voice as he went on, 'I was reminding him of himself—fifteen years ago—when my mother died.'

She felt her hand clutch at him more tightly.

'I didn't know—'

'Her death drove us apart. It shouldn't have—but it did. I went…wild. I can see that now. And my father…he simply locked himself away inside himself. We both of us grieved—but we could not reach out to each other, father to son, to comfort each other. And once the wall was built between us, neither of us could undo it. Until now. It's thanks to you, my beloved heart, that I have my father back as well.'

But still she was troubled. 'He can't want me—'

'Si!' He took a breath. 'I told him, Magda—I told him everything about you. How you took a dying woman's child to care for and love, how your loyalty to your friend, your love for a motherless child, made you put aside your own life, whatever it cost you. And he was as stricken with remorse as I was—he begs your forgiveness, cara. And he asks you if you will accept this, and wear it every day—for him and for me.'

He reached inside his pocket and drew out an antique ring box. There, inside, was a ring glistening with diamonds and sapphires.

'It is the eternity ring my mother wore—my father gave it to her as a symbol of his undying love. And I give it to you—' there was another catch in his voice and Magda's throat tightened in response '—as a symbol of my undying love for you.'

He slipped it on her finger and the tears spilled out of her eyes.

'Let us be happy for ever,' he said softly, and kissed her quietly, lovingly, with all his heart.

There was a tug at his leg.

'Pick up!' demanded a little voice.

Rafaello stooped and scooped up the little boy and hugged him close. And the three of them stood there, in the pouring rain, in the gusting wind, beside the cold grey sea, their arms around each other.

My family, thought Magda, and her heart turned over.

Rafaello hefted Benji onto his shoulders. The little boy squealed with glee and clutched his bearer's hair.

'Ouch!' said Rafaello. 'Benji—don't pull Papà's hair. Now you are my son you must be nice to me.'

He started to walk towards the shore.

'Come on,' he called to Magda. 'We have a flight to catch. My father is desperate to make amends to you, Maria and my aunt are desperate to get Benji to themselves again, and I—I am just desperate for you!'

With the crunch of shingle under her feet she hurried after them, her husband and her son. Her heart was singing, and it was a song that would never end.

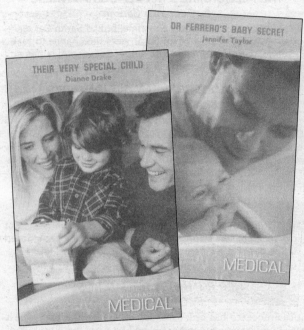

Queens of Romance

An outstanding collection by international bestselling authors

NORA ROBERTS
Summer Delights

4th July 2008

BETTY NEELS
Summer Engagements

1st August 2008

PENNY JORDAN
Jet Set Wives

5th September 2008

LINDA HOWARD
At His Mercy

3rd October 2008

CAROLINE ANDERSON
Baby Bonds

7th November 2008

One book published every month from February to November

Collect all 10 superb books!

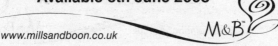

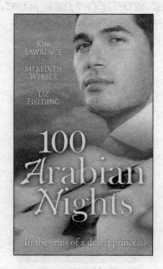

Two men have vowed to protect the women they love…

New York Times bestselling author

DIANA PALMER

Hard to Handle

Hunter

On a top secret operation in the desert, chief of
security Hunter knew Jennifer Marist needed his
protection. Soon he discovered the lure of Jenny's
wild, sweet passion – and a love he'd never
dreamed possible.

Man in Control

Eight years after DEA agent Alexander Cobb had
turned Jodie Clayburn down, Alexander could
hardly believe the beauty that Jodie had become…
or that she'd helped him crack a dangerous
drug-smuggling case. Would the man in control
finally surrender to his desires?

Available 20th June 2008

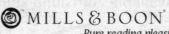